Home Sweet Home

Home Sweet Home

PREETAM PARIKH

 www.trafford.com

North America & International
toll-free: 1 888 232 4444 (USA & Canada)
phone: 250 383 6864 ♦ fax: 812 355 4082

TABLE OF CONTENTS

Acknowledgments

Special thanks go out to God for blessing me. Special thanks for my loving family, Daksha, Paresh, Priya and Purvi for supporting me writing this book. Thanks go out to the wonderful staff at the Berkeley College Library at Garret Mountain campus in Woodland Park, NJ, and special thanks go out to my loving friends.

Dedication

To My Loving and Supporting Family and Friends

Chapter 1
The Beginning/Bar

What kind of beer do you want" said, the bartender and it was at that time I was wondering where the hell I was. I couldn't remember much expect the fact that I have been coming to this broken down excuse of a bar for a couple of years now, and for some reason I never got tired of it. I looked at the bartender who was looking at me with inpatient eyes, and I told him just get me a Bud Light. While I was waiting he gave me a bowl of peanuts that looked like they were fucking rotten or something. But I haven't eaten all day so I ate the whole bowl, they tasted dry as if the peanuts were missing salt but I didn't care. My beer finally came and I was so thirsty I drank it so fast I wanted to fucking puke that shit back up all over the place. I started to get a headache I don't know why all I had was a lousy beer and some peanuts; it's probably from all the assholes screaming at the top of their lungs. Well it's been a fascinating couple of years of my life, sit down and if I have time from drinking another beer and also at the same time about to punch this mother fucker in the face for breathing all over my neck I'll tell you.

Growing up was pretty mild for me nothing out of the usual, except for the fact that me and my "loving" parents, and I use the word lightly because my parents are loving don't get me wrong, but sometimes they feel like pestering little insects whom you want to swat, but anyway let me get to the point I have a tendency of drifting off from time to time. So growing up was nothing short of a walk in the park besides all the moving we did as a family, I swear we moved so much we had the fucking movers number on speed dial. And another thing my parents are not just "loving" people, but also persistent, meaning they kept the same movers card when they first moved when I was a kid. I can remember living in this hick ass town; it was like a ghost town. For the first several weeks I didn't talk to anyone, I don't know if I was just shy or I just didn't give a damn. Anyway let me stop myself before I go into a huge rant on how unsociable my life is. Then something changed I didn't know what it was I saw this girl standing in a line at the local grocery store. Now mind you I was only 13, sometimes I can't even fucking think straight. I wanted more than anything to go over there and talk to her, but it's like I froze, I stood still with nothing to say I don't know what happened, is it because I am nervous she is the first girl that I saw since I've been here, I couldn't figure it out. So I said to myself, "I am just going to go over there and talk to her, what's the worst that can happen". The line starting to grow gradually smaller and I think she was next in line. I made my way up and snuck into the line without anyone else seeing me, I stood right behind her. I was so nervous I didn't know what to say to her, "oh my God" I said, standing behind her gently smelling her hair. She was standing there so elegantly, I mean the dress that she was wearing was so beautiful, I think that was the same age, so it worked out. Her body just standing there was so inviting. I didn't care that I had only one thing in my hand to pay for it was pretty much worth it. When she was done paying for her groceries, the cashier looked down at me and said, "Can I help you sir, sir can I help you, you're holding up the whole line". I couldn't focus, my eyes glued to her body, the way she was walking out of the store to go to her mom's car, I couldn't control myself. When the cashier angrily said, "Sir are you going to pay for that or what, I don't have all day". Then in an instant I looked back up at him and said, "Sorry, I was distracted, I gave him the one item I had in my hand". He rang it up and the bagger put it in a bag and handed it to me. I said to him that I didn't want in a bag, he looked at me as if he was pissed off or something. I grabbed the bag and started walking out the store thinking to myself, what a fucking loser it was one bag like that was such a hard job, he's probably going to go home and play with his sister's dolls.

The store was only a couple of minutes away from this small ass house we lived in so it wasn't that bad. Let me tell you about this house, it was generally big it was pretty much the "stereotypical" house in which you see in magazines and shit. Big, white with a picket fence, even though the fence looked like it had better years. The grass was green, but it looked like it had not been cut for ages, and the backyard looked like a tornado hit the place. Grant it we have been living there only for a short period of time, but I don't know if my parents ever heard of the term maintenance or even watched one episode of home and gardening, but someone had tell these sweet adorable people something. I walked into the kitchen and put the bag on the countertop and opened the refrigerator to see if there was something to drink, and of course all we had was the usual, milk, probably spoiled, half carton of orange juice and beer, that was for my mom and her one of many boyfriends. I grabbed some orange juice and I looked at the carton and got a real monotone expression on my face, because the damn carton had pulp inside the orange juice. Now if was anyone else that would been okay, but I hate pulp I have spend so much damn time getting a drainer and draining all that disgusting crap, so it doesn't fall into my cup, it's so boring. I grabbed the damn cup and went straight to my room not even saying hi to my dog, which was just lying on this cheap ass rug we bought from a local store. I swear that dog ruins everything we buy him, we barley had that rug less than a couple of days and already there is hairs and half the carpet is tearing. Next time that dog is not getting shit. I put the cup on top of my dresser and just plopped myself on top of my bed, which sometimes felt like I was lying on a bed full of stones, I guess it had to do with the mattress since it was so old, my parents never bought a new one they just gave me their old one when they were done. As I was lying there, bored out of my mind, wondering what I am going to do to occupy my time, I couldn't help to think of that girl who I saw in the grocery store. I kept thinking to myself if she lived around here maybe if I can see her again if I have to go to the store to buy something. Now instead of lying here sort of comfortable I was distracted, now she is on my mind. I got up off my bed and walked to my mom's room, when I walked in she was lying there with her BOYFRIEND Jeremy, personally I don't know where my mom keeps meeting all these jerks, but besides the point I asked her if I can go to the store tomorrow and look around if they had some old baseball cards. Ah baseball, the one thing no matter how bad things got, I can go see a game and it will make it all better, especially with my dad he is the only person in the whole world who can understand me. My dad, now if you want to talk about a real man, then you don't have to look any further. Not like these bastards my mom keeps hooking up with everyday. I swear it's like a new man every fucking day; she goes through a new guy more than I do a pair of underwear. Jeremy was rubbing her neck, and I was getting a little irritated at the fact he kept putting his slimy hands on her body. My mom looked at me and said sure, you can go to the store in the afternoon, but in the morning we have to start looking for a school so you can start soon.

At that point I was feeling a mixture of two emotions running through my body, I was happy that I can go back to the store and see if that girl is going to be there and at the same time, I was annoyed that she had to mention school. See there is nothing wrong with school, I just don't want to deal with the whole process of fitting in, and that's always the hardest part. I can admit that I would be perfectly comfortable with being home schooled, I mean my mom is fairly educated, fairly educated meaning she only had a semester of college under her belt and never finished, I think that was the year she met my dad, and one thing led to another, got pregnant and here I am. When I think about it I'd rather take my chances going to school, then stay home with my mom I love my mom, but staying home would mean what Jeremy calls spending quality time, and I rather get a root canal. And you never know this girl might even go to the same school or better yet be in one of my classes, now that would put a smile on my face.

Chapter 2
The Glory of Moving Day Again...

It was getting late, and for some strange reason I wasn't tired, well maybe a little tired but I can stay up a little more. I walked over to my door and I was about to shut it when I heard my mom laughing in her room, I can hear her say, oh Jeremy, cut it out, you're so naughty". You couldn't believe how much that pissed me off, I just shut my door and I locked it because I didn't want to be bothered by the bickering. I walked over to my closet, on it there was a poster of AC/DC, that was my favorite classic rock band, I opened my closet and with hesitation picked out some clothes for tomorrow, I was getting ready for school tomorrow I threw my clothes on top of my bed and my shirt made it halfway before landing on the floor. I didn't care though; it was a shirt and not one of my favorites so it can just sit there. My mom didn't have an iron, so all my clothes were always wrinkled. My mom said there is no point to buy an iron, because your clothes are just going to get wrinkled again, and you have to iron all the time. My mom didn't believe in spending any money if she didn't have too, if that was the damn case we would be millionaires instead of the average American. I pulled out the plastic container that was under my bed, and grabbed some school supplies to stuff into my book bag. I primarily had a list of the things that I wanted to bring, but due to the sheer excitement on my face I didn't care. I think I stuffed a couple of highlighters in there also one or two notebooks, pens, folders, glue and some other stuff. I got my pajamas from my dresser and changed before I went to bed. I was in the middle of taking off my shirt, when I heard a knock on the door. It was my mom, I didn't want to open the door then again I didn't want to get grounded. I opened the door and I continued to change, she came in and sat at the corner of my bed. She looked at me and said "tomorrow is a big day, nervous". I said, mom "I am almost 14, my birthday was coming up soon, I'll be fine". She pulled some money from her back pocket, even though it wasn't her money, and placed it on my dresser. Here she said, so you can grab some lunch tomorrow, my mom I said, always considerate she probably gets that from Jeremy, then I sorted of chucked and grabbed the money. I finished changing and was getting into bed, when my mom leaned in and gave me a kiss on my cheek. Love you, she said good luck tomorrow make some friends. I looked at her and said I will; don't worry at the same time wiping off the side of my cheek with my sleeve. She was about to leave out the door, when she told me that she is going to find a job tomorrow, so Jeremy is going to drop you off to school tomorrow. Now it was at that point where I got really upset, I couldn't believe Jeremy, of all people, is going to drop me off, this would be the first time we spent more than a minute with each other. My mom shut my door and went to her room, now I couldn't sleep, and I was staring at the ceiling for several hours before I started to get bored and I just closed my eyes, and went to sleep.

I felt something pushing me on my shoulder, I woke up to a haze and it was Jeremy on the side of my bed. "Come on champ", he said, "today is your big day you don't want to be late". I can tell you it was a pleasant site to see Jeremy early in the morning, he fucking smelled like beer and cigarettes, but then again when does he not smell like that shit, so it was pretty ordinary I guess. I got up and looked at the alarm it read 6:00 AM, it was too early. Jeremy stood up and said, "Let's go, are you hungry there is some food on the table, eat and take a shower we have to be there by 8:00 AM". I got up and partially made my bed, I didn't care; I was probably going to go to sleep when I am done with school anyway. I picked up my jeans that were surprisingly on the side of my bed, and the shirt that was still on the ground. I grabbed my shirt, and just gave it a quick shake to get all the dust off of it. I grabbed my towel and headed to the bathroom, now the worst part of taking a shower in the morning is the water is so damn cold. I was always paranoid about where I keep my stuff in the bathroom; I just didn't like anyone using it that's it. When I am in the shower, I have a pretty common routine, I always wash my face and hair, and then I use a body wash, then finish up with a face lotion. For someone who doesn't care about his clothes, I care about my face and body, but then again who doesn't. I stepped out the shower and dried off, and put my clothes on. I walked over to the kitchen table, and to my surprise the breakfast was very appetizing, it was left over from yesterday's breakfast, but I wasn't complaining because it's still food.

It was getting petty late if I can recall around 7:30 AM and I should start heading out. I grabbed my book bag from the corner of the table and made my way to Jeremy's baby as he likes to call it, it was just a freaking car to me. Jeremy goes on for days about his precious car, it looked old, and he once told me it was a 1965 Mustang. It was cherry red, but some parts were scratched up and you can see some of the paint coming off. Sometimes I think he treats the damn car better than my mom, but what can you do. I hopped in the front, and for some damn reason, Jeremy got all upset and told me to go sit in the back of the car. He told me that he had some important papers in the front seat. I looked in the back and said to him, there is fucking garbage everywhere it looks like a damn dump. I got in anyway and Jeremy was taking his sweet ass time, like usual. He grabbed a beer from the fridge, and plopped his overweight body in the front seat. He took like freaking 10 minutes to find his damn keys. I got so aggravated, "We are running late, it's almost 8:00 AM". Without saying anything he started the car and finally we took off. He was a pretty quite car ride to my school, I was making sure that I had everything in my book bag, one more quick check you know. We finally pulled up to the school, I don't know if I was nervous but something inside my stomach was not feeling right, hopefully it wasn't the breakfast. I got out, and I said thanks to Jeremy for the ride, he said welcome and drove off. With a big sigh, I stopped and paused, this is it, praying that my first day is good. Looking around the school was pretty big; there were a lot of students hanging outside and around the side near the benches of the school. I was walking toward the main entrance so I can get ready to get situated, when someone bumped into me. I said, watch were you're going, and it was at that point where I looked up and noticed the kid was like twice my age. Great, as I was thinking to myself, what the hell did I just get myself into? Of course, like all bully's, this one was pretty dumb, so that worked in my favor, I think. He grabbed me by my shirt, and pulled me closer and said, "Hey punk, I should knock your fucking teeth out for bumping into me". He threw me to the ground, and started to walk away, laughing like a fat ass. As I was dusting myself off, mumbling, fantastic, first day and this shit happens. I was getting my book bag off the ground, when I heard a voice from a far. "Are you ok; it looked like you took a pretty nasty spill there". I got up and turned around, and to my surprise, it was the girl from the grocery store. It was strange, the whole time I wanted to say something to her, but I couldn't form any words. Then I just said, hi but it was a nervous hi, as if my voice was high pitched. She smiled and walked me to the main office, where I was staring at her the whole time. When we got to the main office, she leaned over and said I have to go to class, hope to see you soon. I smiled at her, and thanked her for walking me, but in my mind, I wanted to see her more and more. I leaned over the counter and said, "I am new here, can someone please help me, it looked like the damn place was dead, and no one was around when I needed them". Finally a lady came up to the counter, she was about 5'11 and she had tan skin, and smooth black hair. She looked at me and smiled; I smiled back and was thinking what she was wearing under her clothes. "Can I have your name please, so I can get your paperwork? I told her my name was Mitchell James, but I rather be called Mitch. She gave me my paperwork and told me to head to English, because that's the class I was supposed to be in right now, if I would've came to school on time. I thanked her for the paper and started making my way out of the office, as soon I was leaving I turned my head for one second, and I saw her turn around and bend over to grab something from the filing cabinet. Her body was so sensuous, I mean the way her black and grey skirt was firmly hugging against her body, her luxurious legs making their way up to her thighs, were only complemented by her tight ass. And in an instant, it came to me; I am obsessed with girls, not even girls but women. She got up as she was holding the paper in her hand, and waved at me as she made her way in the back. I quickly waved back but I don't know if she saw. I hurried and ran to my class, I had totally forgotten, I opened the door and quietly made my way into the front of the room. I usually sit in the back, but since the teacher was a lady I sat in the front this time.

When I sat down in my chair, the teacher was passing out homework sheets for our test, I couldn't wait for that. When I was handing the paper back to the person behind, I noticed that they were not taking the paper. I turned around, and to my surprise it was the girl, I couldn't believe that I was sitting in front of her. When the teacher was lecturing, I wasn't paying attention because all I could think of her, this was the happiest day of my life. When school was over, I waited for her in front of the front entrance; I saw her coming down the hallway. The way she was walking such like a women, with her hair bouncing up and down, her smile was so extravagant, her lips so wet. She made her way down the steps, and walked over towards me and smiled while she sat on the corner of the steps. I slowly walked to her and sat down besides her, and smiled at her. "Class was boring today; I can't believe we are having a test already". She looked at me and said, "I know I don't know what she is thinking, she is pushing us way to hard". I just looked at her, I couldn't find a reply for her statement, but I didn't want to. I just looked at her, stared in her eyes and just smiled. I think that she was waiting for her parents or someone to pick her up. But I wouldn't mind if she had to wait for a little longer. I hurried up and asked before it got too late, or before her parents come. So maybe if you're free sometime, you want to like hang out and play. She put her bag on the ground, looked at me and said, sure if you want to hang out today, you can come over, I live by the old bank on Wood Street, house number 13. It's a big green house, with a tire swing in the front yard. Before I said yes, I asked her what her name was, she said you're so silly, my name is Beverly. An old broken down car slowly made its way up to the side of the main entrance. Well I have to go; it was nice talking to you, that's my parents. As she was making her way into her car, I waved to her and quickly gathered my things. I was waiting for my ride to show up, I wish that they would hurry up already, there are taking forever. I didn't know if my mom was going to pick me up or if it was Jeremy. After several minutes I saw a car making its way up, and to my distain it was a red fucking mustang. And that could only mean one thing, it was Jeremy. He pulled up and opened the passenger door, so I can get in. I got up and walked to the car, "Oh the front seat this time, how I feel so special, thanks for picking me up in such short notice". I think that even Jeremy knew that I was being sarcastic, but he never had the balls to admit when I questioned his manhood or something. Jeremy took a couple of extra minutes to get going, which was pissing me off. I love spending quality time with you man more than the next guy, but can we hurry this up I am hungry. He looked at me, but this time was different, as if he was sad about something. If I had a guess he probably ran out of damn beer. "Listen kid, this might be tough for you to understand, but you have to promise me you will not get upset". All I wanted to do is get the fuck home, but what the hell is this drunken bitch talking about, sounds like a real pussy. "Your mom and I had a long talk when you were at school, and we both waited for you to get out, so we can get your opinion". Great, I didn't like where this was going, "Where is my mom, why is she not here with you picking me up". She's working, but that's beside the point, I want you to listen. "This might come as a huge shock to you, but I think everything will work out in the end". I wish he would just fucking tell me, and stop beating around the fucking bush. "We are moving kid, your mom got a job at an insurance company in Ohio, and we have to start packing up today". Now why couldn't he say our dog died or something, but of all the news this shit. My whole world just felt like it crashed down on me and I am fucking suffocating under all the weight. "What the fuck, Jeremy, why do we have to fucking move, I like it here school is great and I met a nice girl". "Sorry kiddo, that's the way it is, your mom, got offered a great position at the insurance company and its great pay, so we can be financially set". You mean, you can be financially set faggot, I can't believe this, why is this happening to me of all people. I don't know what I am going to do now, I met such a nice girl what I am going to say to her now. Oh shit, I am supposed to come over and hang out today; I have to go see her. Jeremy you know that girl I was talking about, I was supposed to hang out with her today. I am going to go, before we start "packing", and I was wondering if you or mom can tell my mom if one of you can come pick me up. I gave Jeremy the address to the house, so he won't get lost, because God knows he will. Later that day, he dropped me off in front of her house; while we were pulling up I can see her playing in the tire swing in her front yard. It was a mild and warm day outside, as I was stepping out of the car. I turned back at Jeremy and said thanks for dropping me off. "What time do you want to get picked up; we have a lot of packing to do". I call you when I am ready to go and I will wait outside by the tire swing. I walked towards the swing and just stood there as she was flying through the air; I just stood and watched her, the way her body was so proportioned to the tire swing, and her hair blowing in the breeze. "Hey, I have to tell you something important, I am moving to Ohio. "My mom just got a job at an insurance company, so we have to start packing today and leave". She stopped swinging, and slowly got off, "I am so sorry, you just got here to that's such a huge bummer, and I kind of liked you to". Oh great as if everything else wasn't going so smooth, she had to drop this bombshell on me. Now I was so fucking confused, the only logical thing I could say is, I kind of liked you to, but now I am moving, so this is not going to work. For a couple of minutes no one said a thing, we both just looked at her, and in one minute we both just broke out laughing. I don't know what came over us, but I think I had an idea, even though I am moving and I am probably not going to see her again, it's not that bad I guess. We both walked and sat on her front step of her porch, and just talked for a while. "I am going to miss you, hope you have a fun time in Ohio". I laughed and said, "Thanks I'm sure I will, but at least I was able to spend the last couple of minutes with you. When she was talking I hurried and leaned in and gave her a kiss on her cheek. Suddenly she just stopped talking, and I thought I did something wrong. She smiled and leaned in and gave *me* a kiss on my cheek. Now, I know we were both young, but I think that we both can agree that we found someone special in our lives. I went inside and called Jeremy, because it was getting late, I told him I was ready to go home so you can pick me up now. When I walked back outside, I leaned against the side of the door, and watched her sit on the porch. It was such a beautiful night, the stars were coming out, and it was a mild breeze gently blowing in the air. She continued to sit there so innocently, while at the same time, it looked like she was so careless. I wonder what she was thinking about; I wanted to know so much more about her, I was so upset that I had to move. Jeremy was coming up the street, and she stood up and walked towards me, and gave me a hug, crying. I hugged her also, and told her that I have to go, but I won't forget you. I walked towards Jeremy's car, I turned around and she waved sadly, I waved back as I saw her walk into her house. I got in and said hi to Jeremy as we drove off.

When we got home, my mom was just pulling up in her car, I wonder what she was thinking about this whole thing, of course she would me more excited than me. When he pulled up, I quickly got out and ran up to my mother and hugged her so hard. "It's so nice to see you sport, how was your first day of school? I am sorry that I couldn't pick you up today, I got called into work, and I had to put in my two week notice to my supervisor". "It's okay, it's not that big of a deal, I am just glad your home, I missed you". We all went in and, it was a long night for all of us, because we had to start packing up. I ran all the way into my room, and just jumped in my bed, and just laid there for a while, I had to get my mind off the girl. I started taking out all my things and started putting them into the boxes that were in my room. I overheard my mom and Jeremy talking in there room, but I couldn't really make it out that clearly. I didn't let that bother me as I continued to pack. After a couple of hours I got all my stuff in all the boxes, when I made my way downstairs it looked like most of the stuff was already done. I walked in the kitchen and my mom was on the phone with the fucking movers. Luckily for us we have the damn movers on speed dial, so my mom didn't have to waste time dialing the number. I walked out onto the front porch and Jeremy was fixing his car, I was going to give him hand but I didn't feel like it. I sat down, and just waited for the movers to come and take our stuff. After my mom was done talking on the phone, I can hear her coming outside, she sat right beside me. "I know this is tough, son but I know that we can get through this, Ohio is not that bad of a place you know". I didn't want to talk to my mom right now, but I did smile and just nodded. She came closer and held me close, and Jeremy was still fixing his car like anyone even gives a damn. I heard a loud truck coming up the street, and the expression on my face told the whole story. It was the moving truck and it slowly stopped in front of our house. Jeremy got underneath from his car, and wiped his oily hands on a rag that was on the hood of his car. I am going to talk to the movers, start getting all the boxes ready and put it outside on the porch. When Jeremy made his way up to the movers, my mom and I went inside and started to get all the boxes to put them outside. First we got all the boxes from the living room, then the kitchen, my room, then my mom and Jeremy's room. Then we got all the extra boxes from all extra rooms, and the basement and the attic. When we got all the boxes from the whole house and started to load them in the huge ass yellow truck. It took a long time, because we had so many fucking boxes, because we have so much useless shit in this house. After we got all the boxes in the truck, Jeremy walked over to the front seat of the truck and sat down, started to force small talk to the driver. While my mom and I just stood there and let it all sink in for a moment. We gave one good look at the house, and my mom just held me against her. "This is it, I can't believe this is actually happening, we are moving all the way to Ohio". I looked at her, she had a happy but sort of sad smile on her face and a tear fell from her eye. I looked at the truck, and one more time at the house, and at that time I was thinking, time to start our new life in Ohio. And when we made our way into the car to get ready to leave and follow the truck, only two words came to mind when we drove off, goodbye Beverly.

Chapter 3
New Life, New Girl

It was a really long drive, and I was getting tired, I mean looking at the damn scenery for a while gets pretty boring too, but what can you do. The only thing that I was looking forward about this whole move is my birthday, and I am hoping that I get a better gift than last year. My birthday gift last year was so lame, I couldn't believe it, there was one thing that I wanted more than anything. It was these rollerblades, but something about them was so special. They were all black, and there was a yellow stripe going down the back and across the sides, it had four Velcro straps going across the front on both blades. They were not that expensive but moderately $100, but it was worth it. No, you want to know what I got, I got clothes, and not even clothes, it was a fucking sweater with a dog in print going across the middle. I was so pissed; I rather get a fucking video game, than get a "dog" sweater. When my mom gave me the sweater, she said hope you like it, I know it's not much, but it's the thought that counts. The thought, you were not thinking when you bought this were you, but I guess I couldn't be that mad, back then money was tight so it really was the thought that counts. It seemed like forever, I don't know how long we have been driving for, but we finally came to a stop to get something to eat, and fuel up. The diner that we decided to stop at looked worse than our own home. One side of the building, the paint was coming off and you can see the metal. The sign of the restaurant, said Smith's Diner, but some of the letters were not lighting up, probably the light blew out. There was not a lot of people, what I meant to say is cars, besides us there was one black and red pickup truck. I think it was a Ford F-150, but it looked like a slightly newer model. In the back there was a lot of 2x4 pieces, maybe he is doing construction who knows. And on one of his tires, he was missing a hub cap, I know I am going into detail of a truck, but I have a habit of picking out small things. Jeremy was making his way out of the mover's truck, as my mom and I were making our way towards the diner. When we went inside, the outside was looking a hell of a lot better, first of all it smelled badly, and one side of the diner was really dark, light a light blew out on that side or something. But when you are really hungry, you don't let small stuff like that bother you. I walked up to the front and sat down on one of the stools. After a couple of minutes of a waitress came up and said, "Hello, how can I help you today, would you like to hear our pie specials of the day". I don't if it was me, or every time I meet someone, why do they always have to look so attractive. I mean this waitress had to be in her twenty's if not a little older. "Yes, I said, I would like to know more about your pie specials, even though I didn't give a rat ass about the pie that she was serving. For the sake of argument I said; just give me blueberry or cherry if you have it. She politely said, "Sure thing sweetie, just give me one second, and I will have your pie, and I can also tell you our lunch specials". As she was getting the pie, I said "No thanks, I don't want lunch, but my mom, who snuck into the women's restroom, and Jeremy would like to know, he should be here in one second. God knows what he was doing out there, probably looking at the car; he swore he can fix anything. My mom was coming out the restroom, and sat next to me one a stool. The waitress was coming back with a piece of pie, when my mom said, "Excuse me, yes can you please help me, I want to know what you are serving for lunch today". What she meant to say, what is today's lunch specials, but my mom always had a distinct way of saying what she needed to say. As the waitress was putting the pie down on the counter, I got a glimpse of her nametag, it read Kelly. I thought to myself, what an ordinary name, but with all the names out there, some tend to be ordinary. Kelly replied, "Today for lunch, we have three cheese macaroni, Tomato Campbell's soup, biscuits and gravy, country fried steak, chicken fried steak, and she said some other stuff, that my mom really wasn't paying attention too. She stopped her midway, and said, "I will have two plates of country fried steak, and one plate of biscuits and gravy. She looked at me and said, "You're not hungry, Mitchell, I said, "Please mom, I don't like being called that". Sorry honey but Mitch sounds so, as she couldn't give a reason for her suggestion. Fine mom, I guess I am a little hungry, as the waitress was standing there; I got her attention, and said, "On second thought, I would like to order something, just one plate of your biscuits and gravy please". As she wrote down all the orders, she headed into the back to give it to the cook; I couldn't help but to stare at her walking away. She was so young, and she had everything to live for. She was skinny but it was a "good" skinny, thank God she was not a "walking Skelton", she had blonde hair, but it looked more like dirty blonde. She was sweating a little bit on forehead, but it was hot inside the diner. The sweat just dripping off the side of her face, oh my God, I couldn't control my urges. Even something so simple, like the dress that she had on was simply intoxicating, I mean the little, tight, yellow dress that seemed to fit her body so well. I wonder what kind of moisturizer she showers with every day. And with that thought, Jeremy finally walks in; he goes straight into the bathroom. Several minutes he comes out, and sits down next to us. "What took you so long baby, we were worrying about you". I don't know what my mom meant when she said we, and I hate the fact that she is always calling him these stupid little nicknames.

Our food finally arrived, and even though it was a diner, in the middle of nowhere, the food looked half decent. Everything looked edible, but anyway, when the food came all I can think about is the waitress Kelly. When she got closer, I said, "You know you're very pretty, what are you doing working in a place like this you should be modeling". She smiled "Thank you, you're too sweet, but money is very tough right now, and this is the only job that would hire. I only live a couple of miles down the road, so it's not that bad of a drive to come here every day". My mom overhead, as she was being held close by Jeremy, she added her two cents in like mothers always do, that was very nice Mitchell, sorry I mean Mitch. After we ate, Jeremy and I headed to the bathroom, as my talked to the waitress. The bathroom looked big from the outside, but the stalls were really small, it was quite annoying. It looked dirty, but then again so did everything else about the diner. I went into the "cleanest" stall and did my business, and Jeremy I think picked one of the urinals. As I was peeing, I heard Jeremy, as if he was looking for something, then I heard it. It was a lighter, he is smoking again. Man I tell you, this guy smokes all day, all the time; I am not surprised he hasn't died of cancer yet. Boy, when that happens maybe I will be a little more happier, but in tell then I am stuck with this asshole. We finished up about the same time, washed up and headed out. My mom was still talking to the waitress. What the hell they can be talking about for so long, I said to myself, as I was heading to the car. Jeremy stood by, as he went over to my mom and the waitress; I just sat in the front seat, and waited for them to hurry the hell up. My mom got up, and waved goodbye, and both of them left and headed outside, of course, Jeremy headed back to the movers truck and sat in the passenger's side, as my mom made her way into the driver's seat of our car. "What were you and the waitress talking about, you took a long time". "Oh nothing she said, just talked about where she goes to school, and any plans in the future, pretty boring stuff". We all started to drive off, the movers reversed, a little and took off first, and then my mom started the car, and we followed. As I looked one more time, out the window and into the diner I saw the waitress cleaning the countertop. She saw me out the window, and stopped cleaning, and waved at me. I hurried and waved back, but I don't know if she saw me since the car was halfway on the road. We still had a long drive ahead of us, so this would be a great idea for me to catch up on some sleep. Several hours later, I woke up to a sudden brake of the car, an animal was running across the street, and my mom almost hit it. Since I was awake, I looked at my mom and said, "How much longer is this going to be, I am getting really bored". "We are almost there you just got to be patient, it takes some time". With that said, I just nodded off back to sleep, even though the next time I wake up, we won't even be half way there. Hours later, I woke up to a sudden brush against my shoulder; it was my mom, telling me we finally made it to Ohio. Finally, I was getting really restless, and I needed to stretch bad as hell. After being cooped in the damn car, I finally had the chance to get out and stretch, and did my legs thank me. It was quite early in the morning, so I begged my mom if we can go and get some breakfast. Since everyone was tired, or they just seemed tired, my mom told me maybe it is a good idea if we all got something to eat. Now, when you come to a new town, let alone a new state, you are going to have a hard time finding what you really need. It's always a good idea, to ask around and this way you get to introduce yourself to all the nice people that Ohio has to offer. After several minutes of bickering with the town folk, we finally found a diner which consequently reminded me of Smith's Diner, the one that we had to unfortunately leave, but that's all behind me now, so I am not going to let that bother me. After, my mom and I went inside, Jeremy, oh loving Jeremy, walked right behind us. This diner actually looked like a diner, it looked clean, there were people actually inside the damn place, and the bathrooms looked like bathrooms. I don't know what kind of diner's they have in Ohio, but it sure as hell beats the one from home. But then again, every time I think of that crappy little diner, and that crappy little town, I always think of Beverly, I wonder what she is up to now. And as that thought was circling in my head, my stomach was telling me something else, it was growling. I sat down at the counter on top of, what I have to say a really comfortable stool, and Jeremy and my mom sat next to me. This time the waitress was not as hot as the one from the other diner, you know, the one with the little yellow dress and the sweat dripping off her face, but that's beside the point. When the waitress handed us the menus, surprisingly the selection of food looked a little better than the one before. We ordered our food, you can pretty much say that everybody had good taste, or they just know what they wanted. After we ate, we decided that now was a good time to leave. After we were all stuffed, I think now was a great idea to actually look for our damn house, unless we all wanted to spend the night outside in an unfamiliar state.

We finally made it to our house, and to my surprise it was still early in the morning going into the afternoon. When we pulled up behind the large ass mover's truck, I was actually shocked that the house looked like a house. It was much larger than the one we had before, and it looked cleaner, the paint looked new is what I meant to say. There was a shed to the immediate left of the house, and there was a fucking tire swing, that was grand. When we pulled up and everybody started to get out, one thought came and slapped me in the face, we had to unload and move all the shit out of the truck. Personally, I didn't want to do a damn thing, but thinking that would be a little selfish, so I decided to give a helping hand. My mom got out and made her way to Jeremy, God knows what they needed to talk about. If I had it my way, I would put Jeremy in the attic or the Goddamn basement and let that pussy rot, but I am half decent guy. "Hey, help with the boxes; get the big ones first so the little ones will be easier". My mom said screaming halfway down the street, disturbing all the neighbors. I went over to the side of the truck and lifted up the latch and climbed inside to get all the heavy boxes. I walked out with one box, and I noticed a girl coming out her house, it looked like she was fully developed, but she had to be like one year older than me. Well, my birthday was tomorrow, so I guess we should be the same age, I put the box down and started to walk over to her before she went back in her home. I didn't want to go over there with nothing to say, because I would look like a fool, so I thought I would make up a lie. She stopped, like she didn't want to go in her house, but locked her eyes on me walking over there, and I happen to notice so I needed to think of something fast. "Hi, my name is Mitch and me and my family just moved here. I was wondering if it is no problem to you, if I can use your phone, since ours is not installed yet or the wiring is messed up". "Sure, she said, come on in, the phone is right near the kitchen on the right hand side". I yelled at my mom, that I met a friend and was going to make a quick phone call. And if you know my mom, when she is busy or distracted with something, and if you ask her a question or get her attention, her reply is always the same, huh what okay then. I walked in the girls house, it seemed like no one was home, because it was awfully quite. "I am sorry; I didn't catch your name, she said, "My name is Bethany". "Bethany, which is such a pretty name, I bet it, is your mother's name, making up some lame ass speculation". She just smiled and handed me the phone, then she said she will be right back. I pulled out the number that was inside of pocket and called it. It took a minute before someone finally picked up. We talked for several minutes, and she told me that she had other business, but to keep in touch. When Bethany came back, I thanked her for letting me use her phone, and started to walk to her door. "My mom is coming home in a couple hours, if you want to come over for dinner. Just in case your mom has nothing prepared for tonight, she can really cook". "Well, let me talk to my mom, and I will let you know, thanks again Bethany for the phone, take care". I left, walked across the street and made my way in the house, where most of the boxes were already in the living room. There was only one thing that I was looking forward to, and it wasn't my room, it was my birthday.

Chapter 4
Jeremy

I can remember my birthday like it was yesterday, four years has passed since that and now I don't look forward to my birthdays. Last couple of years has been okay to say the least, the presents were getting better but that's because I was getting older, I guess that is bound to happen. It's funny because we are still living in Ohio, I thought we would've moved by now, but since we moved so much before it was good to settle down for a while. The only good thing about being older is you get wiser, well that is what my mom always told me. But if you believe everything that your mother tells you, you never find out anything yourself. I know that sound a little strange but you get used to the idea of figuring out shit yourself, you don't want your mother near you all the time. Being cooped inside that damn house for the whole day, I decided to go out and get some fresh air. The first thought that came into my mind when I went outside was about Beverly, she is the same age as me, and I wonder if she is still back at the little ass town. The good thing about being 18 is I can drive now, even though I have a fucking permit, but I can still drive. I worked most of the summer and earned up enough money to not officially buy my own car yet, but enough. I got a really boring job at a local paint store couple of miles of where we live. I know what you're thinking, a paint store, but you would be surprise how many fucking people in Ohio love to fucking paint. It's like they have nothing else better to do. I can imagine with all the big houses it's a lot of empty walls to paint, and we have a lot of paint. "Hey Mitch, come over here boy, I need you, take out all the Goddamn paint out of the back and put it on the shelves. In case you're wondering who the hell that asshole is that's my "wonderful" boss. His first name is hard to pronounce, or maybe people are saying it wrong I don't know but whatever the case everyone always just calls him by his last name, O'Donnell, go figure an Irish guy working at a fucking paint store Christmas came early for the poor immigrant bastard. I mean that with the up most respect by the way, good guy at heart but just a little edgy sometimes, guy needs to learn how to fucking loosen up sometimes. I purposely took my time getting to the back and grabbing all the damn paint to load them on the shelves. He hates that the most, when I take my time instead of doing my job. But what he doesn't know is I am doing my job, I am taking my time because my fucking job sucks. After several boring hours of stacking paint and my damn back was about to give up on me to, a customer walked in. it's the first one we had all day, what can I say "business is booming". I don't know if she was lost or needed any help, when I saw her face she seemed lost as if she had no idea this was a paint store or something. I walked over there and greeted her and asked her if she needed any help finding anything today. The key is to be as polite as possible even when you have to fake it or dealing with rich, snooty ass snobs but that's another story. She didn't respond at fist just kept on looking around the store. It was pissing me off, but then she finally said, "Yes, as a matter of fact I do need help, I was wondering… and at that time you wouldn't believe who just walked through those off colored double doors, the girl of my life Bethany. I couldn't fucking believe it, "Hey, I think that this lady needs help Mitch, why don't you help her". Oh shit, I totally forgot about Ms. Dumb blonde over here. "Hey can you take care of this, I can get this one, she just walked in, don't worry I know her". I rushed over there, not physically but you know what I mean. "Hey Bethany, how's it going, it's been a long time no talk". I am sorry, do I know you, and anyway I was wondering if you can help me. It's been such a long time, I don't know if she even remembers me. "It's me Mitch; I moved in across the street from your house, I came over one day to borrow your phone to make a call". She had to think about it for a minute, "Oh hey, Wow! I can't believe it, it's been such a long time". "They got you working here now, but that's beside the point how have you been"? Good I replied, I really wanted to tell her so many other things but I forgot I was working and I didn't want to make Mr. speaks with a bad accent angry. "How come you never come out anymore, what I meant to say is how come I never see you around". "About that I wanted to tell you we moved, to a much bigger house in a more populated state if you can call it that, we moved to Texas". I had a blank look on my face, I wanted to say something so bad, and the only word that came out was, why? "My mom got a better job offer and it paid more money than what she was getting now so she decided to pack up and leave". This was a complete shock to me, but I didn't want to keep thinking about that to long because it will remind me of Beverley for some reason, so I hurried up and changed the subject. "You look great, as those my first thoughts that came shooting out". "Thanks, she replied, "How old are you know, completely cutting her off before she got a chance to say anything else". "I am 17, I know what you're thinking, I look young for my age but I am 17". She was the same age as me when I saw her for the first time. The other lady that previously walked in was leaving as she had two bags in her hand; O'Donnell just looked at me and walked into his office. Before Beth, that's what I call her because I hate calling her by her full name its annoying, if you're not doing anything right now you want to grab something to eat or something. She smiled, sure, we are not leaving for a couple of hours anyway lunch sounds good. My mom is doing some really last minute paper work and driving from place to place looking for stuff to put inside the house it's a real zoo. I put down my apron and yelled at O'Donnell, "I am taking my 30, which is my lunch break; I get 30 minutes to grab some food or whatever I need to take care of. I took Beth's hand and walked outside, today was definitely a good day.

I didn't know that many spots to get some decent food, but there was one place near the job, it was small and it sucked but it was better than nothing I guess. I took her there and her first expression was, this is nice, but she said ever so sarcastically I just smiled as we walked in. I couldn't make out the name because it looked like they were doing construction and some of the damn letters were missing. The place looked very much alive, again being very sarcastic; the damn place looked like a morgue. Actually I've seen morgues more alive than this place but I don't care that much to talk about it any further. We walked up to the main counter and looked at the scarce menu they had hanging above us. It was kind of sad that the place was really small, but it's worse when your menu has no damn food on it. I didn't know what to order, I mean everything looked so great, I leaned over to Beth and asked her if she wanted anything. "Um, she said, "I want a number 2, but instead of the soda can I get water". She looked at me, like she was going to say something, I don't drink soda it causes bumps on your face, well there not really bumps but you know what I mean it's like small blemishes or something. Now at that point I just smiled and agreed with her but in all honesty I really didn't give a fuck what causes what, but I didn't want to say that. After we got our food, oh did I forget to mention I ordered a number 9 and that consist of two grilled chicken sandwiches, large fries, and a large coke; pretty good deal if you ask me. There was nowhere to fucking sit in this damn place the only table was near a window, and trust me the view wasn't that great to begin with all we got is a large fucking red pickup truck and some trees near a pole or something. After we engulfed our food metaphorically speaking, I asked her if she wanted to go for a walk or something because I had some time left on my break might as well use them wisely right. We left, and being the ever so gracious guy that I am I left a little tip on the table because I felt bad for the place. "Where do you want to go, you have to remember you only have little time left to be walking around she said". Don't remind me I said to myself, I wanted to take as much time as I needed so I don't have to work. "I don't know, I said, let's just walk it's a nice day outside, anyway I am with you so it's even better". I can't believe I just said that, what was I thinking, I mean don't get me wrong I like this girl but now was a bad time I think. She just stopped walking and just looked into my eyes. I don't know what she was thinking but at that point I didn't care I just wanted her to say something. "You really mean that, what you just said do you really mean that or are you just trying to impress me"? I tried to play it off like I didn't know what she was talking about or something. "What do you mean, what are you talking about"? As we kept on walking and I kept looking at her but when she turned to me

I look the other way. She stopped again and looked at me again, this time she held my hand so I couldn't walk away or pretend I was again. "Hey you never answered my question, did you mean what you say earlier"? She was persistent, I'll give her that, "Yes I did, I am really glad that you are with me today, and I like having you around". She just smiled and looked at me; she didn't say anything but I think I had a feeling that she liked me back too. I asked her the same question sort of, I was more blunt if you can imagine that for a change. "Do you like having me around to, I mean do you like me". Again she smiled and looked at me and gave me a hug, but this was different it was more like a I love you hug and I will never let you go hugs, but I am not a fucking hug expert, in the end I think I got my answer.

Time was running out from my break I only had 10 minutes left and I had to get back to the store to do some last minute inventory and lock up, because for some reason my boss is letting me leave home early. "Hey I have to get back to work to close up and shit and do some other stuff you want to come with me or do you have to go"? "No I can come if I know my mom we will be here for a while, now I can finally see what you do at your job". I do plenty of shit but then again it's a fucking paint store, come on it not like a Goddamn casino otherwise I would be filthy, stinking rich. We made it to my job with 5 minutes to spare on my break, my over enthusiastic boss was standing behind the counter staring at me when Beth and I walked inside. "How is going O'Donnell, pretending to actually give a fuck if he has a nice day or not, the only thing that I like about this guy when he signed my checks at the end of the week. After I checked the inventory and was about to close the store, O'Donnell was coming out of his office with a newspaper in one hand and his wallet in the other. I was hoping you would give me a raise or something, but if you had a boss like the one I have you wouldn't expect much from him. He had the wallet out for another reason, but he wasn't grabbing for anything he was looking at a picture in the right hand side under the plastic covering. He just stared at the picture for a while, and he looked at me then in a split second he left and didn't say anything as he left. With that said, or not said, I locked up the store grabbed my coat and other shit and proceeded to head off. I looked at Beth and asked her if she wanted to come to my house and meet my ever so wonderful mother. She looked at her watch and said "Sure why not I'm always up to meeting new people, hopefully your mother is as nice as you are". Wouldn't you like to know, I mumbled to myself as we left, it's not that my mom is not a bad person but she is a mom and you know how mothers are? But you don't need to here anymore of my mom since I already explained previously. It was getting late, actually it wasn't but I always make a reference to time, and always in a hurry to get somewhere when I am not. I decided to take a cab, it was surprising I found one just parked against the side of the street like that, they are hard to get sometimes. Beth and I got in and the first thing that I noticed is that the damn cabbie was middle eastern decent, now personally I don't have a problem with that because I don't consider myself a racist or anything, but it was just ironic that's all. When we got in he leaned over from his seat looked at me kind of weird, and gave Beth a strange look, he probably never saw Americans so well put together. "Where to, he said, hurry up I don't have all day, and you're wasting my meter". I gave him my address and told him to step on it, I always wanted to say that and he was being a fucking asshole so I didn't want to have an engaging conversation with the bastard. Couple of miles and more of his excessive annoying talking later, we finally made it to my house. My house so wonderful, but not as wonderful as the one we fucking left a long time ago. Every time I see a fucking house I always think of Beverly. She is probably so grown up now, her body probably looks better now than it ever did before. I can just imagine pressing up against her soft succulent skin, and holding her in my arms while looking into her eyes and telling her how I really feel. But now I can't all because of my wonderful mother, oh and if I forgot to mention that before well now I did so I think you are pretty much caught up on my mom.

We made our way into the house and to my surprise my mom wasn't home, but then again it didn't really surprise me that much, because she is never home most of the time, she is out doing God knows what. But what I saw was none other than my main man, and I used that term very lightly, Jeremy. Jeremy was propped up on the couch like he broke every bone in his body or something; I wish I said to myself. Luckily for me the couch was turned away from us, and he was watching TV or something, I didn't really care to explain what he likes to watch while relaxing, there was no need for it. When Beth shut the door, he heard it and got up from the couch; stood up stretched his arms scratched his fat ass stomach and looked at me. "Welcome home kiddo, how was work today"? I don't know why Jeremy keeps calling me fucking kiddo, but it was starting to really piss me the fuck off. "Work was good, I replied, even though it sucked, but I didn't want to tell him that, he would get all upset for some reason. And when Jeremy gets upset he is the biggest mother fucking baby in the whole entire mother fucking world. When he gets upset or I tell him anything bad happened or even if I am having a sort of off day, he would run to my mother and tell her like it was the end of the fucking world or something. He didn't say anything for a second, and looked at me, and then he said, "You're going to introduce me to your pretty little friend there or what". I rolled my eyes and said this is Bethany, an old friend who used to live right across of us, she came to visit". That's nice he said as he proceeded to go into my mom's room and he shut the door behind him. "What was that all about she said, who was that guy, he was kind of weird and shit". That my friend is who we call Jeremy, he is living with us until the time being, or until my mom finds a better excuse of a man. Come on and follow me I said, to her as she was right behind me, where are we going exactly as she said right into my ear. When she was done yelling in my ear, I said we are going to my room, because I enjoy the privacy. Why do you hate the living room so much it seems like a nice place, she continued to talk, she kept going on about the fucking living room, it's just a room I said to myself. I think she was talking about her mom going shopping for some new sofas to put in her living room or something. It might have been something about redecorating or something, I didn't care that much too really pay attention. Anyway this whole entire talk about living rooms I just lost my train of thought, wait never mind just got it. It *was* about a living room, mine to be more exact, and why I didn't give you a reason earlier in which why I hated it. Okay so here's the truth about our fucking living room, and why I am making such a big deal about it. The only reason why I enjoy my privacy, and why I made that statement to Beth because of Jeremy. Yep, that is pretty much it, all because of Jeremy, I hate being in the living room, because his room, I mean my mom's room is right next to it. And I hate spending time in the living room because he can hear everything I do and say, and that's why I made a big deal about my privacy. Now if I can be frank for a second, Jeremy is not a bad guy, just smells bad, is a fucking loser, is a mother fucking alcoholic, smokes too, I forgot to mention that or not forgot, never showers, I don't think, never brushes his hair, always wears the same shit over and over, and leaves the house a fucking mess, but he is not a bad guy. Sometimes I have to give him credit, because if it wasn't for him, I would've been late to school sometimes. He didn't have to get out of bed to drop me off, but he did so that made him okay, still hate the little fagot but that made him okay. I never been this mean or even said this much mean things about one person, because as a optimistic person I try to better myself every day, but Jeremy was different, just because the things he did and said, and how is always touching and caressing against my mom's body, pisses me off. Instead of me talking or thinking of new things to say about Jeremy, why don't I just tell you exactly who he is, or tell you as much information I can from him these last couple of years.

Well, short and simple Jeremy worked for several years as a construction worker, I know what you're thinking, he wasn't what we like to call management type so he worked lower level construction, or that's what he always called it. I think he went to school for construction management or something; he did that for about 4 to 5 years and finally graduated with a degree. I believe at that time he had a girlfriend of sorts but shortly after a year they split up, and Jeremy being the "educated" person he is didn't sign the damn prenuptial agreement, and now that sleazy ass girlfriend took him for everything he was worth. Shortly after that, he got some money that he saved up from his job, and moved into a crowded ass apartment building in the city. And when I mean crowded that damn apartment was crowded, it seemed like every floor and every room had someone living in it. There was people going in and out, all the time day and night, well that is what he told me one day. His room was located on the 4th floor, room number 413, now there was one special thing about his room, the previous owner was a real O.C.D. and he kept the fucking place so Goddamn sterilize. Nothing was out of place, it's like he would blow a gasket if someone touched something or didn't put anything back the way it was. So, the good thing, yea the good thing was he didn't have to clean up when he moved in, since the whole entire, and I mean the whole entire apartment was spotless. After he lived there for a couple of years, he decided to move out, because he found a better job more suited to his status, whatever. And knowing Jeremy like I do, well it's easy to say that when he left the whole place was trashed, there was shit broken and he never reported it or anything. I guess he didn't care that much to pick up a phone and tell the superintendent that some of the stuff wasn't working properly; I mean it's such a hard job. So he packed all of his belongings and left, and didn't look back, the better job wasn't that good, actually it was more a demotion than what he worked for. He ended up working at a construction site, don't get me wrong, but he didn't do anything he learned in school. Although he had all the credentials, his management wanted something else from him, and told him stay right where you are, your fine right there. As you would imagine that kind of pissed me off, where he fucking walked up to his boss said I QUIT MOTHER FUCKER, and punched him right in the jaw. Subsequently when he did that, he broke his bottom jaw and knocked some teeth out. Then the little pussy instead of fighting back he hurried and ran into his little office, pulled out his cell phone and called the damn cops. A minute like 4 patrol cars came, and I am not a fucking rocket scientist but that's a lot for one person. After a lot of complaints by people that he thought were his friends, the cops proceeded to arrest him and threw him in the back seat of the car. When the cops were driving, Jeremy had the last laugh, giving his ex-boss the middle finger and laughing away. After being cooped in jail for a couple of months, because this was his first offense, he was released on bail, and you wouldn't believe who of all people bailed him out, his ex-girlfriend. It seemed that she had a little flame for him after all or whatever the reason. He collected all of his stuff and walked out a free man, until the next time he decided to let his actions speak louder than his words. "You can stay with me, until the time being, don't worry I've cleaned up since the last time we were together". She was right actually, she did clean up, and not the apartment but herself, she cleaned herself up a lot. I think that she used to what's the popular term now a days, oh I forgot "push rocks". Now I don't know how serious she was into all that shit, but it was ugly, some days she would score, and other days business would be really slow. Other days she would have to deal with the big boys, meaning the people who expect her to do her shit properly, and if she would fuck up or not get enough money, or even agitate someone the wrong way, she would pay for it. Now these guys they don't play that well, and if someone they know fucks up, that person get's fucked up if you catch my drift. Sometimes she would get hit, and punched; it was disturbing at times made me want to puke. I remember this one time she fucked up real bad, the person that she was selling to wanted something more, let's just say he had his dinner and now he wanted dessert. And she wanted no part of that; because well she was only interested in business, well you see he didn't like that too much. In his mind he thought he was getting played, so he made a quick phone call to some people he knew and one thing led to another, she was thrown into the back of a white van and they drove off. What happened next didn't get better; they tossed her out and the concrete floor in some abandoned warehouse. They had her hands tied behind her back, and the main guy who wanted some loving on the side walked up to her. He grabbed by her cheek squeezed real hard, and said, "You want to play me like a fucking fool, now you're the one who is going to pay you filthy, stinking, disgusting whore". He let go of her cheek and slapped her hard across the face, she was bleeding a little bit on the lip. Another guy came up and punched her right in the stomach; all you can here is her crying and coughing a lot. One guy ripped off her shirt and started feeling on her breasts, and started to kiss her on her neck and lips. Then the main guy, one more time slapped the shit out of her, grabbed her and threw her in the van and sped off. Minutes later, he tossed her out of the van and on the side of the street. "Next time, when I want something, I expect you to give it to me you dirty bitch".

Jeremy put all of his shit on the side, and grabbed more of his stuff from her car, for one person he had a lot of shit. "Thanks Amber, that was her name by the way just in case you were wondering, "I really appreciate what you're doing, I thought you never wanted to see me again after what happened last time". "Oh come on that was in the past baby today was a new day and I am with my main man all over again". Jeremy didn't complain he had a place to stay, food to eat, water to drink and a pretty decent girl to fuck if he got bored, and trust me Jeremy gets bored a lot. After several months of living with daring sweetheart, he came home from a late night that night, but to him he considered it early in the morning. He was taking his key out of his coat pocket, when he heard a noise. Now this noise was specific, it wasn't like something breaking or anything, but more like a girl moaning and screaming. He opened the door and walked inside, and to his surprise the moaning and screaming got louder every time he got closer to Amber's room. Now at that time he was thinking two things, one she just might be watching another porno, or second, she could be fucking another man. So with any hesitation he opened the door, and it was the second thought that was true. "Oh my God, Amber said, what the fuck Jeremy, I can explain, let me explain". Jeremy looked pissed, like someone blew up his fucking car or something, I thought he was going to kill the little bastard or something. "You know what, you never changed, you were the still the same little Amber from before. "We are through you slut, I am taking my stuff and leaving, have fun fucking bitch". And in a second, Jeremy left without looking back or without saying any last words. He didn't know where he was going to go, or what he was going to do, but he didn't want to spend one minute in that place. Months later, he got a local job working at a grocery store or some type of store, and that is where he met my mom. Now I wasn't happy about that day, and I am not happy up until today either, but I had no say in the matter. I knew that my mom needed to date again since my dad, well you know, but she could've done better than this guy. When I first met the guy, I knew he was trouble and he is still trouble till now. But again, there is something special about him, just have faith is what my mom always said every time I had something to say about him and her decision. I think she was getting pissed that I only had negative things to say about him, and I don't know him like she claims to do. And she always said the same thing, because I didn't think she wanted to tell me off, I don't know if she was afraid or whatever the case, it didn't bother her as much. Months later, her feelings got stronger, and he started to feel the same way about her, always calling her fucking nicknames and shit like baby and cupcake and sweetheart I wanted to fucking puke. My mom, being the free thinker she is, asked him he wanted to move in, and start a family. "I don't think this is such a good idea", I told my mom, "I don't trust this guy, he looks like a huge loser and he smells like shit". "You are always bringing out the negative in someone, for once grow the fuck up and live with it, I need to start dating again and I think I found Mr. Right. He grabbed her hand, as they walked down the street, as he whispered in her ear while she was laughing. So there I was, left with no chance to say one more thing, not enough to defend myself. I guess she was right, about dating again it was a long time, and for a long time she pretended to be happy. All I want is her to be happy, but not with this fuck, I guess my mom was right I do bring out the negative in people, but if you knew Jeremy or even live with someone who acts like a Jeremy, then you can see why I think so negative. Maybe one day I'll take my mom's advice and think more positively, but then again it's just fucking advice. I don't have to listen to her, and in my opinion Jeremy is still a fucking drunk bitch loser, but then again it's just my opinion, as I smiled sarcastically watching them walking away.

Chapter 5
My 18th Birthday Party

This morning I didn't wake up to my alarm clock as usual, no I woke up to a different sound, it was a fucking car. And now who in the right mind would work on a car fucking 7:00 in the morning you would say, none other than Jeremy. At least that's who I saw when I poked my head out the window and saw him cleaning his seats with a dirty rag. I am one of those people if someone disturbers me when I am sleeping, I am awake for the rest of the day, I am a very light sleeper, and on that note I decided since I am up might as well get something to eat and start off my day. I believe my mom went grocery shopping yesterday, and that means we finally have some decent food in this house. Usually when my mom goes shopping or goes out to get stuff for the house she comes back with the job only half done, it kind of gets everyone mad, but when can you expect she's my mom. I walked right into the kitchen, opened the fridge and saw one gallon of fucking milk, and on top of the fridge there were two boxes of cereal, one was full and the other one was half empty. Now I don't like to say bad things about my mom, because I know that would be mean but this women needs shopping lessons, I don't understand, she takes enough money out from the bank what the hell is doing with all that money instead of buying food. So I grabbed a bowl, a spoon, some cereal, and milk and sat down in front of the TV and watched some cartoons.

Now I know what you're thinking 18 and still watching cartoons, well I have an answer for that and that is I don't give a fuck, because there is nothing else on 7:00 in the Goddamn morning. Speaking of cereal, why is it when I write down what kind of cereal I want, my mom never gets the one I am looking for. Grant it she will get the same name and everything but she will get the store brand. I know it looks the same, and tastes the same, sort of, but for once I want the good cereal even if the box is like 5 dollars. I finished eating, and the only good thing about today, besides the car and the cereal it is the WEEKEND, and I can relax all day, while my mom and Jeremy are working, or whatever.

I got and put the bowl in the sink, and I noticed that the dishes were not clean from yesterday's dinner, and Jeremy had breakfast today too, that means there are more dishes to wash, great. Well I am not going to let that ruin what can be such a wonderful weekend, I hope not. When I went into my mom's room, she was already gone I don't know where she went, but knowing her she will be gone the whole day. I was about to back in my room, when Jeremy walked in, he was all dirty from cleaning his car and shit. He walked up to me and said, "Hey kiddo, morning, hope my car didn't wake you up, sorry about that". I hate when he called me that, kiddo I am not a fucking little kid anymore. But I was too happy to let that bother me so I could care less. "Hey Jeremy, how's is going man, don't worry about the car it's no problem at all". Pretending to actually give a shit how he is and about his shit of car, but it was too early to get started with him. I sat down and the TV was still on, I don't know exactly what kind of cartoon was showing but it looked pretty funny so I watched the rest of the episode. After the episode was over I felt disappointed because the episode fucking sucked, but I can't complain. Jeremy was taking a shower, so for like 10 to 15 minutes I can have some freaking peace and quiet. I hopped in the shower down the hall from my room, it was smaller than my mom's but I liked it, I had all the privacy I wanted. And besides it was practically mine since I am the only one who always used it. I had all my stuff in there soap, body wash, and a washcloth. I took a generally long shower because for the first time in a long time the water was hot. I think because I am in the shower while Jeremy was also taking a shower, every time I get in by myself the water is usually freezing. After 30 minutes of cleansing, I finally got out and the whole bathroom was steaming, I wrote my name and some other stuff in the window as I left, I kept the door opened so the bathroom can cool down. I walked into my room and got dressed, I thought the time had passed, but it was only like 8 something. I finished getting ready; putting on my favorite pair of jeans that I always wear, well not all the time but most of the time. Now the one reason that I like these specific pair of jeans is that they fit comfortably around my waist, they don't come down to long near my ankles, and they so comfortable. I remember the first day I got them, my mom and I went shopping at a local clothing store, it wasn't name brand or anything but it was still good. We walked in and the whole fucking store was packed, I mean packed like sardines in a tin can, it must've been a sale or something. The reason why we went shopping is my mom needed some new clothes again. Now we all know how much women love to shop, it's like in their gene or something. Whatever the case, she gave me some money and let me pick out some clothes of myself and that I did. I walked around for a minute until something really good caught my eye, and I found some reasonable sale items on jeans and shirts. Now the shirts were a little tacky, and it's one of those shirts that I wouldn't get caught dead wearing, literally I can think of a hundred shirts that I would die in that the ones they were trying to pass off. But there was this one pair of jeans that stood out. They looked kind of old, but I guess that was the fashion or something. The bottom was slightly messed up like they were ripped but that was the style. It had two pockets in the front and one pocket in the back. Now when I grabbed them from the rack and paid for it, I went into the dressing room and put them on, I didn't want to wait till I got home.

I walked out my room looking like a hundred dollars and smelling like a million, but I don't want to sound boastful. It was getting late in the morning, and I had the whole day to do whatever the hell I wanted. Jeremy got of the shower, walked over towards me smiling for some reason like he just found his dick or something. That was rude I apologize, just kidding I meant every word, anyway he was smiling for another reason I guess. "Hey kiddo, I just forgot I have to meet with someone to talk about this new job offer that just came to my attention". I don't know how many times I have to say it, but I fucking hate that word, Goddamn it. "Fine, I said, that's cool I am going to go out anyway and get some air or something". "Are you going to see that girl, you know the one you brought over last night"? "No, I think that she left already with her mom when she got back home yesterday". I am going to just take a walk and probably do some other stuff; I said as I walked outside and started making my way down the driveway. It was a mild day, or as mild as it gets around here, the weather was kind of monotonous, the winds were very docile, but it did rain some days ago so that's about it. I didn't know where I was going but I needed to go somewhere and fucking think for a while, there are so many disappointing things that happened to my life in these last couple of months. For instance, the fist girl that I met, Beverly, I really liked her and we moved to fucking Ohio. Second, I met another girl I am a little older now so I think I understand these feelings that I am having, she had to go back with her mom to where ever the hell she lives. Every time it seems like I make a friend something happens and I don't have a friend anymore. Whatever, I really don't give a shit because I will meet another girl that will be better than these two. This girl will be special I guess, nothing to extravagant but someone for me, someone who understands me. I want this special girl to be funny, she's got to make me laugh, I want her to be strong, what I mean by that is not body builder strong but emotionally strong to deal with all of life's shit. I want her to believe in herself and never give up if shit goes astray. I want her to independent, good strong moral values, good head on her shoulders. And yes, I also want her to have a smoking hot ass body; I think when looking for a girlfriend that key is always an important factor. I want her to have a good fashion senses, I mean if she does have a fucking hot body I want her to wear clothes, not to show if off like a disgusting, diseased infested prostitute, but to compliment her physique. And other stuff that I cannot of think of right now, but I think that you get the idea, and one day I will meet someone like that and hopefully she will make all my dreams come true.

I walked for several more minutes I didn't know where I was going, honestly I thought I was lost or something. I am glad that everywhere I go I always carry my cell phone and my wallet just in case of emergencies. I didn't recognize a lot of the buildings that surrounded me, I remember correctly my family and I drove down this road before but I wasn't paying attention, now I wish I did. I kept on walking, and I was saying to myself that if anything I am probably in the next town and I can just call someone to come pick me up. Again I kept on walking straight, because there was no point to turn around and go back if I don't know where to turn around to. I saw one car drive by; it slowed down and stopped along the corner of the street. I quickly walked up and was going to ask him where the fuck I was. As I walked closer he walked into a store, great, I said, I can ask someone inside how to get back to my house. Well I am not going to say that but give them the street address and shit, I don't want fucking random people showing up on my doorstep. I walked into the store, and it was a bakery, so I pulled out the one thing that can help me get through this tough situation. I pulled out my wallet, come on it's a damn bakery and I was hungry, I am not going to buy anything you know. I walked up to the counter and started to look inside the glass display. You wouldn't believe how much baked goods this place had, it seemed like the whole place was packed with sweets. As soon you walk in there are 4 tables in the corner and a poster of some city or something right above it. Right in front of you there is the main counter and on each ends there are display statues with sweets inside. On the top right hand corner there are booths and shit so people can sit and eat. On the lower right hand there is a jukebox machine, it looked kind of old, but it still worked. As you walk further into the store along the front window side there are more tables and a few posters hung up there too, all of these posters have frames on them, but they still look nice. And finally the middle had a lounge of some sort, they were couches and a two tables and one TV. This place was fucking incredible, I could've spent the whole day here and never went home. But seriously it was a damn bakery that's it, so I told the person that I wanted a specific piece of pie. For some reason I always get apple but this time I wanted lemon just because I was feeling a little spontaneous or I just didn't give a fuck and I was extremely hungry, maybe that was it who knows. Anyway, there was this girl just sitting behind one of the booths on the far side of the store along the window as soon you walk in and shit. She looked very fucking cute and I was going to go over there and something, but it felt like something was holing me back, I couldn't figure it out; I mean if you saw a smoking hot chick sitting alone you would go over there and talk to her right? I mean I smelled okay, I guess I don't think I smelled bad at all, I was dressed fine nothing to fancy or street like, and my hair was in order. So I don't get it why couldn't I go over there and talk to her, what the fuck. And in the last second it hit me like a 45 slug right in the back of my fucking head, and I felt my body dropping to the ground. For a second I couldn't breathe everything was getting dark and I was feeling cold. I knew I only had a couple of seconds to live before I see the preverbal white light at the end of the tunnel sort of shit. I saw another girl come out the restroom, it felt like time stood still around me and my heart was beating ever so nervously against my chest, it felt like it was going to tear right out. My mouth felt dry, and I had a weird feeling in the pit of my stomach like someone was grabbing my sides and fucking twisting them as hard as they can. She came out the restroom ever so benevolently, everything from the dress that she was wearing to the way her hair looked. I mean I couldn't believe my eyes, her body was so voluptuous, and her smile could light up a room. She was glowing with such beauty and grace, with so much personality in her step. It was like she was calm and collected, but also caring and passionate and proud and aggressive. I took my attention away from the girl that was still sitting at the booth and I stared at this angel that God has sent down from the heavens to let me run into her arms and hold her against my body. I wanted to turn away because my mom always says staring is rude, but I couldn't help it, and I think that girl noticed so I quickly turn my head around and frantically starting to eat my pie which by the was getting cold.

The girl told the other girl that sat down with her something, she leaned over and whispered it in her ear, and a second later the girl who got out of the bathroom got up and looked my direction. She didn't directly look at me, but I knew that she was looking at me it was painfully obvious. Her other friend sat back down and the main girl of my incoherent rambling was coming over my way and I all of a sudden got really nervous. She slowly walked over to me and every step she took my heart was pounding louder and louder, I kept on looking and sort of eating my pie at the same time. She stopped right behind my stool I was eating, cleared her throat I turned around and she folded her arms against her chest. She kind of gave me a look like I know you were staring at us and I want to know what the fuck is up kind of look. "Um, she said, can I help you, because I noticed that you were looking at me and my friend for a long time and it was getting a little childish?" For a second I didn't say anything, and then I said, "Sorry about that, you look very familiar that's it, I thought you were someone else but I couldn't put my finger on it". Even though I was lying, and she did look very familiar and I could put my finger on it. She looked at me for a second, and just smiled, "No problem, I thought you were just staring because you were one of those weird guys who stars at fucking girls and gets off by thinking all these sexual thoughts about them. You have no idea as I was thinking to myself, for a second we didn't say anything to each other, and kind of looked at each other for one second. "You know you look very familiar yourself, you sure we haven't met somewhere before, do you live around here"? I looked at her, "Yes, for a matter of fact I live a couple of miles down from the paint store, it's a big white store full of paint, being sarcastic I thought it was funny". For some reason, you really look familiar I can't my finger on… and on that thought she just screamed out Mitch, I can't believe it. Beverly, I replied as I got up and gave her a big hug how've you been, it's been a long time. "Good she said, my family is in town just visiting my cousins and shit and I wanted to get something to eat, saw this place and decided to come here". "Wow, this a total surprise, I still can't believe it, sit down let's catch up how is everything". "Wait a minute you knew it was me the whole time didn't you how come you didn't say anything or walked up I could've introduced you to my cousin who is sitting along the corner in the booth". "I didn't know if you would still remember me, it was such a long time, and I was afraid that you would have found someone already". "Come on, me find a boyfriend good one, anyway I am single you know that, I am not big on this whole dating shit." As she was saying that, I quickly remembered, hey I know this is short notice but I was wondering, and it would mean a lot if you can come, but I am having my 18th birthday party at my place, but my parents are going to be gone that whole weekend I think they wanted to see the sights or something. So I was wondering if you can come or are you not into the whole birthday shit either, smiling sarcastically as I said it. I can come, and I'll bring some of my cousins too, they need a good time they can be boring sometimes. Okay great I said to myself as she walked over to her table and grabbed her things. Beverly and her cousin was about to leave, and I gave her my address for my house. She looked at it and slid it into her purse well; see you in a couple of days KIDDO. Okay, I will see you soon, take care and keep in touch as we hugged and she left with her cousin.

I know what you're thinking, kiddo, well; you see it doesn't bother me when people I actually like saying it as oppose to people I despise saying it. And I know it always bothers me when people saying it, but if you had a hot ass girl who is almost the same age or maybe a little older than you are saying that, it is such a turn on, right? Oppose to a drunken old fagot bitch calling you kiddo, and I know I shouldn't be calling him that, actually to tell you the truth he is been changing last couple of weeks. Jeremy stopped drinking; he still smokes, not as much as he used to be but a little. But I can't believe he stopped drinking I thought we would have to bury him with all of his fucking beer bottles and shit. And I know me saying all of these kind of makes me sound like a fucking hypocrite, like I say one thing and do the other kind of thing, but I don't believe in fucking morals so I could care less about the whole thing. Shit, I just realized I have to head home, it was getting late. I pulled out my cell phone and called Jeremy to come pick me up, several minutes later he arrived. He parked in front of the diner and I walked over to the passenger seat and hopped in. "Hey Jeremy, thanks man sorry for calling late lost track of time". "No problem man, I was doing other things anyway just sit back and enjoy the ride home KIDDO". I just smiled and nodded my head as we drove off to go home, and I needed to rest up before my big birthday bash, because it is going to be a long weekend ahead.

Chapter 6
Falling In Love

It was morning, it seemed a little early for me but nonetheless it was morning. And when I woke up I felt someone next to me but I didn't remember going to sleep with someone else. Wow, I said to myself it must have been one crazy ass birthday party, I couldn't remember anything, but I didn't drink or I don't think I did. And in that second, I heard a moan, it sounded like it came from a girl or something and when I turned around it did come from a girl. I couldn't believe my eyes when I saw fucking Beverley laying there right next to me in my bed. I didn't know how this happened, I didn't know what I did, I don't think that I did anything wrong in this case. What the fuck, wait okay let me think, breathe Mitch, everything is going to be alright, you can get through this just breathe. In that split second, Beverley woke up and stretched and screamed she looked at me, "Good morning sleepy head, you're finally awake you want to get some breakfast or something". I didn't know what to say but I said what any other reasonable person would say in this situation. "Sure, why not I am a little hungry and I know this great little place just around the corner from the house". We both got up and she put her shirt back on and I started to get dressed also, this was coming at me so fast, I don't remember anything that happened but I couldn't concentrate on that. For some reason I was staring at Beverley, I mean her standing there with no shirt as she was putting it on and getting ready it made me feel so strange inside but happy at the same time. Whatever happened I wanted to know because it was going to bother me for the rest of the day. "Hey Beverley, I said as she was getting ready, um, what happened last night exactly, because I don't remember clearly"? She put her shirt on and her boots and other shit, turned around, smiled and said, "What are you talking about, you don't remember it was your birthday party last night. You had all of these people over and we partied, I think you had way too much to fucking drink". Come on, if you want to get something to eat get off your lazy ass and hurry. I got up as she was smiling, I finished getting ready, but just for a second felt like an eternity, my whole life I wondered if I would see her again, and now she is in my house putting on lipstick and fixing her hair. I always thought what my life would be if she never came back, what kind of person I would be if I never saw her again. But not even seeing her but just looking at her again, and everything she does and says. The way she smiles when something is funny, the way she cries when she think something is sad. The way she looks in the mirror trying to figure out what she is going to wear or how to wear her hair. The way she always looks good no matter what the weather is or what kind of mood she might be in, or what kind of mood someone else may put her in. The way she thinks about things that interests her, how she always puts others before herself. The way she sits down and reads a book, wondering what she might be thinking about, and the way she enjoys herself watching a movie. And in that second, I just realized that I might be in love with Beverley. I didn't know where these emotions were coming from just yesterday I liked her and today I am in love with her. She was standing by the door waiting impatiently, but I know that she was not mad for some reason. I grabbed my keys and my wallet and we left to get some breakfast. "You want to drive, I really don't care, and I really don't feel like driving today". Thank God, I passed my written test before my 18th birthday, because driving with a fucking permit when I am 18 would be fucking embarrassing. I got in and she sat in also, we started to pull out it was still was pretty early in the morning I think it was only like 9 something but I think my watch was broken so whatever. She adjusted the seat, and turned on the radio, it was nothing but fucking commercials. I hate this, she said, no matter what day or time it is every time I want to listen to the radio its always fucking commercials. Even the way that she complains about the radio is so fucking cute, anyway we got there and for a little breakfast place it seemed like there was a lot of cars. Okay like 2 or 3 but still that's a lot I guess, I found a nifty little parking spot right next to a fence and a fucking tree. Great, I said as we got out I hope a fucking dog doesn't pee on my car thinking it is a tree or something or whatever. We went in and the place smelled like breakfast in my house, so that wasn't a bad start I guess. We found a table right next to a window, and the good thing was that I can see the car right outside the window. Her car is so much better than my moms and Jeremy combined, it was a slightly newer model but it looked like it was in good condition. I remember Beverley telling me one day what kind of car she drove. Well it was her mom's car and she gave it to Beverley for her 18th birthday. Oh yeah, that's right she is the same age as me that's cool, I always she was younger or even a year older than me. For some reason Beverley looks older than her age, I don't mean that she looks old like a senior citizen she just looked older than I did, but I didn't care that much about it to let it bother me. But the car was another thing; it was a green color like a dark green, and it had a black hard top. The tires were decent and the inside didn't look bad either, for a nice girl she had a nice car. Our food finally came, and for some strange reason I always order the same thing when I go out and eat breakfast, but when I am home I always eat the same fucking shit. I always get two pancakes; one side of eggs scrambled of course, two hash browns, one sausage, and orange juice. Beverley got some eggs, sunny side up, one hash browns and some milk, to me it seemed like a wimp's breakfast, but I don't pass judgment. About halfway through the meal, she gets up and says I have to use the little girl's room. I say okay and just sit there staring out the window for a minute. I didn't want to continue eating without her it would seemed rude you know, like if she would've came out and all my food would've been gone, and I had to watch her eat that would be kind of weird. It was another casual day outside, where you see people being well people. There were two kids on the corner talking about something, I couldn't hear but they were talking about something. There was a lady walking her dog, make that dogs, I think she had like 4 fucking dogs. There was another man smoking a cigarette on the bench on the other side of the street. There was another lady, she looked like she was waiting for something, and she kept looking at her watch and kept looking down the street. Minutes later, Beverley came out and sat down, "What are you looking at"? She said. "Nothing, I replied, just staring out the window just waiting for you to come out". "You ready to go, I am getting bored of this fucking place, let's leave we have the whole day". "What about the food, should we just leave a tip and go"? "Just leave something who cares let's go I am getting bored, leave a decent tip would you"? And that I did, I left like 5 or 6 dollars, I know that's a lot of tip but the waitress was really sweet, and I know that she tried even though business wasn't booming if you know what I mean. I had no idea where the fuck we were going, it was getting pretty late in the morning it was almost noon, and my parents still not were coming home for two more days, see they told me they are coming home Monday. Oh, and when I met parents I met my mom, not that lying sack of shit Jeremy, but I guess he's a good guy. We left, and started walking down the street; I didn't know, but for some reason it didn't stop Beverley to wherever she was taking me.

We finally made it to a park that was near around where my house was, now since we have been living here I never knew about this park, maybe I need to get out more. The park was nice, and she picked the right time to go because the weather was just right and there weren't a lot of people, and it was pretty early in the afternoon we still had the whole day to ourselves. We found a little bench near some trees, and there were some rose bushes near both ends of the bushes. It looked like something out of a magazine, but what do I know. We sat down and Beverley was looking around, it was such a nice day outside the wind was blowing in the air and the birds were chirping. Just looking at her staring in the sky I just wondered what she was thinking about, she seemed so peaceful. I wanted to tell her so badly how I felt, I wanted to grab her hand and look into her eyes and tell her I love you. I always loved you, and I will always love you. I wanted to look into her eyes and tell her that everything was going to be alright, and she never had to worry ever again. I just wanted to look into her eyes and tell her so badly, but I couldn't for some reason words wouldn't form. There were so many things that I wanted to say to her, but I couldn't find the words. I didn't know if she would understand I didn't want to bring her into my world with all my problems, I couldn't stomach to see her face and the feelings that she is going through. There were so many things that were bothering me, that sometimes it was unbearable and I can't take it. It's not that I was afraid of telling her how I felt, but I couldn't not right now, not now when I have so many other things to sort out in my life first. Where do I begin, I mean my mom first, she is such a strong, independent, beautiful person, and yet at the same time she never understood what it meant to really be in love. And not even love you know, but to be with the one person that you can spend the rest of your life with. To be with the one person that makes everything alright and always brings out the best out of you. To be with the one person that you can talk to if you're having problems or just to talk to. To be with the one person that makes you excited and afraid and happy and sad all at the same time. The one person that you can hold tightly and never let go. That is how I am feeling right now with Beverley, God, why can I tell her how I feel. Don't forget Jeremy, for some reason he is mixed in all of this to. I know that I get on his fucking case a lot but if you fucking met the guy you would give him a hard time to. Sometimes he tries you know, it's not like he is totally helpless, and yea I have to admit he does come through when I can't depend on anyone else. And Bethany, the other girl that is involved in all of this shit, every time I think of her I think of Beverley. And I know that is wrong because she is such a nice person, she is full of life and has such a great personality. She understood me for who I am and what I can become understood me so completely sometimes I was surprised. I know that she was the second girl that I met, and Beverley was the first girl that I met, and I can't help to understand that no matter what I do, I always have these feelings for everyone that I ever met or loved. But no matter what happens in life and what kind of obstacles that life puts me through I can always overcome. No matter how I feel on a particular day or what kind of mood someone puts me in I can overcome. No matter how I feel about someone or what kind of mix emotions I have someone, inside I know that everything is going to be alright. And today sitting on this park bench looking at Beverley I know that I cannot be afraid anymore of what happens. Sometimes in life you have to take your shots and don't be afraid of the risks that lie ahead. My mom always said, "No matter what happens in life, always listen to the one thing that is going to help you get through even the hardest situations, listen to your heart". And for a while I never knew what she meant by that, but today I understand what she was trying to say and I had to listen to my heart. And out of instinct maybe or my mother's words don't know to surely, but I grabbed Beverley's hands held them firmly and looked into her eyes. She just smiled, "What's up Mitch, you want to say something"? And as I stared into her eyes for one more second I just said it, everything that I have been going through my whole life, all my emotions, thoughts just everything. "Beverley took a deep breath looked at her and said, I love you Beverley". She was still smiling, but it kind of disappeared in the day, she looked at me grabbed my hands that were holding hers, a single tear ran down her eye and just glided gently against her cheek, she smiled once again and said, "I love you to Mitch". It was at that moment that I finally understood what my mom was saying all of these years. Everything that I was feeling, everything I went through as a kid and experiencing as a man is finally making sense.

Beverley and I stood up from the park bench and we held hands as we walked away, she leaned over and softly placed her head against my shoulder. I turned my head as we continued walking, looked at her, and I know that deep down inside my heart everything was going to be alright, I knew that she was going to be answer to all my questions. I just smiled as we walked out of the park, holding her tightly never letting her go.

Chapter 7
Mother

After I expressed my inner most feelings for the girl that I can spend the rest of my natural life with, now the hard part came. I know what you're thinking; telling someone how you feel after such a long time isn't hard? But it was it was the hardest thing that I could've done, because there were so much negative thoughts going through my head at that time, but I did it and I couldn't be happier with my decision. And you're probably thinking what can be harder than true love right; well she hasn't met my mother. Now when it came to finding the right special girl that I need in my life, which was hard to tell her that I love her and to hear those words back. But when it came to actually bringing someone home to meet my family with the exception of Jeremy here is the challenge. It wasn't that family and Jeremy was embarrassing or anything, but whenever someone comes over to visit or anyone brought someone over they get over excited to easily. I always have the feeling like they never met human beings before and they are treating them like a science experiment. Okay maybe not that extreme but you get the picture, they make the person feel, well over comfortable and sometimes in my family that can be a bad thing. Yesterday it was kind of late so I decided to crash at Beverley's house just until the morning and then I have to head home to go back to work before my parents get home. I got a text message from my mom that night, and it read, "Hey sweetie, it's me, I just wanted to tell you that we will be home tomorrow afternoon, we decided to get home a little earlier than planned got a little homesick, see you soon bye love you". So you know now why I have to head home the next day pretty early and get ready to introduce Beverley to my mom and Jeremy. Morning had finally arrived and for some reason I was in the same bed as Beverley in her room. I was feeling two different things right about now, one I was freaking out a little bit because her parents were home. When Beverley brought me over to sleep over her parents didn't mind because it was late and I appeared tired. I didn't think that I would actually be sleeping in her room nonetheless in her bedroom with the door closed. I was sleeping on the pull out couch in the living room, but for the life of me I don't know how I got in her room and on top of her bed. The second thing was what if her parents wake up decided to wake up and see that I am not in the sofa or not in the living room. Or what if they decided to knock on Beverley's door, or see me coming out of her room in the morning. Beverley woke up and stretched, looked at me and just smiled, "Good morning sleepy head, hungry I can make some breakfast or something". "Beverley what if your parents see that I am not in the living room or see me coming out of your room". She just laughed as she put her head back down on the pillow, "Don't worry my parents went to work already, we were sleeping when they left". I was breathing a sigh of relief maybe I made a big deal for nothing; I have a tendency of doing that from time to time. Breakfast sounds good I said, "Get up and get dressed, and don't take forever like you usually do". As I laughed walking out her room to go in the bathroom, I can hear yelling shut up as I walking in. I took a quick shower because I wanted to make it home before my mom and Jeremy made it home. It's not that they didn't trust me but I promised them I would be home before they get home. Well I promised my mom, I don't promise shit to Jeremy, because he is the type of person that would fucking snitch and tell the whole world if he had to. After a quick cleansing I got out and I opened the bathroom door and I saw Beverly walking around with bra and panties on. I just stood on the edge of the bathroom door and just whistled as I laughed to myself. She turned around dripping wet from when she got of the shower, looked at me for a second and went into her room to get ready. Just standing there in my 2 dollar towel and imagining Beverley coming out the shower dripping wet, with her bra and panties on, and just imagining the moisturizer slowly sliding down her soft smooth skin, and the warm water gently caressing her body, and her hands touching herself while she gets clean, rubbing softly against her body. That moment got me thinking that I am going to hang out with her more often and if I can come over more often too. She finally got out and was three quarters of the way dressed just needed to put on her socks and shoes. I finally went in and since I am a guy it took me fucking record time to get ready. I put on some deodorant, sprayed cologne, put on my socks, followed by jeans, a belt, my shirt, and finally my shoes. I finished in like a minute and thirty seconds. When I got out she was done getting ready, she had all of her stuff waiting by the door. As I grabbed all my belongings and headed out, I told her that I needed to hurry because it was almost the afternoon before my mom comes home, and yes Jeremy. It was a far walk from her house to my house, and we decided to take a cab or something to get there faster. I was low on cash, hard to believe when you have a great job working in a paint store, but I tend to blow my money on useless shit anyway. "Hey I am low on cash, do you mind splitting the rate"? "How are you low on cash you just got paid like a couple of weeks ago, okay I split it with you". We both got in and the cab smelled pretty badly, I argued with the cabbie to open a window or something before he has two rotten corpses in the backseat. I didn't think that the cabbie even understood fucking English, because he looked at me like I was speaking another language. So I asked him again polity, again he looked at me and said "Where do you want to go, tell me where you want to go"? I was thinking to myself great another cabbie that doesn't speak English and it is from some Middle Eastern country or something. No more Mr. nice guy, I said, "Hey fuck can you open the window and can you get your ass moving". I think he understood that because he started to go, he sped off pretty quickly actually thank God there were no cops behind us. I gave him my address, and minutes later he pulled up in front of the house. Beverley and I split the cab ride, as we walked up the driveway to my home. "What a fucking loser, couldn't even understand simple English, and we live in America, I said to Beverley". "It's not his fault you know, people of his ethnicity are always looking for work and shit". In some demeaning way she was right, even Mexicans are always looking for work to, and they will get whatever it is suitable and earns them an honest living, even when most Americans put them down for working such low credible jobs. We walked in and sat down on the couch, I grabbed the remote under the half empty bag of potato chips and shook all the crumbs off of it. I turned on the TV, and just for the sake of argument we have a really old ass mother fucking TV. And sometimes it really pisses me off, because when you turn it on after a long time of being off, it takes like a million years to turn on. The TV itself is small but not ridiculously huge or anything but it still sucks. Just last month the fucking color tube broke it just stopped working and everything was either in black or white or the color intensity was all wrong. I don't know I am not an expert or anything, but it just pissed me off. Well the TV finally came on after like 20 seconds of stand by and the channel that I was watching yesterday was all fucked up. The color was too bright or to dull, whatever I turned off the TV and just laid my head back on the couch. We laid on the couch for several more minutes until Beverly got up looked at me and said, "I am bored, what the hell Mitch, when are we going to do something fun for change before your parents come home". "Hold on one second, that bastard fuck Jeremy is not my dad okay; my dad is in heaven got that". She just nodded and walked into the kitchen, as I completely stretched out on the couch and took a deep sigh. I heard her opened the refrigerator door, that's when I got up and walked into the kitchen to. It's not that I don't care if she is hungry or thirsty, I don't want her to eat all the fucking food or something. She started looking for something to eat, and she was making me hungry so I decided to grab something to eat also. As we were buried in our fridge for food, I heard a truck or something pull up I walked out of the kitchen and peaked through the blinds. It was my mom and Jeremy, there were coming out of the truck with some bags and shit, great there home now the real fun begins.

I walked back in the kitchen and told Beverly that my mom and Jeremy were home, if you still wanted to meet my wonderful family. "It's cool, no problem I still want to meet them though, and they seem like interesting people". When she said that it brought a smile to my face, and for some reason it brought happy memories when it used to be my family. And when I mean my family, I mean my dad not that leech

Jeremy. Times were so much happier back then I think for everybody, or it was for me. It's like my whole world came crashing down when I realized that my dad had passed, and my mom took it the hardest, she was an emotional wreck every night was so painful for her to bear. Your mom is always going to be your mom, no matter what happens in life or how old you get. She is still going to be your mom and she is still going to love you no matter what you do. And sometimes it felt like I was taking that for granted because I acted out on occasion, I was getting in trouble I was labeled a problem child by my school. It was hard for me to lose my dad, and I know that this sounds like a fucking pity case, what makes me so special than anyone who lost someone they loved. I mean I met people who lost their dad or mom, or even the entire family, and I was making a big deal out of my dad. But it was different; I don't know I felt like we had a special connection or something. It was like we could talk about anything, I remembered I would run up to him when I was little and tell him everything. If I ever needed anything I would always run up to him and ask him, no matter what it was it could've been something little to. Now I can't even do that, and I am not saying that my mom is dumb or anything, but she never got me like my dad did, we sort of just clicked, well it was more than any other father son relationship or that's we he always told me. My mom and Jeremy came in the door and I walked out to greet my mom, and casually said hi to Jeremy as they came in. Beverly walked out the kitchen with a sandwich in one hand, a can of soda in the other and a great big smile on her face. "Hi, she said, you must be Mitch's mom, well let me tell you it is a real pleasure to finally meet you". I didn't know what so phony the smile on her face or the way that she greeted my mom when she walked in. My mom was a little surprised to see a girl in the house; she just thought it would've been me. I thought it would've been funnier to not tell her that I am bringing someone over until she got home, bad idea on my end. Jeremy strolled in and put his bags down in the same spot he always does, took of his cap and smiled. "We have company kiddo, you going to introduce me to your little friend". I cleared my throat, and said, "Jeremy, mom, this is Beverley". I didn't know if they looked stunned or they forgot, mom do you remember when we first moved from that little house, and I made a friend. And when I had to say goodbye to this friend Jeremy dropped me off to her house to say I was moving. Well this is her, this is Beverley she surprised me a couple of weeks ago when she walked into my job; I knew right then and there it was her. My mom stood there for a second with a deer in the headlights look on her face, and a second later she screamed, "Oh my God, Mitch I can't believe it, wow Beverley you look so fantastic, look how much you've grown, it is so nice to see you again". I think that my mom just beat Beverley with the fakest greeting to another person, but I could be kidding myself she might have meant it. Jeremy just walked into the room, and said hi to Beverley as he shut the door behind him, he looked fatigue or something, and he tends to get bad-tempered. "Come on Beverley, come in the kitchen you have to tell me everything about you". They sat down and Beverley said, "No I want to hear about you first, Mitch has been going on about how much a wonderful mother you are to him". I couldn't believe she just said that, I do talk about my mom, but it is generally the truth, and sometimes that truth sounds negative or positive, depends on how perceive it. And some it sounds like pure sarcasm, but she criticizes me, and I know that she is doing it out love. When I talk about my mom, and when I harass her no matter how it sounds when it comes out, or how she takes it I am doing it out of love. Mothers can be a pain, but I truly do love her and I don't know what I would do without her.

I walked in the kitchen, pulled up a chair and sat down next to them, because my mom was going to talk about herself, and I didn't want to miss for the world. When my mom goes off and starts to explain her life story she always has this routine, I guess you can call it a tradition because of all the countless times she has done it. Before she starts talking she waits a second, looks around the room, or whatever room she is in, takes a deep sigh, and starts talking. She once told me that it builds emphasis on the speech or something, but I personally don't care, because the speech is always going to be the same even in her case. Anyway before I start getting on my mother's case of oral communication let me shut up now. Growing up life for me was pretty good, I never had the privilege of going to a nice private school, my family wanted me to get more socialized and go to public school. That was not that bad some of the people I have met were pretty nice, and some were rotten to the core. I never put to many blame on the rotten kids, it wasn't my fault that they had poor upbringings, I always tried to be nice to everyone I met. Growing up, and going to more public schools as I got a little older each time, I tried talking to more people even if they didn't talk to me. My mom always told me "Lauren, the only way that you are going to get noticed, is to talk to people; you have to trust me on these things". And trust I did, I have met so many people but some rejected me and some accepted me. As long as I had a few good quality friends down the line, I never worried too much about anything else. That was until I was about 14 and my mother was taken away from me. I am not exactly sure, the police reports said it was a car accident but you know cops always fucking covering shit up. Anyway, life was hard growing up, I don't know too much, I don't try to think about it too much it bothers me. Let me see, she paused for a minute scratching her chin, I skipped school a lot, I just wanted to hang out with my friends all day. I really didn't care that much to go anymore; it felt like my whole world just came crashing down after my mom died, so I stopped caring about the little things in life. I stopped caring so much that all my teachers started calling around and low and behold the local authority even had a hit of it. It got so bad that sometimes I would've to be escorted by police themselves to go to school, it was so fucking embarrassing. After several months I finally started to go to school again, you wouldn't believe how much Goddamn work I had to make up on account of all the weeks I had missed. But in spite of this entire damn trauma there was one good thing, and his name was Ronny, but everyone just called him Ron. You see Ron was different than any other guy I had met. Well, actually Ron would be the only guy that I would meet at that time, I never had a good track record when it came to guys and or relationships, but that's a different story. There was something special about Ron; it was like he was trying to be like every other guy and at the same time he presented himself with such attitude. He always rode his bike to school, I have never seen him get dropped off by his parents or even get picked up after school. And it was that when rumors started to fly around the school, everyone was talking about what kind of relationships Ron and his family were having at home. And it wasn't like a onetime thing it happened like every day one day it so bad that he didn't show up for 3 days. He finally showed up on the fourth day and he looked a little different than before but nothing physical. When everyone was labeling him and treating him differently I was falling in love with him. I think it was the first serious crush I had for a guy, and mind you we were only in middle school, but a crush was a crush. As time went by I got older and moved up the chain in the public schooling, I was in the 10th grade, my sophomore year in high school. I went to this little has high school, just a couple of miles away from where we lived. The actual school wasn't that bad, it was a nice decent size, and it looked better than my middle school. I enrolled in the moderate classes first, I didn't want to take to easy classes then I wouldn't be learning shit. It wasn't about half way through my sophomore year that I met Ryan. Now Ryan was a little different than Ron, and no one including me ever knew what happened to Ron. There were so many rumors flying around it even spread throughout the town, I felt bad about Ron. People say that he murdered his family or something, because he was so independent all the time. Another rumor was that he disappeared, because no one heard from him for months, and it's not like Ron was popular or something, I mean it wasn't like we could go to one of his friends or something to see where he was. Ron never had the luxury of having a lot of friends, but Ryan was so much different, he was more outgoing. Ryan would talk to everybody and he was always smiling, and I think that he played on the school's football team or basketball, he played some sport. And do you want to hear something funny; it was actually harder to talk to him than it was to Ron. I never really talked to Ron like that but I did say like hello to him this one time, and I mentioned it was raining to him in class one day. But Ryan was so beautiful I was so nervous, but I walked up to him one day he was standing by his locker, and I tapped him on his shoulder and I said hi. Okay maybe I was a little more nervous than I thought, because I actually stuttering, but I got back in control, took a breath and said hey. He just smiled and said hi, and then he said, "Hey your Lauren right, I think I sit behind you in like bio class or something right?" "Yeah, you do that class is like really tough, and the teacher is really boring to". He just smiled and walked away, as I stood there leaned on the side of the locker, clutching my notebook with a big smile on my face. Weeks later, we spoke again, but this time it was in class, I think he asked me to if he can borrow my pen or something.

Months went by until we spoke again, I don't know if he was ignoring me or what but in some weird way it kind of bothered me, because I wanted to know if he liked me back or if he was talking to someone else. And wouldn't you guess, months went by and I just heard he moved or something. Well, let me see, she was still scratching her chin I couldn't believe Beverley actually wants to hear all of this; she sat there with an interesting look on her face. I went to college for about 2 years it was a community college couple of miles away from my old high school I went to. The campus was so quiet and so beautiful, even in the spring when the weather was so calm and peaceful. Through the first couple of weeks or so going in the first couple of months was really hard, and I didn't know anybody. High school to me was a real help, I know that some people say that high school is a joke and it will never help you through college. But I believe that it will, it all depends what kind of classes you take and how much extracurricular activities you are in, is what most colleges look for, and don't forget GPA and your SAT scores. Well to sum this boring story up, because I know you crazy kids want to go something I'll wrap it up. I graduated college with an associate degree in Business, and met my first boyfriend, but things didn't work out to well. After about a couple of years after, I met Jeremy and we sort of clicked you know. It wasn't anything big but we had something special that only two people can share you know. I think I can see myself marring him, but the talk never came up, so I really don't bring it up. Well that's a little about me, hopefully it didn't bother you too much sweetheart. "No problem, Beverley said, "I must get going though". "It was nice talking you Lauren hope to meet up with you some other day". My mom never cared as much if you use a first name basis in the house; she said she wanted to be more of the cool mom whatever the hell that means. I told my mom that Beverley and I were going to go out and catch a movie or do something together; I was getting kind of bored at home. As long as my mom knows where you're going, who you're going with, and tell her a reasonable time you're going to be home, she never really put a second effort of caring where you go in the first place. Beverley grabbed her things, and grabbed mine we walked out the front door and started to walk down the driveway. I was supposed to go to work tonight, but I am going to call out. Work is important and everything but I wanted to spend some time with my girl before I head over to work. "What are we going to do it is pretty early in the evening"? "You want to go see a movie or something there are some really good movies playing and it's my treat". "Sure, why not as long as you're paying I have no problem with it, none at all". I just smiled as I held her close as we walked down the street holding hands in the sunset.

Chapter 8
Just another Fine Day

Movies! Is a topic that always comes to mind when you are going to see such a particular film. You want to make sure that you see *a* movie, and not even *a* movie but *the* movie, otherwise you're going to be disappointed on what you picked trust me. When I say trust me I say those words lightly because I can tell you about this one time I saw a *really* bad movie. It was one night and my mom wanted to do something different in the house, like we have any traditions or we did anything different in the first place, but anyway she requested that she wanted to go and see a movie. Now normally we try to go out and actually do shit as a family but if it's not me complaining then someone is always is. But since everyone was so fucking bored out of their minds we decided to go and try to enjoy ourselves. There is one thing you should know about my mom, she is not much of a planner. What I mean by that is when or if she has an idea she kind of goes with it with no second hesitation. We got up all changed, Jeremy for some Goddamn reason took the longest, and we all just left. We were all packed in the car like sardines in a tin can, but it's different when everybody weighs differently and shit. Then in an instant we all just heard, "Fuck, the car is almost out of fucking gas, great what the hell." That was my mom, got to love it, Jeremy added his two cents into the mix "Fuck it, just go I mean the movie theater is not that far away we can make it and come back". Way to be fucking optimistic Jeremy got to love his enthusiasm. So with words of inspiration, we took off like a fucking torpedo, and we got there in record time. We all got out; I got out first followed by my mom and Jeremy and last but not least Beverly, who at one point didn't want to go. I mean she is the one who requested to go see a movie, but then again I kind of see her point. I guess when she said that she wanted to see a movie, I am sure she meant just the two of us; don't ask me how my whole family got involved into this fucking ordeal. We walked up to the entrance and made our way to the front of the counter to purchase our tickets. You wouldn't believe the fucking selection that they had; I mean what will ever pick. They had movies called: The Weekend, Twins, some foreign movie, a chick flick called Like Me for Me, Love Me Forever, and some other shit. So staring at the selections for about a minute I decided to see something scary. I made a decision to see something scary because it would fit everybody's movie needs; scary movies have suspense, a villain, a hero, a mystery, and most importantly blood and guts and gore. That's why I like horror movies for the sheer over dramatic scenes of blood and guts and gore, but the mystery is always good. We got our tickets and made our way to the concession stand, and let me tell you something about my family. When we go out anywhere in this particular case to see a movie, my mom always brings extra cash for some reason. I guess she has some idea we like to eat out more than we like to eat home, go figure right. We ordered so much food we had to make two trips, okay not exactly but you can impinge that right. We probably spent like $30 on food, that's still a lot but what can you do. This is what we got, I got a large popcorn, large soda, and like five snacks. Jeremy also got large popcorn, soda, large nachos, and three snacks. My mom got medium popcorn; she is trying to cut back on eating too much junk foods, two sodas, and two nachos. So much for that theory, and Beverley got small popcorn, small soda, and one snack. Now there is a reasonable eater, or she must've eaten earlier, but whatever the case she is the only person who didn't struggle to carry all the food, it was quite funny. When we walked into the theater on the screen was that annoying ass voice telling everyone to please turn off their cell phones. I don't know why they have that because you know no one listens; there is always that one asshole that picks up his Goddamn phone. We chose seats almost center to the screen, well that is where I sat, I wanted to get a good view, and everyone else sat to the left and right of me. Beverley sat to the left of me, she got situated and put her head on my shoulder and smiled, I held her close and waited for the movie to start.

After a grueling two and half hours, the movie was finally over Beverley and I were quite pleased, even though she was clutching my arm and closing her eyes but she said she liked it. My mom was kind of scared but she got over it, and Jeremy fucking fell asleep like one hour into the movie. We woke him up and left, there weren't a lot of people seeing this movie so there was no line to the exit. And the first thing that happens when you walk out of a dark theater for two hours and come to light, everyone starts freaking out and holding their eyes. Luckily for me, I was used to that so it didn't bother me that much. We all got into the car and just drove off, we arrived at home and everyone seemed pretty tired, of course Jeremy fell asleep in the car ride home and the damn theater was only like a couple of minutes away. My mom pulled in, turned off the car and everyone started to get out. I had to awake Jeremy again, he fucking sleeps too much, my mom got out and Beverly followed. I walked up to Beverly, "Hey what are you going to do; it's kind of late do you want to crash here and go home tomorrow"? "Yeah, that's cool let me just tell my mom, do you mind if I use your phone real quick". "No go ahead, you know where it is; turn on the lights so everyone can see". We all walked in and the first thing that Jeremy did is took off his shoes and plopped right on his bed. My mom went into the bathroom and turned on the shower, Beverley just sat on the couch as she was calling her mom. I took off my jacket and put it on the coat rack on the side of the wall, took off my shoes and sat near Beverley. Moments later she hung up leaned over to me and said that it was okay for her to stay here but she had to go home the very next morning. Okay, I said, as I just relaxed and took a deep breath as I turned on the TV. When I am tired, but I can't fall asleep TV always does the trick and it especially when you watch something boring like the news. Beverley got closer and snuggled up against me as we both watched the news together. When we woke up again it was morning, I couldn't believe it we spent the whole night sleeping on the couch, and neither of us changed. I woke up Beverly who looked so cute sleeping all curled up, she woke up in a panic. "Shit, I can't believe its morning;

I have to get out of here". She frantically gathered her stuff, and said that will call me later when she has the time. She gave me hug as she ran out the door and down the street; I think she was taking a cab or something.

I turned off the TV, since it was on the whole night, and took off my shirt grabbed my towel and hopped in the shower. I am guessing that my mom and Jeremy headed off to work, since I didn't see any cars in the driveway. After my shower, I grabbed some breakfast I was hungry, I couldn't believe it because of all the food I ate the movies. I didn't want to make anything big so I just made a bagel. I also made a bowl of cereal and turned on the TV again, I can never just sit there and eat my breakfast I always eat faster when I am watching something, I guess because I don't have to focus so much on my food. After I ate I finished getting ready, I was eating with boxers on only, and I felt a little cold. I sat down on the couch, and I started to channel surf because I was so bored. It was early morning, around 11:00 AM I think. As I was channel surfing I couldn't figure out what the hell I wanted to do, I mean I have to go to work today, but that's not until 6:00 PM. I talked to O' Donnell to let me also work nights on some days so I can spend time with my friends during the day. From 11 to 6 I was completely and utterly bored, I didn't want to call Beverley just after she left, because I didn't want to sound too persistent to see her. I just continued to sit on the couch, I finally found something good on, it was some documentary on Prisons and Gangs, and it seemed interesting so I kept it. I laid back on the couch, took another deep sigh, it was like a I am so bored and I am tired sigh, and just said to myself out loud, this is just another fine day.

Chapter 9
Work

It was almost 6:00 PM, and I was hesitant to go to work, but I needed the money for obvious reasons. I mean its common sense, we all need money, without money we cannot buy anything that we need. For example, you need money to buy a car or you need a line of credit to buy a house. Credit cards are different but they are still considered money. I needed money for one reason in particular, and that can be spelled with one word, Beverley. I wanted money so I can take her out where ever she wanted to go, I wanted to buy her things. I don't know what it is with this girl but every time I am with her I feel so special. Anyway before this gets any more boring, I decided to head into work a little earlier, I was getting bored standing around. When I walked in Mr. O'Donnell wasn't pleased to see my face, I think, I mean he kind of looked happy and in one second all that just went away as soon he saw me come in. I didn't care what kind of mood he is in; it's a fucking paint store for Christ sake. All that man is good for is signing my damn checks when it comes time to pay me. Just as I would've thought work was slow, only one person came in the span of like one hour and I still had seven more hours to go. I was going to tell him that after 5:00 PM if I can go home early but I would already know what he would say. Besides if I leave home, and leave work early I will not make enough money, and if I don't make enough money I can take Beverley out anywhere, so I gritted my teeth and stayed. Maybe it won't be that bad anyway, maybe no one will come in and it will be a really slow day. And wouldn't you know it that as soon as I said that four people came in, and to my delight there were all women. Okay now I know that they didn't come to buy paint because first they were dressed to nice to be in paint, and they didn't seem interesting in paint. One of the girls walked over to the counter, I walked over there. "Hi, can I help you"? Yes, she said, "I was wondering if you can tell us how to get to the highway from here." "You see I made a wrong turn somewhere and now we are completely lost". Unfortunately, I didn't know too much about directions so I couldn't do much but I had an idea. "Wait one second; I am going to get someone who can better assist you". I walked over to O'Donnell's office and told him the situation; he got right up and walked over with a cheesy ass grin on his face. I am guessing this is the first time he has seen a decent women in years. When he was giving them directions I went over to the counter and pulled out today's newspaper. After a couple of minutes and some laugher later the ladies went on their way O'Donnell made his way towards me smiled and said still got it. I just nodded my head as he went inside his office and halfway closed the door. I was too focused on my newspaper in hand for him. I finally had the chance to see the paper, because the store was not that busy. I looked at the classifieds section of the paper to find a better job, because I didn't want to work at a fucking paint store any longer. And another reason is that I wanted to get out of this miserable ass town with these miserable ass people. It seemed like fucking forever because I couldn't find anything that I wanted or anything that was close to where I lived. I pulled out a pen and started circling shit that I seemed was interesting or something. They had some ridiculous jobs in the listings such as working in waste management, I hate picking up my own shit what makes you think I am going to clean someone else's shit. Someone wanted a maid or something, I said no to that, another one was a babysitter. Now I circled that and drew an underline underneath because babysitting seemed easy. I like kids so that was an option, but it always depends two things one the kid and second the pay. I kept on looking and didn't find anything, so I went and looked on the second page and still didn't find anything. I put the paper down and told O'Donnell that I was taking my break. It was a little earlier than my original break time was scheduled but since work was so slow for obvious reasons he didn't care as much. Honestly the reason that I needed to take a break is to find a better job, I wasn't hungry or anything but I was walking around the area of the paint store to see if there were any other jobs that were hiring or anything. And you wouldn't believe I didn't find anything, and it probably came to me that if I wanted to find a job I would to go out of my way to look for one. That means fucking drive somewhere miles and miles away from my house to go to a job that I might or might not like. But then sometimes you have to make sacrifices in life and I was willing to take a risk by looking over there. You never know they might have some really good jobs but at this point anything is better than working in a Goddamn mother fucking paint store with a disgusting prick for a boss. But he did hire me to work there and I do make a decent pay and he lets me take my breaks whenever I want when business is slow so he's not that bad of a guy.

Well I headed back to work because honestly I was bored and I didn't know what to do with the rest of my time. I walked in and O'Donnell was on the phone talking to a guy for putting in new tiles or something. I can hear him screaming at the guy on his end, poor guy must have been deaf or something, but if he wasn't before, now he is. I walked over to the counter and I saw magazine cut outs spread all over. I picked one of them up and he had some ads circled for new shelves and some new carpet to be put in. I have to give credit for one thing I like that he is taking the initiative to at least sprucing this old place up. Hours went by and I thought nobody was going to come in, but as soon I turned my head the other way I heard the door open. I couldn't believe my eyes the most beautiful women just walked in the paint store. O'Donnell came out and as soon he laid eyes on her he was flabbergasted, he didn't know what to say. I walked over for the sake of being embarrassed by O'Donnell. "Hi, how may I help you today"? I just stared at her waiting to say something so I can hear the sound of her voice. "Yes, you can help me I am actually having trouble finding a specific type of paint". I couldn't believe it someone who walked into the paint store not to ask directions or offering to sell something, but actually buying some paint. "What kind of paint are you looking for" I said, trying to stir the conversation a little more. "You see I just moved and some of the walls in the house are painted a light peach color, and I need to paint over it with a more vibrant color". "Okay, I said let me see what we have in the back of the store just give me one moment I will be right back". "Okay she said, as she started to walk around the store. I walked to the back and O'Donnell came over to me, "What did she want" smiling as he asked the question, I said "can you believe it, she wanted some paint". I was trying to look for this paint but I kept on looking back and the second time I looked over she was looking at some paint and some paint samples on the bottom shelf. That means I caught her bending over, this lady had some of the finest pair of legs I have seen in a while. And the rest of her body wasn't that bad either; her legs were only complemented by her hips and ass. She came in wearing this red dress that was tight all around her body; she had some black heels with straps that came halfway up her legs. She had a black purse on her left shoulder and she was holding a cell phone in the other hand. Her face was covered with makeup and she had lipstick on, and her hair was straight but it had volume and bounce. It wasn't like every other girl's hair that I have seen who only have straight her and it's so flat. She also smelled like perfume, and the scent was simply intoxicating. I found some paint samples that she can pick and choose from. I walked over to her and said, "Okay, from what you told me I have found these samples of colors you can pick and choose to cover up the peach color". She looked at for a while and made her decision, she picked the one in the middle. The middle color was like a midnight blue purple color, it looked really good especially when sun hits it. "Okay, I'll get your paint in one moment be right back". I walked over to the back and it took me a couple of seconds to find the paint because not a lot of people pick that color, actually a lot of people don't know specifically what color they want. I found it and also I threw in a smaller can of a lavender color as a bonus, thinking that she might want that or something. I got her attention and told her to walk over to the counter so I can ring her up. I rang all the paint up and told her the total was $23.30, pretty expensive for paint in my opinion, but I only work here so. She gave me two twenties and I gave her change back. She smile and said thank you as she collected her bags and walked out the door. I just can imagine her going home and painting the house, and getting undressed, slowly taking off her dress as it slides little by little down her body to her ankles. Standing there for a second naked with her breasts exposed, as she slips into clothes she can paint in. Slowly stroking the paint brush in the can and sliding it across the wall. Watching as some paint spews off the paint brush and splattering tenderly on her skin. When she is done hops in the shower taking off her dirty clothes and running hot water. Step by step she walks in as the warm water caresses her body as she sighs in relaxation. I can imagine her picking up her luffa and pouring body wash on it and rinsing it in the water, as she massages her body with the warm exhilarating sensation of the body wash and the warm water. She turns off the shower and steps out dripping wet with body wash left over and water gliding down her body as she dries herself.

And then it hit me, wait what the fuck I have a girlfriend and her name is Beverley and I love her. I can't be thinking about other women like that, I don't want to ruin possibly the best thing that will ever happen to me. It was almost closing time, and Mr. O'Donnell walked over to me and handed me an envelope. It was my pay for this month, all of a sudden I was in high spirits, because I have enough money from this paycheck and some money saved from my allowance I can take Beverley out on a wonderful date. I grabbed the envelope, and grabbed my coat as I put it on. I thanked O'Donnell, as I was about to walk out the door, but before I took another step he said, "Hey Mitch, I was wondering if you can work next week, I was going to ask you if you wanted to work tomorrow but I am going to redecorate this place". "I going to close the store for this week and open it next week with a new look and possibly some new stuff". "Sure, no problem, I can come in next week, and I told him jokingly, this place needed some sprucing up in the beginning". He just smiled as he walked in the back room; I made my out of the store and walked down the sidewalk to go home. As I walking down the street to go home, I saw a building that was only a couple of blocks away from where the paint store was. It was generally smaller than the paint store but it was big on the inside. I walked in and who I thought to believe was the owner was sitting behind the counter with who I thought was his daughter or something. The place was a vintage clothes store, and I was actually surprised, because you find any decent clothes store anywhere and these guys had all the classic and retro clothing. Now they didn't have any bell bottoms or anything from the 60's through the 80's but vintage clothing. It's the clothing that you would see celebrities and people in Hollywood or even people with good fashion sense wear. The reason that I walked in isn't because I wanted to buy some clothes, even though they had everything I liked, but I saw a help wanted sign in the front window, and I was looking for a new job anyway. I walked over to the guy who was counting the money in his cash register, and I told him about the sign. He put the money back in the register and closed the door, and he walked over to me from behind the counter. "Yes, he said, we are looking for someone who can work part time with my daughter here to help her run the store. After several minutes of talking he looked pretty interested in me, and he told me that I had the job right off the bat. Wow I couldn't believe it, who would ever knew I was walking down the street and saw a sign in a window walked in and got a job. And for the first time it was a job that I could see myself actually enjoying the fact that I have to come to work. Don't get me wrong I did have a job at the paint store, and even though sometimes O'Donnell can be mildly annoying, he is still my boss at this point. I had to tell him that I was going to put in my two week notice, because I found a better job, well a more interesting job. I told the owner of the clothes store, I will come back tomorrow and let you know what I think. I still needed some time to think this over, even though there is a good chance I am taking this job at the clothes store I needed to tell O'Donnell.

I left and walked back into the paint store, and O'Donnell, who was cleaning up around his office, I knocked on his door, and he was surprised to see me. "Mitch, hey what are you doing, weren't you supposed to go home a while ago". "Yes, I said, I have to talk to you about something, now this is not easy to say so I am just going to say it". And before I said another word he interrupted me and said, "Let me guess you want to put your two weeks in because you want to quit". I couldn't believe it he was right, wow that was pretty astonishing I couldn't say anything. "How did you know, I said to him still shocked that he knew what I was going to say. "Trust me, he said, I have hired a lot of kids like you who work hard but at the end want to work somewhere else". At one point I felt kind of bad, "Well you're right, I did find another place that sort of caught my eye it was a vintage clothing store just a couple of blocks away from here". "I told the guy that I would come back the next day and tell him my decision, but before I did that I told him I had to take care of something". And that something was coming to the store and telling O'Donnell that I am quitting and going to work somewhere else. "Hey don't worry about it, Mitch, I am not forcing you to work here if you want to work somewhere else you can". "Thanks Mr. O'Donnell thanks for being so nice about it, and sorry for quitting so abruptly, you're a nice guy and it was nice working for you for these last couple of months". "No problem Mitch it was nice having you here, you really helped me out a lot". And on that note we shook hands as we parted ways, he went back in his office as I walked out the store. I walked back into the clothing store and walked right up to the manager and told him that you have found you're guy. "Great he told me, when can you start", he seemed pleased he finally found someone. With no hesitation I told him I can start tomorrow or later that week whenever was best for him. He said okay come back tomorrow and I'll make sure to set you up and make sure you are comfortable with everything. I shook his hand, I couldn't believe it I found a better job and I'll tell you his daughter is cute, but nothing is going to happen because I am in love with Beverley. I walked out and was going home, all the time working in the paint store, waiting for an opportunity to work in a better job came. Now as I go home, I think that everything in my life is finally coming together, now I finally believe that my life has a purpose. I just smiled as I walked down the street and said to myself, I have a job, I have a job.

Chapter 10
Making a New Friend

Finally the next day has arrived and I was looking forward to going to work, and having the chance to meet that girl, tell you the truth I was pretty nervous. But it was like I was nervous in a good way not really in a bad way, because besides Beverley whom I adore I was pretty optimistic of meeting someone new. The manager didn't really give me a specific time to come in so it was pretty early in the afternoon so I thought to myself I would wait a little while. I didn't want to come in to early and I didn't want to come in to late then. So I waited like an hour or two before I would show up, now this gives me time to do whatever the hell I want. I hope the manager is not walking around wondering where the hell I am. Because it was in the afternoon and I am probably sure that he opened already, and wondering where the hell I am. So after like 30 minutes I left and I made my way down to the clothes store, luckily for me there was a car in the driveway. I am really glad that my mom didn't have to go to work today. I walked in and there he was behind the counter, his daughter was putting some clothes on the rack just in front of him. I walked further in and he came from around the counter and gave me a hug, I would've preferred a handshake but okay. So glad you can come in today, I thought you weren't going to show up and decline my generous offer. He introduced himself, my name is Mr. Taylor and this is my daughter Alison. She came up and said hello and just smiled and went back to putting on clothes on the rack. He walked me around the store and showed me where everything is and what goes on. He was pretty lenient about the uniform since his Alison was dressed in a black shirt with a jean skirt and black pantyhose. She also had some pink bracelets on each hand and a gold and blue and yellow necklace. And on her shirt were a pair of huge glittery pink lips, and on the back a blue glittery guitar. I can tell already that this girl was different just because she didn't dress like everyone else she had her own style, which I thought was pretty cool. Mr. Taylor gave me my name tag which he made in his office in the back, and told me that I was in charge of the cash register for a while, you know probably to start me off. I was a little surprise that he first off offered me a job so quickly and then he told that I was in charge in the cash register. I mean when I started in the paint store for the first time, O'Donnell made me unload boxes, stock shelves, and sweep the floors, and this guy is making me run probably one of the most important positions in the store besides inventory and all that other shit. Now I knew there had to be some sort of a catch so I walked up to him as he was fidgeting with some papers in his hand. "Mr. Taylor, I really appreciate the job on such short notice and I am going to a fine job sir, but I was wondering why you chose me to work the register all of a sudden, I mean it's my first day". "Good question, he said, I have to leave on a business conference in Los Angeles, I am so sorry but I have to leave". "I never got your name son; you know that's a vital part in our relationship". "Yes, I am sorry, my name is Mitchell, but you can call me Mitch sir". "Okay Mitch, well I have to go I have to make it to the airport to catch my plane it leaves in one hour". "Don't worry Mitch, when I am gone I always put my daughter in charge, she has the keys to the store, I think that she is the same age as you are". And just like that he grabbed his newspaper his cup of coffee, his two suitcases and left out the door. I was a little stunned, because I never experienced my boss leaving the very first day where I thought he would go over the ground rules with me. I just shrugged my shoulders and walked behind the counter, and waited for some people to come in and start shopping, it seemed pretty slow outside so you can only hope for the best. I couldn't happen to notice that in the far end of the store was Alison unpacking some boxes and putting some clothes on the shelves.

Now I know I am not to suppose to feel anything because I am in a committing relationship with Beverley, but for some reason when I look at Alison I feel something entirely different inside. It was sort of bothering me inside that I am having these mix feelings for another girl, so I walked from behind the counter and walked over there to talk to her. When I approached her she was taking clothes out of a box and putting them accordingly on the racks. "Hi I said, my name is Mitch just in case you didn't get it before, you must be Alison right"? I know that wasn't the greatest introductions, I mean I already knew her name I was just being polite. "Hi, she replied, I already knew your name when my dad told me that you were coming to work here". "It must be really fun to work in a clothing store with your dad as the manager". "Okay first of all, the store is called Vintage Equals Retro, and honestly the truth about really working here it is not all that great. "Don't get me wrong, I love working at a clothing store but with my dad as the manager it really can really stressful at times". She put the second box down and headed into the back room I guess she had a lot of free time on her hands because it was a couple of hours in and still nobody came in. to be more approximate was one hour in and nobody came in. I walked around to my side of the store just waiting for someone to come in so we can have some fucking business. Now there was one thing that kind of caught my attention and that was the name of the store. I mean I know it is a clothing store and I know that they sell old fashion clothes and even classic clothing, but I could've came up with a better name for the store. But I didn't have any say in this because I don't own the store I just work in it, and so far I like it. Even though no one came in it makes my job that much easier so I don't have to deal with those annoying ass customers. Sometimes people can either be a really big help or they can be the most fucking annoying people in the world. I can remember this one time working with O'Donnell, this lady came in and she looked like the typical lady who didn't know what the fuck she was doing. I mean when she walked in she was clueless and her facial expression priceless, like the preverbal deer in the headlights look. She came in wearing fancy ass clothes, I mean when someone usually walks into a paint store you don't see them dressed so nicely. I thought she was going somewhere and forgot to buy some paint or needed some and this was right on the way. No that wasn't the case she actually came into the store looking to buy some paint, I found it freaking hysterical. She looked around the store as if fucking Jesus Christ was walking around. She came up to the counter and said the most ridiculous question that I have ever heard. "Excuse me; I was wondering if you can help me I was looking for some paint". And I know what you're probably thinking she was probably looking for a specific paint or something like that, but she was actually looking for PAINT.

That was the highlight of my day I can tell you that, I went home that night with some good memories and a laugh on her expense. After some time had passed, three people came in the store and luckily for Alison and I they were all relativity young, I say about two were 17 and one was about 20. Finally an age group that I recognized, well it sure as hell put a smile on Alison's face because two of the three people that came in were guys, and for girls that's always a good thing. They started walking around the store, I don't know they if they were going to buy something because they were walking around for like 5 minutes. Finally one of the guys came over to Alison; he had two pair of shirts and one hat in his hands. He said, "Which of these shirts would really look good with this hat"? I just shook my head, because I even knew that guy didn't care about looking good as much he did talking to Alison. She said, "I think the first one, and the first one being the red and black in his right hand and the other one was grey and purple in his left hand. The hat that he had with him to match the two shirts is black with red graffiti designs in the background and the sides. It was common sense of what shirt to pick to what hat even when they fucking both match. But I didn't care, he was talking to Alison, and it seemed like they were hitting it off pretty well. On the other hand, out of the three came in two were guys and the other one was a girl. She seemed pretty quite I didn't hear her talk but just watching her walking around the store and watching her pick up clothes and put them back, seemed pretty shy. She wasn't but so skinny but she still looked okay for a skinny girl, like I haven't ranted about skinny girls in the past. She finally picked up two pair of jeans, one scarf, three shirts and other shit and walked over to the counter. "Hi, she said, may I have a tag for the dressing rooms please; I would like to try these clothes on". "Sure, I replied as I gave her a tag and told her where the dressing rooms were". Now she can obviously read for herself because when you walk in the first things you see are all the clothes, people walking around and a huge sign for the dressing rooms in the corner. I just wanted to be a smart ass but more importantly I was really trying to spark up any conversations with her, that didn't work out to well as she grabbed her clothes and headed for the dressing rooms. She turned back gave me a smile and went inside; I just shook my head and went to see if that other guy needed any help. I was walking to him and he was walking to me, we almost bumped into each other, he was ready to purchase. He only had one hat and one shirt, not a heavy shopper this guy. We walked to the main counter and I rung him up, he grabbed his bags and walked outside. I guess he had to go somewhere important because he didn't even tell his friends that he was leaving. The girl came out of the dressing room and she had all of her clothes that she wanted to buy folded up in her hand. Great, I said to myself, I have to take the time to unfold all of the clothes and re-fold them just so I can put them in a bag. She walked up and pulled out her wallet from her purse, she pulled out her credit card and some cash too. "I like to pay for this half with cash and the other half with credit please, if that's not a problem". "No, I said; don't worry about it I'll take care of that for you right away". I was trying to be as cheesy as hell so I can come off as a nice guy so maybe she will talk to me or something. I rung her up and put all of her clothes in a bag, while the other guy walked up from behind and started to count how much cash he had on him. As soon I was done with the girl she waited over by the chair near the door, as I rung up the other guy. He got his clothes in a bag, and grabbed the receipt and walked over towards the girl by the door. They looked over for one second what they bought and walked out.

After no customers for a while, the store got pretty boring; all I kept on thinking about is Beverley, and what she is doing right now. And also what time and day Mr. Taylor was coming back from L.A., because it is crazy running a store without the manager here. But in the end I know that it's going to be a challenge but I am looking forward to it. And the best part is I am not alone, if I am in trouble with something I know I can get the help of my new best friend Alison, she will take complete care of me.

Chapter 11
Dreams

After a long and exhausting day at work, Alison decided to pack it up, we had some people come in buy some things return some things pretty common routine. She came up to me and said, "You did well today you know for a rookie, she smiled, nice job come back tomorrow I think that my dad should be back from L.A. in the morning". We said our goodbyes and I grabbed my coat and decided to go home and get some sleep, because I was dead tired. I was so fucking tired I had to wake myself up, I decided to get some coffee from a local convenient store just around the corner. Sometimes I ever wondered if they ever got any business, because it seemed like no one was ever in the place. I mean I did see some people walk in and out but no steady flow of traffic when it came to customers. The food there was really bad, that's why when people do go there they never leave with anything to eat. It is either for gas or there world famous coffee, which to me is just coffee. So I got a cup and to tell you the truth I was pretty surprised, the coffee actually tasted good not like other cheap coffees I had in the past. Sometimes when I get coffee from other places it taste like shit, but this time it tasted rich and full of flavor, and it was a relative good price. Well now that I am satisfied with coffee I decided to head home and get some sleep. I got home I decide to take the long way back so that way I can just get myself pre relaxed before I get 100% relaxed and don't do shit. Besides the fact of going to work tomorrow that fact doesn't bother me as much it did working for O'Donnell. Don't get me wrong he is a nice guy but a fucking God forsaken paint store I know now why they never get any business, there is not a single person who needs paint every five minutes anyway. I finally got home and when I pulled up to the driveway I noticed Jeremy's truck was in the side, and he had some pieces of lumber in the back of his truck. I got out and walked to the front door, and I heard some noise coming from my mom's room. Now needless to say I don't want to repeat the noises that I heard, but anyone with a fucking brain can figure out what was going on. My speculation is after Jeremy was fine tuning his automobile he got bored and went to go fine tune my mom. Well I congratulate him for being like the tenth guy who was able to get my mom out of her panties and into bed. Now I was a little upset because I couldn't watch TV in the living room because the TV's volume isn't loud enough to drown out their screaming and shouting, well it's more of my mom screaming, but I don't want to get into that. I just walked into the kitchen because I was hungry, for some reason I always get hungry before I get tired. I opened the fridge door and looked in, and to my surprise well not really there was no food. All there was two cartons of milk, one orange juice carton, some cheese and meat, no fucking bread, and some fucking beer. Oh also some containers that had some other food inside but I was smart enough not to go anywhere near that radioactive waste they call food. I was forced to eat some cereal, but I wasn't that upset because I wasn't that hungry in the first place, I just needed something to fill my stomach. I grabbed the box from the top of the fridge got some milk and a spoon and started to eat. Jeremy came out walked into the kitchen and opened the fridge. He grabbed a beer and turned over to shut it and looked at me and said, "Hey kiddo, when did you get home I didn't even hear you come in". "Just a while ago, I said, just eating and probably going to sleep I have to work tomorrow". "Cool, he said, well I have to go your mom and I are watching a movie or something. "Okay, I am just eating and probably go to sleep I am kind of tired, I have to go to work tomorrow". Have fun he said as he walked away and went into the room. I just nodded my head and quietly said out loud yeah you too, because God knows I know they will. I finished eating and put the bowl in the sink with all the other dishes that were just fucking piling up like a mountain. I guess no one really cared to do the dishes around here and because I was so bored I thought I would actually give a helping hand and do the dishes. Now I think it was painstakingly obvious that my mom knew that Jeremy never did any work around the house, and some how she never really cared. It's like all the work that needed to be done always came back to me. And I don't know I guess for some reason I never really cared about taking the credit, it's not like when the job is done I am going to feel really excited or something about telling my mom I did it. So I give the credit to Jeremy so my mom at least knows just a little that he actually doesn't do shit around the house, I just make it seem that way. I took off my shirt it was so fucking hot in my house, and I kind of just softly threw myself on top of my bed. I was so tired I can sleep for days I closed my door and took off my socks, then my jeans. I put on some sweats and closed my blinds and turned off my phone so I can get some sleep. I crawled under my sheets and sighed for a second and closed my eyes.

The next time I woke up it was like hours later I looked at my alarm clock that sits on top of my dresser, it said like 5:30 P.M. I couldn't believe slept that long, I thought for sure it was the next day. I really don't remember what time it was for sure I actually went to sleep but it was pretty early in the afternoon. I was still tired I could go back to sleep if I wanted to but the only reason that I woke up is my mom came in the room and kind of woke me up mid sleep. She told me that I was sweating and really cold, and was kind of tossing and turning a lot. She told me that I was having a nightmare or something. But I didn't remember anything when I woke up, I couldn't really make anything out it was all a huge blur. My mom was still standing by my bed side as she was talking to me but I was still half asleep half awake, you ever get that feeling, it was like I can hear what my mom was saying but I really couldn't make it out sort of. "Honey, are you okay, my poor baby you were having a nightmare". I finally woke from this and quickly responded, "It felt so weird, like it was so real, mom how long have you been in my room"? My mom was just looking at me for a while and just smiled and said quietly, "Honey I came in to check up on you and you were talking to yourself and clutching your pillow very tightly". I got up and threw my pillow back on my bed and told my mom that I was going to take a shower or something. I needed to wake up get refreshed because I still feel a little tired and maybe this whole entire thing is just one huge dream or something. I went into the bathroom and got undressed as I hopped in the shower and turned it on. I usually take cold showers because it can get really hot and mucky in my house, but this time I took a nice hot shower so I don't feel so damn tense. I guess I just needed to relax or something, it felt good just letting all that water hitting me as I just stood in my shower for a second. I didn't do my usual routine in the shower as I usually do when I get in there, I just took this time to just relax and take a shower. When I was finished I got out and wrapped myself in my towel and headed in my room. I quickly put on my clothes disregarded my hair, it was still wet and I kind of dried it off by my hand. I looked at my clock and it was like 6 or 7:00 P.M. I couldn't see I had my shirt covering half the time. I put on my jeans and told my mom I was going to out for a while, I get this weird dream or whatever the hell that was out of my head. So I grabbed my wallet, keys, gum and put on some cologne, just in case. I was about to walk out the front door, when fucking Jeremy stopped me. "Hey kiddo, what time are you coming back, don't forget you have to go to work tomorrow". "Yeah, I know, don't worry I will be home soon I just need to clear my head". "Tell my mom if she needs me to call me, I have my phone with me". And with that said I walked out and made my way to the car in the driveway. I opened the car door and got in, I didn't know where the fuck I was going all I knew I just needed to go away. And following my heart I pulled out my cell phone shut the car door and called up Beverley. I know it was late but I needed to see her because I know she is the only person that can help me with this, whatever problem that I am fucking having. It rang like four times then she finally picked up, "Hello, who is this" she said that in the most innocent cute voice I have ever heard. "It's me Mitch, Beverley what's up I need to see you". "Oh my God Mitch, wow I never knew you had a cell phone" laughing in the background, hold on for one second. I didn't know if she was home or not I guess I got pretty lucky when I called her and she picked up, I think that she told me she was going out for a while to a whole bunch of places for school or something. "Okay back, sorry I was talking to one of my friends, umm what were you talking about something about meeting up right?" "Yes, wait I thought you were doing that thing for school." "Now that isn't for a couple of weeks silly, come on we went over this you never pay attention to what I have to say. I just smiled and chuckled a little bit and said I was sorry maybe I should listen to her more often. "Hey are you busy we have to meet up now, I know it's late and it is short notice but I have to see you." "Okay you want to meet up in the same place we always meet up in say like 20 minutes or so." "Cool I said, I know where that is, I can be there in 20 minutes, I will see you there." I strapped in my seatbelt and started to reverse and I took off. Oh by the way that place well it is nothing really special, Beverley and I always meet up in a park near a hospital on one corner, and a photo store on the other. It was about 20 minutes and I just pulled in, I parked my car near a rusty broken down Chevy and got out. As soon I got out I saw Beverly sitting on the bench where we sit all the time. She saw me coming up and screamed my name as loud she can. I just smiled as I walked over there, it was pretty cold outside as we were both dressed in jackets, she had a scarf I just had a hat. We hugged and sat down on the cold park bench. Before I could the next word out of my mouth, Beverley said abruptly, I am leaving. It took me a second to register that because maybe I wasn't hearing her right. "What, I said, what are you talking about, what do you mean you are leaving"? "Look it has been fun, and I really like you and over these last couple of months I have really fallen in love with you." But do you remember when I said I was only town for a couple of days or so, well it turned into months and in that span I have got to know you and fall in love with you, but I have to go." "But why, we were so good together, you know I thought we had something special, why is this happening." "I am so sorry Mitch, baby you know I don't want this to happen either but it's not my choice it was my mom. I guess whatever the reason she came into town for she is done and we are leaving, maybe moving to another place I am not sure". I couldn't say anything I was so shocked I just looked at her with a blank face. She got up and I got up too, "Don't worry, I will write or call you every day, I have to go my mom and I are getting some stuff arranged." "Okay then if you have to go, I'll guess I call you tomorrow or something I don't know but I call you." She gave me a hug and kissed me one more time under the cold air and gave me a smile and told me that everything was going to be alright. She started to walk off near her car as she stopped turned around and gave me a wave. I waved back as I started walking to my car too. I couldn't believe it after all this time she was leaving, she was the one you know I was going to ask her to marry be one day. I got in my car and just drove off without even thinking of what just happened and without thinking of her, because I don't want to feel the pain. I got home and Jeremy was watching TV in my mom's room because I recognized the TV show and he had the door halfway opened. I went in my room and got on top of my bed and just lied their thinking about what just the fuck happened, because it was so fast I didn't see it coming. I was in so much pain I just closed my eyes and maybe if I fell asleep I can feel somewhat better in the morning. I closed my eyes and I just cried myself to sleep. I woke up again, but this time it wasn't because of Beverley it was that dream again, I couldn't figure it out. All I remember is I am at my home, my first home before we moved and it is really dark, and I see a door halfway open, and there is a light in the room, so I followed the light and walked in. and I see a person laying there in the bed, wearing a night gown and just smiling at me. I walked in further and sat down on the bed as she was rubbing my shoulders, caressing my hair. She said, don't worry everything is going to be alright, I won't let anyone hurt my baby. I thought it was Beverley that is who I thought I was dreaming about, but it wasn't because this person had a deeper voice. She threw me on the bed, as she got on top and started to rub my chest, she kept on repeating, don't worry everything is okay, I won't let anyone hurt you." I think she was drinking because there was an empty wine bottle on the floor and she had a wine glass in her left hand halfway full. She started to rub herself as she was making moaning sounds, I really couldn't understand what was going on, or who it was exactly. I thought it was just a figment of my imagination, or all of this couldn't be real. I couldn't make sense of any of this, everything was happening so fast; all I can think about was Beverley. She got closer and put her lips near my ear as she whispered something to me but it wasn't what she was saying all along this time it was more personal, like it hit home or something, but she said low I couldn't make it out all I got from it was, don't worry baby, I am here and I am never letting you go. She said something else but I didn't catch it, I thought I was making this entire dream up as if this person didn't exist. But it felt too real to be made up, I felt a connection with this person but I couldn't understand why. She got back up again and started untying her night gown, she had a black bra on, and she grabbed my hands and placed them on her chest. As she used my hands to feel around on her breasts, she made me squeeze harder as she just smiled, laughed and screamed ever so pleasantly. She unhooked her bra, as she was exposed again gently touching herself over and over. She leaned over and started to softly kiss me on my lips. I was so confused at this point, I couldn't even think straight enough to get this person off of me. She started to take off my belt buckle and started to loosen my jeans. She made me take off my shirt as I was laying there half naked as she got up from me and stood up. She took the bottom part of her night gown off, and then she took off her black panties. Now she was standing there naked as she slowly crawled back into bed and again right on top of me. Now she started to rub my chest a little harder and started to kiss me more vigorously. She leaned in closer and took off the rest of my jeans as she threw it in the corner with her night gown. She started to kiss me on my chest and slowly working her way down, and then she came right back up and started to kiss me on my lips again. The room was to dark I couldn't make it out, I couldn't see the person's face. She said something but I didn't catch it, and I was so confused I couldn't recognize the voice but it sounded so familiar. She leaned over and slapped me hard in the face as she screamed and stared to kiss me again. She leaned in and put her breasts in my face as she grabbed the back of my head, she had a hand full of hair as she made me kiss her nipples. I tried to push my head away but she had my hair in a tight lock, she made me suck her breasts as she just moaned and screamed so softly, smiling as I did it. She aggressively threw my head back on the pillow, as she started to pleasure herself; she leaned in to my ears, and just said ever so gently but with a lot of meaning, FUCK ME. She rose up from my ear as she pulled me further away from her, and she started to take my boxers off as she was still moaning. She grabbed my dick, and started to play with it a little, as she slowly went down and put it in her mouth. She rose up and got on top of it, as she moaned and kept saying FUCK ME, harder and harder. She looked into my eyes and said, "Don't worry baby, I won't let anything happen to you, I will never let you go Mitch. How did she know my name, this was all so confusing. "Don't worry baby, momma's never going to let you go, she is never going to let you go." I had a fucking pale expression on my face, and the last thing I remembered was she leaned in and gave me a kiss on my cheek and said, "I love you honey, and I will never let you go". Then I woke up fidgeting, screaming, and in a panic I was cold, sweating, I couldn't make sense of any of this, it happened so fast. I was crying, because this dream it felt so real. This was the dream; this is the dream that I have been having the last couple of days. But why, I couldn't figure it out, I just sat in bed with a blank look in my eyes as I try to piece all this together, and the last thing I remember me saying in spite of everything that happened was, it was my mother.

Chapter 12
The Shrink

I didn't go to sleep at all that night, and when the morning came I wasn't that tired I guess I wasn't really thinking about sleep. Luckily for me when I woke up from this fucking dream my mom didn't hear me screaming, otherwise she would've ran in the room and it would've been a little awkward. I got up from my bed, it was around 8 or 9 in the morning, and I didn't have to be at work until 4:00 P.M. so I had time. I put on my house slippers and headed for the bathroom; I turned on the faucet and splashed some cold water in my face, so I can just wake up. I stayed a little longer in the bathroom, because my fucking mom and Jeremy were both home and after the dream I had last night I didn't want to rush and greet them this morning. I got out and quickly walked into the kitchen, and just nonchalantly poured me a bowl of cereal just trying to pretend like nothing happened. As soon as I sat down Jeremy walked into the kitchen, said hello opened the fridge and grabbed a beer. He walked back into the room, as my mom came out wearing the same night gown that I pictured her wearing in my dream. She came in the kitchen, as I just frantically got up and put my bowl in the sink. It still had some cereal left over but I needed to get away from the kitchen and away from my mom at this point. I told her that I needed to get to work early for inventory and set up some new displays and hang up some new clothes with Alison. I hurried out of there without a second's hesitation, because I didn't want to be around my mom for one more second. I felt kind of bad; because I never blew off my mom like this because I thought we always had a good relationship going on, at least better than most family members, at least better than some mother and sons. But I had no choice, I needed to leave and just get to work at least I know that everything is normal there, and I just can concentrate on making some money for the weeks ahead. Man, I was Goddamned bummed because of this whole Beverley thing, and this whole dream. I just needed a couple of days to get this whole shit sorted out; I think that would be best for me now. I know that I didn't have to get to work for a couple of hours, and it wouldn't be surprised if I went there and there would be no one in the store or it was closed. So I had some time to spare, I just decided to walk around for a while and get used to this fucking town. Living here for a couple of years now, I pretty much driven everywhere around here, but I haven't seen most of the town so I took the chance to go sightseeing. I drove around for a while and the only thing that kept coming to my thoughts were my mom and that night, and her undressing, and her on top of me saying those words. Not even paying attention to the road I almost crashed, it was a red light and I drove by and almost hit a SUV. We both stopped and got out and I told him if he was okay, he wasn't like every fucking asshole that almost gets into an accident and goes all berserk, he was pretty cool about it. After I told him that it was my fault because I wasn't paying attention to the road. He drove off and I took a second to get into my car and I just parked it along the side of the street, and sitting in my seat I turned my head to the right and there I saw a building for a psychiatrics' office, you know a shrink. I thought about it for a while and after that everything happened, I thought it would be a really good idea to go in there and try to make an appointment or something. I stopped my car and got out and walked into the office. When I walked in I could tell that this place was meant for a shrink's office, the interior scheme was really bland. I don't want to go into it because it is too much shit for one person. I walked up to the main counter and there was a young lady behind the desk. She was on the phone when I walked up, she had to be no less than mid twenties, young and beautiful, and I wondered why she would want to work here. "Hi, I like to see the specialist please, if he is available". "Do you have an appointment, if not then you need to fill this out and wait for the doctor". I filled out the stupid paper work, I hate that shit it is always useless information sometimes, like they will ask you are you dying from anything or something. Now I know it's not that serious but come on its fucking ridiculous sometimes. I finished and handed the clipboard with all the papers to the security, as she just smiled and said wait for the doctor.

At least two painstaking hours went by, and finally my name had been called. When the doctor called me he wasn't what I expected, actually the doctor was a she. I can't believe that I have a female doctor, to make things worse of what happened to me already. I got up and followed her into the back, where there were plenty of empty rooms; some had people in them I guess they were waiting for their doctors. She finally showed me into my room, and told me to wait for a couple of minutes as she was busy before I had arrived and needed to get something done. She came in several minutes later, I was lying down on the couch, and I got up immediately when she walked in and closed the door behind her. She pulled out another clipboard and set it aside on the table as she pulled up another chair and sat next to me. She began the session with one question, "Please take this time and tell me a little about yourself, if you don't mind, so that way I can get a better understanding of what I am dealing with." I hate when people use that term what I am dealing with, she is making me seem like I am serial murderer or a rapist or a pedophile or something. But I knew she was only trying to help so I didn't want to give her such a hard time. Well how do I begin, I said to myself, well my name is Mitchell James, but everyone calls me Mitch, and I live in Ohio, recently moved from little town somewhere don't really know. Umm… let me see, oh, I work in a clothing store called Vintage Equals Retro, good place I like it. I live with my mom and my step dad his name is Jeremy, he is an okay guy sometimes gets on my last nerves but an okay guy. My dad passed away a while ago, and it's been hard on my mom and me, but I think she moved on because she dated like 10 guys before she met Jeremy, once calling him the one. I have a good relationship with my mom and a on again and off again relationship with Jeremy. "Why is that, why do you think you have a better relationship with your mom and not with Jeremy"? Well, I said, "Because he tries to be my dad, and he can never fill those shoes, and he is so phony sometimes and my mom never sees through that. I try to help my mom out sometimes and try to tell her that Jeremy sometimes can be a royal pain and he never does anything around the house. Well enough about him, I am starting to get a headache. Oh yeah, I did meet a girl, well she was actually a very special girl, I think she might have been the one. "Interesting she said, as she was writing down some notes on her clipboard, she paused for a second and said, tell me about this girl". "It seemed like you guys were pretty close, what happened". "Well, I liked her for a long time, then we started dating last couple of months ago and then I just completely fell in love with her. And she had felt the same for me too; I mean we were perfect for each other. There are so many things I can say to describe her or even what she does. Every time I think of Beverley I always smile, she is so smart, pretty and charming. She carries herself in such a way that it would be hard to believe that is the same age as me, which is 18. She is so graceful, always smiling, and helping people out. She is always in a good mood, but sometimes she does have an occasional mood swings, but every girl has been through that. She is so beautiful, and special I could just spend the rest of my life with her. But that's what I thought; just recently we met at a park where we always meet to getaway and talk. And before I could say the next word, she told me that she was leaving. And she left, that was yesterday I think now I don't know if I am ever going to see her again. I don't know what I am going to do without her; you know I don't know if I am going to find another girl like that. "I am sorry to hear that, I know it can be tough losing someone you really love due to heartbreak. I just recently got divorced for the first time, and I thought he was the Mr. Right, but apparently I was wrong. I am sorry, here I am the doctor and I am telling you all my personal problems. "Its okay don't worry about it, I guess we are in the same boat". "Well, is there something else bothering you, you can tell me anything, because no matter what we discuss in this room everything is confidential a hundred percent." "Okay there is one more thing that bothered me; well it really freaked me out. I had this dream last night, and well I really don't want to explain it in full detail, but I can tell you the short and sweet version of it. The dream took place in my house, and it involved my mom and I felt really confused; because it wasn't a happy go lucky dream it was a nightmare. Basically I walked into my mom's room and she was lying in bed wearing a night gown, and I sat down next to her because I wanted to give her company. And the company turned into SEX. The psychiatrist looked shocked and puzzled at the same time, because she looked at me for a second and didn't say anything. "Okay, some mix emotions and feelings about your mom, go ahead and explain the rest of your dream to me please". Okay well, she threw me on top of the bed, and started undressing she got completely naked and got on top of me and made me take off my shirt and pants, then my underwear. "When you mean "made you" what do you exactly mean by that, did she tell you aggressively?" "Now she forced me to take them off, so I got completely naked, and then she grabbed my hands and made me squeeze her breasts and then she made me suck on her nipples. Then she started to kiss me on my lips, and chest area. She started to erotic moaning and screaming sounds, as she started to work her way down to my dick. She started stroking it, up and down continuing to make moaning sounds. At one point she put my dick in her mouth and started sucking pretty soft and sensuous. Then she stopped kissed me some more and then she got on top and started to ride me and she kept on moaning and her screaming got louder and louder. She kept yelling FUCK ME, over and over again; she kept bouncing up and down, and her breasts bouncing while she was screaming louder and louder. Then I woke up really cold, sweating and screaming and shouting, luckily for me my mom didn't hear all that screaming last night.

I felt kind of relieved telling someone, because I needed to tell someone. The doctor just looked at me with very perplexed eyes, I think she was a little upset because I went into such great detail, but that was only half of it, I told her I was going to keep it short and sweet. "Okay, give me a minute to let this entire dream sink in, oaky so this dream was pretty lucid and very much real. And I know you stated previously that you had a good relationship with your mother. Okay, I am going to ask you some questions, and give me your honest answer okay, so that way I can understand what I am dealing with here. Okay are you ready because he is your first question. She paused for a minute to write some stuff down on her clipboard, she wrote down a lot of stuff because she took about 2 minutes. "Do you love your mother?" I said without thinking, "Yes" "How often do you spend time with your mother?" "I try to spend every day before and after I get out of work" "Have you ever seen Jeremy do anything to your mother at any point in your life?" "They had sex once or twice I think that is how I remember it" "Have you ever been sexually assaulted when you were a little boy?" "I can't remember."

"Okay, with that said I think the only thing that we can say from all of this is you have to come back and see me once a week starting today." "It is very imperative that you can make it to these meetings on time and come every meeting. Are you going to tell your parents what happened last night with the dream"? "Probably not, I mean I will feel really uncomfortable telling them, I think they would never understand, and I don't want to freak them out. "Okay, so you can leave but come back next week, okay don't forget you have to come on time and you have to come every week now. I got up and we shook hands, as she gave me some papers and a card with her work number, fax number and her cell phone number she had written down on the back. I have never been in a doctor's office before where they put their cell phone number on the back of the card. I guess probably during this whole session, she probably wrote it down somewhere and thought it would be important to do so. Regardless, I would feel kind of uncomfortable calling her on her cell phone, I mean we just met it's not like we have been friends for years. She showed me out of the office, and told me once again about the rules. We shook hands one more time as I said see you next week as I was leaving out the door. I headed for my car got in and felt a bunch of emotions coming from me. One of them was kind of nervous, because now she knows the whole story and I kind of don't want to know what she is going to say next week when I go in. And the other feeling was well, I felt relieved because can you imagine what would've happened if I didn't tell anybody what kind of person I would've probably turned out to be, I would've probably sexually abused my own children, or someone else's children. I can't even think about that right now I started the car and drove off, I checked my time on my car and it said 3:15 P.M. Great with all this shit that just fucking happened, now I have to go to fucking work. Well there was one good thing about this and that was at least I don't have to go home and spend the afternoon with my mom and Jeremy. I think they are both off today from work, speaking of work, it's like they are home more than I am before I go to work. I don't know what kind of work schedule they got but it is really weird.

I decided to head into work a little earlier, all this talk about work and my family it was only like 3: 23 P.M., and I still had some time. But I didn't to waste it driving around somewhere possibly wasting all my damn gas. I pulled in and when I got out I saw Alison walking across the street, she was walking alone with keys in one hand and like 3 small bags in the other. I met and greeted her as she walked up the street. I helped her with the bags as she opened the store, as she was getting ready I took a chance to look around, and there were a lot of people walking around, so I guess we can have pretty good business today. We walked in, and I asked her, "Hey where is your dad this time on another important conference meeting"? "No, she replied nicely, he is talking to some people to get some renovation done to this place, you know try to get some young people in. "Cool, I said, as I walked behind the counter to get ready and man the cash register today. I guess that's my new thing when Alison's dad is not here, but I didn't mind at all. Alison walked over to the main door and flipped the closed sign to open, I guess she wanted to start early today, and then she walked back into the office to work on some paperwork. I just stood behind the counter beating my hands against the marble making a beat, just waiting for people to come in, I looked outside the window one more time, as I quietly said to myself, business is booming. Several minutes went by and then all of a sudden like so many people just started to walk in it was unbelievable, I guess they really wanted the store to open early. It was like watching fucking rat's running around for cheese everybody was just going everywhere picking up different pieces of clothing and stuff. At one point it was quite amusing, but then the real serious shit started happening. I left from behind the counter to make sure that everybody was doing okay, or if they needed any help. Then I quickly returned because I don't want to be the reason we get robbed on some stupid shit. When I got back people already had already what they wanted, some had a lot of clothes in their hand, then like three people left the line and went back to the racks. I only had to ring up one person; she was kind of cute you know for an older chick though. I mean she had to look really cute when she was young, well sort of cute; I just smiled while I was putting her clothes in a bag. She collected her stuff and walked out, then I got to thinking, maybe if she has a daughter or something, she is probably cute as hell. Two more people walked up and one guy was listening to music through his I-Pod I guess, it was so loud the lady behind him was just shaking her head from side to side. I quickly rung the people up and told them to have a nice day. It always helps if you're polite and always smiling to the customers, it always makes them coming back for more. I rang two more people and they got their bags and left, after that the store was kind of quiet for like 20 minutes. So I had some time to chill, I walked over to Alison to see what she was up to and to ask her how her day was going. When I got there I noticed that she was crying, so I was a little concerned "Hey, are you alright, is there anything I can do to help?" She quickly looked up wiped the tears from her eye with her sleeve gracefully smiled and said, "No it's alright don't worry about it okay, I am fine." Okay I said, "Well let me know if you need anything okay, I am here to help". She smiled again and said okay as she got up continuing to wipe the tears from her face as she headed in the back, I guess to take care of the shipment that just came in and in that second, her dad came in the door with two guys wearing like overalls. I guess those where the guys who going to help fix this place up a little bit. He just handed them some papers and an envelope as they gave him a card, it looked like a business card and they shook hands and they left. I guess he just made the deal, he started walking my way. "Hey Mitch, how is my favorite cashier doing on this fine day?" I smiled, "Good, I am doing good sir". I didn't want to tell him about Alison because whatever was bothering him it wasn't really any of my business, and I didn't want to go and run up to her dad telling him what happened, like a tattle tale or something. Alison came from the back room, and walked up to her dad and gave him a hug, "Hi dad, you finally done with those guys, did you make the deal yet?" "Yes, he said, hey I have one more piece of business to take care of, I am sorry I can't stay but this is very important". "Okay don't worry I just look after the store like I always do when you're gone." He gave Alison a hug and smiled, grabbed some papers from the back and left. Well, Alison said "I guess we are on our own again, I don't know how long he is going to take this time but I am sure we will be fine." "It's cool, I have no problem I said, I kind of like working here anyway so that makes up for it. Good she said as she grabbed her I-Pod from her pocket, put her headphones to her ears and turned the volume all the way up as she was dancing all around the store, taking inventory.

Several hours went by and people came in and out, so I can say it was a nice and steady pace today. This one lady gave me a twenty dollar tip, just because I was polite, see what I mean by always being nice to people it helps. It got pretty late afterwards, and no one was coming in so Alison decided to close up, it was a couple of minutes before the actual closing time, but she told me that she had something to do. So she closed up and I grabbed my coat as she grabbed her stuff, we got to the door and she stopped and gave me a hug. "What was that for, I couldn't figure out why she hugged me for." "Thanks for being such a good friend earlier, you know when I was crying and stuff". Don't mention it I said as she left and I was a little confused but kind of delighted. I mean it was just days after Beverley left and I never saw her again, I mean she was the girl that I was going to spend the rest of my life with. But I guess I needed to move on, and I was thinking to myself could I have feelings for Alison, I mean I don't even know her. Everything was happening so fast I couldn't control it, I had to see the psychiatrist, but she told me to come back next week. I wondered if she was still in, I mean it was only like 8:30 P.M. I got in my car and drove to her office, as soon I got there she was coming out from her office and the lights inside were turned off. I got out of my car, and walked up to her, "Hi doctor... I paused for a second, because I didn't even know her name. She gracefully said, my name is Doctor, Elizabeth Ross, but you can call me Dr. Ross. "Okay Dr. Ross, I need to speak to you, and I noticed that you were coming out from your office, and I know this is in short notice, but I was wondering if I can speak with you. She noticed that I was serious about the matter; she grabbed her keys out and opened her office door. Thank you I said, I apologize once again, I know it's late. Don't worry about it, she said as we walked in and I closed the door behind me. She took off her coat, and she had a tight white top, with a black skirt on, with black high heels. I know that she is a shrink but come on, do you have to dress provocative for her sessions. But who I am I to complain; I mean I rather have her dress like that then unappealing. I sat down on the couch as she pulled up the same chair she did last time, and placed in front of me again. She started off her session a little differently this time. She placed a tape recorder on the table and pressed the play button, as she leaned back in her chair and cleared her throat. She paused for a second, looked into my eyes and then she started. She started the session the same way, I guess she does this for all of her patients, anyway she asked me how I was feeling today. You know the usual psycho babble bullshit, if there was anything bothering me or if I was upset about anything, if my relationship at home wasn't going the way I expected, questions like that. I told her that everything was going good, and I had no problems. Even though I was going through a really tough time with the whole Beverley break up thing, I still couldn't believe she dumped me. But that's not what she is calling it, she said something about a long term relationship, but I think it might have been too long term. She asked me if anything new happened at work today, if I met anyone new. That's where the fun had begun, I thought to myself, as I just smiled and thought of Alison. I told about my job and how great that was going, I was making really good money and working in a place I actually feel comfortable. I also told her about Alison, and ever since that first day I could never stop thinking about her. I went from sitting on the couch to actually laying on the couch, because I was more comfortable lying down. When I told her about Alison, she smiled, "Have you had these feelings for Alison, before or did they recently start?" I told her that they recently started, I told her that Beverley was special, but Alison was different you know. It was just a way that she carried herself, she was so strong, you know so independent and free at the same time. I kept going on and on about Alison, I sounded like a little school girl going on and on about her first boyfriend. We talked for several hours, I kind of felt bad because I wasted so much of her time; I mean she probably had to go somewhere. I mean we talked and talked by the time we were done it was 10:42 P.M. It was getting late, and that's when she cut it off from there. "Well it's like you got a lot of issues and I am glad that you came to express your feelings today." "I am glad too, and once again I am sorry to bother you, I know you probably had some plans." "You don't have to worry about that I wasn't going to do anything anyway, just go home and watch some old videos." "So don't forget *next* time come once a week, I was nice enough to see you today because it seemed like you needed to get some things off your chest." "Okay I said, made a mental note about it, I won't forget." She walked me out and she got in her car and drove off, I waited for a second and just thought about going to work the next day, not because I like the job or working the cash register even more, I wanted to see Alison again, and I wanted to spend more time with her. I am not too sure what it was, but there was something about her, I just never wanted to be away from her. It was so strange and everything was happening so fast, maybe just maybe I think I am in love with Alison.

Chapter 13
Alison

When the next day finally arrived, I couldn't stop thinking about Alison, and how much I wanted to see her. When I woke up I checked the alarm and it was pretty early, so I decided to go back to sleep. I rolled around and tossed and turned for minutes and then I got up, I couldn't sleep a wink. I decided to get up and just relax in the living room and watch some TV; I had to keep the volume low because my mom and Jeremy were still sleeping. Did I tell you the good news, my mom who was working originally at her old job doing, well I never knew what she did, but anyway she spent all day looking and interviewing for jobs and she finally nailed one. And Jeremy was so pleased he actually got off his lazy ass and started to look for another job, I guess working at the damn construction field wasn't cutting it for old Jeremy. I think he told me yesterday that he wanted something more fulfilling, whatever the hell that meant. I tuned on the TV, and I probably flipped through the channels for about 10 minutes, I couldn't believe that there was nothing on. I mean grant it, it was early, and it was a Friday, but come on there has to be something on. Well I guess when you start gearing for the weekend, the cable company always waits and puts all the good shit on Friday nights and Saturday nights, that's when all the good movies come on. I turned off the TV and went into the kitchen, I was going to make a bowl of cereal but when I opened the fridge door I noticed that my mom had finally gone shopping. I saw so much food; you swore she robbed the hell out of the grocery store. I pulled out the egg carton, and some bread, I decided to make an egg sandwich. It seemed like so long that I actually had something good to eat. I grabbed a plate and the skillet under the counter and turned the gas on high. I got a bowl from the top cabinet and placed 3 eggs in there. I opened the drawer and took out the mixer and a spoon and a fork. I broke the eggs against the side of the bowl and placed the eggs on the skillet. The smell of fresh eggs sizzling was so good I couldn't wait until I was done. I put the bread in the toaster oven and set it for about 4 I didn't want it to get burned badly. I am so glad we have a 4 slot toaster; I don't understand people when they only buy the 2 ones. I mean an average family household has more than one kid, and I bet they all like eating toast. I mean it just cuts the hassle of putting 4 pieces of bread in their one at a time. Anyway fucking arguing to me about fucking toasters and shit, and my eggs were ready. I took them off and put them on a plate and my toast popped up at almost the same exact time. I grabbed them and opened the fridge and low and behold guess I found, butter. I grabbed a knife and buttered my toast, for the only like the second or third time I can actually have a real good breakfast. I put the plate down on the table and poured me a glass of milk and orange juice. I can never decide what to drink in the morning so I poured both.

I pretty much devoured my breakfast, it was so good, and I got up and washed the plate and put in the sink. I couldn't believe the dishes were actually done this time, not one single fork or spoon or whatever in the sink. There was something happening differently in this sometimes dysfunctional house of mine. My mom and Jeremy were actually shopping, and the dishes were being done. I felt kind of delighted; maybe just maybe that everything is going to finally start picking up, maybe we can start being a real family. It's been ages before that happened, I mean sometimes my mom will go to sleep fucking screaming and crying because that asshole Jeremy would piss her off. Then being the tough guy that he always he fucking thinks he is, fucking runs out the door, hops in his car and drives off. There are two places that you can always find his ass, either in a bar drinking away his pain and sorrow or in a strip club with some degenerate prostitute getting a lap dance for a dollar. I grabbed my towel and headed into the bathroom, I needed to take a shower because I usually take one when I get off work but last night I forgot, and I smelled bad. I looked under the cabinet for a new bottle of body wash and to my luck I found one all the way in the back. It wasn't the kind that I liked to use, but body wash is freaking body wash. I turned the shower on hot and I let it run for a while, I got in and it so soothing and calming. I grabbed the luffa sponge that was on the hook on the side of the wall. I poured a little body wash on the luffa and started to cleanse myself. I did that for about a minute and then I washed my face with some soap and then I used a face lotion, that I put on directly after washing my face with soap. It helps to make my face smooth, and it doesn't over dry like most lotions when you use them. I got out dripping wet and wrapped myself with my towel and hurriedly ran into my room without getting the floor to wet. I opened my dresser and pulled out some fresh boxers and an undershirt. I opened another drawer and grabbed some socks and a new shirt that I was waiting to wear for a long time. I grabbed a pair of khakis, because I was getting a little tired of wearing jeans all the time, it made me feel one dimensional in my style of clothing. I put on some cologne that my dad gave me before he passed away, still surprised that there is some left, I thought I would've finished it by now. I remember waking up when I was little, running through the kitchen, and going to my dad and watched him get ready to go to work. He would shave with a razor, and I mean one of those old fashioned razors. Sometimes I can smell the shaving cream in the morning; I would watch him for hours getting ready. I wouldn't care that I was a little tired I would just go back to sleep when he left, and he always used to say the same thing before he left to me, he would say as he is leaving, "See you when I get home kiddo". Now fucking Jeremy started calling me kiddo, but it's not the same, it's just not the same. I quickly put the rest of my clothes on, and glanced over to the alarm clock, it was around 12:00 in the afternoon, so I decided to go out and do something. My mom and Jeremy were still sleeping so I decided to leave them a note just to tell them where I was going, but I didn't write down who I was going to hand out with. Man I tell my job has some of the weirdest hours, when I first got hired by Alison's dad, he gave me a schedule with work times and days, but it was so confusing to read the first day. But I guess since he owned the store and was taking about opening up more stores around the world, and possibly even opening up different stores, he didn't care what time it opened or closed. This is my work schedule for the week, and you will be surprised, well I work the whole week, and I can choose what days that I went off. I couldn't believe how amazing that was no longer will I have to worry about missing anything anymore? Well, on Monday I work from 4 to 10, Tuesday I work from 2 to 8, Wednesday I work from 3 to 9, Thursday I work from 1 to 7, Friday I work from 4 10 and on Saturday I work from 4 to 12. Saturday is the only day of the week that the store opens late, but no one ever comes in that late. It is just kept opened late because Mr. Taylor can get some extra work done around the store and some inventory. You probably figured out why I didn't mention Sunday, well the store is closed that day so I usually go home or hang out somewhere. I got in my car and drove to the store, maybe I will get lucky and see Alison inside, I want to start hanging out with her more and more now. I needed to get over fucking Beverley, man she was the one and she is going to fucking blow me off like that. I couldn't believe her and how mother fucking selfish she is. All I wanted to find someone who will not leave me, and can understand me; I just wanted to find someone special. And I think that in spite of all what happened, everything that I have been through with Beverley, and my first girlfriend Bethany, in the end it didn't work out. I just didn't want that again, this time I was willing and able to make it work no matter what it took I will work at it for me, but more importantly for the girl that I got to know, and want to get to know even better, Alison. I pulled up to the store and there was nobody inside, so I guess it was still pretty early and Alison was not around. I drove off and I was driving for a while until I started to get a little tired so I decide to stop and pull over. I parked my car at a street along the side; I couldn't find any parking anywhere I had to drive in the fucking boondocks to find a good place. I got out and looked around, I wasn't really familiar with this part of town and luckily for me the store was only 15-20 minutes away so I don't have to drive that far back when I go to work. I walked around and saw a pet store, and did that bring back memories or what. I remember one time my mom surprised me with a little puppy that she got from a pet store one day coming home from work. My little eyes lit up brighter than a Christmas tree, I was the happiest boy in the whole wide world that day. I can still remember it like it was yesterday, my mom came home and had a basket with a big red bow tied to both ends, and the basket was moving. At first I was a little confused, but when she lowered that basket and I saw the puppy for the first time I started smiling. The puppy was small and scrawny, but I loved it to death, I played with it for hours and hours every day. The hardest part was naming him, but one day I woke up and the dog was running around and chasing his tail, and wagging his tail, it was so happy and independent. It rand up to me, I crouched down and it jumped on my chest and started to lick my face as it would bark. The dog had the cutest bark I have ever heard, I still couldn't believe how small and furry it was I decided to name him Harry. Man I loved Harry so much, I practically raised him from a pup myself, I loved him until my mom got really fucking drunk one day got in the car to go to the market for some cigarettes. She got in and didn't even know that Harry had snuck out in the middle of the night and was in the driveway. My mom got in the car, and started to back up, she reversed so Goddamn fast, Harry had no time to move, and she hit and killed him. It was days later I found out, but my mom told me that he ran away. I was so devastated, and it wasn't till I think a day later I was playing in the backyard and fell on a huge hole. I dug the hole up halfway, and saw Harry, my mom came out and noticed that I found out and she just cried. I never forgave my mom for that; I don't think I ever will.

I walked in and I heard a girl talking in the back, she was quite loud arguing over something with the owner. I walked back there to see what all the damn commotion was and I couldn't believe it, it was Alison. She was here, I walked up and said hi, she turned around and then quickly turned around again to the owner. The owner got mad and went back to the counter, as Alison let out a sigh. She turned to me and said, "I am sorry, about that Mitch, the store owner was being a pain in my ass." "What are you doing here, are you looking for a dog or something too?" "You can say that, I said, "No I am here because I didn't want to be at home that's why so I decided to drive around and I found this place." She smiled at me and then said, "Now tell me the real reason why you are here." "Okay, I paused for a second; I once had a dog when I was little until my mom ran it over with her car, and stepping in here brings back memories." "That's more like it

Mr. Mitch, now let's get out here shall we, I know this great little place just a couple of miles away." I didn't want to say no, because this was my time to finally spend some time with Alison alone, and I wasn't going to miss the opportunity. We left and started to walk towards her car, would you believe her car was better than mine. Even though my car was old and I drive like shit, but still I was kind of jealous. We reached her car and I walked around and sat in the front seat, she got in and buckled up. She reached for her CD case from under her seat, don't ask me why it is under her seat but it was, and she grabbed a CD to put into the disk tray. "Sorry I don't have my I-Pod player to play songs through there, we have to use old fashioned CD's." "Don't worry about it, it's cool, I like CD's anyway its better than listening to tapes or something." She smiled as she started her car and drove off. Okay, this girl is perfect because she even drives faster than I do. She is like me but different in every way, one thing is that she is a female, and the other is that she is so free spirited. We drove for several miles and, it was good because it was only like 2:00 in the afternoon, and I didn't have to be at work until later anyway. She stopped and pulled up; I didn't know where we were or recognized any of the landmarks. She got out and told me to get out too, she walked over to me grabbed my hand and told me to follow her; I guess she was leading me somewhere, but I didn't know where. We finally got to wherever the hell that she was dragging me, and when I saw what she sees every day I couldn't speak. It was something beautiful, there was a lake surrounded by big rocks and lots of trees. The sun out and the sky was blue, and the birds were chirping. It was really peaceful; she took me to the highest point where there was a huge rock. "I come here once in a while just to get away from everything, it helps me relax." "I can see, I said, wow just look at this place it looks like it goes on forever." We both laid down on the rock just staring at the sky, and listening to the birds as they chirp. She turned her head and looked at me, "Hey you know we have been working together for a while now and well I am glad that my dad hired you." "Thanks, I said, I am glad that your dad hired me too I like working there and I like spending time with you." Shit, I thought to myself, what I just said I couldn't believe I just said that. Alison paused for a second, she rose up and leaned towards me, got closer and said, "I like spending time with you too we make a great team."

Then she leaned in closer and kissed me, I was confused I didn't know what to do, so I did the only sensible thing that any teenager would do, I held on to her gently flipped her around and kissed her back. We started kissing, and my hands were behind her head, I took one of my hands and slowly rubbing her stomach, I went lower still rubbing her body, and then I kind of pushed her off. "What's the matter, did I do anything wrong?" "No, it's me, you see I really like you but I don't want to rush into this I want to get to know you a little better first before we do anything hasty." She got up and grabbed my hand as she pulled me up, and she just gave me a hug and held on to my body for a minute. "What was that for" I said. "Well that is being such a good friend, and also respecting me at the same time." I smiled and just held her close to me as we just stood there. For the first time, I don't have to rush into anything I finally found a girl that I can be myself with, I am in love. We decided to leave because it was almost time for work; we walked down and walked to her car. We both got in as she started the car up; I pressed play on the CD, as we held hands as she drove off.

Chapter 14
Our First Date

We got back to work and with only 15 minutes to spare too, we were both pretty relieved. We sort of spruced up the place before Alison opened the store. I went over to my station as Mr. Taylor would say and counted the money and wrote it down in this notebook he always makes me write it down, so he can keep track. Alison opened the store, and she saw a guy coming from the street, she kept the door opened because he was obviously coming in. "Are you guys open, I just need to buy a couple of things." "We are now sir, come on in and help yourself, I am sure you are going to love our selection today." The gentlemen came in, he looked average, and he had a New York Yankees baseball cap on, a black T-shirt with a green khaki jacket over it, blue jeans and black shoes. He was carrying a coffee mug in one hand and a newspaper clutched his left armpit. I noticed when he walked in that the gentlemen had a ponytail, and it was like a dark but dirty blonde color. He proceeded to look around the store going about his day and sipping his coffee every couple of seconds. The gentlemen walked around for a couple more minutes, pulled out his cell phone and proceeded to make a call. I think he was calling his wife, and the only reason I can make the observation is two reasons one, he was talking quite loudly, and the other one was he was using words like honey and baby. Or I could be wrong it probably isn't even his wife it's probably his girlfriend or something, because there is nothing wrong with a guy who looks like he is late 30's going on 40's to possibly have a girlfriend right. He hung up the phone and put it back in his pocket. He picked up one piece of clothing, and it wasn't for him, he had a girl's top. The top was probably medium sized going on by the length and width, it was all black with a black lace going on the sides, and it had small white diamonds (fake) going all around the top boarder following the bottom boarder. Must have been a gift for his wife or his girlfriend, or I could be totally wrong again and he could be really, really kinky and he is buying that for himself, to go home later tonight and try it on. I just had a really disturbing image, and I needed to turn my attention towards something else or better yet someone else. I quickly rung him and put her top I mean his top in a bag and told him to have a nice day, as I handed him the receipt. He smiled and took another sip of his coffee as he walked out the store, I walked over to Alison, to see what she was doing, and she was in a corner of the store where you can try on shoes, she was sitting down with her back faced away from me. I walked over and gently tapped her on her shoulders, I guess she didn't hear me coming; she shot right up and dropped a book on the ground. I picked it up for her not asking her what it was, because it wasn't any of my business. She thanked me for picking up the book and handing it to her, but again she was crying, so this time since I got to know her a little better over these last couple of weeks I decided to ask politely. "What's the matter, I said, if there is anything wrong you know you can tell me?" She just looked at me and said, "I know, but it's very complicated and I don't want to bore you with all the details of my life." "I don't mind, I am sure I can keep up." She started going on and on about her life growing up, and how she could never find a steady boyfriend. "It is so hard finding someone you know, you think that you found someone but they turn around and fucking stab you right in the back." She was probably going on about her old boyfriend, man that guy sounded like a fucking jerk to do that to such a sweet girl. "I know what you mean, I liked this girl well I mean I really loved this girl and she loved me back, we were supposed to spend the rest of our lives together. But one day we met up in the park at the same spot we usually meet up, and before I can even get the word in, she left and I never saw her again." "I guess we are in the same

damn predicament, and in the end it didn't work out for us to well."
I just smiled and shook my head from side to side saying you can say
that again, as I walked over back to the register. And Alison went about
her business. For the first couple of minutes the store seemed empty
then soon it hit around like 5:00 to 5:30 P.M. we got bombarded by a
whole bunch of girls. Now at this point I would be smiling my ass off,
and trying to help all of them, but I didn't do that, I really liked Alison
and I wanted to show her that she was the only girl for me. They all
headed for the back I guess that's where all the good clothes are kept,
but I really wouldn't know I just run the cash register but I help from
time to time. They all grabbed a whole bunch of clothes from the racks
and came running up to the counter asking for the key to the dressing
rooms. I handed the girl in the front the key and she ran back got all
of her friends and went inside. I can hear them laughing, and giggling
inside, as they were changing. Alison walked up the counter and just
laughed, "Man those girls really know how to shop huh, and they must
be extreme shop addicts." "Yeah, I said, hey I paused for a second;
after we close up do you want to go out to get something to eat, or
grab some coffee or something." "Sure I would like that; it would give
us a chance to get to know us a little better." "You're right, that would
be nice to get to know us a little better, so we be can ready to take this
relationship to the next level." Alison smiled as she went into the back
and walked over to the dressing rooms, she asked if everything was
okay, one of the girls replied, yes we are done. All the girls came out
and walked over to the counter; one by one they all pulled out credit
cards and waited. And one by one I swiped their credit cards through
the machine, and one by one they left with their bags in hand all and
all of them on cell phones. I swore that they were an exact clone of
fucking Barbie or something, I guess all they needed to make this day
perfect was Ken.

After that was all said and done, the store got pretty quite again,
and that was my change to talk to Alison. I needed to come up with
suggestions to where she wanted to go, because I didn't know yet what
she was into. She was in the same corner that she always is, but this
time she was reading. "You really love this corner of the store; you are
here all the time." "Yeah, you can say that, it's the only part of the store
where I can get privacy and I don't have to worry about people seeing

me." "Hey I was wondering, where you wanted to go, if you wanted to go somewhere special or just somewhere in random." "It doesn't matter; you can take me anywhere you want, as long I am with that is all that matters." I smiled and walked back to the register, again the store was pretty quite. I told Alison that I am going to the corner store just to get a bite to eat real quickly. She said okay, as I left and started walking across the street, and made my to the store. Wow, I thought to myself this store seems pretty quiet, I walked in and started to look around. I looked for a couple of minutes but I couldn't find anything that I liked, and went I walked into the back of the store were all the beverages were kept, you wouldn't believe who I bumped into. It was my psychiatrist, Dr. Ross I couldn't believe of all the corner stores she picks the one that is miles away from her office. I walked up to her and said hi, I think she was quite surprised to see me here. "Hi Mitch, wow, what on earth are you doing here, I can't believe it." "I just work across the street and I just came in to just get something to eat real quickly." "Okay, how is everything else going on with you, how is your job and Alison, how is she doing?" "She is doing well, we starting dating, and I really like her, actually we are going on our first date tonight, so I am pretty nervous." "I don't know where to take her you know it's our first date, and I want to make a good impression. "Well can I give you some advice, just be yourself, don't try to overdo it on the first date, and just take her somewhere where you think the both of you will have a fun time." "Thanks, I think I am going to be fine thanks you Dr. Ross, you always know what to say at the right time." We said our goodbyes until next time and I walked out the store, I wasn't that hungry anyway so I didn't bother to pick something up. I went back inside to the store, and Alison was helping out some people, actually she was ringing them up at the cash register. But she didn't seem to mind at all, I guess she likes really helping people, or probably wondered where the hell I was. I walked around the counter and towards Alison, and I gave her hug and thanked for helping these people when I was gone. "Okay, I thought of a perfect place we can go and just talk for a while, so that way we can really get to know each other." "She seemed oaky with it because she smiled and winked at me as she headed towards the back again. It was getting late, and we still had some time before she closed up the store, so we were completely alone for the time being. I walked up to her, every time I wanted just a minute for myself, I saw me being drawn closer and closer to her. I knew that right then and there I wanted her in my life, and I would sacrifice anything to make sure that worked. She was drinking coffee and reading a newspaper article. I kind of pushed down the newspaper down so I can see her face, she seemed pretty distraught that I did that, I quickly apologized. I grabbed her hand and lifted her up and held her close to me. She was surprised of my actions even saying at one point, "Hey you, miss me." She just laughed while I just held her in my arms for a minute or two. She smelled so good, I couldn't resist her anymore, it's like I can't live my life without her. And it was then when I figured out that I was over Beverley, I just hope that I don't get hurt like last time, but I was determined to make it work. Time had run out and it was time to close the store, she tried to tell me that she needed to lock up, but I playfully held her closer preventing her from doing so. Finally I let her go, so she can close up, while she was walking over there I told her if had any ideas of where she wanted to go, I asked her if she wanted to go anywhere in particular again. She just shrugged her shoulders and just gave an inconspicuous hmm… and said how about to a restaurant or something, I always wanted to go somewhere nice. I looked back at her, "That sounds like a great idea, now it gives me the reason to actually dress up." "My mom bought me this shirt and pants combo one day, and it came with a tie." "Fancy, she replied, now it gives me a chance to actually put on some decent makeup." I just gave a little smile, and then went on about my business, didn't know what that was, but it was something. Alison grabbed all of her stuff, as she told me to hurry up or she was going to leave me in the store. We left, the night was pretty fair. The winds were calm and the streets were quite, it was a nice breeze flowing, so that felt good. I turned towards Alison and said, "Hey, I am going to go home and get ready, you know take a shower and stuff, where do you want to meet up at?" "Umm… she paused for a second, come pick me up at my address." "You mean your home address, I said shockingly." "Yeah, where do you think I go after work all the time, duh come on Mitch?" "Okay, I am just surprised that, I paused for a second, never mind, so I will pick you up at." I waited for Alison to give me a time, because I didn't want to show up too late or too early. "Umm… she paused again, come and get me around 8:30 or 9:00 a clock if that's cool for you." I agreed as she was writing her home address down on the back of a napkin, and handed it two me smiling. I just looked at her if she was serious, like I am not going to lose this one piece of napkin, but I folded it quickly and put it in my pocket. She turned off the lights as I quickly ran to the door; she shut the door and locked them. "Don't forget, you have to pick me okay, please don't forget, I need that time to get ready." I want to look nice tonight, I never get a chance to look nice, and I more importantly I want to look nice for you." I just smiled as I grabbed my keys and told her "I will be around 8:45 P.M., so you will have enough time to get ready and look your prettiest." She just smiled, as she started to walk to her car, I offered to walk her to her car just to be safe. There are a lot of sick people walking the streets late at night. She got in and started the car, and told me one more time to don't forget, as she drove off. I walked back to my car, turned on the radio, but nothing good was playing. I shut my door, and turned on the AC, even though it felt good outside it was hot as hell in my car. I kept that on for about a couple of minutes before I drove off to go home. After getting cooled down, I put the car in drive and took off. Luckily there were no cops patrolling the area because I was speeding, I wasn't going that fast but enough to get nailed with like a $300 ticket or something. It was almost time to pick up the love of my life, okay maybe I am jumping a little too ahead of myself, sorry about that, but I did like her that part was true. And another part of me did really love her, I don't know if I really did or if that was just mixed emotions of Beverley and possibly of everything that had happened in my life, up to this point. Well, before I bore you with details, I slowly turned the corner of where Alison lived, and proceeded to look for her house. When she told me what kind of house she lived in, it seemed like every ordinary house, but since it was night I had a hard time finding it. I finally found it and slowly pulled up to the house and to my surprise the house was huge, okay it wasn't like a mansion or anything but it was big. I didn't want to be rude and honk the horn, so I turned off my car, got out and walked to the front door. I waited for a second or two, I looked my watch and it said 8:47 P.M. so I was on time. I took a deep breath and rang the ball, after a couple of seconds Alison's dad answered the door. He was pretty pleased to see me and not some punk kid, taking his precious daughter out for a date, as he likes to say. He asked me if I wanted to come in, I gracefully accepted and made my way in, I took off my coat and hung it on the rack. Alison is still getting ready, just make yourself at home, and let me know if I can get you anything to drink. I just smiled and said thank you, as I made my way into the living room, and patiently waited. She finally came down, and let me tell you she was absolutely breathtaking, I mean the dress that she was wearing was so gorgeous, she had a dark blue dress that came midway down her body, and the back was crossed all over going all the way down. She had dark black heels on, and she smelled positively intoxicating, it had to be the new perfume that she bought. She made her way down, and hugged her dad as I got up and followed her to the door. I shook Mr. Taylor's hand as I told him I would take care of her daughter and make sure that she would return home safely. I always believe that when I am going out with a girl it is important that you treat her nice and also show her a good time. Who knows if this night is over she might want to go out with me again sometime so that was important. We walked to my car as I opened the passenger side door for her; she got in ever so gracefully as I walked around to the driver's side of the car. I got in and buckled up, and turned around to Mr. Taylor who was standing halfway out the door, and honked my horn. I waved and started the car as I started to reverse and then we left. We stared driving and Alison had no idea where we were going, so adjusted the seat a little, pulled down the mirror in front of her and started fixing her makeup. It was just amazing because I would never picture her for being so into her looks. I mean when I saw her for the first time, I knew that she was really pretty and she had an extraordinary body, but just seeing her from how she usually dresses to tonight it was fascinating. We drove for several more minutes; she pulled out a CD and put it in the tray. She waited a couple of seconds for the player to read and hit play. "What did you put in there?" I asked still driving. "Just something that we can both enjoy its new I just got it". It started to play I recognized the sounds of the instruments for a while but I still couldn't get it. I let it play and then I started to say a bunch of random band names out to see which one was the correct one. Alison wasn't telling me on purpose because when looked over I could tell that she was having fun with me guessing and getting them all wrong. "Okay, give up now stop guessing and I will tell you" she said. "Okay I said, I give up are you going to tell me now?" She just smiled and just said in the most playful voice, The Clash silly. Oh, I replied really not knowing but had an idea of who it might be, I knew it sounded familiar. The Clash was a punk rock band from Britain I believe from the early 1970's to the 80's, if I am right. We finally pulled up to the restaurant that I was taking her to, and it was special. Not because it was just another restaurant, you can always claim that a restaurant is special but this was more sentimental. Because my mom used to take me here all the time, there was one were we lived before we moved? I slowly pulled in and was looking for some parking, and finally I found some in the side of the building. We got and she couldn't stop awing over the fact that it was so big, and it looked pretty expensive. I just nodded my head as I held her hand and we walked in and made our way to the front. When we got there was a waitress who was going to sit us. She was young probably in her twenties, she had her hair up and her bangs were down. She had on the usual uniform for most waitresses in a restaurant; she had a white button up polo, and a black skirt. She gracefully asked us how many, I politely said just two, we followed her to our table and she gave us our menus. She said if she can start us out with anything to drink, and Alison went first. "Can I just get some raspberry iced tea please, that's my favorite". And I chipped in and I said I will have the same thing but I didn't want the lemon on the side of the cup." She smiled, "Okay two iced teas, be back in second." I opened the menu and started to look around. "Did you find anything that you liked, as Alison was looking through the menu herself trying to find something?" "Umm, she said I'll guess I will have Chicken Alfredo, because that's my favorite". When the waitress came back with our drinks, she placed them down, pulled out a white notepad with a pen. She was ready to take our orders; I let Alison go first because she knew what she wanted, as I had already made up my mind when she was coming with our drinks. Alison gave the waitress her order and I went next, I told her that I wanted the Chicken Marsala. She wrote down our orders and took our menus as she walked away. I just stared at Alison for a minute she noticed and quickly smiled, "What why are you staring at me like that" she said. "I can't help it you just look so beautiful tonight; I can't take my eyes off of you. She just kept on smiling and just said "Then don't" as I held her hand waiting for our food to arrive. The atmosphere for the restaurant was pretty nice, it seemed that everybody was having a nice time, and it seemed pretty busy because all of the employees were running around attending to every one's orders. I felt bad for them because sometimes they will get ridiculed for something that they didn't even do. A waiter came and he gave us some breadsticks and salad, it was complementary, the salad looked really good and the breadsticks smelled great. We ate that and talked for while; I mean we didn't have any conversation topics or have any idea what we needed to talk about. We just talked, and to tell you the truth it kind of flowed that night, I didn't know what it was. About 15 to 20 minutes went by and then our food finally came and we both were exceptionally hungry and couldn't wait.

Again we just ate and talked, I mean the whole night we were just laughing and smiling, it felt like I can be myself with her, like how I talk to her on a regular basis without the feeling of pressure. I can say that we had a great time we spent the rest of the evening just eating and talking about whatever. It was pretty magical, besides Beverley, I have never felt this way about anyone before. I just smiled to myself and called for the waitress, she walked over and I asked her for the check. I could see that Alison was going to pay for this, but I talked her out of it and insisted that I would take care of it. I took out my wallet and my credit card and placed it on the bill that the waitress put on the table. She took the bill and we waited for to come back, we got up, I started to put on my coat as I helped her. The waitress came back and smiled and told us to have a good night, before we left I placed a tip on the table. I believe that our bill came to $50 so I left like $10, I wasn't really good at math but I thought it was reasonable. We left and started to leave, we got in the car and I told her that I was going to take her somewhere else. It was getting late in the evening so I didn't want to waste too much time. I decided to take her to the park so we can talk. I wanted to take her to same bench that I used to take Beverley. It wasn't anything out of proving a point, like this will make me feel better or I am trying to get back at her or something. I thought that I can finally move on, and just try to live my life with happiness and love, something that I haven't done in a long time. We pulled up to the park and when I parked the car, I turned off the car and opened the door. I sat in the seat for about a second until I got out and walked around and opened Alison's side door. She got out and took off her coat and placed it in the front seat. She said something I think about the weather, about how nice it was, but I wasn't really paying attention. We shut the door and stated to walk to the bench, it was really good weather I had just noticed. We got to the bench and just sat down, and we just looked at each other. I just smiled, I really wanted to tell her everything, you know just tell her so much about everything, but the time wasn't right, besides it was such a nice night I didn't complicate things. "This is such a nice night, it's so peaceful and relaxing, and don't you agree?" she said. "I just looked at her and said yes. I grabbed her hand and took a deep breath, "Alison, I had a wonderful night tonight, and I was wondering that you wanted to do this again." She smiled and held my hand and just said yes. I smiled back at her and we just continued to talk about whatever came to our minds. I asked her what were her hobbies and she asked me what my favorite music was. Stuff like that, which I didn't mind at one bit because it was like back at the restaurant, I can just be myself with her and not try too hard.

It was getting late and I think it was about time that we leave so I can drop her off home safely as I promised Mr. Taylor I would do. We walked to my car and got in, she hit play on the CD that she was previously was listening to. I started the car and reversed, and drove off; she was rocking out to the CD as I just continued to drive. We got to her house as I slowly pulled up to the driveway. She stopped the CD , I got out and walked around to open her door, she stepped out, I walked her to her front door as I walked up to the top step. I held her hand as I looked into her eyes. "Tonight was fun wouldn't you say, we should do this again sometime." She smiled and said yes we should, without any wasted motion I was about to say one more thing and she leaned in and kissed me. She quickly pulled back like she did something wrong, I grabbed her and kissed her back. I gave her a hug and wished her a good night, she got her keys out of her pocket and opened the door, she was going to go inside until she came out and hugged me one more time. She walked inside her house and shut her door; I smiled as I grabbed my keys too and opened my door. I got in the car started it up and just drove off, it was a long night ahead of me, I was getting pretty tired and I need to concentrate on the road if I wanted to get home safely. And the best thing about this whole night was I knew when I go home and no matter how upset Jeremy was about something and how much my mom was going on about something. When I go to sleep and wake up the next morning I will be happy. And that is because I will get to see Alison again.

Chapter 15

First Episode

When I woke up I really couldn't remember much of anything, I didn't know what time I went to sleep. I think I still had my shoes on, if that's the case I must have been really tired. I was still a little dazed, man I was so tired for some Goddamn reason but I didn't care as much, because I was so hungry. I got up and I felt something on my wrist, I was still wearing my watch. I sat up and scooted to the edge of the bed, I took a deep breath and took off my wrist watch and placed against an old photo frame on my dresser. I took my hands and just placed it over my face for a second and then ran through my hair with the finger tips. I got up and stretched; I yawned, and rubbed my eye with my finger. I wanted to take a shower because last night being out for a long time I really smelled. I don't know what it is every time I go somewhere I always ending up smelling bad, I mean it only happens when I come back from the place and wake up the next day. It's sort of weird maybe I should take my showers at night. I walked into the kitchen and the first thing that I saw on my table were brochures for school and shit. That just put a damper in my mood, because it's school, I mean who gets excited for school, its fucking school. But I needed to go or do something "educational" as my mom would always say. I mean she means well but I didn't like school, I went to school previously growing up and shit but I really didn't care to a point where I just stopped going. And the really funny part was that neither Jeremy nor my mom really cared as much as other parents would. They knew that school wasn't going to work out for me; they were both worried that something stupid may happen like I would get into fight with a student or a teacher and get expelled. And another reason was that they both knew that I was going through some tough shit, and they kind of just eased off my back enough to not ask if I was going to back. But now seeing the brochures on the table, it was all coming back to me now. But I think my mom said it's never too late to go back, maybe you can learn a trade or something. Yeah, learning a trade that sounds funny, because I was a good learner but if it was something that I hated or was not interested in I really didn't give a shit. After all this shit I was so heated that I couldn't even think straight, man if took up smoking at a early age I would be outside smoking all my mother fucking stress away from this whole world. But I didn't, because unless like Jeremy I care about my body because I want to live and live a long life. I couldn't even eat now because of all of this shit; I needed to make a decision about all of this shit. It took me a minute to think about all of this because like everything in my life everything was happening so fast. I had made up my mind, since I have been out of school for a while, and when I tried to go to school it really never worked out. But on the other hand if I never went I would never have the opportunity to meet any girls, so I guess it worked out to my favor. I thought about it for another minute still wondering what the hell I was going to eat while staring at these papers, and then I came to a conclusion. I decided that I am going to go back, might as well I mean if somehow I can balance going to school hanging out with Alison and going to work then I can do anything. Now with all of the excitement of school, yeah excitement, but anyway I didn't want to eat anything big so I just made myself a bowl of cereal. I noticed that the red light on the answering machine was blinking, but I didn't hear the phone ring in the morning, I must have been knocked out. I pressed play and waited for the message, it read, "Hey Mitch, it's Alison, hey listen up you don't have to come to work today I know you were scheduled but you can take the day off. My dad and I are heading to my aunt's house so the store is closed today." I deleted the message and went back to my cereal, I was kind of disappointed because I won't get to see Alison, but on the other hand I was relieved, man she has been working me like crazy and now I can finally relax. It was still early so I decided to take a shower, with Jeremy and my mom still sleeping, or I guess they were I didn't know if they were up or not, but anyway I can take as long as I want today. My mom bought me some shampoo and body wash and some other stuff because I was running low. When I went into the bathroom and looked inside the shower to see what she had got me, I couldn't believe it she actually got me the stuff I liked. I really am picky about the scent that the shampoo and the body wash give away. I went back into my room and grabbed my towel which was hanging on the rack near my window. And I walked back into the bathroom I closed the door and turned on the shower. I always waited until it got hot before I hopped in so that way I don't have to stand in the shower and wait as it gets hot because it is always cold in the beginning. I started to take my clothes off as I was whistling a tune I heard from the radio, I really liked that song but couldn't remember who sang it but I did remember the name, it was called "Goodbye To You", I am pretty sure it was a sappy love song. Steam started to come from the shower so it was ready; I slowly stepped in and closed the curtains. I'll tell you the water was so warm I could've stayed in the shower for another hour, but I needed to get out before I prune up. I always make sure to dry off completely because my mom hates when I just get out of the shower dripping wet and run to my room. Even though I always tell her that it wasn't that much water on the floor, she still gets upset. But today because they were sleeping I decided to dry off somewhat and then make a run for it to my room. Water was dripping off my leg and some got on the floor but it will dry up eventually so I didn't have to worry about it. It was getting pretty late in the afternoon I would say around 1:30 P.M. I didn't get a chance to look at my clock. I quickly dried off and when I turned my attention to my alarm clock to check the time, I was pretty close it was 1:38 in the afternoon. I had the whole day ahead of me while I was still getting ready. I quickly put on my clothes, first the essentials boxers, socks, undershirt then I put on my jeans and a T-shirt I grabbed from my closet. It looked really old, but I guess that was the way the T-shirt was made. I never took the time to iron any of my clothes because sometimes I really didn't care about that much. I guess the only time I do iron any of my clothes is if I am going somewhere really special, in that case I would've have to wear a suit or something. I sprayed some cologne on my wrists and left my room. As I entered the living room I noticed that my mom's door was halfway open so I figured that they were awake. I guess they were watching TV or something because I heard talking. As I was about to leave and go enjoy my day, Jeremy came out the room and smiled at me. "Morning Kiddo, what's up, what are your plans for this glorious day?" "Nothing much really, I said, probably just going to go outside and drive around for a while and stuff." He continued to smile as he walked into the kitchen he opened the fridge and started to take out some food. And that was my cue to leave as soon as possible before my mom wakes up and starts hammering me with 21 questions. I grabbed the keys and walked out the door, well Jeremy was right about one thing it was a really nice day outside. If I had to guess it had to be around 70 degrees and the winds were really peaceful. I had no idea where the hell I was going or what I was going to do. I unlocked the car door and sat in; I didn't close the door at first, because I wanted to get some of that fresh air. And for the strangest reason I just started to think about random ass shit. I didn't even start the car or anything I was just seating in the driver's seat still parked in the driveway. I don't know I just wanted to start the car and just drive away and enjoy my day, but there was something holding me back. I tried not to think about everything all at one time because it might give me a headache but I couldn't help it. I thought about Beverley, and why she just left me like that waiting in the blistering cold. Why she would just leave and never call or write or anything. I just couldn't understand I thought I was doing everything right that she would be the one that I could marry and be with for the rest of my life. She never told me anything that day and when I tried to call her that same night, it's like she didn't want to talk about it or something. Every time I would try to understand why she did what she did she would hurry up and change the subject. Then she said she had to go and then she would hang up the phone and never call back. I know that there are people out there who lose someone they really love but at a young age this really hurt me. I couldn't help to believe that I was in love with her and I would give up my whole life for her, but now she's gone and I would probably never see her again. Then I started to think about my mom and Jeremy, I don't know why but I think that my mom was happy or at least she thought she was. She never really complained that much about Jeremy. Of all the things that I hated about that bastard my mom loved him; she thought he can make her life happy or something. I thought about how my mom was bouncing from job to job and trying to find something that would make her happy, instead of working there and making excuses about being happy and shit. And Jeremy, the last time he had a job was when he was working at the construction site couple years ago. He was doing well you know working hard every day and making a steady paycheck. I thought he would finally get his life back together and shit but knowing Jeremy he would self-destruct and fucking blow everything out of proportion. And his ex-girlfriend shows up out of nowhere, now he was dealing with all that bullshit. Honestly it was too much shit for me to handle or even think about right now.

I closed the car door put the key in the ignition and started the car; I reversed slowly making sure that I didn't hit anything. I started to drive; I still had no idea of where I was going and what the hell I was going to do. While I was driving I couldn't help to think about Alison and what she was doing now. I mean I am sure that she was kind of bored at her aunt's house or I could be wrong, but anyway I was wondering if she was thinking about me at all. The town was pretty busy there were a lot of cars going up and down the streets, but not a lot of people walking around though. I was getting a little hungry so I decided that maybe it would be a good idea if I would stop off and grab something to eat. I drove around looking for a deli or something, and then I found a small restaurant on the corner of Green Street. I looked for some parking, at first I couldn't find any and then I finally found a parking space behind an old red Ford pickup truck. I slowly parked behind the truck making sure that I don't hit the bumper. The good thing that it was only two blocks away from the restaurant, so I didn't have to walk that far to get something to eat. I walked from my car to the restaurant and it only took me a couple of minutes, I walked in and the place seemed pretty busy. There were some people sitting on the stools that were in front of the counter, and more people in the booths all around the place. I walked in and sat down waited for someone to bring me a menu or something. Again I was thinking about everything again, maybe I am thinking too much about everything all the time, but I couldn't help it. I thought about when I am fucking 21 that I am going to leave this God forsaken place and actually do something with my life. Maybe Alison will still love me still, and then she can come with me. I mean I want to get away and start my life with Alison, and just live happily ever after. A waitress was coming my way and she was holding a menu, "Hi there sweetie, how are you doing on this fine day, can I get you anything, she said handing me the menu." "Can I just get an iced-tea for now without the lemon please?" Okay, she said as she wrote that down on her pad and headed into the back. I flipped open the menu and started to look around and to my surprise they had some really decent food, I mean everything sounded good so I guess I would be the judge when it actually came to my table. I looked around the menu flipping through its 3 pages and then I found what I wanted to eat. I put the menu down and waited for the waitress to come over my again. I stared to think about all the times I went out to eat either by myself or with my family or with my friends, and how every time I thought that all these little diners always looked the same. I thought about the happy times when it was my *real* family going out to eat once in a while, when it was my dad, mom and I going out as a family and enjoying each other's company. Now every time I go out and eat I have to go with my mom whom I don't mind because of all that happen in her life she is still my mom, and Jeremy. I know Jeremy is trying hard to make my mom and me happy but he is not my dad and no matter how hard he tries he is never going to be. I tried to think happy thoughts about my dad but something disturbing was racing around in my head. At first I tried to play it off like it was nothing serious, and not try to think about it. The waitress made her way to my table with a smile on her face, "Made up your mind yet sweetie, tell me what you want?" I smiled back at her, "I would like your famous Southern Style Cheeseburger with Home Cooked French Fires please." Again she wrote that down in her pad and smiled, I handed her the menu as she grabbed it and walked away. I was still confused about that image racing around in my head, I tried not to think about it again but it was so strong and vivid that every time I would try to think about something else it didn't help. All I can picture is that dream that I had, I really never thought about it that much until right now, and I still haven't put all the pieces together. I mean the dream happened so fast all I can remember from that night was my mom sexually abusing me in a way I would never thought possible. Grant it, I knew that it was a dream but still it was my mom and she was having sex with me that night, and Jeremy was nowhere to be seen that night. That was another thing why wasn't he home, I mean from that construction job he hasn't worked in years and he is always home with my mom. My food finally came and it was a huge plate, the burger was stacked with everything and the fries looked so good. She put the plate and my table and said enjoy honey as she walked back into the kitchen. I grabbed the ketchup bottle and doused my fries and the inside of my burger. I like a lot of ketchup on my food; I always believe that it gives food that extra kick or flavoring. I started to eat the burger taking the top bun off and stuffing my French fries inside to a point where it was falling out the side when I tried to pick it up and eat it. I thought it was pretty funny because my mom said I used to do that when I was little, I guess old habits never die hard. I made short work of my sandwich and finished it off by drinking two glasses of iced-tea. I waited a while so the food can work its way down before I get back into my car and drive off. I noticed that there was a girl sitting all the way on the other end of the restaurant, and when I glanced over real quickly she looked like Alison a little from the back. And when I noticed that I thought what Alison was doing at this point in time, I hope she was having more fun than I am right now. I asked the waitress for the bill and I pulled out my wallet in the mean time. She came back and the bill was relatively cheap it read only $9.75, so I pulled out $10 and placed it on the bill. I didn't worry about the change because it was only a quarter. Too me it was nothing really that important to stress about and ruin my whole day. I grabbed my coat that I had placed beside me when I was eating and put it on. I made sure that I had everything because sometimes I would forget shit and be upset, and when I try to go back it would always be gone. I had everything and made my way out the restaurant, I was satisfied because the food was really good and it was cooked very well. But even with a full stomach I still wasn't feeling well at all. So I made a hasty decision and decide to go see Dr. Ross, my psychiatrist and bother her with all my problems. I walked to my car and unlocked the door I got in and started to search the glove compartment for her address. I quickly found it and placed it a side, I started the car and drove off. Luckily for me I didn't have to work so I can see her as long as I want to and when I looked at her address she was only a couple of miles away from me, so it wasn't that far of a drive.

I drove through and I had to stop probably like 3 or 4 time because of red lights. That's the thing with red lights, it's like whenever I need to get somewhere important there are a hundred fucking red lights, but whenever I drive just to pass the time the lights are green. But I didn't mind one bit because I couldn't stop going on about the weather. I finally got there and parked my car on the side of the street. I took a deep breath because I was actually supposed to see her today. I was nervous for some reason; I know that she is my psychiatrist and shit but still talking to her about my problems always made me a little nervous. I walked in and walked right to the counter and told the girl that I had an appointment today to see Dr. Ross. Well, okay I really didn't have an appointment but I needed to see her regardless. She took a second to flip through her log and found nothing. "I am sorry sir, are you sure you have an appointment today I don't see you here." "Yes I am sure I made on last week to see her today, maybe you should try looking one more time." She smiled and started to look again as I waited, and then Dr. Ross came out her office door talking to one of her patients. She quickly noticed me standing in front of the counter and walked towards me. "Hi Mitch, how are you doing today?" "I am fine, actually I am not doing that well, I was supposed to see you today I need to see today." She looked upset or something or worried about me so she said follow me and took me into her office. She closed the door when she entered and turned on the lights, she walked to her desk and put some papers into her drawer and locked it. She grabbed a chair and sat even closer to me than usual. I sat down on the couch I was to uncomfortable to lay down this time so I was going to sit up. She had a notepad and then she got up and put it on the table she sat down again and looked right at me. "We're going to do this a little different this time, I hope you don't mind." "No, I said, really having no problem with it because I am the one seeing her." "Tell me your problems Mitch; we are going completely off the record for this one." I didn't know what she meant by that, was this going to happen all the time. "I am sorry, I said, I don't know what you mean by that." "What I mean by that is just talk to me about whatever is bothering you, I am not going to think or even talk to you like a psychiatrist, but more like your friend. And I believe that you and I can get a better understanding of what is really bothering you." Okay, well I started to talk to her about how I started to think about Beverly, and about that dream that had that night with my mom. "Everything is happening so fast you know it's like I can't slow it down, this whole situation with Beverley, I think messed me up emotionally and mentally." She looked at me concerned with every word that I had said. I think how seriously she was taking this matter which she cares more about me in a professional viewpoint than any other of her patients. I told her that some days I would feel fine and then other days I would just breakdown and start to lose it. I wouldn't go out of control or anything but it was more like why is everything is happening to me sort of feeling. "I didn't know what I did wrong with Beverley, I thought that I was doing everything that I could to make it work and then she just left." "Maybe you are still having strong feelings for this girl, and that is causing you to stress out at high levels she said." I told her about that dream and for some strange reason I swear that it means something. Because regular people just don't have dreams like that, this dream felt so real and lucid. I didn't say anything for a minute because I needed time to think about this, maybe if I start putting all the pieces together it would start to make sense. "I have all of these questions that I always ask myself and I never have any of the answers to them." "Maybe this dream isn't just about that night, maybe this has been going on my whole life and now since I am a little older I can start to make some sense of this and put together all the pieces." She again looked very concern and moved the chair a little a little closer to me. "Okay I can see you are dealing with a lot of stress right now, and still trying to figure out this whole dream." "Can you excuse me for one second please, I will be right back I am terribly sorry." She got up and left her office, I didn't know where she was going or what she was doing. I was still sitting on the couch with hands on my face looking down. I can hear her walking down the hallway; she suddenly stopped and knocked on someone's door. I can hear her talking to someone, they talked for several minutes but I couldn't make out what they were saying. I heard them walking down the hallway again, and it was getting closer. Minutes later she came back into the office, she was with someone else. He looked at me for one second and walked towards me. "Hi Mitchell, can I call you Mitch is that alright?" I just nodded my head and smiled at the stranger. "My name is Dr. Carson and I am child psychiatrist here at this facility." "I was wondering if I can help you with anything, or if you want to talk about anything I am here for you." Dr. Ross came up to me and sat next to me on the couch; she looked at Dr. Carson and looked back at me. "Mitch, she said, Dr. Carson is going to be seeing you now, I think that whatever you are going through you need to see a professional. I am just a psychiatrist and I can only do so much to help you." "Dr. Carson is a professional child psychiatrist and he can be more help to you than I can right now, I am sorry." I was fucking confused, "I thought I can come in and talk to you, I thought you and I had an understanding." "Now I have to see someone else, I don't think that I am comfortable with all of this happening so fast." "I know right now it is really confusing but he can help you, you have to trust me on this." She got up from the couch and walked back to the corner of her office. Dr. Carson sat down next to me on the couch and started to talk. "Son, he said, I am afraid that everything that has happened to you in the past and the events that have taken place in these last couple of weeks, you are going through a mental disorder." "Now I know that sounds bad but you have to trust me that is very common, most of the time it is because of stress at work or school, love ones, there are plenty of reasons, but I need you to trust me." He got up and walked out the office, he had the door still open, because he was coming back. I looked at Dr. Ross with a blank expression, as she just whispered to me I'm sorry. Dr. Carson came back into the office with a piece of paper, he had written a prescription for some medication for me to get to help me ease with this whole situation. He handed the prescription to me and told me to get that filled as soon as possible, the sooner the better he told me. He smiled, and put his hand on my shoulder, "Everything is going to be alright don't worry, and these things have a way of working themselves out." He stood up and thanked Dr. Ross as he left the office closing the door behind him. Dr. Ross came and sat next to me again, "Hey I know this is tough because you are still young and you have everything to look forward to when you get older, but I want to help you A.S.A.P. before this problem gets any worse." She stood up and I got up to from the couch, she just smiled at me and walked out of her office. I just stood there for one minute still trying to figure out what the fuck just happened.

I looked at the prescription that Dr. Carson gave me and he wrote down that I should come back in 2 to 3 days. I folded up the piece of paper and put it in my left coat pocket along with my phone and some gum I had. I walked out the office and made my way out of the building. I didn't even want to think about anything right now, about Beverley about Dr. Ross or Dr .Carson, about my mom or Jeremy, about Alison and her dad, about anyone. I took the keys out of my right coat pocket and walked over to the driver's side of the car. I unlocked the door got in and closed the door, I started the car turned on the AC, popped a CD in the disk tray and fucking drove off.

Chapter 16
Alone

I continued to fucking drive not thinking about anything, this point I didn't care where I was going or what the hell I was going to do. I glanced over at my watch to see what time it was and it was getting pretty late in the evening, around 5:35 almost 6:00 P.M. The only thing that was certain right now, the only thing that I needed to do is just get away. I didn't care where, but right now all I wanted to do is just be alone. I continued to drive and I noticed a lake or something to my right. The good thing was that the road that I was on was completely empty, there wasn't a car in front or behind of me. So I decided to slow down to see the lake more clearly, and I think it was the same lake that Alison took me one day on top of the stones. I started thinking maybe I should go there because I knew where it was and I wouldn't get lost if I decided to drive up any further. It was a couple of miles away from where I was so I needed to drive a little further. Luckily for me I had enough money in my wallet just in case I run out of gas and be fucking standard somewhere. Actually with that being said, I quickly came to the conclusion maybe it would be a good idea if I went to go fill up, since I haven't filled up in a long time. It seemed like fucking forever, but I finally found a gas station in the middle of nowhere. I pulled up and the first things that I noticed is that the gas prices were very reasonable, I tell you if you get gas in the city it would about twice as much I am glad I live in nowhere. I pulled up towards the pump and turned off my CD player. I waited for someone to come out and of course they were taking fucking forever. I was about to get out of my car when I saw someone coming from the inside. He walked towards my car and I rolled down my window a little more. "Hi, can I get $20 regular please thank you." He took the twenty and went to the gas pump, he took out the pump and inserted in my car gas valve. The good thing that I will finally get gas and the lake was close because there was a sign that said it was only 2 miles on the right. He finished up filling up and he walked around to my window and smiled and said, "There you go buddy, now you are good to go on the road." I smiled back started up my car again, and said thank you as I drove by. The meter went from almost empty to full in one second, I felt good now I don't have to worry about being stuck somewhere. There were no cars on the street so I decided to speed a little, well okay I was actually speeding a lot but come one there was no one on the fucking road, it's no point to observe and follow the rules now. I finally got to the lake, and when I got closer to it I noticed that I saw the same boulder that Alison took me one day, and I was right those were it. It's been such a long time since we have been up there and last time I think she drove so I wasn't really paying attention of where the hell we were going. I drove around and parked my car along the side of the path. I purposely didn't grab anything, well more importantly my phone. Because everything that just happened with Dr. Ross and Dr. Carson, I didn't want to get distracted with anything right now, especially someone calling me out of the blue. I grabbed a bottle of water because it was so hot outside it was almost unbearable. I hope my car can stand the heat just being parked out here for a long time; I didn't see any shade or anything that I could've parked it under. I walked slowly towards the rocks; the weather was so calm, so peaceful. The water was so calm and the birds were chirping and there was a breeze flowing, it was really a nice day outside. I sat down on the pathway and just stared into the horizon, the clouds were so blue. I lay down and took a deep breath I didn't want to think about anything right now, I just laid there for several more minutes and let it all sink in; I finally got up and made my way up to the stones. I forgot how Alison showed me last time to climb up here, it would suck if I slipped and broke my leg or something, because I am the only one here and my phone was in my car. I slowly climbed and within a couple of seconds I made it to the top, I couldn't believe how amazing the view was. Last time I went with Alison I really didn't get a chance to actually look beyond the rocks and into the horizon because I was paying attention t her. Now that's not a bad thing but now I can finally let this entire moment sink in and without any distractions. I sat down and put both my arms on my knees and took another deep breath, focusing on not trying to think about what those Dr.'s said to me back in the office. Even though it was lurking around in the back of my head and I couldn't really put it away.

About an hour went by and the weather was still calm, the breeze starting to pick up but it was not cold. It was just right because the sun was still out and the birds were still chirping and flying around the lake. I was still lying on the rock and now it was getting a little uncomfortable, I got up and I noticed that I was lying on a small pebble, I picked it up and threw it has hard and far as I could. I saw it fall right into the lake and, I just smiled and laid right back down. Several more minutes went by and then I got up and decided that I should be going home now. All I needed was just time to think, and I am glad that I came here to do that. I slowly started to climb back down, and along the pathway I would pick up small rocks and throw them into the lake. I smiled and grabbed my keys; my poor car has been sitting out in the sun for hours. Soon as I opened the car door I can feel the heat coming from inside I quickly started the car and turned on the AC on full blast. Since I had already filled up on gas I didn't have to worry about wasting any right now. I closed the door so the air doesn't go outside, I made sure that I didn't get any missed calls or any new voice messages on my phone. I looked and I didn't get any so I was relieved that this time alone I actually got to spend alone. I reversed and started to drive home, I was a little anxious about going home to tell you the truth. Don't get me wrong I wanted to go home, but after what the doctors told me, and what they told me what I had was pretty common. As I continued to drive I was getting hungry it was such a long time since I last ate, well actually ate something good. I drove some more and I noticed a small diner just on the outskirts of town, or wherever the hell town I was in, I wasn't really sure anyway. I pulled in and slowly parked my car. I got out and put my hand over my stomach, I can hear it growling. I grabbed my wallet from the side of my car door and shut my car. I grabbed my keys and turned on the alarm and went inside the diner. As soon I walked in I could smell the food being cooked on the grill. I quickly found a seat and sat down waiting for a waitress to come my way. As I was sitting there I thought to myself that this was good. I can eat in peace and go home and worry about all that bullshit that happens in my house later. I looked around the diner and took out a picture of Alison that I had in my wallet; I looked at it for a minute and just smiled as I put it away.

Chapter 17
Our Second Date

It was pretty funny because it seemed like the diner I was in wasn't that busy but the waitresses were running all over the place, maybe it was lunch hour. I didn't know all I know is that I was especially hungry today. Finally a waitress came over to me and she looked as if she hated working here or something, she kind of had this look on her face like she wanted to get fired or quit or something. Well, she came up to me and right from the beginning I could tell that her greeting was fake, and not to mention two other things on her were fake, but that's another subject. She handed me a menu as she told me what I wanted to drink, I smiled and simply just told her that I wanted water. I opened the menu and looked inside, everything looked so great I was hungry I could eat one of everything. But I didn't have the money and the time; I kept on looking until I found something really good. It was all the way on the bottom of the page. Steakhouse Special is what it read, and it came with your choice of corn, potatoes, corn bread, or apple pie. Well I don't know about you if you can get decent steak and some sides and desert, I see why the hell not. And the other good thing was that it wasn't that expensive. The waitress came back to give me my water, she told me if I had found anything and I told her that I wanted the Steakhouse Special. I also told that I wanted the potatoes and the pie with it too. She smiled, again reiterating that she was being phony and wrote down my order, she grabbed my menu and walked back into the kitchen. I waited patiently, but I couldn't stop thinking about Alison, and then for some strange idiotic reason I thought about Beverley. It was so funny because the more I wanted to spend time with Alison, always trying to be around her. I would call her so we can talk late at night and so I can hear the sound of her voice. I couldn't help to wonder what was Beverly doing, or how she was. If she met anyone new or is she still single, or if she did meet someone is that person treating her right. It was so confusing why is it that I am still living in the past I was trying so hard to move on but I guess a piece of me will always stay left behind.

My food finally came to my table and I could see all the steam rising from it, and to anyone's knowledge you know it is going to taste really good. The waitress put the plate of food on my table smiled at me and quietly walked away. I looked at the food for one second I didn't jump into it like I usually do when I eat something, I decided to do something differently this time. I moved the plate up a little further away from me and placed the cup of juice that I ordered further away too. I put both my elbows on the table and folded my hands together, for the first time in a long time I prayed. Now I never pray, or I can't recall I time I did ever pray except when I was in church but that's mandatory. I sat there because I had never done anything like this before, I mean I quickly opened my eyes and looked around and then quickly closed them again and I could feel that people were watching me, and I was feeling a little uncomfortable. I sat in my booth for several more minutes still with my eyes closed. I could smell the steam coming from the food, it was really good. I had no idea what I wanted to pray about or for whom in that in case. It is different when you are in church because you are mostly praying with or for the same thing, God, but sitting here I couldn't figure it out. So I quickly started praying for everything but in bits and pieces. I prayed for my mom, I just want her to have a happy and healthy life, I prayed for Beverley that one felt kind of weird. Well not really weird but should I pray for her after what she did to me. But I guess everyone deserves a second chance no matter what they did. I prayed for Alison and her dad, just because no particular reason. And yes, I even prayed for Jeremy, that one put a little smirk on my face, even though sometimes I hate his ass he comes through and I appreciate that I guess. I smelled more steam coming from my food, I quickly said amen, and moved the plate closer to me. I grabbed the napkin that was on the side of the table and unfolded it and put it on my lap. I grabbed the salt and pepper shakers and sprinkled a little of both all over my food. I picked up my fork and knife and started eating. Everything was good as I took small bites so I can savor the flavor. I finished the steak first then ate all the starch later you know the potatoes and bread.

I finished up and drank the rest of my juice as I put the cup back down and lay back against the seat. Everything was so good I haven't eaten like that in a long time. I should tell my mom that she needs to cook like this more often. My mom doesn't have the greatest expertise in culinary but she is okay. She usually surprises everyone especially me when she out does herself in the kitchen and makes something really delicious. I grabbed the napkin I used to lay against my lap and wiped my face and hands and put it on the plate in front of me. I waited for the waitress to come back around so I can get the check. The place didn't look that busy, there were a couple of trucks and cars parked outside. And inside there were only a few people and one waitress on the phone on the other side of the restaurant. Finally someone came she walked over to my table smiled and picked up the plate, I asked for the check before she walked away. She walked away and came back with the check placed it on the table and walked away again. I picked it up and it read $12.74, I am glad that I had money in my pocket; the meal was a little more expensive that I would've imagined. But it was so worth it; I can't stress how good everything was. I left about $13 and got up and proceeded to walk out the restaurant and just walked down the street. I had no particular idea of where I wanted to go but I just needed to go somewhere. I glanced over at my watch and it was pretty early in the afternoon the sun was glaring over it so I really couldn't get a good read, I believe it read 12:00 in the afternoon. Honestly I had no idea of I had to work today, I didn't speak to Alison in a while; maybe I will give her a call. I took my cell phone out of my pocket and scrolled down in my address book until I found her. I called her and waited for her to pick up, it rang for several seconds. Then I heard a hello on the other side. "Alison, it's me Mitch, hi how are you doing, hey I have a question, and I wanted to know if I work today honestly I don't know if I do?" She laughed for a second and told me to wait for one second. I continued walking down the street not paying attention to where I was going. She came back on the phone and just laughed again, "Of course you are working today silly, I am about to go to the store and open up you want to meet me there?" I glanced over to my watch again only five minutes had gone by, "Okay I will meet you at the store, don't wait up." She laughed again and said bye, I put my phone back in my pocket and stopped walking and looked around. I had no idea where the hell I was; I guess I really wasn't paying attention where I was going. I pulled out my wallet and luckily for me I had some money left over, I guess the restaurant didn't break my wallet that bad. I pulled out like twenty dollars I didn't know if that was going to be enough but it was better than nothing. I waited and then I chased down the next cab that I saw. He saw me and slowly pulled up next to me, "Where to, he said in the most inviting way. I got in and hurriedly told him Vintage Equals Retro, it was a clothing store. Apparently he knew where it was because he has been there one time before; even though I really give a damn about that but whatever as long he can get me there on time. Seconds later he drove off and within minutes we arrived to the store. I saw Alison walking across the street, I yelled out my window as the taxi was slowly creeping up to a stop but she didn't hear me I guess she had her headphones on. I paid the cabbie the fair and thanked him and told him to have a nice day. I got out and walked across the street, I jokingly crept up and grabbed Alison from behind and covered her eyes as she was laughing, and knowing who it was already. She turned around and just smiled, "Hey you made it finally I thought you were never going to show." "And what not get to spend the whole day at my favorite job with my favorite girl, come on I wouldn't miss it for the world." She smiled and turned back around to open the store we both walked in as I turned on the lights. I was going to ask Alison a question but she started to walk to the back office, I will just tell her later it wasn't that important to bother her right now. I walked over to the main door and flipped the closed sign to open and waited for the bum rush to start. I was going to walk to the cash register but I walked towards Alison, she was getting some paper work together. I knocked on the door and waited outside, I didn't want to come in and bother her it would be rude. She came out and handed me an envelope, "It's your paycheck I think that you have earned it wouldn't you say. "Hell yeah I said, very enthusiastically, and put it my pocket. "You are not going to open it and see how much money you made." "That's not important right now; actually there was something that I wanted to ask you." She stood there playing with her hair as she waited for me to ask her something. "I was wondering well since we had so much fun on our first date, I was wondering if maybe sometime I can take you out again." She didn't say anything for about a second and just smiled, "Sure I would really like that, I am sure we are going to have a great time." I smiled back and said great as I walked back to the register. Before I got halfway to the cash register someone came in the store. I walked over to the person and asked her if she needed any help looking for anything. She said no I am just looking and continued walking around the store. I just shrugged my shoulders and walked back to the counter. The lady was still looking and picking up garments of clothing and putting them back down, she would pick up some clothes and hold it against her and put it down again. I found an old magazine that I started to flip through because I was so bored. After several more minutes the lady had a variety of clothing in her hand and walked to the counter, she asked me where the fitting rooms where. I told her in the back left hand of the store, I gave her a card for the rooms. She politely grabbed the card and proceeded to walk to the far end of the store. She picked the first door and closed it behind her locking it to make sure. That gave me some time now I walked from around the counter and went to go see what Alison was doing. And of course she was in her little corner of the store just reading. Yeah just too make to make something extra sure, our store is really not that busy that's why we have to figure out other shit to do to occupy our time. Okay now that you got that straightened out, I tapped Alison on her shoulder as she didn't jump up this time; I guess she had gotten used to it. "Hey I was just wondering two things, first when you wanted to go out again and the second where you wanted to go." "She stood up and took two steps toward me and said, "Well then how about after work or something it's not point of waiting around for it right?" "And about where I don't know, come on do I ever no, but anywhere is fine I really don't care remember." I smiled, "Okay then I know a great little place couple of miles away from here, actually it's like only a couple of minutes away from my house." I will pick you up at your house later tonight I said walking back to the register. "Hey I will meet you at your house okay we will take my car that's not a problem." I was a little confused, "Why I said walking back to her trying to figure this out." "My dad is home she said, and I don't want him to know I am going out this late to get something to eat you know because he made dinner for me when I get home." "I don't want to hurt his feelings if he figured out that you came over to take me out to get something to eat." "Oh okay, I said its cool don't worry about it, it's fine." I started to walk back to the counter I pulled out my cell phone and called up the restaurant to make reservations. Even though the restaurant was small it was pretty expensive and busy all the time, so you can't just go in there and expect to get a good seat. You would've have to call at least an hour in advance and sometimes more, but nothing ridiculous.

Several more people had walked into the store as I was standing behind the counter greeting them as they came in as some greeted me back. They were pretty much distinctive in their own way more of their clothing then anything. They dressed sort of like mixed punk rock with old fashioned clothing from the 80's. As they all started walking around the store I kept thinking to myself that I liked how they dressed. It was three girls and two guys; I really didn't give a shit about the guys they looked like your everyday preppy Ivy League bastards. But the girls were different, sort of, they looked like they go to private schools too but they were not as stuck up as the guys perceived to be. There were two blond ones and the brunette is the one that caught my eye. I could tell that she was different than any of her so called friends, she didn't dress so loudly like the others but she had her own style. The group spent several more minutes looking around the store. As the brunette walked past the counter she saw me noticing her and I quickly turned my head like I wasn't looking at her. At that moment I was hoping that Alison wasn't looking because I didn't want to ruin anything with her it was finally working between us. The girl walked up to me well to the counter and cleared her throat, but she did it in a way like she wanted me to look at her or something. I looked up at her and said, "Hello, my name is Mitch, welcome to Vintage Equals Retro can I help you with anything?" she smiled back at me and turned around placing her back toward the counter. She leaned in closer backwards supporting herself with her arms on the counter. She smelled so good like strawberries or something. I moved in a little closer and smelled her without her or Alison noticing. She turned back around and I quickly backed up so I wouldn't freak her out being so close to her. "Yes, you can help me with something, I want you to give me advice if these clothes that I have look good on me." I didn't know what to say did she wanted me to follow her to the dressing room and tell her how good she looks in clothes she picked out? "Um, I don't mean to be rude or anything but why don't you ask one of your girl friends to help you with that." She laughed, "I just need a guy's opinion okay." "Okay, I said well you did come in with two guys maybe they can help you." "Those guys she said, they don't know anything, besides one of them is my brother, and the other is his best friend and he is not into that kind of shit." "Okay but what about the cash register I just can't leave it out in the open like that. "Just get your co-worker to cover it duh, I mean it's not like she is doing anything anyway." I guess you're right, I thought to myself as I just walked over to Alison and trying to figure out how I am going to say this to her, without making sound weird. I walked to her little corner and gently tapped her on the shoulder, of course she was sitting there and reading something, I swear it's like she has nothing better to do sometimes. But I wasn't complaining, I mean if I did I wouldn't have a job. She put the book down and just started at me with her blue eyes. "Hey I know this may sound a little strange but I was wondering if you can watch the cash register for a minute or two, this customer insisted getting advice on how she looks in clothes." She stood up at first she didn't say a word, I was getting nervous, then she just smiled and said sure. "It's been a long time since I have been back there anyway no problem Mitchell." "It's Mitch" I said back to her, I hate when people call me by my full name it drives me crazy. She started walking towards the register as the brunette girl started walking back to me smiling and looking at me the whole time. I tried to play it off as if she wasn't looking but I knew she was I just hope Alison didn't find out that I was looking back. I mean there is nothing wrong with looking back, it's not like I am going in the dressing room to help her undress or anything. She walked over to me with a lot of clothes in her hand, and by the look in her eye I knew that this was going to be a long day. She leaned over to me and said, "Well aren't you coming, I need your help taking these clothes off, I mean they are so dirty I have been outside all day." What the fuck I thought, she really did want me to come inside, she started making her way to the dressing room and kept the door halfway open on purpose. I didn't know what to do here, on one hand Alison was my girlfriend, but on the other hand I really wanted to go inside. In strongly didn't want to do it but there was something inside of me telling me to go and undress her. I walked over to the door and just knocked even though she knew it was me. "I don't think that this is such a great idea, Alison, my co-worker is my girlfriend and I really love her you see." She just laughed as I can hear her taking off her boots, "Come on, she said she doesn't have to know she is all the way on the other side of the store." "Don't be such a baby I know you want to see me naked, it's obvious the way you are looking at me when I walked in." I was stuck again on what to do I wanted to go in so badly but I wanted to be faithful to Alison. "I am waiting, she said, as she was taking off more of her clothes." In a split second I had made up my mind, I peaked around the corner and just looked what Alison was doing, she was reading a book. I opened the stall door and went inside, I knew that what I was doing was wrong but then again it felt so right, I couldn't explain its like frenzy when I am around girls, especially the more attractive ones. I closed the door and locked it, she pulled me in closer and my lips were almost touching hers. I was staring into her eyes as she was starting back into mine. I could hear the rest of the people talking to each other in the store; I wondered if they knew where their friend was. "I didn't catch your name, I said, trying to be polite." She smiled at me, "My name is Kristen." "That's such a pretty name I said, again being polite as we came in closer. She leaned in further and kissed me on the lips, I backed away for a second kind of shocked everything was moving so fast. I leaned in kissed her back, and then we started kissing; my hand was on her shoulder and slowly moving down. I moved my hand further down slowly touching her breasts and moving down to her stomach. My hand made my way to her pants as we were still kissing. She had one of her hands on my hair and the other around my waist. I had my hand on her pants slowly unbuckling her belt and slowly pulling down her zipper. We stopped kissing for one moment and I took off her shirt, she had a black bra on I believe it was silk, as she took off my shirt too. We started to kiss again as it was getting more intense by the second. This felt so good, I mean wait, in my mind I knew that what I was doing was so wrong, and then she grabbed me and pulled me even closer. I couldn't resist and then I went all in, and then I pushed her back against the wall. "I am sorry this feels uncomfortable, and everything is going so fast. Look I have a girlfriend and I really love her okay I know that might not mean a lot to you but it means a lot to me. I apologized to her and left, I was such a wreck I didn't want to leave all I wanted to go back in there with her and kiss her again, she tasted to good and her scent was so… I had to go. I ran up to Alison, "Finally, hey did you tell her how *good* she looked in her new clothes." She just smiled and nodded her head, "Hey I am so sorry I have to go I can't explain right now but I will. And about our date I don't think that tonight is going to be good." "Trust me it's not you, something has come up last minute and it is really important." "I will call you tomorrow okay I promise I'll take you anywhere you want to go okay, I am sorry I have to leave bye. And before she said her next word I left, I didn't want to turn around and see her face it would make feet at unease. I was crossing the street and I could hear the store door open, I quickly turned around maybe it was Alison, but it was the brunette girl Kristen and all of her friends. She seemed prettier, what was I thinking. She saw me and she didn't give me any attention, I guess she didn't want to cause a scene or something. But she just looked at me and I looked back at her too, then I turned around and started walking. I just crossed a street and took a random corner just to get away from everybody. I stopped and saw a bench just a couple of feet from me, I walked over to it and sat down. What was the matter with me, I didn't know what was going on now with all the girls that I had ever met or kissed in my life, it's like I want them all but I know I can only be with one. Sometimes life isn't fair, my dad said to me when I was little, and I guess he was right. But who'd ever guess it would lead up to this, from Bethany to Beverly to Alison now Kirsten, what the hell was going through my mind. I am in love with Alison, and now Kristen, I didn't know her that well, but I wanted to get to know her everything was so confusing. I felt bad that I kind of bombed on Alison and our date; I was really looking forward to that. I needed to talk to somebody, I needed to talk to somebody, and then I realized that maybe Dr. Ross is in today. I grabbed my cell phone and called her office, after a few rings her secretary picked up. "Hello, I know this is on short notice, I was wondering if Dr. Ross is in or if she is available?" "She is in and she is available, would like to make an appointment today?" "No thank you can you just tell her that Mitch is going to come and see her it's an emergency, she knows who I am." "Okay, she said, I will let her know that you are coming". Thank you, as I hung up. I looked at my watch and it was about 5:00 P.M. I had enough time to go see her. I grabbed my keys and started looking for my car.

After several minute I finally found it, I got in and started the car, I didn't wait for any reasons I just drove off.

Chapter 18
Love Triangle

I didn't know how long I drove for, maybe for a couple of minutes but it felt like a couple of hours. I even got fucking lost because I wasn't paying attention to where the fuck I was going. When I finally got on the right street there was a lot of traffic, I guess a lot of people were coming home from work. There was a lot of cars and it stretched for fucking miles, great I thought to myself by the time I get there she might be gone and then what I am going to do, talk to my mom about my relationship problems. Oh shit, my mom I completely forgot, luckily for me there were no cars behind me and I made an illegal turn and drove around the other way. Thank God I didn't see a cop, I have been driving for a while and so far so good I didn't get a ticket yet but I didn't want to jinx myself. The reason that I am freaking out is because I haven't spent quality time with my mom in a long time. Quality time, I said it, no matter how many times I may hate my mom or say shit to her or behind her back, I still love her she's my mom. And the real reason is I think or I believe it is my mom and Jeremy's anniversary coming up. Actually it is supposed to be my parent's anniversary, let me reiterate that one more time, parents. As in my mom and my dad but my dad is passed and now my mom and Jeremy have been together for a long time so they are celebrating what would be in this case my mom and dad's anniversary, get it. I hated it more than anything in the whole fucking world, but I wanted to be a good son to my mom and sort of be a good friend to Jeremy also. I contented to drive down the road, I didn't want to call Dr. Ross and tell her that I have to cancel whatever appointment we had. But I guess totally standing up her up would be a little better, which would teach those fucking doctors for what they said to me last time, assholes. I finally got home and with plenty of gas left, well half a tank but it's better than nothing, I will just fill up next time I get a chance. I pulled into the driveway and Jeremy was sitting on the porch with a beer in one hand and a magazine in the other. And not to my surprise he had a six pack of beer next to his left by his feet, well five, the one is his hand. I didn't want to stay in the car because he would just stare at me the whole time; I stopped the car and slowly got out. I shut the car door and walked toward the porch, saying hi to Jeremy as I walked to the door. He was sipping his beer and just waved at me as I walked in and the screen door shut behind me. I took off my shoes and put them near the coat rack; I took off my jacket and placed it on the side of the couch. I hated hanging up my coat because if I ever need to grab it again it would be easier. I went into the kitchen and grabbed a bottle of water and opened it and started drinking. I almost drank the whole bottle without stopping I was so thirsty. I yelled for my mom, no answer, I waited and yelled again, no answer again. Maybe she was in the shower but I walked to her room and I didn't hear the shower at all. I was a little confused, but not worried because my mom is an adult and she can take care of herself. I went outside to Jeremy, who was taking out a cigarette from his pocket. "Hey have you seen my mom, man I didn't see her in the house?" Jeremy pulled out his lighter, placed the cigarette between his lips and lit it. He took a deep inhale and breathed out all the toxic fumes, "Yeah, she went out kiddo, with a friend she met at bowling alley." "Oh, wow she met someone that's cool I guess, I always told myself that my mom needed more friends." "Hey kiddo, your mom won't home for a while so it's just the two of us, why don't you say we go have a guys night out it will be fun." Now this situation was completely new to me, I don't recall ever Jeremy ever asking to hang out with me, I am just a kid, but deep down this will give me a chance to actually bond with Jeremy and see what kind of person he really is. "Sure sounds like fun man let me know when you want to go out so I can get ready and eat and shit beforehand." "Sure thing, sport, I will let you know like in an hour, first let me finish all these damn beers." Jeremy just laughed as he picked up another drink and put it down and took another breath of his cigarette. I went into my room and then I noticed something, did he just call me sport. That was different he didn't call me fucking kiddo this time, because he always does. As much I hated being called that, to tell you the truth sport sounds fucking worse, now I hope he doesn't call me that from now on. I turned on the radio, I always leave my radio pre set on my favorite station, it's like a mix of rock and roll with oldies music it's not bad but I heard better. So I turned up the volume loud so I can drown away any of the other thoughts that was going through my head. I just plopped myself on my bed and took a deep breath. Great I said now I am fucking stuck in this stupid love triangle with Alison, Kristen and I. There were so many different thoughts going through my head, it was overwhelming I couldn't even take it anymore. I just closed my eyes and tried to go to sleep, there is something about a good nap that always makes me feel a little better when I wake up. I closed my eyes and took a deep breath, and then another and followed by one more and then I went asleep.

When I woke up Jeremy was in my room going through my hat collection. I woke up pretty refreshed, see it always works. "Hey need something, I said, without being rude because Jeremy was obviously in room going through my shit. "No just looking for the perfect hat the one that I have is to old and getting worn out." "How long was I sleeping for, I said, not looking at my watch for the time." Jeremy laughed, man you have been sleeping for about two and half hours." "What the fuck I said, pretty surprised, you're not serious I thought you were going to tell me to get ready or something." "I was, then I saw you sleeping and I didn't want to bother you." "Thanks man, really mean thanks great, I said what time is it now." Jeremy laughed again it is about 7:30 P.M. if you still want to go out we can it's your decision." "Of course, I still want to go you just tell me next time if you want to anywhere and if I am sleeping please wake me up." Sure thing he said as he walked out of my room. Well since I am awake now thanks to Jeremy might as well go take a shower. I got up and quickly got undressed and grabbed my towel and wrapped it around myself. Jeremy was in the kitchen when I opened my door and walked outside. "I am taking a quick shower I just need to calm my nerves." He smiled and said okay kiddo, as he had another beer in his hand. Kiddo, fuck now is he going to call me both, great another nickname. But I didn't let that bother me, well how could it since I had so much other shit going on already. I walked into the bathroom and shut the door; I turned on the light and walked over to the shower. I twisted the faucet until the water got hot enough. I unwrapped myself of my towel and I was standing there naked for a second. It was cold in the bathroom; I couldn't wait to jump into the shower. Before I got in I always make sure that everything of mine is in its rightful position, because Jeremy sometimes uses my stuff and it pisses me off, he has his own shit to use. Everything was there just how I left it, the water was warm enough and I flipped up the metal switch so the shower can start. I slowly got in and let the warm water caress my tense body; I took a deep breath and closed the curtains. I did my usual routine in the shower, but I hurried this time I didn't want to spend all day in the shower and keep Jeremy waiting. All in all I think I spent about ten minutes, much shorter than my usual time of 15-20 minutes, I like to take long showers for some reason. I got out dripping wet and like I do sometimes the towel was sitting on the toilet seat so I had to run and run back to the mat and dry myself off. Luckily I didn't get that much water on the floor just a couple of drops. I quickly dried myself off and wrapped myself with the towel and opened the bathroom door. I walked out but I kept the door opened the door this time so all the steam can leave, and it won't be hot when someone walks in. I walked to my room and lowered the volume to the radio, because I forgot to turn it off before I got in the shower. I lowered it just enough where I couldn't hear it, that was the point I guess. I put on some deodorant and then sprayed somebody spray all over myself. I grabbed one of my favorite shirts and put it on. My hair was still wet, I always let it air dry sometimes I use the towel but not today. I grabbed a pair of boxers and put them on, I told my mom that I wanted the ones without the tag in the back, and she finally came through. I put on my jeans, grabbed my wallet and slipped it into my back pocket. I grabbed my watch and put on my left wrist, my mom got me one of those old stretch watches that the band of course stretches, and I can't wait until I have the time to get a decent fucking watch. I was almost done, last but not least is a necklace my dad got me. It wasn't much it was one of those surfing shell necklaces you can get at the boardwalk, but it is really important to me because it is the last the thing he got me before he passed away, I wore it all the time ever since that day. I left the room feeling clean and tense free and smelling even better. I walked to Jeremy to see what he was doing, I knocked on the door. "Come in, I am almost done getting ready." When I walked in and when I saw Jeremy I almost didn't even recognize him, I couldn't believe it he actually shaved. I thought he was never going to shave and be one of those Middle Eastern people who let their beards grow out ridiculously long and shit. Because to tell you the truth even though I hated spending time with him even if we were not in public, if he went out looking like that I would die of embarrassment. "Are you ready, I am done so what do you say we go out and have a fucking rocking time." I smiled, maybe Jeremy is not that bad after all, and I mean he tries hard to make me like him. "Where we going anyway, you haven't told me all day where we were going, come on tell me." "Okay well since you are 18 and you have a valid driver's license, I am taking you to your very first strip club. I noticed that you were having girl troubles, just the look in your eyes and your posture and other stuff too." Okay now it is official I fucking think that Jeremy is a great guy I guess we had to find something that we had in common. And I think that it mine are a little more complex then Jeremy's but who cares he is taking me to a fucking strip club. Finally I go into a place and not think about Beverley or Alison or Kristen. Jeremy grabbed his keys and his wallet; he also grabbed a pair of shades. I don't know why it was like 8:00 at night; I guess he wanted to look really cool. We headed out and he walked to his truck, which I have to say is looking really spiffy. Probably the new paint job that he got looks really nice. He got in the driver's seat and I walked around to the passenger side. I tried opening the door and I realized that the door was jammed in and you had to try extra hard to open the door. I finally got it open and Jeremy was laughing, it was pretty funny though if you think about it. I hopped into the seat and closed the door, mistakenly slammed it. Jeremy started the truck and we drove off, I asked him where the strip club was, but he cut me off mid sentence and said, "Hold on first, I am going to go to a local corner store and get some beer. Do you want anything, I am buying." "Beer, I am under the age, besides beer is disgusting." "Okay suite yourself I am going to stop in and get some let me know if you want anything." We drove for a while and we finally arrived, the place was really small but it was packed. He pulled in and parked near a broken down Acura, the car was so beat up two of the four hubcaps were missing and it had two different paint jobs. Whoever owned this car made a wise fucking investment buying this piece of shit. Jeremy got out and I didn't want to stay in the car so I got out too. "So you are getting something after all, I knew that you wanted something." I smiled and shut the door, it was cold and I forgot my damn coat all I had on was a long sleeve shirt, with a short sleeve on top of that. And it was cold as hell, okay I know that's an oxymoron but you know what the fuck I mean. We both walked into the corner store, and the first thing that I noticed is that there was a smoking hot girl working behind the counter. Fucking great I said to myself, here I am trying to not to think about any of the girls, and *she* shows up. But this girl was different, even though she was blonde and probably dumb as hell but she was hot. Jeremy walked over to the section where they keep all the beer and shit and started smiling. I think I was the only one who knew that fucking Jeremy was driving drunk. Okay not like drunk but intoxicated enough where if he got pulled over he will get busted. I guess he has done this before because he is showing no signs of being intoxicated. He is talking regular, his stance is normal, and other stuff I can't remember right now. I started looking around for some food and drinks but their selection wasn't great just their actual store size, pretty ironic wouldn't you say so. I found some soda and some chips so I grabbed a can and two bags and walked up to the main counter. There were two people working the girl and some fat guy, and I was hoping I get the overweight dude rather than the girl. I really don't want to deal with another girl it's been overwhelming as it is. As soon I walked up there was another person in front of me and he was being helped by the fucking dude. Great you know what happens next, I have to get the fucking girl. I walked up there and I didn't want to be rude so I said hello. She said hello back and started ringing up my items. "Okay, it comes to $5, would you like a bag with that sir?" "No thank you, I will just carry it." She gave me my stuff and smiled; I thanked her and walked back toward Jeremy. Another person walked up to the counter, and was being helped by the girl. So it wasn't as bad as I expected that to go, glad I got the girl after all. Jeremy was about done with all of shit, I can't believe it he had two cases of Bud Light in his hand. "I am done man I think this should be enough let's go we have to hurry, I don't want to be late." I just smiled and nodded my head as he walked to the main counter. As soon he walked up Jeremy ended up getting the damn dude, but knowing Jeremy he didn't give a shit. As long as he gets what he wants, especially beer or cigarettes it doesn't matter if a girl is bald and fat selling him the shit. I guess that's what Jeremy means when he always says he needs to get his quick fix. He bought for his stuff and we left, as soon as we walked outside it started to rain. It wasn't poring or anything but just drizzling, and I always thought that those were the worst, because it will rain a little bit and then just start fucking pouring without any warning. We hurried and got into the truck, and Jeremy like a fucking mad man reversed the car all fast and shit I nearly spilled my damn soda all over my fucking shirt. I guess he was in a real fucking hurry to get to this strip club; I couldn't wait to see the lineup. Oh I was being sarcastic by the way, it was like a random fucking day in the middle of the week, and I really didn't know what day it was anyway. But I can tell you it's not like it was the weekend, where you are expecting to see some really hot fucking girls or something. But no we are probably going to get the bottom of the mother fucking shit barrel. Girls with all types of fucking diseases and shit, great I am go in clean and come out with a S.T.D. and without even having sex. Sorry for all the fucking cursing I have a real bad headache and I am still kicking myself with this whole love triangle bullshit. I can't believe that I went in that dressing room with Kirsten. Even though she was so fucking hot and she tasted so good, but what the hell was I thinking. I am in love with a beautiful, smart and talented girl Alison. How I am going to explain what happened to Alison when I go into work tomorrow. I hope she is not mad about fucking ditching her and leaving her there. I hope she didn't get all upset and tell her dad, I really need that job and next to Beverley, Alison is the best thing that happened to me in a long time. I picked up my cell phone and called her, by this time the store is closed and she is probably home or out. I was afraid of calling her house because I didn't want her dad to pick up and get upset that I left his daughter cold and dry. So I decided to call her on her cell phone, I found her name and put her as one of my first speed dial options. I called her; it was ringing I was so nervous, it kept ringing and ringing. I hope that she isn't ignoring me on purpose, like she can see me calling and still not picking it up. But then it went to voice mail, so instead of hanging up I left a message, "Hey Alison, it's me Mitch, I am so sorry for leaving you at work by yourself you know that I never wanted to do that. It's just something really important came up and I had to take care of it. If you get this message please, please call me back so I can explain. Look I really love you oaky Alison, and I will never do anything to hurt you. What I did today was on short notice and it may seem like I was being rude but I can explain. Well I have to go me and Jeremy are about to go hangout at a bar. So I will call you later if you don't call me first, okay baby love you goodbye." The only bad thing about that whole message is two things; the radio wasn't on so there was no background noise to kill the talking. And the second thing fucking Jeremy heard the whole thing. But he didn't say anything about it, for the first time Jeremy was actually minding his own business. You know I don't know what happened to Jeremy, the old Jeremy would have never been this nice to me if he wanted or needed something. And the old Jeremy would always but into my fucking conversations too, that got really annoying fast. I didn't know what was going on with Jeremy, but hey I fucking loved it.

Finally we arrived to the strip club, and I have to tell you the place was actually busy. I mean there are a lot of cars and trucks outside. But a lot of cars really doesn't mean shit, I wanted to see how the girls looked like inside. We drove around for about a couple of seconds, and then we finally found a spot. We got out and I stretched my arms and closed the door, Jeremy was the next one to close the door. "Are you ready for this kiddo; this is my favorite strip clubs in this fucking town." "Sure I am ready, are you ready is the real question, being a smartass one of my very good qualities." He just laughed and started walking toward the club, I followed trying to cover my head with my arms as you guess it, it was still raining and now it was coming down a little harder. We rushed into the club and the bouncer even knew Jeremy, he told him that I was 18. I showed him my driver's license and he let me in. "I can't believe you know the fucking bouncer." "Yeah, I and he are old construction buddies from back in the day." We got in and I was fucking shocked, the girls were really fucking beautiful I couldn't believe it. Every girl was really hot looking, all I wanted to go up to all of them and introduce myself, and I wasn't even worried that I might even get something. I started walking around and as I walked toward this one girl who looked Spanish or maybe a mix, I heard Jeremy say have fun kiddo. I walked up to the table where the Spanish chick was dancing and sat down. I pulled out a five dollar bill, something small. Jeremy walked over to my table and handed me some money, just in case I run out or something. I was going to thank him but he had already walked away and started to talk to this black chick with big ass breasts. I got my five ready and stood up she leaned in and I placed it between her bra and breast. She smiled and said, "Hey are you new, I haven't seen you here before, and well I never see that many kids here." "I am new, I am with my friend over there to your right, and I am 18 so don't worry." The music that they had playing in the background was really fucking pitiful, but who the fuck cares when they had hot ass girls like this. She started dancing and then she came to me again. I grabbed another five dollars and placed between her lips ever so gently. She said if I wanted a lap dance and it was usually $20, but she will give it to me for $10. I said yes as I pulled out a 10, as she started making her way down from the ramp. She came from around the corner, and the only thing that was going through my mind at that time was I am hoping I get to fuck the shit out of this girl. She grabbed my hand and took me to a back room, as we were passing by I saw Jeremy putting money in some girls ass crack. I whistled and gave him thumbs up as he smiled and gave one back. She continued to lead me to a room, we finally got there and we walked in. She shut the lights behind and closed the door; there was a small lamp that was lit up on the far corner. She pushed me into the chair and turned on some music. She started dancing, and she grabbed my hand and placed it on her waist. I can tell already that this wasn't like an ordinary strip club; the strippers actually let you touch them. She started dancing more and turned toward me. She put one leg on my leg and the other on the other leg, she leaned in closer and grabbed my other hand and undo her bra. And right in front of my face where a pair of the most delicious big breasts I have ever seen. She leaned in a little closer and stated rubbing them in my face. Now I don't know about anyone else but usually when a girl does this to you or anything sexual, your dick usually gets hard, and ladies and gentlemen, my dick is hard. She stood up again and started pulling her g-string down her smooth, thick hips all the way to the floor. She again put her legs on my legs and grabbed my hands and placed them on her breasts. She made me squeeze them, "How they feel baby, she said as the music was playing and she started sensually moaning. "They feel fucking great baby, so soft and so smooth." She laughed and once again leaned in closer and she put her big, wet, juicy lips on my lips and fucking kissed me. Her hand slowly started making her way down my shirt to my dick, and she started unbuckling my belt buckle. She stopped kissing me, and she started to unzip my pants. I got up quickly threw them off, and then she got on her knees and she grabbed my dick. She started sucking the fuck out of it, and it felt so fucking good. She was going nice and slow and then she sped up a little. Fucking spit was coming from her mouth, she stopped sucking for a minute and spit on the tip. She started stroking my dick and then she started sucking it again. Now, at this time I thought she was only going to give me a lap dance but this was so much fucking better. She started sucking my dick so good, it felt so fucking good. I used my right hand and caressed the back of her head and started moving her head back and forth. I started slow and then I sped up a little bit. The whole time she was sucking my dick I can hear moaning sounds coming from her mouth, but you couldn't hear it to well because her mouth was pretty full. At the same time she was playing with herself, she was sucking my dick and playing with her fucking pussy, what can be better than this. Then something stated happening, I started to feel all numb inside and I started to shake all over the place. I think that I was going to cum, I told her that I am about to cum, I didn't want to say nothing and be rude and cum in her mouth. She stopped sucking and started stroking again, "Yeah, give me that mother fucking cum all over my fucking big ass breasts. She let go of my dick, and I didn't care that there was spit all over it, I started to stroke it and less than a second, I can feel it. "Yeah, baby you ready I am going to cum all over those big ass juicy breasts of yours." And within one second, I came and it shot all over her breasts, and I felt so good after it all came out. She started laughing, "Yeah, baby that is what I am talking about, you're fucking cum baby." I started to clean myself up with a fucking napkin and she got one finger and swooped up a piece of cum and licked her finger, "Ah yeah baby, I like the taste of fucking cum in my fucking mouth." I grabbed her head and put her lips back on my dick, "Lick the rest of that cum baby I want you to swallow all of this shit." And she did, she started licking the rest of it of my dick and then she showed me as she swallowed the rest of it. She stood up and started to clean herself up, she just smiled and laughed as she was wiping the cum of her chest and mouth. Now I know it was only ten but after what she did I decided to pay her fucking twenty dollars. She got finished getting ready as did I, and I pulled out twenty dollars from my wallet and handed it to her. "I didn't get your name, I said, after all that it was funny because I wanted to know her name." "My name is Spanish Ice, come back again okay sweetheart so I can do this again, it was fun." "Sure thing, I said, as I opened the door and walked outside. I walked over to where Jeremy was last, and I didn't see him. And then I saw him by the main door talking to the bouncer dude. I walked over there, "Hey your done that fast, I said loud as hell, I think everyone fucking heard." "No, he said I had some business to take care of, you know talk to some people." "Hey you ready to leave it's getting late and your mom should be home soon." I said bye to the bouncer as we walked to his truck, he got his keys and opened the truck. We both got in and he started the truck, as he started to drive off. "Hey whatever happened with you and that Spanish chick?" "Dude, you wouldn't believe it, she brought me to the back room and I thought she was going to give me regular lap dance and shit. But then all of a sudden she started to undress, and then well short story she started sucking my fucking dick, and then I came all over her breasts and face. And then she licked the shit and swallowed the rest of it. "Jeremy's reaction was pretty much expected, "WHAT THE FUCK DUDE, he said, she did that shit wow I don't believe it." "Aren't you glad I brought you out, you needed to get out and enjoy yourself? "Hell yeah I am glad, thanks man I really appreciative this, but if you can do me a favor and don't tell my mom about what happened." "Sure thing buddy, don't worry I won' tell your mom anything." I smiled as we pulled into the driveway, and turned off the car. We both got and shut the doors at the same time. I grabbed my house keys and opened the door, as Jeremy and I walked in. My mom was lying on the couch; she was surprised to see the both of us coming home late at the same time. Jeremy walked into the room and closed the door, I heard the bathroom door open and then he closed it. "Hey baby, where have you guys been, it's late?" "Hey mom, I said, sorry since you were gone, Jeremy and I went out bowling and then went to a pool hall." "Okay that sounds great, did you guys have fun?" "Oh yeah, we did, but I especially had a great time." "Goodnight mom, I am not going to take a shower I will take one tomorrow, I have to work anyway." "Goodnight honey, I will see you tomorrow." I walked to my room and threw off my shoes and took my jeans, and shirt and boxers and threw them into the hamper. I grabbed a new pair of boxers and shirt, just something to sleep in. I turned off the light, and threw myself on the bed; I just smiled and closed my eyes.

Chapter 19
Kristen

I finally woke up, and for some reason my dick was sore, but I didn't care last night was so fucking amazing. That reminds me, I have to thank Jeremy for an awesome time again, and if it wasn't for him none of this would've happened. I just got up I really didn't care that for some reason I was still fucking dressed in my jeans and shit. I tell you sleeping in jeans like I have my life are really not that bad, I don't know why people complain all the Goddamn time. But I guess they are right when they say it really depends of what kind of jeans you can buy. The jeans I had growing up are so old and worn to shreds that sometimes I would cut them up and use them for shorts and shit. But now since I am a little older I can finally get the jeans that I want, and when I go to the mall or wherever I get the most comfortable but reasonably priced jeans I can get. I am not about to spend over a $100 on a pair of fucking jeans no matter how comfortable they are. I took off my shirt and smelled it, it smelled like fucking cigarette smoke; I rolled it up to a ball and threw it in my hamper. I opened my dresser drawer and put on some deodorant, as I was doing that I walked to my window and peaked through the blinds, Jeremy's truck was gone. Maybe he went out somewhere; I thought to myself, I finished putting on my deodorant. I took off my old socks and put fresh clean ones on. I changed boxers too, but this time I decided to wear briefs, I wanted to feel how they were different than boxers. I put them on and slipped them all the way up. A second later I started walking around my room to test them out and let me tell you they were comfortable then boxers. I grabbed a piece of paper and a pencil and wrote boxer briefs on it. I finished getting ready and left my room, I wasn't that hungry to get something to eat so I decided to go into my mom's room. She wasn't home either, okay now I was wondering where the fuck my mom and Jeremy were. It was early and I didn't fully wake up, I was still a little tired. I walked to the kitchen sink and turned the faucet on, I let the water run on cold for about a minute. I just stood there and looked at the wallpaper in disarray. My mom and Jeremy were both gone, and I still had some time before I went to work. There was something bothering me but I couldn't put my finger on it. I didn't know what it was, I mean I am 18, I have a car, I have a driver's license, I have a banging job and hot ass girlfriend. I love spending time with my mom and I am starting to like Jeremy, I think that Jeremy and I are finally bonding. And that is something that honestly both of us can say would never have happened. But there was something else, in a spur of the moment thing I walked back inside my room and grabbed a piece of paper from my wallet. It had Bethany's number, my very first girlfriend before I moved. I was hesitant of calling her I started asking myself all these questions, how about she doesn't remember me, or how about she didn't want to talk to me anymore, or worse she met someone else. I shook my head and put both my hands under the running water and cupped some water and splashed my face. The water was so cold that it woke me up for a second, and honestly that felt good. I turned off the faucet and walked over to the towel. I grabbed it and quickly dried myself off before I started dripping all over the place. I put the towel back on the rack and walked back to the living room. I sat down on the couch still holding the piece of paper in my hand, now I was more hesitant of calling her. Then I just did it, I grabbed my phone and called the number I was so nervous, how about she picks up what do I say. It rang for several seconds and then it just went to voice mail, "Hi this is Beth, I am not here right now... I hung up the phone. I was never big on leaving messages, but this time I guess more anxious than anything, so I didn't want to leave one. I just continued to lie on the couch really not moving at all, I was too bored to even watch TV, so the remote just sat there on the table. It was still early so I decided to kill time I was going to take a nice long shower, that way I will be at least relaxed. I got up from the couch and started walking back to my room, I got completely undressed and grabbed my towel and walked to the bathroom. I do what I always do when I am in there and by this time I guess I really don't have to explain. I stared into the mirror and it was so fucking dirty I can barely see my own reflection. I grabbed a washcloth and wet it a little bit, I cleaned the mirror and it was clean. I opened the door and kind of threw it with all the other cleaning supplies in the back. I lifted the toilet seat and took a piss. After I was done I flushed the toilet and washed my hands. The water was warm enough so I unwrapped myself from my towel and slowly walked in. I did what I always do when I am in the shower so there is no reason really explaining the shit.

When I got out I got my towel and dried myself off, I walked to the door and opened it, closed the light and shut the door this time. Since no one was home there was no point to keep the door open. I walked to my room and quickly got dressed, I don't know why I was doing everything so fast but there was no hurry to do anything. I finished getting ready and dried off my hair, walked outside my room and walked to the kitchen. I looked at the time and it was early in the afternoon around 12 so I still had time before work. In pure boredom I grabbed my car keys and I walked outside the front door. I closed it behind me and locked it, I walked to my car and pressed the unlock button. I opened the door and sat in, I didn't close the door right away because it was really nice outside and I wanted to get some fresh air. I looked at the car time and only ten minutes had passed, I closed the door and started the car up. Now I was getting hungry so I quickly drove out my front driveway and looked the nearest fast food joint before I fucking starve to death. I only drove for about another ten minutes and I finally found a place, it was a small burger shack, nothing great but it's fucking burgers. I drove for about another minute and turned on my right turn signal, and then turned into the parking lot. Thank God there wasn't that many people because I always hated finding parking anywhere. I parked near a blue Honda, the car itself was really nice as if it was brand new or something. I turned off my car and got out; I closed the door and walked over to the blue Honda. I couldn't believe how nice the car was, it was better than my piece of shit. When I was looking at the back I noticed that the license plate was from New York. Wow who in the right mind would leave New York just to come to fucking Ohio? If you compare the both I am pretty sure that New York wins in the things to do category, but whatever I didn't care it wasn't me so. I walked in the burger shack and made my way to the main counter. There was a small line so I didn't mind waiting; I was more hungry then worried about being inpatient right now. I was waiting when I heard a group of girls laughing and then one of them started talking pretty loudly. I wanted to kind of check it out and see for myself what the hell was going on, but I didn't want to lose my spot. Then I heard someone that sounded just like Kristen, and now I left the line and walked over to the group of girls. I was getting closer when all I heard was Mitch, hey come over here. It was Kristen and she was with a group of friends, and they were all girls. I walked over to them, "Hey Mitch, how are you man, how have you been?" "Good, I have been good, wow it is nice to see you again Kristen, you look good." I wanted to be polite, because I told her that I am in love with Alison. "When did you get here, she said, I didn't see you pull up." "I just pulled in I parked next to a nice ass blue Honda." "Wow small world huh, running into each other in the same burger place, and that's my blue Honda you parked next Mr. so you had better not scratched it." I can tell in her tone of voice that she was joking around but she was still serious. "Wow that's your car, don't worry I didn't scratch it, its fine, hey you got a really nice car." "Oh I am so sorry, where are my manners, let me introduce you to some of my friends." This is Jessica, Michelle, Robin and Victoria. "Hi ladies, I said nice to meet you all, my name is Mitchell, but everyone calls me Mitch." They all said hi, I told Kristen if I could see her for one second. She said sure, we walked over to an empty table, and both sat down. "Hey about last time we met, I think you have some explaining to do, I mean that was crazy what you did wouldn't you say so." I don't think it was crazy, she said, I was following my instincts, I like you. And if you want to talk about crazy you started kissing me back remember, so I think you owe me an explanation." "The only reason I kissed you is because you kissed me first, if I didn't kiss you back and walked away what the hell would you think and I would've felt like a pussy for not kissing a girl." "I see, she said, well let me say bye to all my friends real quick, stay right here don't go anywhere." I smiled as she got up and walked over to all her friends, she said she had to go and take care of something really important. I can hear them all wining and shit, saying please don't go, and please stay. She hugged all of them and walked back over to me. "Hey what are you doing for the rest of the day?" "Nothing I said, why I asked her." "Nothing really what time do you have to be at work?" "I believe today around 4 but I am not a 100% sure." "Let's hang out; I don't think last time we never got a chance to really sit down and talk." "Tell me about it, I just smiled, okay sounds cool I was just about to go back home and pick up a few things. If you want, you can follow me and come see my house or I can meet you somewhere." "It's cool I'll just follow you home, so I can see your place is that cool with you." "Sure you don't even have to ask, oaky ready to leave." We left and walked to the parking lot, she got in her blue Honda and I got in my crappy ass car and I reversed slowly, making sure I don't hit her car. I started driving and she was following me right behind.

We drove for several more miles until I have finally came home, and still Jeremy's truck still wasn't in the front driveway. I didn't know where the fuck he was, and to make matters worse I didn't have his number in my phone. So if anything it's not like I can just call him and make sure that everything is alright or something. I pulled in slowly and Kristen followed and parked right behind me. She got out first and I got out second, I walked back to her car as she was getting out. She closed her door and I walked over to door and closed mine. I got my keys and walked to the front door and opened the door. I walked in and Kristen walked in right behind. I closed the door, and walked into my mom's room, she wasn't home either. Then I thought to myself that I get the whole fucking house to myself, it can't any sweeter than this. Kristen walked further into the living room and she sat down on the couch. She took off her coat and placed it aside, she I walked into the kitchen, as I heard her get up and she walked into the kitchen too. She was wearing this tight black T-shirt with white and red stripes going down the front, with air brush effects on the back. She had a pair of tight blue jeans; she looked so fucking hot in what she was wearing, I can barley control myself. I offered a drink and she told me she wasn't thirsty, as she was looking through my drawers and shit. I took out a soda and closed the door. "On the other hand, I am a little thirsty, do you mind." "No not at all, I said to her, smiling and taking out two glasses from the cabinet." I opened the soda and poured two glasses; the fizz rose all the way to the top of the glass and slowly made itself way back down. I threw the soda bottle in the recycle bin and closed the lid. I grabbed my cup and I started sipping first, and I gave Kristen her cup second. "Thanks, she said, you know you have a really cool house, it's so much better than mine." "Thanks, well it's nothing really; I mean it's just a house pretty regular." She just smiled and started walking around, so I decided to give her a tour. I showed her the living room of course, and then the dining room. I showed her my mom and Jeremy's room next followed by the kitchen, which we were just in. I showed her the bathroom down the hall and my room. She was quite surprised when she saw my room, because I guess she never seen a room so clean before. The expression on her face was pretty much readable, it was quite funny. "Wow your room is so clean; do you like clean everyday or something?" I just laughed, "No, but I like to keep a clean room, it makes easier to find shit when I need it." "And I take the cleanliness after my dad; he was sort of a neat freak." "Where's your dad, is he working or something, I didn't see any cars in the driveway?" I paused for a second, because it is different when I am not trying to think about my dad. Kristen is the only girl to ask me about my dad; it just took a second to sink in. "My dad, passed away when I was a little kid, I live with my mom and her boyfriend Jeremy." She didn't say anything for a second, "Sorry I didn't know, I understand how you feel, my dad passed away when *I* was little too so it's hard I know." "It's okay, can we change the subject I am not in the mood to talk about it, okay." She just shook her head yes as she continued to walk around my room and looked around more. She looked inside my closet and then she sat on my bed. She fell back and just laid there for a second. "Let's do something fun she said, I am getting kind of bored." I looked at her, lying in my bed, "Okay what do you want to do, I don't have any ideas." She thought it about for a second, "Let's go out and get something to eat if you want." "What, you ate at the burger place remember your still hungry?" "I never ate actually, not a fast food place but like a restaurant or something, somewhere nice so we can eat and talk." "Okay sounds like fun, just give me a second to change, and we can leave." And when I said that I knew that wasn't leaving so I had no other choice to undress in front of her. Something about undressing in front of your mom when you're a little kid is cute, but a hot girl is really weird. I took off my shirt and then my jeans; I had a pair of boxer briefs on because they were so comfortable. "Have you been working out, you look nice?" I just smiled and threw on a dress shirt and a pair of nice jeans. I sprayed some cologne and buttoned up my shirt; I put some moose in my hair and styled it, I am ready, you ready to leave. "Wow, impressive I have never seen anyone get ready so fast and look so good without taking a shower." I smiled; I took a shower this afternoon, but thanks." I grabbed my credit card from the drawer and some extra cash just in case because you never know. Kristen got up and walked with me out from my room to the living room. She grabbed her coat and walked to the front door. I looked at the time and it was about 4:24 P.M. it was getting late in the afternoon. I walked to the front door and opened it, Kristen walked out first and then I did. I closed and locked the door. She was already making her way to her car. I didn't go to my car at first, I walked to Kristen, "Hey it's only 4:25, you sure you want to go out and eat now. Let's go see a movie first and then we can go to a restaurant sound like a plan." She said "Sure it's cool, but there is no point of having two cars, leave yours here and hop in mine." "Trust me I don't drive like a madman, that's only when I have road rage." I just laughed and walked to my car to make sure it was locked, and then I walked to Kristen's car and got in the passenger's side and closed the door. She started her car and reversed and then drove off. "I know where a good movie theater is around here, it's the one that I always go to, and it's pretty cheap. I am glad she knew where the theater was because I have no idea where the hell it is.

We drove for a couple of miles, hitting a few red lights along the way and finally we made it to the movie theater. I have to say it was pretty big, and it looked new too, I couldn't wait to see what kind of movies they were showing. Kristen found an empty spot and parked the car. We both got out, and she said, "See I told you that I drive normally and no road rage this time." I smiled and nodded my head and closed the door. We walked around to the main entrance of the theater and walked inside. When we walked inside, the place was big and kind of chilly. I am glad that I took the time and changed shirts to a full sleeve when I had the chance. Kristen and I walked up to the front and there was no line so we didn't have to wait. When we got to the front there were so many movies playing we didn't know what to see. We looked around for a minute she turned back to me "What do you want to see?" "I don't know I didn't want to see anything in particular, so it's cool whatever you pick." Okay as she turned back to the selection and chose. Okay can I have two tickets to The Neighbor; I heard that is supposed to be really good. The person working behind the counter gave Kristen two tickets as she started walking to find where it was. "What's The Neighbor supposed to be about, I have never heard of it?" "It's about this creepy teenager kid who just moved into this neighborhood, and he just found out he lives next to a girls house. And over several months he starts watching her and stalking her and shit. I don't know the rest but it's like a suspense movie or something." Interesting, I said as she found the place, we walked and the previews were playing, so I was glad that we didn't miss any of the movie. We walked in and started looking for a seat, for a movie that I have never heard of the theater was packed. I guess the preview for the movie itself was better than what Kirsten was telling me. We finally decided to sit in the middle of the theater and watch the movie. And then it was at that time I finally fucking forgot I was supposed to be at work. I told Kristen that I was going to be right back; I had to make a phone call real quick and it was very important. I walked out of the theater and walked outside to the front. I hurried up and called Alison, luckily there was no miss call from her, and otherwise I would've felt really upset. I called her, she picked up after several rings, "Alison, hi it's me Mitch, hey sorry I can't come to work today something came up on such short notice, I am so sorry for not calling you earlier but it just came up out of the blue, and I have to take care of it." She didn't say anything for a minute, "it's cool I had to take care of something with my dad anyway so the store was closed. I tried calling you but my battery was bad." "Oh okay well I hope everything is okay with you and your dad, but listen I have to go but I will call as soon I get done." "Sure that sounds nice, and hope everything is fine with you too." She hung up the phone and I walked back inside, I didn't want to miss the movie. Luckily for me it was on more preview showing, I quickly found my seat next to Kristen, and some fucking asshole was trying to sit hit on her from behind. "Hey, she's with me man, okay so back off." "Sorry bro, I didn't know I thought she was alone, my mistake I am going now." "Thanks Mitch, he wouldn't stop bothering me it was getting annoying." "It's cool, don't worry about it, I hate fucking punks like that anyway it annoys me too." "Who you call, she asked as I sat down next to her and she wrapped her arm around me." I had to call my mom, and figure out what the hell she was doing and what time she was coming home, nothing serious or anything." She just smiled and put her head on my shoulder as the movie started playing. I felt really bad, how in the hell did I end up getting myself into this kind of shit. This is the fucking second time that I blew off Alison just to hang out with Kristen, don't get me wrong she is incredibly hot, but Alison's my girlfriend. Was I cheating on her with Kristen? I mean we are just seeing a movie and getting something to eat as friends, we don't know each other. Honestly I don't know anything about her in the first place and we made out in Alison's store, and I ran out of there without explaining anything to Alison. And now, well the store was closed but instead of staying home and relaxing I am out with Kristen again. I don't know what it is I want to stop spending time with Kristen but for some reason I can't. I couldn't figure it out, it's like she has this power over guys and me. She never says a lot, but then again she doesn't have to, her looks say enough. I mean she is hotter than Alison, and more developed, but was she interesting like Alison is. I had no answers for all of these questions, I just put my head back and sat close to Kristen and watched the movie.

About two and half hours went by and the movie was finally over, that was such a long ass movie but it was really worth it. It was suspenseful every second I couldn't wait to see what happened next. The lights came on and everyone started getting up and walking out the front door. Kristen got up and stretched and yawned, "I am very tired for some reason I don't know why, I am going to go home and get some sleep." She grabbed my hand and we started walking out the door with everyone else. We walked through the crowd that apparently looked like they were coming in; we made our way to her car as she grabbed her keys. She kept yawning, she was really tired. "Let me drive, give me your address and I will drive you home, you look tired. Go to sleep in the front seat. Actually I am a little tired, yeah its cool you can drive just don't crash my baby." She said laughing as she handed me the keys, she walked over to the passenger side as I unlocked the car. She got in and closed the door, she buckled herself up and put both her feet on the seat and closed her eyes. I guess she didn't want to wait until she got home. I got in and closed my door; I put the key into the ignition and started the car. "I am sorry we didn't get a chance to get something to eat, I know you were hungry." "Its fine, I will just get something to eat when I go home, if I am dead tired before that." "Hey what's your address so I can drive you home safely?" She yawned once more and said 1333 Bruce Street, Hill Rock Boulevard. I started slowly leaving the movie theater and trying to find the street. I got on and started driving, I checked the time on Kristen's radio and it was almost 7:00. It was getting late I wonder if either my mom or Jeremy was home yet. I was going to call my mom again but I am bad when it comes to driving and talking on the phone I was always afraid of crashing or something. I remembered the address she gave me 1333 Bruce Street; I had no idea where the hell it was. "Kirsten, sorry to wake you, how do I get to your house exactly, I don't want to get lost." "It's easy, she said, just keep on driving straight and take the left when you see a fast food place called Taco King. Once you are on that, drive for couple of miles, and when you see a home gardening store on the right side, make that turn. And then finally drive for couple more miles and then you will see Hill Rock, I live in one of those complexes and just drive up to 1333 Bruce Street." "Okay I think I got it, thanks go back to sleep I will wake you up when we get there." I was driving and then I saw the Taco King, and I got into the left hand lane. I took that left and started driving again and I hit a red light. It was kind of hot so I rolled my window down just a little so some air can come in. I waited for the light to turn green but it was a long light. I peaked at Kristen and she was so cute sleeping in her seat I smiled and the light finally turned green. I started driving again and there was a slow ass truck in front of me. I swear it was going like fucking five M.P.H. and it was really pissing me off. The driver stayed in front of me for about ten minutes and then he finally switched lanes. Thank God, I was about to honk my fucking horn and shit and tell him to hurry up. I continued to drive until finally I saw the home gardening store on the right, luckily I was in the right lane already and didn't have to switch. I drove up and made that right, great, I said more driving, but for some reason I didn't mind at all. Another red light, and Kirsten was still sleeping, she was all curled up she looked so cute, I think she was snoring and I didn't even mind it. I drove down the street and about I would say another half an hour I saw Hill Rock Boulevard and drove up to the entrance. When I drove up to the front there was a guy in a booth, "Excuse me sir may I help you?" Wow, he was good other security guards don't even know who goes in and out. "I am here to drop off Kristen; she is tired so she fell asleep in the front seat." I moved back so he can see her, to make sure that I wasn't lying or anything. He saw and noticed her, "My apologizes sir, yes go ahead." He lifted up the gate and we drove in, it took me a second to find 1333 Bruce, because every house looked the same. I drove around in circles and then I finally found the place, and Kristen was so cute snoring louder now. I slowly pulled in; I saw another car in the driveway. That must have been her parent's car; I hope they don't see me driving it. I pulled in a little further and stopped the car. I tapped Kristen on the shoulder and told her that we made it, she was still sleeping, I waited another second and said her name Kristen, I tapped her on the shoulder again and then finally she woke up. She was a little dazed but she finally came through, "Did you have a hard time finding the place?" "No it was easy, I had no problem." "Like I said, she said as she rubbed her eye with her hand. Kristen's mom and dad came out the front door and started walking towards the car. Great, what the fuck, how I am going to explain this one, and Kristen fell back asleep on the seat. I slowly opened the door and kept it halfway opened; I walked to Kirsten's parents. "Hi, they said, may we help you." At least they nice, well so far, "Hi my name is Mitch and the reason that I am driving Kristen's car is we saw a movie together. And she was really tired so I offered to drive her home so she doesn't have to." Kristen woke up and saw me talking to her parents; she got out and closed the door. "Hi mom, hi dad what's going on, when did you come out?" "Just a minute ago, Mitch here was telling us he offered to drive you home after you two saw a movie." "Yeah mom, I was really tired and I couldn't drive back so he offered, he is so sweet." I just smiled and didn't say anything; honestly I didn't know what to say at this point. "Well aren't you the sweetest boy ever, for driving our baby home from the movies." "Mom, I am not a baby I am almost 18; I am growing up before your eyes." "I am so sorry Mitch, were our manners of course we are Kristen's parents my name is Jill and my husband is Jeffery Hills. "Would you like to come in, can I offer you anything to drink; I know you had a long drive?" Okay, yeah that sounds good thank you very much." I walked over to the driver's side and closed the door and locked it. Kristen and I and her parents all went inside, it was getting dark and it was going to rain soon. When Kristen and I got inside she showed me around her house. It was big and inviting, and it was clean, not like everything had to be in a certain spot clean, but clean fresh. She showed the entrance where we were standing, and I closed the door behind me and locked it for her. Her mom came back from the kitchen with a glass of lemonade and gave it to me. I thanked her as Jill and Jeffery walked up the stairs and walked to their room. "Your parents seem like very nice people." "I think your being polite, don't get me wrong they are loving people but they are parents and you know how parents can be, especially dads." "Oh I am sorry, I forgot, I didn't mean to say that." "It's okay I know it was an accident." She showed me the dining and living room, it was very nice. She showed me the kitchen and the two bathrooms. Oaky I have to say one thing about her two bathrooms, they were big and spacious. She took me upstairs and showed me the other bathroom and then finally the good part. She showed me her room, and she walked in first and then I walked in second, and her room was really nice looking. She had posters of old movie stars and rock and pop bands. I thought she would've had a really girly room but I thought wrong. She walked to her bed, "Can you close the door, and I hate when my parents come in and see what the hell I am doing." I closed the door and walked to her bed and sat down. "Shit, I just realized that I drove you here and remember I left my car in my driveway. Will your parents freak out if I ask them to spend the night, more importantly is cool with you." "Well, it's cool with me, but let me go and ask my parents if it is okay." She left and walked outside to her parent's room, as I waited penitently on her bed, I looked around her room again her room was so much better than mine. That reminds me I have to buy some posters or something for my wall because it was so boring looking. Kristen finally came back into the room and she told me that it was okay that I can spend the night; I am more excited than they are. "They told me that you had to sleep in the guest room but since I am their baby girl I convinced them that you can stay in my room. I don't have any sleeping bags, because my family haven't gone camping in a long time, so you would have to sleep in my bed." I didn't know what to say, I don't think that I have ever slept in the same room let alone in the same bed with a girl. "That's cool, I have no problem let me know when you need to change so I can just leave." She walked to the door and locked it and turned off the light and turned on the little lamp that she had on her dresser. She took off her socks and shoes and took off her coat. "What are you doing, tell me you're not going to change in front of me, if you want me to…" "I am going to change in front of you, remember you saw me without my shirt in the dressing room." She started taking off her pants and then her shirt, she threw the dirty clothes in the hamper, and then she just stood there in her langrage. "Like what you see, you want to see more?" I was baffled, was she going to do what I thought she was going to do in front of me. She walked closer and unclipped her bra, and threw it in the hamper she was just watching her standing there with her breasts out in the open. They were so natural so voluptuous, she walked back and took off her thong and threw it also in the hamper. She opened the door and grabbed another pair and slipped them on. She grabbed a T-shirt from the drawer too and put it on. She still had the light on and she walked towards me, and crawled into bed. I took off my shoes and socks and that's it. I didn't want her parents to walk in the morning and see me sleeping with their daughter in the same bed. "You coming to bed, I know you're pretty tired." I crawled into bed with her and pulled the sheets over the both of us. "Hey I am glad that you are spending the night with me, I hate sleeping alone." "I have no choice, saying sarcastically; my car is back at my house." "I know but I am still glad though my parents are loving people, but they are pretty controlling, and they never let me have anyone over, especially a boy, so I am glad." "I am glad too that I am here, it's nice spending time with you." She smiled and turned around and said she was going to sleep. Again I was in the same situation that I was in before, I am in love with Alison, and now it went from meeting Kristen in the store, and kissing and making out with her in the store, now I am fucking sleeping with her in her bed in her room in her house. I had to promise myself one thing that no matter what happened, I cannot tell Alison about this, I love her to much to tell her something as devastating as this. But I know if I don't tell her that the guilt of Kristen hanging over my head. I lifted up my hands and placed them on my face and took a deep sigh. Kristen woke up, "Are you alright, you still awake, I thought you were sleeping." "I am going to sleep now; I was just thinking about something, good night Kristen." "Oh okay, well good night Mitch, see you in the morning."

It was morning, I can hear the birds chirping outside and when I sat up Kirsten wasn't in the bed. I got up and walked outside from her room to the middle of the hallway. She came out from the bathroom, "You scared me, when did you wake up?" "Sorry, just now like a second ago, where are your parents?" "Luckily for us my parents both left early for work so they didn't come in and see us sleeping in the same bed." "I am glad too, for the both of us, I mean I would probably never be allowed over again, and your parents would've made you never call me or something." She walked back into the bathroom and she had the door open I walked to the side, and she was brushing her teeth. She finished and then walked outside; she started walking downstairs, so I just followed her downstairs. She walked into the kitchen and starting going through the fridge. She couldn't find anything so she closed the fridge door and walked to the cabinets and starting looking through them. "You must be really hungry, you're looking around everywhere for food." "I am hungry, and there is never any food in this house, sometimes it is so frustrating." I have an idea, I am going to take a shower and we are going to go out and get some breakfast. I know this place where you can get breakfast 24 hours a day and you can also get lunch and dinner too. "That sounds great, okay you take your shower and I will chill out and watch TV or something." "Okay sounds like a plan, so you better get going it's almost 11 and I know how long it takes girls to get ready." She noticed that I was joking by the tone of my voice, as she walked by and sarcastically gave me the middle finger. She walked upstairs and then she said, "Come on up I don't want you to be down there all by yourself, you are going to get bored, I know how you guys are when you are not doing something sports related." I laughed as I walked upstairs, and she was standing there in the middle of the hallway. I was trying to get by and she was blocking my way. "Cute, what you're doing, come on stop playing around." "If you want to get across you have to kiss me, then I will let you pass." I smiled as I leaned in and kissed her on the lips. She smiled and walked into the bathroom and turned on the lights, and then she turned on the faucet. What was I doing, now I am voluntarily kissing her and every time I do it I can only think about Alison. But there was something that I couldn't figure out, I thought that it would never get this out of control, but I can't help it, her lips are so juicy. I love the way that she smells, I love the way that she tastes, but inside I know it was wrong, but outside from that I wanted to spend more time with her and know her story. She twisted the faucet and the water started pouring. I heard her move the curtains and get in, "Mitch, if you are still there come in the bathroom I left the door open just for you silly." Now she wants me to come in the bathroom and do what I presume, hope not get in the shower with her, I didn't bring anything to change into. I walked into the bathroom and closed the door, hoping that her parents don't come home from work early and see me standing in the bathroom while their daughter takes a shower. "I am in, what's up why am I in the bathroom?" "So I can talk to you silly, that's why, why else would I call you in the bathroom. I smiled for a second, "Oh okay so what do you want to talk about?" "Nothing really, when I get out I should be done in a few, I will get ready and we can get some breakfast. Or if you need to get home I can drive you home, let me know okay, so I know what the plan is. I thought it about for a second, "Kristen I really loved spending time with you and meeting your loving family, but I need to get home, I didn't tell my mom where I was. She is probably worried, she didn't even call me the whole night, and she probably thought something terrible happened." "Okay I am done now, so can you get my towel its right behind you, thanks." I handed her the towel as I can hear the last drops coming from the faucet, she smelled so good. She opened the glass sliding door and when she stepped out, dripping wet, and that look in her eyes, I could barley control myself. I wanted more, I know that I love Alison, but Alison didn't have the body like Kristen did, and she didn't have the spontaneous but exciting way of thinking like Kristen did. I love Alison because we have so much stuff in common, but I like Kristen because of her sexuality and her body. I wanted so more to be with her in that shower and watch her lather her sweet, warm body, and slowly and gently see how the water rinses it away. I wished so much that I can be the luffa sponge, to get a chance to rub all over body, to rub against those perfect breasts. She stepped to the other end of the bathroom as she got a blow dryer and stated doing her hair. "Can you go in my room and get those clothes that I have laid on my dresser please?" I walked into her room and found it I handed her the clothes as she slowly closed the door halfway, as she was getting ready.

About 15 minutes later she was done, and when she stepped out she smelled better than when she stepped out the shower. Her scent was so intoxicating, I wanted more and more taste her. She walked down to the living room as I followed, she grabbed her keys and coat and walked to the front door. "I am going to drop you home; I don't want your parents to worry about you all day. I have some errands to run so I am going to be in the neighborhood, let me know if you want to hang out again sometime." She opened the door and walked outside to her car, I followed her closing the door behind me. She was already sitting in car and I walked to the passenger's side and got in. She grabbed a CD from the compartment she had above the steering wheel, and put it in the CD player. "Hope you like rock music, because that is all I listen to." "It's cool I like that kind of music too, it's my favorite kind." She smiled as she reversed out from the driveway. She started driving as she turned up the music louder; I sat back in the chair smiled at Kristen. I thought to myself, great this is going to be fun, how am I going to explain this mom and Jeremy; more importantly how am I going to explain this to Alison, as I still see it she is still my girlfriend. At this moment I didn't worry about that, I just rested my head on the seat took a deep breath and listen to the music all the way home.

Chapter 20
Girl Trouble

I didn't know if she knew where the fucked I lived so I had to tell her my addresses before we get lost. "Hey do you know where I live, I don't think you do." "No, I was going to ask you for your address back at my house I forgot. But there is something I have to do; I have to meet up with someone first, and then I will drop you off. I am sorry I just remembered you're not mad are you?" "No don't be silly, you're driving *me* homer remember, there is no reason for me to be mad at you." My address is 1500 East Garden Street, that's where I live, I hope that's not hard to find?" "No, I am sure we can find it, it will be fun I can finally see what your house looks like." Yeah it will be fun, I can invite her in and give her a tour and introduce her to my erratic but loving mother, and Jeremy the man of the hour or sort of speak. "There is one thing that is bugging me and I always forget to ask you. If you're from New York originally, what are you doing all the way in Ohio?" "I was waiting on that question all day; well my mom and I are visiting my sister who lives up here. She said she was going to meet me there after she gets home from work she was going to drive up there, both my parents. That's why I told you I had to meet someone earlier, but I will still drop you off. I just have to go in and say hi and hug everyone." "Sounds like fun, if there is one thing *I* always hate it is visiting family, I don't know what it was honestly but every time I went anywhere I always had a boring ass time." "Well my sister is not boring, she is just like me. Kristen's sister is just like her, Kristen was so hot and she tastes so good, that can only mean one thing, that her sister is probably hotter and taste even better." About an hour went by and we finally made it, not to my house but to Kristen's sister's house. It was so big, and there were a lot of cars parked around it, I would say between 5 and 6 if not more. Must have been some sort of party or something, I see a lot of people through the blinds. "I forgot to mention, it's my sister's birthday today, so I know she doesn't know you but just wish her a happy birthday for me." "Sure no problem, I can do that for you." We arrived and she pulled in closer, Kristen turned off the car and we both got out. The first person that came running out the door was probably Kristen's sister, one would guess. She ran to Kristen and gave her a hug, thanks for coming, and I see you brought someone with you. I walked over to her, "You must be Kirsten's sister, hi my name is Mitch I am Kristen's friend, happy birthday." "Thank you, but how did you... Kristen told you to say happy birthday to me?" "Yes, you're not upset are you, because it's kind of awkward because we don't know each other?" "I am not upset, trust me, I am fine don't worry." Brooke, Mitch and I have been hanging out a lot lately and we went out on our first date haven't we Mitch?" "Yes, we have, Brooke, Kristen is a very special girl, and I love spending time with her." "Brooke listen, I can't stay long I have to drop him off back home his mom is getting worried." "Are you sure, you can't stay longer, please?" "I am sure trust me but I will call you later okay I promise." "Before you go let me ask you a question, excuse us Mitch for a second." "So you and Mitch huh, he seems cute, so are you guys like officially boyfriend and girlfriend material yet, tell me everything." "Brooke, I love you happy birthday, but I have to go, and I promise I will tell you everything okay I have to go." "Okay, well thanks for stopping by, have a safe trip, don't forget call me." I will, Kristen's sister made her way back into the house, as Kristen made her way to her car. "Hey what did she tell you, you were giggling it had to be funny, if you don't mind me asking?" "Nothing really you know just girl stuff, so come on I will drop you off." "What are you going to do when you drop me off?" "Come back to the party say bye to everyone and my mom and I are going back to New York, back to our house." She got in the car and I made my way in the car also, "You have to go back so suddenly, when I will see you again?" "I don't know let me give you my number so we can call each other and talk late at night." I grabbed my cell phone and added her to my list, Kirsten. "My number is (973) 223-8530, now when you call me I will store your number in my phone, and now we can talk to each other as long as we want." I smiled as she started the car and drove out of her sister's driveway. She took the CD that was in the player out and put it back where it went. She grabbed another CD from the holder she had above and popped it in. She smiled at me and pressed play, noticing by that it would be something that I liked, but I have been wrong before. The CD started playing and at first I didn't recognize it but as soon as the song got further into the chorus I knew who it was. It was funny because it was The Clash, well at least Kristen and Alison have one thing in common, same likes in music. Well okay, one artist but it was better than nothing. I randomly called Kristen, because I still had my cell phone out in my lap. Her phone started ringing, and of course she was driving so she didn't see who was calling. I grabbed her phone and looked at it, "Who is it, who is calling?" "Me, now you have my number silly so I am going to save it as Mitch, my name so you can call me and we can talk late at night." She smiled and thanked me as I put her phone back down in her lap. I don't know how long it was going to take from her sister's house all the way to my house. I decided to call my mom and at least try to get a hold of her, because she never called me yesterday. I called her and for about a couple of seconds no one picked up, and then she did. "Mitch, baby you alright, you never called yesterday and I didn't see you all night, are you alright?" "I am fine mom, it's a long story, and I am getting a ride home with my friend she is going to drop me off. I will explain everything when I get home I promise." My mom took a deep breath, "I am just glad that you are alright, now I can tell Jeremy to stop freaking out. Okay honey, I will see you soon, love you." "Love you too mom, and tell Jeremy that I am okay and I will see him soon." She hung up the phone, and I just sent a quick text message to Jeremy to tell him that I was okay and I was coming home. "What did your mom say; she sounded pretty distraught about the whole situation." "She was just glad that everything was okay, more importantly that I was okay, you know how mom's are, I said sarcastically." "Okay, sorry I didn't mean to make your mom upset in anyway last night, you had no ride home I thought it would be a good idea that's it." "Don't beat yourself up it wasn't your fault, I am glad that I stayed so it worked out. When I get home I am just going to have to explain to my mom what happened. But I promise I won't tell her everything, it's no one's business but ours." She smiled and grabbed my hand as she continued to drive. I smiled back at her and held her hand firmly in mine, but in my mind I wasn't smiling. In my mind I felt fucking stabbing myself repeatedly with a large knife. The reason that I felt like that is because I was in a fucking love triangle, I am in love with Alison and now I think that I have feelings for Kristen. I don't know who to let go, because in all good judgment you cannot have two girlfriends, it would never work out. I would always have to sneak around and see the both of them, and how about I have to see them both at the same time. I knew that inside this shit was eating away at me, and I couldn't take it. I had to figure out what the fuck I am going to do fast before this shit gets any worse.

After hours of driving, well we would've got to my house earlier but I think that Kristen made a wrong turn; she is so cute when she is hopelessly confused. I didn't want to waste your precious time, so I am not going to fill in the details, of when we stopped to get gas, and once more to get something to eat. Because I thought that kind of fucking information would be really fucking useless. She stopped at the side, because she didn't have any time to pull in and pull out. I got out and thanked her again for driving me home and, especially thanked her for last night. She smiled and said she will call later and she turned the car around in the street and drove off. I grabbed my keys from my pocket and before I could get to the front door my mom came running out the door and she gave me a huge fucking hug. "I missed you; I hoped and prayed that nothing terrible happened to you." "Mom I am fine, I am sorry for not calling I knew if I told you, you would freak out and overreact. But I should've at least called because it would've been the right thing to do. "I am just happy that you're alright, come on in I bet you are hungry." Actually I wasn't, while I was walking with my mom going back inside. She closed the door behind her and didn't even lock it like she usually does. She is probably happy that I am home or in one piece. My mom has a tendency to fucking overreact and jump to conclusions about everything. Like I can remember this one time I was eleven, and I spent the night at my friends Justin's house. I forgot to tell her, and she thought I got fucking kidnapped. She went around the Goddamn neighborhood putting up fucking flyers and shit. Then I came home the next morning before she went to work, and when she saw that I was okay she started freaking out and hugging and kissing me, she wouldn't stop crying. I tell you I am glad that she is a little older and doesn't fucking cry and overreact to everything that happens to me now. Jeremy came out the kitchen, and like a typical guy he smiled, "I am glad you're okay kiddo." That is all he fucking said, and went back in his room with a beer in his hand. Jeremy has never been big on the sentimental bullshit like every other girl I have met, especially my mom. My mom just smiled and hugged me one more time and walked into her room. I can just fucking imagine if I came home like bleeding or with a leg or something missing, my mom would've killed herself and Jeremy probably would've gone fucking insane. I walked into the kitchen and grabbed a soda, after everything that just happened I think that I deserve a cold drink. But if there is one thing that I hate more than anything is that every time that I need or want something to drink or eat we never have it. But whenever that I am not hungry we have all the food in the fucking house. It was so hot in the house; I swear they had the thermostat like on fucking 90 degrees. I was literally sweating all over the place, and my shirt was sticking to my back. I walked over there and it was on fucking 75, now I don't know about my mom or Jeremy but I was hot. I turned to a cool 60 for a while then I will put it to 70 when it gets nice and cool around the house. I walked back to my room and shut the door all the way; I really didn't wanted to be bothered right now. I am not in the mood for another fucking distraction. I don't think that emotionally I can handle that kind of stress right now. I unlaced my shoes and threw them off on the side of my dresser, I was so tired that I didn't even care about my mom worrying her ass off, and Jeremy pretending like he doesn't give a shit. I didn't care about Alison right now, or even Kristen, both of them at the same time I couldn't take it anymore it was so fucking stressful. I didn't care if I had to go to work today, I can just tell Alison that something came up with my mom; she wasn't feeling well or something. I didn't want to tell her the truth not yet, it's not like I am cheating on her with Kristen but I don't know what the fuck all that was. I mean from the meeting in the store to her house everything happened so fast. The only thing that I cared about right now, the only thing that I wanted to do is go in my bed and go to sleep. I took off my shirt, and crawled back into bed. Eventually someone will come out and turn the thermostat to 70 or higher but I didn't care about it right now. I got all the way under the covers, threw them over my face and just fucking closed my eyes.

When I woke up my eyes had to get adjusted to the light, because my mom turned on the fucking brightest light in my room. Apparently she was looking for something, and my mom always looks for something when I am sleeping or studying. She never gives me a reason why she is coming in my room, but I have a pretty good idea. I guess it's her way of checking up on me, even though I am fucking 18 and not a baby, it never stopped my mom. In her eyes I always been her baby and she is afraid that one day something terrible is going to happen. She swears she can see the future, and predicts all these things happening to me. She never says if they are good are bad, but throws out these hunches all the time and sometime they are annoying but comedic at the same time. I don't know sometimes I feel like I can't help myself in certain situations. Since my mom was going through all my shit I decided to get up and use the little boy's room. I didn't bother to ask my mom the real reason why she was in my room early as hell in the morning, it's not like I am hiding shit from her and I never want her to find it or something. I guess whatever she is looking for has a reason for waking me up early as hell in the morning. I walked to the bathroom and noticed the time from the microwave that was sitting on the counter. I was so upset, because it was only ten in the morning, and now I am going to be awake for the rest of the day. See I am one of those people who if I am disturbed for any reason when I am sleeping and whatever time I wake up in the morning, I am awake. I know that's not common for most people, but sleeping was never my best friend growing up. I barely got any and finally all those years of staying up all night caught up to me. I did what I usually did in the bathroom and about five minutes I was done. I came out and walked into the kitchen, and everything was out of order, the fridge was moved back from its original place. The cabinets were opened and most of the dishes were out. There were empty boxes everywhere, as if like we were moving or something. Then all of a sudden a terrible thought just came into my head, of all the thoughts I ever had, this one had to be number one at the top of the list. I thought to myself a hundred times over we can't be moving. I didn't want to believe it; I managed to walk away from all the boxes in the kitchen to find more boxes in the living room. There were also tons of tons of newspapers on the ground too. I went back in my room and closed the door, and covered my face with my hands. Why is this happening I kept saying to myself over and fucking over again? How many times do we have to move, then I got up and thought maybe I am overreacting to this whole situation, maybe my mom is just packing shit up to give away, you know to people or something. I stood up and walked outside to the kitchen were my mom was working. She just smiled, of course, and went on her marry way. I calmly walked up to her and asked her the most important question that she would here. "Mom, I said, are we moving?" She didn't say anything at first I guess she didn't hear me so I asked her again. "Mom, I said one more time, are we MOVING?" "Moving, she said, yes we are moving, I am so sorry I wanted to surprise you but you probably had noticed from all the boxes. I didn't say anything and ran back into my room and slammed the mother fucking door. I was so fucking pissed at my mom, why the hell do we have to move again. Fucking again I said we have to move again this is great, I swear it's like every time I meet someone new and start to like them we move. I can't tell you how many times we had to do this, and this routine is starting to piss me off. Now I am stuck in this stupid ass love triangle with the girl I love Alison and the girl that I can't help but to stay away from, Kristen. What am I going to tell them both that I am moving, I guess I can finally tell Alison that I have been spending time with another girl, but it didn't mean anything, she was just a friend. But in my mind it did mean something, I loved Alison, but I had all these feelings for Kristen, and I never felt like this about anyone, except for Beverley, and look where the fuck that got me. It got me dumped in the middle of the night, snowing in our most favorite spot a park, sitting on a park bench. I got up from by bed, and I can hear my mom taping all the boxes up in the living room, and Jeremy was helping. "Mom, why do we have to move? She really didn't give me an honest ass answer, "It's just time for a change, that's it, and I think that everyone deserves to start over don't you?" "We moved the first time and it almost crushed me, and now we have to move again after I met someone special." "Oh you're talking about Alison, how is she doing?" "She is doing fine, but look that is not important, I just don't want to move, okay what about school?" "Well, aren't you going away to school or something, I forgot what you told me last time." "I nodded my head, and thought about all those fucking brochures that my mom had brought home. Some of them were actually for pretty good colleges but they were too far, and a couple of them were really expensive. But out of all them I did manage to pick out one of them, it was a little less expensive than the others but expensive nonetheless. It was a typical four year college, but if I stayed the for the summer semesters and took extra classes when I could I can graduate in three years instead of four, which will give me a whole extra year to work and earn some serious fucking money. And a good thought ran through my head, at this time I think it would be a good idea to go and try to explain things to Alison. Before she gets the idea to fucking fire me and leave me jobless. I still felt kind of bad that I didn't talk to her for a long time and ditching her twice at work. I didn't think about school or the thought of my mom packing up in the living room. I grabbed my keys and coat, without saying a word I walked out the front door and walked toward my car. I saw my mom walk to the door with the corner of my eye but I didn't turn around. I had nothing to say her, this is like the fucking second or third time we moved and she told me fucking last minute. I guess she has always been like that, telling people at the last minute what the hell is going on about anything. But you know, she fucking never thinks that it affects anyone that once she has said something everyone is just supposed to compromise and get on with it. Well, mom, I don't think it is supposed to work like that so when are you going to get it through your thick head of yours. I unlocked the door, got in, and started the car and fucking drove off. I wasn't thinking about anything important or whatever because I wanted a clear head when I talk to Alison. I didn't want to start talking to her with Goddamn clouded thoughts and everything. Because I get all fucking distracted and I hate that shit, when I am trying to think of something and it never comes out the way I want it to come out.

I finally reached her store; I drove around for a block or two just to find parking. I swear to God, you can never find a Goddamn parking spot whenever it is very important. But whenever there is nothing the fuck going on there is like a hundred empty Goddamn parking spots available. I finally found a parking spot near an old, red Ford 150. I stopped the car and got out; luckily I was only a block away from the store, so I wasn't going to run down the street like a jackass. I reached the front door, and walked in the store, to my surprise Mr. Taylor was there. I walked to the counter, "Hi, Mr. Taylor, is Alison around?" "No, he replied she is at home, she is pretty upset at something, and she is not telling me what." I probably have an idea, man I hated myself right now I completely messed things up with Alison. "Is it okay, if I go and visit her, just to make sure that she is okay and to help in anyway?" "Sure, you know you don't have to ask, you are a good friend to her." I smiled and thanked him as I left the store, such a good friend to her I remembered what he said. Okay if I am such a good friend to her how come I feel all guilty inside? I walked a block to my car, and the weather was so fucking hot, but I know that wasn't important right now. I unlocked the door and got in; I started the car and drove off carefully making sure I didn't rear end someone. The last thing that I needed is to talk to some asshole, and hear that person complain about their car. I really didn't know what to say, I wanted to make sure that I don't bring up Kristen in anyway. But I felt really bad, Kristen always said that it wasn't cheating we were just friends. But come on am I the only one who can see here that we fucking made on numerous occasions. Now tell me what kind of person is committed to another and goes around and kisses another girl. Me, that's who and the verdict is I am CHEATING! I arrived at her house, and her car was parked in the driveway. So I am glad that she was still home and not out anywhere. I pulled in and parked my car; I quickly turned it off and sat in the seat for about a minute. I could see her window perfectly from my seat, and then I saw her peak her head out and then she quickly closed the blinds. Going from that reaction I am probably guessing that she is not happy to see me right now. I got out and walked to her door; I took a breath and rang the doorbell. I knew that at first she wasn't going to answer, but if I kept on ringing the doorbell she would have to come. Eventually she did, and she opened the door, and said, "What do you want, what are you doing here?" She was dressed in this old ass T-shirt that looked like it has been through World War III, and a pair of low cut denim jeans. "Why are you so upset, what did I do wrong?" She thought about it for a second, "You left me twice at work, and I had to help out all the customers and close up by myself." I felt bad for leaving her, but I couldn't tell her about Kristen otherwise she will be really mad. "Sorry, I said in my defense, I told you something came up and I had to take care of it. Can I come in, I just want to talk that's it okay." She let me in the house as I closed the door; I sat down on the couch as she walked back to her room. I was going to get up and follow her but I guess she needed her space; she came back with a decent looking T-shirt this time, but still had the same jeans on. She walked towards me and sat down on the couch, she looked right into my eyes and said, "Do you love me?" I didn't know where she was going with this was this one of those trick questions. "Of course I love you, why would you say such a thing." She smiled politely; I was just wondering you have been acting really weird lately that's all. I didn't have an explanation for that but I couldn't tell her, it would absolutely kill her. "I am fine, everything is okay, I love you and that is the most important thing right now." She smiled again and gave me a hug, she stood up, and "I am going to take a shower we have work today. You can watch TV or go on the computer if you want or if you're hungry you know where the kitchen is." I just smiled and said thanks as she headed down the hallway and I heard her room door open. I stood up and shouted that I had to get something out of my car real quick. She said okay as she walked back into the living room, I was about to leave and then she said, "My dad will be home soon, does you know you are here?" "I told him when I stopped at work looking for you, so he knows." "Okay" she said as she headed back down the hallway. I opened the door and started walking towards my car, I didn't know what the fuck I was looking for but I just needed to get out of the house. I sat in the car and I stared up at Alison's window, wondering if she was going to peak her head out, she didn't so I guess she was in the shower. I left from my car and grabbing a piece of paper and putting it in my wallet. It was Dr. Ross number, I didn't want Alison or Kristen to know that I am seeing a shrink; it's just weird you know. I walked back inside the house and she was getting ready, I could hear the blow dryer. I walked to her room and knocked on the door, she said come in as she was finishing getting ready. I just stood beside her door, and watched her still blow dry her hair at least she had the rest of her clothes on. I tell you girls take so long to get ready it's unbelievable, but I guess it's always like that. I wanted to tell her so badly, about everything, but I knew that she wouldn't understand. So I decided to keep it a secret until I feel a little more comfortable about telling her.

She finished getting ready as she grabbed her belongings as she walked past me without saying a word. I don't know why she was giving me the cold shoulder. To tell you the truth liking two different girls at the same time is so stressful, I don't know how anybody can do it. I walked back to the living room as she was waiting by the door, with her coat in her hand. I grabbed my stuff as she walked out the door without saying a word again. I walked outside and proceeded to my car. She unlocked her car door and got in, she shouted that she was going to run some errands, and her dad should be home in three minutes. I said okay as I got into my car and shut the door. She drove off first, and I just continued to sit there for a second and then I reversed and drove off. I could still see her car in front of me as she made a left turn, and I made a right. This is a perfect time for me to clear my head, and not think about Kristen or Alison, I needed to see Elizabeth. I called her office number to see if she was still in, her secretary picked up. "Hi, is Dr. Ross available, it is an emergency I need to speak with her." "She is with a client, do you have an appointment?" "No, are walk inn's available, otherwise I can wait until she is free, it's not that big of a deal." "Okay, come on in and I'll see what I can do." I thanked her and hung up and continued to drive. I wonder what the hell was bothering Alison so much, why was she ignoring me today. Usually she is more energetic and everything, and today she kept on walking by without saying a word. This whole thing with Kristen is really messing up everything; I didn't know what to do anymore. After I felt guilty about myself I arrived at her office, and parked around the corner. I got out and walked around the corner and inside the building and walked up to the counter. "Hi, I called earlier my name is Mitch, I called in reference to Dr. Ross, is she available?" "She is still with a client; if you want you can have a seat and wait I believe that she is almost done." I found a seat toward the corner of the wall, away from everybody. I waited and waited patiently until she came out of her office and walked to the counter. I didn't want to get up and walk up to her, because someone else may be in line and it will be rude to cut in front of them.

Then I heard her call my name, so I got up and walked toward her. "Hi, Dr. Ross, how are you? I hope you are not busy at all." "No my session just ended come on in." "I can't stay long because I have work later today and I don't want to be late." I sat down as she closed her office door. It was hot in the office today, and she had a window open but that was doing no justice. She walked toward me and took off her jacket, she was wearing this multi colored top and it was like a tank top, but it looked really good on her. I guess she had the figure, most women wear clothes that don't fit their figure and they wonder why they look bad in them. But this top was really proportionate with the rest of her slim body. "Tell me what you are going through this time, Mitch." She said pretty sarcastically, as she got comfortable in the chair she was sitting in. "Well, where do I start, everything is bothering me and I don't know what to do. Alison and I are getting more serious but lately she is been giving me the cold shoulder, and she doesn't want to spend time with me like she used to. I mean this whole thing with Kristen, I just met her and everything is going at a fast pace." "It seems like you have to choose between Alison and Kristen, I am sorry to put you under so much pressure but if you continue to date the both of them, you are going to go crazy." "I know, I don't want to date the both of them but I am love with Alison, and I really like Kristen. See, Alison and Kristen are different in their own ways." "Alison is so full of life and energetic, and Kristen is so spontaneous and has such a great personality." "Well, I know what I am about to say isn't that hard to figure out but you have to choose, and it seems like the choice you make might affect your personal and love life." She was right, in spite of all this shit, I had to pick one, but more importantly I had to tell Alison everything. I had to tell her from the day that Kirsten came into the store, to present day. "So sorry to cut this short but I have to go, I think that you have been really helpful." I think I just have to tell Alison the truth, I mean in the end I will feel a lot better." We both stood up and shook hands, as I left her office and walked out the front door. I felt somewhat kind of happy I went, even though what she told I could've figure out. But I guess it was nice to get a different perspective. I got into my car after a block of walking and checked my watch. I wondered if Alison was at work, she told me that she had some errands that she needed to run. I decided to go to work and she if she was there. Man I was so nervous; I didn't know what to say or how I should approach it. I regret even meeting Kristen; you know I fucking blame her for all this shit, but I couldn't hate her all the way. Because if you really think about it I blame myself getting involved, and going to her house, and making out with her. I guess that is another thing different about girls than guys, they alluring, and you can't take your eyes off of them.

I arrived and for the first time I finally found a good parking spot, I drove up and parked my car. Fuck, I said I was running out of gas, it was amazing how far I have driven this thing and now it running out of gas. I hate filling this piece of shit up because of two reasons, one the car itself is pretty old, and gas is expensive. Like a quarter of my paycheck goes to gas, and the rest I spend on like shit for myself. I got out and quickly walked to the store, and immediately walked toward the counter. I didn't see Alison there, and then I remembered her spot in the corner of the store. I walked over there and low and behold she was there, but she was just sitting there looking into space. I didn't want to wave or anything like that so I sort of moved in front of her vision, if you can say that, and stood there. Like any obvious person she noticed and got up, thanks she said sarcastically as she started walking away. "Hey, wait, why have you been acting really weird lately? You know giving me the cold shoulder and ignoring me lately, what gives?" Alison stood there with both of her hands on her hips and waited for a response as if I was going to say something." "My dad told me that you have been hanging out with another girl lately, and he also told me that he saw you with the same girl on numerous occasions." "What, you're telling me that your dad is spying on me, is that it." "No, she said, he drove by all the time and saw you with some fucking girl holding hands. Now you have one chance to explain yourself right now." I guess that now is the best time to tell her, I mean it is now or never and I didn't want to hide it anymore. Honestly all this secrets was killing me, but I am not going to tell her the whole truth because I want to see her again. If I told her everything that happened I am afraid that she will never want to see me again. "Okay, I don't know about the holding hands thing, even though I was lying about that I mean we did more than hold hands but that was beside the point, I was spending time with another girl." "But when is it wrong to have another friend who is a girl?" "There is nothing wrong with that Mitch, come on its obvious that she is not *just* your friend. Why don't you just admit it that you were cheating on me with another skank." "Okay, I think you need to calm down and breathe or something, first of all I wasn't cheating on you, again I was lying, she is just a friend that I spent some time with that's it." "Oh, spent some time with what the fuck does that mean. Let me ask you something, did you kiss her?" Now I couldn't lie, I could've easily as lied to her but I have to tell her some truth. Even though this is going to be hard, but I guess she backed in a corner. "If it will make you happy, I kissed her once, but it didn't mean anything I swear." "Yeah, that is what they all say, please I don't want to hear it right now, and I just want you to leave now." "What, leave like leave, and where do you want me to go." "I don't know, please leave I don't want to see you right now, okay." "Fine, you're blowing this totally out of proportion, if you want me to leave I will leave that is no problem. But if you really want to know something all the time I spent with her, it didn't mean anything, okay she is just a friend I care about you." I didn't care what she had to say next, I was so fucking frustrated about everything right now I just left. I couldn't believe how she overreacted to this whole thing. But then again it all comes down to me; I felt bad lying to her about the first things. I wanted to tell her everything, but now seeing how she overreacted I am glad I didn't. I didn't want to go anywhere but home now, no matter how bad things got I could always go home and it will feel better. I walked to my car and got and drove off, I was so upset that I didn't even noticed I was speeding a little. I couldn't even think straight, now what the fuck am I going to do, Alison is all upset and I didn't even tell Kristen yet. I didn't know what the hell I was going to tell her, hey Kristen umm you kind of fucked up my relationship with Alison I never want to see you again. That would never work, and that would be mean to tell her. I got home and drove up toward the driveway, I parked and got out. I walked to the front door, opened it and walked inside. I took off my shoes and threw my coat on the sofa and walked towards my room. I didn't bother to check if my mom or Jeremy was home, honestly at this point I really didn't give a shit or what they had to say. All I wanted right now is just to be left alone; I didn't want anyone to bother me. But I guess in my family that sort of problem doesn't exist, whenever someone has a problem it's always someone's job to find out. And get all the information about it so they can pretend that they are helping and making everything better. But they are not, I don't blame my mom for being caring and wanted to make sure that everything is okay, but I think sometimes she cares to much and it gets on my fucking nerves. I feel like a fucking baby, but I guess in her eyes I will always be her little angel, and well that wasn't that bad as I thought it would be. I just lay down in bed and closed my eyes and wished that the whole fucking day would just go away.

I awoke and I was still pretty tired, I am always tired whenever I go to sleep and wake up again I don't know why. But anyway, I was still pretty pissed that fucking Alison got so totally mad about everything. I did kind of bring this upon myself, I felt so bad hooking up with Kristen behind Alison's back but it's not like I meant to do it. I mean accidents happen and I made a huge one. I stood up from my bed and just picked up my comforter from the corners and sort of shook it then placed it on my bed again. I never cared that much of making my bed because I was always going to fall asleep in it anyway. I guess this way it will save me the trouble for later. I walked outside and headed toward the front door, my mom and Jeremy were in the room because I can hear them talking and watching TV. I was going to go inside and bother them, and sort of apologize about what happened last night, but I didn't want to get into that again. I walked to the kitchen opened the drawer and took out a piece of paper and a pen. I wrote, Mom, I am going out to talk to Alison and whatever. I didn't want to get too much into the whole fucking process on a post it. I grabbed the note and placed it on the dining room table, that way whenever my mom or Jeremy come out they can see it. I still had to Alison and Kristen that we were moving. I was so Goddamn upset at my mom for telling me last minute. Before I left the house, I walked to my mom's door and knocked and walked in. "I want to know where we are moving to?" It was a second until any of them said anything, but then my mom finally spoke. "Sorry honey, for not telling you earlier but I got a supervisor job at a nationwide insurance company." "I stood there for a second, "That's great mom, but you didn't answer my question." "We, I mean you me and Jeremy, are all moving to New York City, I know that you are not used to the city. I remember your dad taking you the city when you were little, but that was a long time ago." I was so shocked and pissed at the same time; I just walked out of the room and walked out the front door. I headed toward my car, and got in; the weather was so hot I put my ac on full blast. My mom told me to never do that because it uses up all gas, but as hot as it was I really didn't care right now. I wonder what Alison's mood will be when she sees me, I am sure she is still going to be pretty mad but when I tell her that I am moving, then what. Will she be sad or will she even care. I drove off not knowing what I am going to say, and how I am going to say it. All I knew that this was the time that I had to say everything, because I was moving and there was no reason not to hide anything anymore. I continued to drive and I am glad that I had enough gas in the car otherwise I would've been fucking screwed. I was so nervous, how about if I get there and she slams the Goddamn door in my face. Man everything was buzzing around in my Goddamn head, I was getting a headache.

I finally arrived and still with enough gas in the tank. I noticed that Alison's dad's truck was parked in the driveway. I was hoping that he didn't find out that I cheated on Alison with Kristen. I cannot afford to get fired right now; everything was going so good with this job. I pulled in and stopped the car; I opened my door and got out. I walked to the door and rang the doorbell. I waited for a second, and was about to ring it again until I heard someone from the other side of the door. I pulled away from the doorbell and put my hands in my pocket. The door opened and it was Mr. Taylor. He didn't look please when he saw me, it he didn't say anything, but Alison is upstairs. He let me in as I walked inside and thanked him for letting me in; I thought he was just going to throw me out or something. I took off my shoes and walked up the stairs towards Alison's room. I knocked on her door without being rude and just walking in, I can hear her moving around in the room, but she didn't hurry to answer it. She probably saw me pulling up and decided that she didn't want anything to do with me right now. "Alison, please open the door, it's me Mitch. I want to talk and explain myself." Still no answer, I didn't know what the hell to do she was acting like a Goddamn baby. Not answering doors she was acting immature. "Alison, please I said one more time I have something important to tell you." Finally about a second later she opened the door and her first reaction was WHAT. "I am sorry for whatever I did okay, being with Kristen the whole time I was thinking about you honestly. She was just a friend, and I am sorry for kissing her one thing led to another you know how crazy that shit can get." She sat down on her bed and didn't say anything for a minute; she just looked at me and folded her arms. "Look I know you have every reason to be mad at me right now, but I have something to tell you." My mom got a supervisor position at a nationwide insurance company and now we are moving." "We are moving to New York, I don't know when exactly but my mom started packing up all the boxes and everything. I just wanted to tell you so you won't have a reason to be mad at me anymore." She stood up and walked toward me, she didn't say anything for a second, and walked toward her door. "I am sad that you are moving, but you did what you did, and I don't know if I can forgive you for that right now. I have been hurt before in the past and I don't want to get hurt again." "I am sorry that I hurt you, I never meant to do anything like that I promise, but you have to believe me I never meant for any of this to happen it just sort of did. What do I have to do to make it up to you." She didn't say anything and walked toward me again, she hugged me and looked at me, "Please don't hurt me again that is all I am asking of you." I won't I said as I held her close. "I have to go, sorry I have to help my mom finish packing up the rest of the house and shit." "Okay, call me later okay I'll tell my dad that you are moving so he will give you the last paycheck." We hugged again and I left her room, and started making my way toward the door. I guess her dad was in the room because I heard the TV coming from the other side. I'd figured that I will let myself out, so I don't have to bother Mr. Taylor. I walked toward my car and I just realized that I just made up with Alison and I just fucking lied to her again. I wasn't going to go help my mom with the packing. I was actually going to see Kristen that I was moving and could never see her again. I called her as I was making my way into my car. She picked up, "Hey, Mitch what's up?" "I need to speak with you it is important, and I need to tell you this now." She seemed pretty worried in what I was going to say next and before I got the chance, she said come on over I am home. I hung up the phone and placed it on the passenger's side. I started up my car and one more time I looked at Alison's window one more time to see if she would peak her head out or something. I waited and then nothing, so I guess that this was really the end. I didn't know how much my mom got done with the packing, as far as I know it the whole house could've been done by now. Kristen was next, and then I had no idea what the fuck would happen. I had no idea what chapter in my life would come out and what friends I would make or anything of that sort. While I was driving, my phone was ringing and it was Kristen. I picked up, "Hey, I left the door unlocked because I might be in the shower if you get here and no one answers." "Okay, no problem that's fine, I said, I am almost at your house just a couple of more minutes." She hung and I once again threw my phone on the beaten down leather seat. I couldn't believe how piece of shit that my fucking car was. I mean I know it wasn't that new but at the same time it wasn't that old either. A few Goddamn red lights later I finally arrived and hurriedly parked my car in her driveway. I needed to tell her that I was moving before shit starting to get weird again between us. I stopped my car and got out and walked to the door. The door was locked so I guess she hasn't gone in the shower yet. I rang the doorbell, and waited, and then she finally came down in a tight raggedy T-shirt and these cut denim low shorts. While she was standing there even in the most awful of clothing, I couldn't believe how fucking sexy she looked. One part of me wanted to tell her that we couldn't see her again and that this would be the best way. And the other part of me wanted to walk inside the house and slowly undress her and watch those low short shorts slide down her tone sexy hips. And I wanted to take that shirt that she was wearing and just pull it over her head. Grab her by her hair and look into her eyes and kiss her. But my instincts are running wild again, and I needed to stop before things start getting out of control. "May I come in it is important." "Sure, you sounded pretty upset on the phone." I have to make this quick because I have to go back home and help my mom finish packing up." "You are moving?" "Yes, I am that is what I wanted to tell you about, I am sorry to tell you this Kristen but my mom got offered a great job and now we are moving to New York." "I wish this didn't have to be because we could've been great friends." "Just friends, she said looking at me with sensitive eyes." "Yes, friends I am in love with Alison, you know that, but we could still be friends." "Hey I am sorry that I have to go and leave you like this with so much shit going through your head like this." "I am sorry Kristen but I have to go, maybe one day we can meet again and hang out because I would really like that." She still stood there, leaning on the side of the door about to cry, because her eyes were watery. We hugged and she didn't say anything, I don't know if she didn't want to say anything or if she was too upset to say anything, but in the end I did feel awful about what happened.

I walked to my car and unlocked the door, and got in. Kristen was still standing by the door as I waved to her and just smiled. She smiled back at me and slowly closed the door; I started my car and drove off. I never said that I would cry no matter what the situation was but losing two people that I care about is really hard. I continued to drive down the street; I picked up my cell phone and called my mom. Several rings later, of course, she didn't pick up; I left a quick message and hung up. I angrily threw my phone on the seat where it bounced and fell on the ground. I guess this was it then, everything that I worked for with Alison is now coming to an end. And Kirsten is a great girl and if things never would've worked out with Alison. I knew that Kristen would be the girl for me. The only good part of this was the drive home; there were two different ways to get home, the short way and the long way. I took the long way because I wanted to appreciate the drive home as much of it as I can get. The drive was pretty silent, so I turned on the radio. Of course all I got was fucking commercials, so I took a CD from the compartment and popped it in. The Clash started playing and I just smiled and listened to them all the way home.

Chapter 21
New York City

I pulled in still blasting the radio, at this time I didn't want to leave my car. I got and slammed my car door; I walked toward the front door and unlocked it. I walked inside the house and I saw my mom still working and packing up everything. I walked up to her, "I still can't believe that we are moving, this happens every Goddamn time." "Sorry Mitch, and watch your mouth, but this is a great opportunity for us, for me." "Where's Jeremy is he helping you pack up all this shit?" "He is around somewhere the last time I saw him he was in the attic emptying some old boxes and stuff." I walked away from my mother for a second, because I couldn't stand being with her right now. I walked into the kitchen and opened the fridge and grabbed a soda, I was so thirsty. I walked back to my room and half of the shit was already in boxes. I was so upset, because I hate when my mom or anybody comes into my room and starts messing with my stuff. I didn't know where the fuck my mom put anything now, now I have to go back and ask here where the hell she put everything. I specifically told her to never come in my room and start going through my shit. I remember this one time she came in and starting going through all my shit. I was outside playing with a bunch of my friends and I came back to notice that she had taken out all my old clothes and placed them on the floor, and replaced them with new clothes. Now that part I didn't mind at all, because it was new clothes and I didn't care who you were no one is going to argue new clothes. But she never put the old clothes the way they were before and I lost some of my favorite pairs of clothes because it got mixed up with some other old shit that she had. Now all of a sudden I come in and I see Goddamn boxes everywhere and my room is almost half empty. Now I didn't know where anything was. I was so fucking upset that I just crawled into bed and wanted to close my eyes and make it all go away. I got halfway into bed until my loving mother came knocking on the door. I got up and answered the door and she wanted help packing up some other stuff. I walked to the living room with her and Goddamn Jeremy was sitting on his lazy ass watching fucking TV. But I really couldn't say anything because I don't know how much he actually got done so he might have done a lot, I wasn't sure. My mom called me into her room to help her clean out the closet and some stuff under her bed. I grabbed the stuff from under her bed, and let me tell you it was nothing but Goddamn shit and some old newspapers. I don't know why my mom collects shit and never fucking throws it away, that part of her life always got on my nerves. And you think that she had a lot of stuff under her bed, she had more stuff in her closet. The closet door was already opened and it was jam packed with shit that you couldn't believe. On the top shelf they were old board games about four or five of them. On the far right hand side they were old clothes, mostly dresses and stuff. On the left hand side on the floor, there was an old dust buster and some old rags. And finally there were about two to three boxes labeled clothes and other stuff. Emptying all of this Goddamn shit is going to take all day and honestly I didn't have the energy to even do it right now. But I had no choice because if I don't do it today my mom will just make me do it another day. I guess this move wouldn't be that bad. I started emptying all of the shit out of the closet, first I started with the boxes with the clothes. I took the top one off first then I grabbed the second one, I placed them both on the side of the wall. I grabbed the rest of the clothes and put them on top of the boxes, so that way it won't get mixed up with other pieces of clothing my mom had lying around. I grabbed all the board games and placed them on my mom's bed. Now normally my mom would freak out because I would grab something that had dust all over it and put it on her bed. But since her bed was completely stripped down, she didn't mind one bit. When I grabbed the last of the stuff from the closet, I just realized that that the entire carpet was fucking filthy. I grabbed the small vacuum that was already outside and plugged it in. The Goddamn vacuum didn't even start, I had to flip it around and clean all the Goddamn hair and other shit from it. It was a really boring, and I ended up getting dust all over my Goddamn shirt. Finally I flipped the vacuum over and started it. It started working and before waiting I started vacuuming, and it was a miracle, everything started to get sucked up. I cleaned the area, and my mom being the type of person that she is told me to vacuum the whole carpet. My mom always does this every time I am cleaning something my mom always makes me clean the whole fucking house. Now in this case she wants me to vacuum her carpet. And what next, I can just imagine her now, Mitch, can you be a dear and vacuum the whole house for me please? Great mom, that's exactly what the fuck I want to do right now. I want to bend over backwards helping you fucking vacuum the whole entire house. It's not like we live in a shitty ass house, where the house is really small and there is no space. No, we live in a decent house, and inside this decent house we have fucking decent rugs that I had to vacuum too. Now that is going to put a smile on my face. I grabbed the vacuum, and started to clean the living room. I wanted to clean the house, before my mom said anything because she was going to say something anyway. I started cleaning up the living room; I moved all the chairs and tables around so I can get around the tough places. I vacuumed the rugs and around the coat rack. I got around where the sofas where, and got under the sofas too. I stopped to vacuum and put all the chairs back and moved back the tables to where they needed them to be. Well I said to myself the living room was done, and most of all the boxes were already packed up and ready to be loaded into the truck. Shit, the Goddamn truck we don't even have a truck unless my mom called a truck and it is coming on the way. I walked over to my mom and saw her cleaning up her room still. You would be surprised how much shit this lady had, it was fucking crazy. "Mom, I said, did you call the movers?" "No, I forgot and Jeremy is still cleaning up, can you please call them for me?" "Sure, I said I will do that in a minute just have to clean up my room." She didn't say anything so I didn't wait for a response or anything. I walked to the kitchen and opened a drawer where there was a bunch of mover's numbers. Now came the best part, I had to skim through all the fucking numbers and pick the best ones. Then I had to choose by process of elimination and pick the best one. I don't know if my mom still had the fucking mover's number from before but I didn't want to bother asking her. I found a random movers company, and the reason I picked it because the advertisement looked appealing. Well, actually it did really look reasonable, with the prices and the size of the truck. But the name wasn't trustworthy, but who the fuck cares what the name of the Goddamn moving company is called. As long as they come to your damn house and take all your shit. Danny's Movers is what they were called and it was two brothers. At least they were fucking brothers instead of two friends who go around and fucking rip people off or something. The price like I said wasn't that bad they charge you by the mile so I guess that was cheaper than most moving companies. I didn't know how many miles it was from Ohio to fucking New York but I am guessing it was a lot of fucking miles. I got bored at looking at these guys ugly faces and wrote down the number down on a piece of paper, ripped it in half and placed it on the table. I wanted to see what Jeremy was doing because I haven't seen him since I got home; I just heard he was around doing something. I walked into my room and he wasn't there, then I heard some noise coming from the laundry room and I decided to check that out real quick. And to my surprise he was there fucking cleaning up a storm. "You need any help?" "No, thanks man I am almost done though thanks."

I went back into my room and closed the door; I didn't slam it hard or even closed it fast I just closed it. I felt so many things right about now; I was starting to get a fucking headache. I still couldn't believe we were moving, what the hell I did to deserve this kind of shit. I covered my face with my hands and just took a deep breath; I eventually got up and started walking around in my house to see if my mom or Jeremy needed any help with anything, I asked my mom who was still packing and she said, "Mitch, can you please call the movers and tell them that we are almost ready?" I went back into the kitchen and grabbed the number that was on the counter and called Danny so he can deliverer us a truck as soon as possible. It rang for a minute than finally someone picked up. "Hello is this Danny's movers?" The guy on the other end said yes. I need a truck, I gave the guy our address and told him that we were moving to New York, and we are done packing up." He wrote down some information that I gave him and then he said there will be a truck at your house in 30 minutes. I hung up the phone and told my mom that there will be a truck here in 30 minutes. As soon as the truck comes we will be done packing up and ready to move. I went outside and walked toward the patio, I sat down on the swing that my grandmother gave my mom and took another deep breath. I started swinging but not too fast otherwise I get really nauseous and fucking puke all over the place. I still couldn't believe that we were moving everything is going so fast. I guess I am going to have to get used to shit like that. My life hasn't slowed down in a long time, and sometimes I feel like I am completely and totally fucking lost. My mom came out and took a deep breath and sat down next to me. She smiled and put her hand around me, and said, "Mitch, I am sorry for telling you last minute. But this was such an exciting offer for me and I couldn't pass it up. I hope you would understand." "It's okay mom I was a little upset at first but I will get over it, trust me everything is okay." She smiled again and got up and walked back inside the house. If there is one thing that you must learn about me is that I lie a lot. I am one of those people what they call pathological lire, because it comes easy to me. I lie to hide my real emotions, I lie because I don't feel like talking about something, and I just lie. There is no real reason why I do it, I want to tell the truth but I can't. I know it's not me but I lied again, and every time I do it I hate it because I feel like it is tearing me apart little by little. I lied again to my mom when I told her that I was feeling okay, but honestly I wasn't. I wasn't feeling alright because of Alison and Kristen, well not so much of Kristen but Alison. I never had the best of luck finding a special girl, see sometimes I can be a real dick, and I know that some girls love that. That's cool I get it but I don't want to be a sarcastic asshole my whole life. I want to settle down and find someone special just for me. I tried so hard first with Bethany, that didn't work out so well, and then Beverley. She fucking broke up with me in our favorite spot, every so often that eats me alive. After her I thought I was never going to find someone special for a long time. And then out of nowhere Alison shows her face and I absolutely fall head over heels for the woman. And then it happened, you know after working with her and getting to know her for a while we hit it off. I was able to talk to her and tell her stuff that I couldn't even tell my mom. And now I am moving, I had to break it off again; I never meant to hurt her with this whole Kristen situation. You know that shit sort of just happened, and then Alison got all irate with that shit, primarily because of me. I never meant to get involved with her, and I had no idea it would go this serious. The only thing that I could do now is just put all that shit behind me and think about my future in New York. And possibly go to school, and get a great job and make lots of money and get married. I want to live in a good house with my wife and kids and drive a nice ass car. I want so many things for myself and I guess I just have to start looking at that right now as my main focus.

I heard a loud truck coming down the street and got up and walked inside the house. I walked over to my mom and told her that the movers are here, and we have to get everything ready. She came out and told me that everything is packed and ready to go. Jeremy came out from the kitchen with you'd guess it a Goddamn beer and a Hustler magazine. He is such a typical guy, but thank God he is looking at naked women in magazines instead of… never mind. I poked my head out the window and the movers parked the car in the driveway. The stopped the truck and got out, one of them was walking toward the door. I stepped out and met him halfway and greeted him. "Hello, my name is Mitch, you must be Danny's Movers. "Yes, are you guys ready to load the truck up?" "Can you just give me a minute, I will be right back." I walked back inside the house and walked to my mom's room. She was in the bathroom, "Mom, are we ready? The movers are here to pick up the boxes." "Tell the gentleman that we are ready, start putting some of the boxes in the truck. I will be out in a minute just freshening up." I walked back outside to the living room and out the door. The guy was still standing there; I told him that we are ready. Him and his brother, who came out moments later, lifted up the hatch and lifted up the door. The truck was actually big, and I can see the inside from the window and it was huge. Jeremy came out from my mom's room. But I didn't see him when I walked inside that means he was in the bathroom. Great, now I know what my mom meant when she said she needed to freshen up. Great, now I am going to have that thought running around in my head. I picked up a box and walked to the truck. Jeremy came out with two small boxes and loaded it into the truck. I went back inside and I saw my mom come out of her room, with a box. Wow, this was crazy I didn't have to tell them to help or anything. I think that this is the first time they actually did something by themselves, well congratulations. We got more and more boxes and loaded them into the truck, everything was working like clockwork. I think that we were making perfect timing. I mean we got all the boxes in the living room. Now it was the other rooms that were going to be a problem. I started to walk to my room and grab some of the boxes from there and walked back outside to the truck. I told Jeremy as I was coming back in to start getting all the boxes from his room so we can be finished. I walked back to my room and grabbed two more small boxes, stacked them on top and put them on top. That reminded me, I think that we have a dolly somewhere in the pantry. I went to go check and sure enough we did; now moving is going to be so much easier because I don't have to go back and forth all the fucking time. I brought it to my room, and stacked the remaining four or five boxes on it and carefully pushed it through the living room to the porch. Now it was easier I took one box and brought to the truck and again and again. Until the dolly was empty and brought it back inside, I swung by and gave it to my mom so she can use it. She had a lot of boxes in her room, but luckily enough Jeremy had taken most of it and put it in the truck. She put the last of the boxes on the dolly and pushed it towards me. I grabbed it and slowly and carefully brought it outside. One of the movers finally got off their lazy ass and started to grab some of the boxes off the dolly. I went back inside and grabbed some of the boxes from the kitchen and brought them outside. The other brother walked inside the house and started to grab the boxes from the rooms down the hallway, as he walked back out and put them in the truck.

After several more trips we were finally finished, and let me tell you if I never remembered about that dolly we would've been fucking screwed. My mom did one more check and grabbed her cell phone and called the real estate agent. They talked for about a minute and then she hung up. "The lady who is going to sell the house will be here in two minutes. She said she was in the neighborhood and is going to swing by." "Okay, I said, as I walked around and looked everywhere for one last time. We had all the boxes in the truck; I stopped and stood in the living room and looked around, it was just crazy that we were moving, the whole house looked empty. The lady who my mom just got done talking to drove up and parked near the truck. She got out and started walking toward the house. My mom walked outside and met her halfway; they shook hands and talked where they were standing. I on the other hand walked back to my room to make sure that I had everything, and didn't leave anything behind. Nope, I said everything was in the truck and ready to go. I walked back outside and Jeremy was talking to the movers and my mom was still talking to the lady. I walked outside and sat down on the porch, as the movers were taking the last of the furniture which was my grandmother's old swing set thing. The lady again shook my mom's hand and gave her the keys as she stood near her car and waited. My mom walked back to me and I stood up and Jeremy came back outside, and we stood next to each other and didn't say anything to each other. I guess in this situation you couldn't see anything, you had just had to cherish this moment. Jeremy walked to the movers and told them that we were ready, because they got in the truck and started it up. My mom got the keys and walked toward the car, she looked back at me and smiled as I walked toward the car and waited for my mom to unlock the door. We both got in and Jeremy was walking back to the car and got in the passenger's side and shut the door. I sat in the backset behind my mom's side, because that is my favorite side. Because my dad used to drive when I was little and my mom used to sit in the front seat and I used to sit behind my dad. We waited for one more second, and then drove off. My mom pulled out and waved at the movers and then they stared following us, and just like that we were moving. This was another chance for me to start my life over again, I kept on saying to myself that I know things were bad now but tomorrow I am going to make it better. The lady drove off the opposite way, which is another good thing about being in the back seat; I can see everything behind us. I didn't want to think about Alison or Kristen, but forgetting them is going to be really hard, but I know if I want to start my life over fresh that is what I had to do. We continued to drive as my mom turned on the radio and Jeremy grabbed her hand and held it close to his. I just placed my head on the back of the seat and looked out the window, and simply said two words, good bye.

Chapter 22
Surprise

The drive was taking a long time because there was a lot of traffic. People must have been coming off from work or something, I wasn't too sure of the reason. But I really didn't give a shit why there was so much Goodman traffic, all I wanted to do is get to New York and see our new expensive house. I can imagine just moving into a house or an apartment that costs as much as owning a Goddamn football team. Mom kept on driving and Jeremy was talking about something, I wasn't really paying attention to what he had to say. It is funny I thought I hated the fuck out of Jeremy, but then we became friends. And sometimes I hate him because he is so annoying, I hate myself because I can never make up my mind on anything. We hit a lot of red lights on the way and it was getting annoying, because we kept on fucking stopping every two seconds and it was getting annoying. I told my mom how long it was going to take, and she told me in the calmest voice a couple of hours if that. I had no choice of waiting and waiting and going to sleep. I was tired but I couldn't sleep, I guess I was too excited about moving, even though on the inside I hated it and it made me sick to my Goddamn stomach. I told my mom that I was hungry, and then she answered back that she was a little hungry too. I think that Jeremy blurted out he was hungry to but no one was listening, poor Jeremy. So I think that it was a good idea for us to stop and get something to eat. I felt sort of bad for the movers because they have to stop and wait for us to eat and shit. My mom called one of the movers because I gave her the number, and he picked up. I saw him pick the phone because he was literately right behind us. "I am sorry but everyone is complaining that they are hungry, do you mind if we stop and get something to eat? We will be happy to pay for you if you want something, it is the least we can do." "No thank you, but we were talking and we would like to take a break we weren't sure if you wanted to do that's all." "Okay then it is official the next rest stop we will stop and get something to eat and drink." My mom hung up his phone and said that the next rest stop we are going to stop and get something to eat. I think at that time it brought smiles to everyone's faces especially mine, because I think I was hungrier than everyone else in the car. It felt for hours until we hit the next fucking rest stop, but we saw one just one mile down and got into the left hand lane. We turned into the left lane and made the left turn into the rest stop area. My mom was driving around in Goddamn circles to find a spot and then we saw this yellow Chevy pull out and we decided to park there. Now we fit in perfectly now the truck on the other hand, I didn't know where the hell they were going to park. But low and behold they found a parking spot near a green Honda and a red Pontiac. It was just a couple of feet away from us, and the first thing that everyone did when they got was stretch. I know that it wasn't that long of a drive yet, but I don't think that we were going to get another opportunity to stop. So you might as well stretch and feel good now. They started walking toward us as we waited for them; it was looking like it was going to rain soon. The clouds were getting dark and it was getting a little chilly. We all met up and walked into the building together, now I know what I wanted to eat and that was some pizza, but everyone else I had no idea what the fuck they wanted. "What does everyone want to eat? Because I know what I want to eat and that is some pizza." My mom shouted out I wanted Chinese, and Jeremy said pizza too. And the movers said it didn't matter as they said they ate before they left. As soon we all made up our minds on what we wanted to eat everyone went their separate ways. Thank God that someone likes pizza, because sometimes I hate eating alone it is so boring. Jeremy said he wanted extra pepperoni and sausage on his pizza. Me I am more with vibrant colors I wanted pineapples and green peppers, pretty original but I don't like eating meat on pizzas. Which is weird because I like eating meat, I am not Goddamn vegetarian those guys are fucking wimps. But something eating it on a pizza I don't like, I know that doesn't make any sense but that's the way I guess I always been. When we got to the front, oh we had to wait in a long ass line, but anyway, the girl that was working behind the counter was fucking hot. She was blonde or dirty blonde, couldn't really tell just speculating. Anyway she was about 5'5 and I would say about 130lbs or a little more. She had an amazing body though, and the uniform she was wearing was a little tight, so you can see her figure better that way. Well that is what I thought anyway, me and every other guy who probably seen her today. We gave her our order and she wrote down a piece of paper and gave it to the guy that was working and making the pizzas. Jeremy and I just walked around until we found a table that was close to the actual restaurant. I had no idea where the hell where my mom went or the movers went either, or what the hell they were ordering. They said they were getting something I forgot, but anyway someone finally came to our table and brought us our pizzas. When she laid them on the table I can smell the steam coming from the steam, it smelled so good. Jeremy being the genius put the pizza in his mouth and took a bite. See when something is steaming that means it is hot, and you don't have to be a rocket scientist to figure out you are going to burn the roof of your mouth. And that is what poor Jeremy did, and seconds later he regretted the decision. And not a smart one if I might add. After the pizzas cooled down we devoured them, and washed it down with a couple of sodas. We were cleaning up, and about to get up and throw all our trash away then my mom and the movers came our way. "Mom, did you get something to eat?" "Yes, I had Chinese food and the movers said they weren't hungry." We got up from the table and headed back outside toward the car. It didn't look like it was going to rain, because the clouds were clearing up and the sun was coming out. I guess it was going to rain but it didn't which is a good thing because, I hate driving in the rain. Even though I am not driving, but you get my point. The movers got back into their truck, and my mom Jeremy and I got back into our car. I decided to switch it up this time and I sat behind Jeremy. My mom got in followed by Jeremy and they closed the door as we were off again. Now I asked my mom how long it was going to take, and this time she gave me an answer simply saying, "I don't know honestly, probably another hour or two or three." Great I thought to myself, probably another three hours sitting in the back of car being all cooped up and have no room to stretch my Goddamn legs. I hated going anywhere and never having the opportunity to stretch my legs, I swear that I am short because I never had the chance to grow. I blame my mom for this for buying a car that had no fucking leg room, and I am genius for also buying a car with no room. Well, I guess the only thing that I can do now is go to sleep for a couple of hours and hopefully the next time I wake up we will be in New York.

The next time I fucking woke up, we weren't even there, but my mom nailed down the brake, because the mother fucker in front of us cannot drive for some reason. "Is everyone alright? My mom said worried and breathing heavily." Jeremy said that he was alright, and looked back at me and asked me if I was okay. I replied by saying I was okay and then my mom started driving again. Luckily for us the movers didn't rear end us, otherwise we would've been screwed, and had to call the insurance. And everything would've got really boring and complicated. I put my head back on the side of the seat, and grabbed the blanket, that belonged to my mom and covered myself. I was so tired from moving that I never got a chance to actually relax and get some sleep. I was so tired I just closed my eyes and went to sleep. This time I am hoping I don't wake up with my mom slamming down the Goddamn breaks and almost killing us all half to death. I woke up again not only a few seconds later, and threw the blanket off of me and put it on the side. I just couldn't sleep, I don't know why, I looked outside the window and the sun was going away. And the clouds were getting dark, and it was getting late in the afternoon, around 4 if I am correct. And seconds later rain starting pouring but it was only drizzling. Great rain, it's not that I hated the rain, I mean when I was little I used to go outside and sit and watch the rain for hours. Well that is what my mom told me, but I just don't like being in the rain or any cold weather. Well, since I was awake now, I grabbed my book bag that luckily I never put the bag with the rest of the shit that is in the truck. I grabbed my old worthless MP3 player and praying that it still worked. I call it worthless because I had it for a couple of years, and I am surprised that it still let me transfer all my songs on it. I can't remember all the times that I had dropped it or accidently sat on it or even left it in the rain. I guess for being an old MP3 player it was pretty tough. I got pretty bored and started looking out the window and shit. When you are not driving, FUCK, FUCK, FUCK, I totally forgot about my car. "Mom, my car, I parked it at home and no one... "Don't worry about it, I had one of Jeremy's friends drop it off at our new place. I gave him the new address so it will be fine." I was a little relieved, but another person driving my car I can't stand when someone else drives my shit. It's not them, because they say it never is I am just paranoid about that kind of shit. I am always worrying that something bad might happen to it or something. Yeah, now when I think about it, I didn't feel bad because it is being delivered to the new address whatever the hell that is. I just hope that mother fucker doesn't scratch the fuck out of my car. Or if it is a woman, then I won't feel bad I don't know I am just saying. "What is our new address mom? You never told me before." "Sorry, honey I was so into packing and everything I totally forgot. Our new address is West Side above 59th street, Building One Central Park West and Columbus in Brooklyn" What the fuck, Brooklyn! I am not afraid that I am going to get mugged or something, I am just afraid I am going to get mugged every day. Well maybe I can't even say that, maybe just maybe I will only get mugged like twice a week. I am hoping that my Goddamn car is alright, and nothing happened to it, because it's not like I can get another car or something, you know I bought thought with my money. Or I think I did, sometimes I can't even remember what I did five minutes ago. And speaking of work, where the fuck I am going to work and how far is it going to be from the house. Man it's like all this shit is going really, really fast; I need to slow down. Maybe everything is going to change and maybe everything is going to work out and everything is going to be okay. You know you really can't speculate on shit like this, my mom always said that everything happens for a reason. Now I know that she didn't make that up, because everyone says that shit, but it is true when you really think about it. I still had no fucking idea how long it was going to take to get to New York; I swear this drive was taking a long ass Goddamn time. It felt like we have been driving for hours and hours. I asked my mom how long it was going to take to get there and she still had no idea, great I said. I hate for driving for fucking hours and hours. I mean well the drive wasn't that bad because there wasn't that much traffic as there was before, or I don't know I wasn't paying attention. And the weather couldn't make up its mind, one minute it would rain and the other minute it would be sunny again. And the other good thing is that there wasn't a lot of red lights, so we didn't have to stop that much. So the drive all in all was pretty smooth, but we would've made more progress if we didn't stop for food or anything. But you really can't fault that on anyone specifically because everyone was a little bit hungry. When you are driving, well not me, but when someone is driving you tend to get a little bored. And that sometimes leads to people getting hungry and eating. And the worst part was my mom didn't turn on the radio. I think she knew that I still had my little ass MP3 player and didn't turn on the radio. Well I think that a boring car ride to New York, you think at least my mom would turn on the radio, for her and Jeremy's sake. I can't imagine how Goddamn bored he is right now, well maybe he likes really, really boring car rides for hours. But I guess not turning on the radio wasn't that bad of an idea for them because even though I was listening to music, I can see them talking. But I never really cared what the hell they talked about because it was always boring. See my mom, I don't know about Jeremy, never tires to talk about someone behind their back, unless they absolutely deserve it. And another thing is that my mom never talked about me, unless it was about something good. Yeah, she once in a while talks to her friends about something bad I did, but nothing serious. But all that shit always comes in passing; she never intentionally says bad things about me. So I always feel a little comfortable and never have to feel paranoid if my mom is talking about me behind my back to someone. So, to a lighter side they always talk about some bullshit, and that is always boring, I guess. I didn't know and didn't want to know they were talking about this time. The only thing that I saw is that they were both laughing a lot so it had to be something funny. And Jeremy kept on making Goddamn hand gestures, he does that a lot when he is into the story he is telling. My mom never does that she finds that annoying when people talk with their hands. And I find that moderately annoying too, but it never bothers me that much. But my mom, for some reason it bothers her a lot, I don't know why she never gave me a reason for it. I think she said one time it's hard trying to talk to someone and all you see is their hands flying around all over the place. It is funny because I know that is not the reason that my mom wanted to give me, and I never bothered her for the real reason. But I see her point, I can never talk to someone who talks with their hands, I would get dizzy watching their hands fly all over. But like I said, it never really bothered me that much so I don't give a fuck. All this Goddamn thinking I was getting a headache, and I didn't feel good to make matters worse. I don't know what it was, I felt exhausted and weak at the same time, and maybe I am coming down with the flu. Or maybe I am a hypochondriac, you know someone who always believes that they are sick all the Goddamn time. I always found those people funny as hell, for some reason. And I know that was mean to make fun of someone, but if you really think about it I was never making fun of them. I just found those guys funny, because they think that there is something wrong with them when in actuality there wasn't. In some weird way I guess I was like that, sometimes I swear I get sick all the time and the next day I feel fine. And I guess in a way that makes me some sort of hypocrite, well who the fuck cares. Everyone is a Goddamn hypocrite, and there is nothing you can do about it. Man how long is it going to take to get to New York, and soon as I was getting more frustrated, it was a miracle. I saw a sign, and it wasn't like one of those Goddamn spiritual signs, but an actual sign like the ones you see when you are driving on a major highway. I was so happy, it said New York, was only a couple of miles away I was so happy.

I told my mom just in case she missed the sign, but she told me that she saw it, and she knows what she is doing. Oh yeah, that is another thing with my loving but sometimes toffee-nosed mom, she think that she knows everything. She won't get mad but she will feel a little upset that you are trying to how they say talk over her. And I was never the one to get smart with my mom, because in a weird way my dad raised me to be better than that. I can remember this one time, that there was a question I asked Jeremy and I knew the answer to it. Well, I thought I knew the answer for it and Jeremy didn't know so he asked my mom. And she swore all high and mighty that she knew what she was talking about. And before Jeremy could the whole question, my mom answered it and says that it was the correct answer. And the answer that she gave both Jeremy and I knew that it didn't make any sense. But she is the type of person if she got something wrong she will get all upset and complain about it. Oh yeah, so Jeremy ended up knowing the answer to the question, and my mom of course got all upset. She said that it was a stupid question and got mad at Jeremy when he started laughing. He wasn't laughing to be rude, he was laughing because my mom was getting all upset over a question. And honestly it wasn't that big of a deal, but knowing my mom she is very competitive with that kind of shit. Well enough of this endless Goddamn bullshit, the important thing is that we finally, let me repeat finally, reached New York. That put a smile on my mom's face and Jeremy was happy so, he can get up and stretch. Poor Jeremy was all scrunched up in the front seat, but he was a warrior he didn't complain one bit. I had a feeling that everything was going to be alright, even though it sucked because for the like hundredth Goddamn fucking time I have to pack up and move all my shit. You know the one thing that my mom has done is never put my feelings in consideration, about how I feel about all the moving we did. She never once considered what I had to say, or if she did it was fucking brief. But then she always apologized and said that everything was going to be okay. Well I have something to say mom, everything is not okay, because I always have to leave when things are starting to get good. Shit, she does this all the time and sometimes I get so fucking pissed at her but what can I do. I am at the age where I can leave and live on my own, I just need some fucking money, and hopefully then I can leave. I left Alison, after Beverly I thought I was never going to meet someone special again. And then it got all complicated with Kristen. I know I say and complain about the same fucking things, but I can't help it. How would you feel if you met someone, and it got really weird because you started talking and messing with another girl? Some people may say that is cheating, but I don't see it that way. Yes don't get me wrong, I did kiss her but it didn't mean a Goddamn thing, and I don't know how many times I need to fucking explain myself. I had to say to both of them and I didn't want to admit it but I was about to cry. I mean come on, it's Ohio you know what the hell is there in Ohio, but know I had to meet two amazing girls and ruin it with both of them. Fuck it I didn't care, there was something about New York that I thought in my mind I was going to be alright I hope. We finally made it to New York, and the fucking traffic there was insane, you couldn't even get around Goddamn corners. My mom had a hard time finding the exact address of the new place we were supposed to move into. And Jeremy fell asleep so he was no help; man that guy is so freaking lazy sometimes. That was pretty mean, but it is true good guy in heart, probably but I don't care. Anyway we continued to drive and drive, my mom stopped the car and she couldn't find the place. She parked the car along the side of the street and let the movers get in front of us. I think that they would know where the fuck the place was. I don't know why mom insisted of driving first. It's the fucking movers, they of all people know where the fuck to go. But like I said before my mom wants to do everything her way, and freaking insisted of driving first. She knows where New York is, and how to get there she just sucks when it comes to finding places. The movers got out after they parked the car and walked toward the car. My mom rolled down the window and spoke to them. "I am sorry I am having a hard time finding the place that we are supposed to be moving into." "Don't worry about it, I know where it is. I remember I got a call from the real estate lady a couple of hours ago, and she told me the address." "Oh, then I have an idea, why don't you drive and we will follow you and you can show us where the hell our building, apartment, trailer, house or whatever the fuck is." The drivers smiled and walked away, and that is like the first time in a long time that I heard my mom curse. I guess she was pretty tired of driving too and wanted to fucking find the place as much as me and Jeremy. The movers got in their truck and starting driving off, and then we followed. I don't know why the Goddamn movers didn't tell us that the fucking real estate lady, or whatever she did, the lady called and gave them the address. See I had a feeling that my mom was going to have a hard time finding the place, that part was obvious. So we starting to follow them and they were driving fast. I guess they wanted to go home or something, I don't know, I didn't care. We were paying them it's not like going slow or going fast was going to affect anything like that. Fortunately they found the place, and it was half decent, it took a while but I think that I was the only one who was FUCKING pissed at the excuse that was staring us in the face. I mean my mom or Jeremy didn't say anything about it at first, but come on I know they were a little mad. I blame the Goddamn real estate lady; I mean she described the house to my mom when they were talking in the front yard. You know when she came over and they were talking and shook hands and everything. There my mom didn't seem to have any questions or anything of that sort. And the lady was being real descriptive; I heard some of what she was saying, and she was building this house all high and mighty and everything. And to tell you the truth, the house that we were moving into was pretty decent, but it was just a little smaller than the one we left in Ohio. The Goddamn lady didn't even show us where the house was, my mom said that something had come up and it was a true emergency that she had to take care of. I mean she still couldn't show us where the fuck the house was. What lady who works with selling and buying homes doesn't show you where the hell the house is. I think that I was the only person that was generally upset about this whole thing. We got out and walked to the movers, who were parked along the side of the street. My mom and Jeremy got out first then I got out next and the first thing that we did is stretch because our legs really needed some of that. "What the hell mom, aren't you just a little upset that the house that we have to be living in really, really sucks." "I know that the house isn't what we expected. And I am a little upset that the lady didn't show us the house, but it is our new home and we have to make the best of it." Again Jeremy didn't care one bit; I mean I don't think he cared. He had to care just a little bit this was the place that we were living for now. Well that is if my undeceive mother doesn't decide to move again, then this is the place we will be living for now. We walked toward the house, and the movers already lifted up the hatch and the sliding door and started unloading the boxes in front of the house. My mom took out the keys that the lady had gave her, and walked toward the front door. She opened the door and pushed it all the way open. And she was sort of surprised how big it was, I mean the inside of the house was big. So I guess that was going to be good, well even though it is only three of us. Well maybe two, depends if I go to school. Man school, I don't know what went wrong with that shit. I am like fucking 18 and I haven't been in school in such a long time. Maybe I'll get lucky enough and get accepted somewhere, let's just hope they are pretty accepting of me. Because I went to school when I was little I think I remember that, but I got home schooled. And that was for a long time, honestly I don't know how long. I wouldn't even know what to fucking major in if I got accepted anywhere. And before all that shit how about if I have to do high school like start from there and work my way up or something. Man I have no idea everything is so confusing.

We walked inside the house and kind of gave our own selves a tour since they was no lady or anything. I made my way further into the house first, and made my way upstairs. When I walked upstairs I noticed that there were three bedrooms on this floor. I walked into the biggest one and that must've been the master bedroom. On the right hand side of that there were the other two bedrooms. I walked inside the one that was the farthest away from the master, and I noticed that it was the same size of the room that I had before. The layout was different but it was welcoming. So I guess that would be mine. And there was the other bedroom; I don't know what my mom would use that for, probably a study or a guest room or something. I walked inside my bedroom, and checked the closets and everything. The closet in this room was a little smaller but it didn't seem to bother me. Thank God for me I didn't have that much stuff to begin with. I walked out from my room and walked downstairs, my mom and Jeremy were already checking out the rest of the house. I walked inside the kitchen because every good house needs a good kitchen. And it was decent, a little bigger than the one we left back home, but I don't think that my mom is going to complain about the size. I walked out the kitchen and starting walking around the rest of the house. I made my way to the backyard, and it was a little bigger than what we had. In the left hand corner there was a tree, so I guess that was good. There was enough room to build a shed, just in case if we wanted to put some extra stuff in there. I walked from the backyard to the front, there wasn't a front yard just the front and the street and shit. There weren't a lot of cars driving in the street. Actually it was pretty quite so that was good; I don't like a lot of noise. My mom and Jeremy must've been still walking around the house, I wonder if they saw their room yet? I walked to the movers and starting giving them a hand, they were pretty fast workers and they were almost done too. I grabbed the boxes that they had placed on the ground and starting bringing them in the house. Jeremy came down from wherever the hell he was and started giving me a hand too. I don't know what the hell my mom was doing, but she finally came down and decided to help for once. We all stated putting boxes inside the living room area. The good thing about this house it was like super clean, who ever must have lived here before really cleaned the hell out of this place. And another good thing is that the living room had wood flooring. And it wasn't the cheap ass Goddamn wood like in most houses; no we had the expensive wood. Grant it, it was a little dirty but nothing that a little polish and a buffer can't take care of. The only thing is that we needed buy a buffer, and no one knows how much they run. Or where the hell to buy one, I think that my mom tried to buy one from some place don't really know of the name, anyway it wasn't working so she got pissed off and threw it away. Instead of doing what normal people do in these situations, like either getting it fixed or returning it. There were still some more boxes outside, and all the boxes were gone from the truck. My mom walked to the guys, and paid them their money, and said thank you, as they smiled and walked away. They walked to the truck and got in, hoping that they don't reverse and hit our Goddamn car. They left, and we were left with a couple more boxes and a lot inside the house. The weather was starting to get good again the sun was coming out, but it was getting late so I don't know if I had time to do anything. "Mom, where is my car? I wanted to drive around today." "Look in the garage she said, as she was bringing more boxes in the house." I frantically walked to the garage; the stupid garage door was locked, so I had to walk around and lift the actual garage. And thank God my car was there, and nothing happened to it. I guess in the mist of all of the moving, and everyone having mixed feelings about the move. Everyone just forgot about the car, but it was fine. I asked my mom for the keys and walked back outside to the car. "Don't come home late, we are going out to eat dinner tonight." I said okay, as the last of the boxes where being brought into the house. I unlocked the car door, and got in, I made sure that nothing was stolen and fortunately nothing was. I had to thank that person who ever fucking decided to drive my car in the first place, for safely bringing it over here and without stealing anything too. I slowly drove out of the garage and got out so I could close the garage door, which reminded me I need to tell my mom we need to buy an automatic garage closer thing, whatever the hell there called. So that way no one needs to get out of their car and close the God forsaken piece of shit. I had no idea where the hell I wanted to do or where the hell I wanted to go, the only thing that was certain was, I needed to make some changes in my life.

And probably this city was going to do that for me, it was too early to tell anything like that anyway. I checked my wallet, and I had enough money, to buy a decent camera. You know since I am in New York I might as well buy a digital or one of those really good photographer cameras. Well, I didn't have that much now that I think about it but I did somewhere in the ball park of $70 to $100. And with that I should be able to buy a camera from a bargain place. I kept on driving and I finally saw one, it was only a few miles away from our new home, so the drive all in all was about 10-15 minutes not bad when you think about it. There weren't a lot of cars, there was traffic but not a lot so I was able to successfully turn into the lane and pull in and park along the side of the street for this camera place. And just when I got out and was about to go inside I saw someone that looked very familiar to me. She was going in the same camera place that I was going into so I followed her. I know that's wrong, and I wasn't fucking technically stalking her or something but she really did look very familiar. I went in and tried looking for her not really caring about the camera right now. She was at the back of the store looking at films and different types of stuff. Even from the back she looked very familiar, it was weird, and I felt like I was having these feelings. Like I met this person before, there was only one thing to do I walked up to her and tapped her on the shoulder. She didn't get scared or jump or hesitate or anything of that sort, she simply just turned around and said hi. After seeing her face, my heart was pounding, I felt like it was going to fall right out of my chest. My palms were sweaty, and my mouth was dry, I felt like time and space stood still, and the only thing that I said. The only word that came out of my mouth was, Beverly?

Chapter 23
Second Chance

I couldn't believe it, it was Beverly, but she was smiling at me but looked confused. I guess it was such a long time that she forgot. Beverly I said again, "It's me Mitch, remember? And it took only a second and then it clicked, "Oh my God, she said, she hugged me, what are you doing here? "I live here now, my mom got a better job and we moved so I live just a couple of blocks down from this place. I believe it is 144th and 15th street in Brooklyn." "What are you doing here? I said to her happy to see her again. "My mom and I are just staying for a couple of days here in town, we are visiting relatives. She sent me to buy some film and possibly a better camera. My mom wants to get a new one, because our family loves taking pictures, and I was driving for a long time until I found this place." "That is so crazy, I said, I was driving too and I needed a camera too for all the sights. See I been to New York when I was little with my dad, but that was such a long time ago. And things probably changed so I wanted to go around and take some pictures of N.Y.C." "So what time are you heading back? Or can you stay for a while?" "I am not sure; I still have time because I told them I wanted to go shopping to so it might be a while." "That's cool, maybe we can hang out or I can go shopping with you." "Yeah, you go shopping with me, real funny. I thought boys hated going shopping especially with girls." "I found my stuff, hey meet you at the register?" I said okay, and then I realized that I didn't buy the camera that I wanted. I wanted to buy it before Beverly left, I searched and I searched then I found one that I wanted. I quickly grabbed it and rushed to the counter, luckily Beverly was still there. I waited behind her as she was pulling out her wallet for the stuff. It is crazy, I thought never in a million years I would see her again. And here we are in a video store we bump into each other. I guess fate works in mysterious ways sometimes. But there was one thing bothering me, as she was finishing paying for her stuff, I wanted to talk about why she left me in the first place. I mean she really didn't have an explanation or anything. All I wanted to do is just talk about that night, and sort of get some reasoning about why she did what she did. But here lies the problem, did *she* want to talk about it. She has to feel some sort of way about that. Beverly finished paying and I walked next. The guy behind the counter grabbed my camera and rung it up. I paid the guy and he put it in a bag, as he gave me my change. I took the bag, smiled, and walked towards Beverly, as she was waiting by the door. "Is it cool I come with you while you go shopping, my mom is just moving everything in the new house? And we can catch up, you know talk." "Sure, but first I need to get a few more things for my mom, so if you want to tag along you're more than welcome to." I just smiled and walked with her as we walked outside. I didn't care where we were going or how long everything was going to take. The only thing that I cared about is her. We crossed the street, and the weather was getting cold. The night was coming and the wind was picking up. I guess being in a city you have to get used to cold nights. The only thing that I don't want to get used to is cold and lonely nights. "My car is right here, hey why don't you get your car and meet me here. Or you can pull up and I can meet you somewhere." "Okay she said, as she crossed the street." I waited and just thought about everything that happened with us. I wanted to know why she did what she did, there had to be a right moment to bring that up. She started driving up, and she honked, so I got inside my car and pulled away from the side of the street. She pulled up and I got behind her. I had no idea where we were going, but there was something inside of me that didn't care. I feel like my whole life is changing now. I mean everything that happened with Alison back home, and then Kristen that was so confusing with the both of them. There were so many special things about the both of them, but I feel strange inside like none of that mattered. I felt like this was fate, destiny like I was meant to be with Beverly, I strongly believe that. I don't know what it is, I want to be with her but I wanted to be with Alison and weirdly enough I wanted to be with Kristen too. I feel like this is breaking me in two and at the same time I don't seem to mind one bit. I guess being with Alison and Kirsten brought me to this point. I guess it was in my heart to be with Beverley, and I liked that. I know that things at this point where still a little uncertain, and she probably doesn't want to be with me right now. Or she may have found someone already and things may be a little too late, but I don't care about that. I blame myself for letting her go, if I loved her as much as I said back then why did I let her go. Io should've fought for her, and tried to make her see things straight. I should've made her seen that I was the guy that she was looking for the whole time, and I was never going anywhere. We finally made it to the place where Beverly needed to go and it was a bank. I guess she had to make a deposit, or a withdrawal. She parked along the side of the street near all the other cars and got out. I was fortunate enough to find a parking spot behind her car, and pulled in. I got out and walked up to her and walked with her inside the bank. The line in there wasn't that bad only a few people and it seemed like it was moving. Sooner or later Beverly made it to the front of the line, after a few exchanges she got some cash and headed back out. "That was quick" I said, walking with her back outside. "Yeah, I am surprised that the line today was short, usually I have to wait for hours." She headed back to her car, but I stopped her before she got in. "I know that this may be the wrong time to say this, or to even talk about this." "What is it?" she said, looking right into my eyes. "I know that you had a good reason for leaving me the last time we were going out. But I don't want you to leave again. What I am trying to say is I loved you back then and I love you more now, and I want to be with you always." She continued to look at me, almost crying and not saying a word, she was clutching her keys in her hand, as the night got colder. She leaned in closer and hugged me, but she didn't let go. I got my arms and wrapped her close to me. Just standing there in the cold New York City night, in front of her car as other cars and people walking by can see everything. She looked up at me, still hugging me, then she let go and she just smiled and kissed me on the cheek. She got into her car, as I closed her door for her. I walked to my car, and got in. I closed my door and just smiled. I guess everyone deserves a second chance.

Chapter 24
Starting Over

Beverly started driving up again; maybe this would be a good time to call my mom. She tends to worry a lot if I don't call her, tell her that I am alright or even come home to late. I grabbed my cell phone from my coat pocket and quickly scrolled down the address book. I called her number and waited for the ring, and waited for the ring, and then she finally picked up. "Mom, it's me, listen I bumped into Beverly, you know her right, but anyway we are going to go hangout. So I will call you later and let you know what time I am coming home." "Okay, she said, that's nice Jeremy and I are just painting the house, don't come home too late." I won't I said as I hung up the phone, and continued to follow Beverly wherever she was going. She finally stopped, and wouldn't you know it she stopped at her house. This was great, I am always sort of nervous when I have to meet new people, how about I make a fucking mistake or something. She pulled in and so did I, she turned off the car and got out and walked toward my car. "Let me just give these things to my mom real quick, you can come in if you want?" "No, thank you, its fine I'll just wait here for you." She smiled and walked back to the front door, she took out the key opened the door and went in. I just continued waiting, I really didn't care how long it was going to take, because I think that my mom and Jeremy had the house under control and they should be finish painting and cleaning up very soon. I still couldn't believe it, you know I always thought what if I never see Beverly again, and it was such a coincidence that we bumped into each other in the same store, in the same city. But now I feel like what is Alison and Kirsten doing right now, I wonder if they are still thinking of me. I had both of their numbers in my phone, and if I called them would I be cheating on Beverly. Because I said that last time with Kristen, oh we are just friends and look how out of control that shit got. I mean I could call, Beverly is in the house, and she wouldn't have to know. And besides if she did find out who cares we are adults and I can make a phone call to friends if I wanted to, I don't have to feel weird about anything. I picked up my phone and called Alison, I was a little nervous we haven't spoken since the day I told her I was moving. The phone was ringing, and it rang for about a second more and then her voice mail came up. I hesitated and didn't leave a message, it's not because I was scared I just didn't know what to say. I placed my phone back into my coat pocket and waited for Beverly to come out. Man girls take the longest time doing whatever they need to do it is really funny. Well it's not that funny on the opposite viewpoint, we guys have to wait for the girls to take their time, and for some reason we never mind waiting. Beverly finally came out and she changed her top, I guess that's why she was taking so long. She walked towards my car and opened the passenger side door and hopped in. "So, where we going?" I just smiled at her, "You're leaving your car here?" "Yes, there is no point for us to follow each other everywhere we go; besides I'll give you the address so you can drop me back off, that way, well you know." She just laughed as she closed the door and I took off. "Are you hungry? I said I know a great place that makes good pizzas if you want some." "That sounds like fun; I can go for some pizza. Honestly I haven't had pizza in such long time, I am so hungry." I laughed as we drove around New York finding a pizza place. And then it hit me, two things first, we are in New York, and second there are like a hundred pizza places on every corner. But here lays the hard part finding the right one. "There are so many pizza places, Bev which one do you want to eat at?" "It doesn't matter, I am just hungry pizza is pizza to me, they all taste the same. Now, I was going to argue my point that not all pizzas taste the same, but I don't feel like arguing and over something as Goddamn stupid as fucking food. We found a place, and the place was kind of small but it didn't matter to the both of us. We parked behind a huge ass truck; we couldn't even see anything in front of the stupid shit. I turned off the car and we both got out, as soon we both stepped out we can smell the pizza, it smelled good. We closed the door and walked toward the pizza place. We walked inside and walked toward the main counter, there they had a menu that Beverly and I both looked at for a second. They had all types of pizzas, and you can load them up with all types of toppings too. I waited and then the person who works behind the counter finally decided to show his ugly face. I know that may be a figure of speech, but the guy really had an ugly face. I told him that I wanted a slice of plain. I wasn't in the mood for any toppings and I didn't want to pay extra either. Beverly was next and she ordered a plain slice too. I guess she didn't want to spend extra on the toppings either. Pizza places in New York tend to get pretty expensive, so that being said. He took the slices that were out and placed them in the oven for them to get hot. We stepped to the side so the next people in line can order. "So, how have you been what have you been up to? " I said. "You know nothing really, just hanging out, and trying to go to school in the fall." "Oh that's cool, I am trying to go to school to, my mom has been home schooling me for a long time. She didn't want me to go to a public school she didn't think that I was ready and she couldn't bear to see me go." "So that's that I have been in school and out of school more times than anyone I think. And besides we moved a lot so that didn't help matters." "Sucks, she said, what college are you looking at right now?" "I don't know I still have been looking, and I found some brochures so I was going through those." Our pizzas came and the guy put them on plates and gave it to us. We took them and found a table and sat down, it was good because the table was sort of far from everyone else. I don't like to eat when there are a lot of people around. It's not them I just to like my own privacy when I eat food. The pizza was steaming so it was a good idea for the both of us to wait, until it cooled down. But that didn't stop Beverly. She grabbed a knife and a fork and piece by piece she ate the pizza. I can see her blowing inward every time she took a bite. And it was right there while she was putting another piece in her mouth, I had to ask. "Hey, I have a question, why did you decide to leave me the last time we were dating?" She was chewing on the bite that she took, and then swallowed. "I don't know, I guess I felt like I was rushing into everything to fast, and I needed some time for me." "I understand, I am just glad that you're back even if it is just for a couple of days. We finished eating our pizzas and decided it was getting late so we decided to leave. "Hey what's your address, it is getting late and my mom worries a lot." She just smiled and said, East Side Building One between Fifth and Madison." We made our way to the car, and I unlocked the door, she got in and sat down. I sat down next and drove off. That damn truck was still in front of us, but luckily for us there was no car behind us. So reversing wasn't that big of a deal.

We drove for about a minute and then we finally reached her relatives place. The building that they lived in was really nice. I never really got a chance to look at it before. She got out and thanked me for a lovely night; she gave me her number so we can do this again sometime. I quickly saved it to my phone before I forget. I got out and walked around to her, we hugged and she said bye. She walked to her front door and rang the doorbell. Someone came and let her in and she walked inside. I walked back to the car and sat back inside. I drove off and couldn't wait to see what the house looked like. I remember dropping her off seeing a shortcut for going home and wouldn't you know I took it. After several minutes I was home, and I pulled in the driveway. The garage door was closed so I couldn't even pull into the garage. I turned off the car and got out. It was pretty quite outside. I walked to the front and rang the doorbell; I didn't have the keys yet. Jeremy let me in and I walked in and said hi. I shut and locked the door when I came in, and everything looked nice. I guess Jeremy could tell by my face that everything was done. "Yep, he said, we finished unpacking, painting and cleaning up and it only took a couple of hours." I walked upstairs to my room, and I was pretty excited about the changes that they did. Everything is just how I wanted it to be, and it was spacious too they way they organized everything. Everything was put away and my bed was made, I left and looked around in the other rooms. Wow, I said, everything was so clean. I have to give them their congratulations. I walked back to my room, and I just lay down in my bed. I couldn't wait until tomorrow. Not because of the new house, or I get to see Beverly again but one reason that was more important than that. It was my mom's birthday, and this time it was my turn to do something special for her, because she has done a lot for me.

Chapter 25
Happy Birthday, Mom

I didn't mean to fall asleep, but that is exactly what I did. I woke up and it was fucking morning. I was so upset all I wanted to do is just to take a nice long nap and wake up. Well, since I am up now might as well see what the hell everyone is doing. I got up from my bed, heard a noise, and walked downstairs. I heard it coming from the kitchen, I peaked in hoping that no one was trying to fucking break into our house or shit. And it was just Jeremy making a Goddamn racket early in the morning. He was rearranging some dishes that my mom put away. There were some empty boxes lying around on the kitchen floor. Some were labeled and some weren't. I wonder if Jeremy knew that it was my mom's birthday today, so I decided to ask him. "Jeremy, do you know that today is my mom's birthday?" "Of course, kiddo, there is that Goddamn word again, if he keeps calling me that I am going to KILL HIM, I bought your mom a card and something special." I smiled because I wanted to be polite, Jeremy fucking buying something for my mom he has been broke for the longest time. I don't know where he got the money from; he hasn't worked in a long time. Since he got fired from working at the construction site, he has been trying to get work but I guess it is really hard for him. I left and started looking for my mom, she was still somewhere in the house, she just had to be unless she was out. But I would've someone come in or at least

211

saw a car pull up. I walked toward the back yard area and she wasn't there. Then I decided to walk up the stairs and check her room, and like I guessed it she was there. I can hear her working in the bathroom. I knocked on the door, to see what she was doing, and she was cleaning around the sink area. There were more boxes on the floor; I guess she was rearranging shit too. "Morning mom, I said, waiting until later today to tell her happy birthday, because it was too early." "Morning honey, she said, Jeremy, you and I are all are going out to eat soon for breakfast so don't eat anything now." Okay, I said as I walked back down the stairs, and back into the kitchen. I was so hungry; I hope we have food in the fridge or something. And when I looked inside nothing, then I remembered we were going to go out and eat. But when how much longer was it going to take, I walked back upstairs to my mom. "How much longer mom, I am hungry." "Soon, let me finish up in here, and clean up the bathroom real quick. Go help Jeremy, he is down there by himself, go spend some time with him." Fuck, it was cool when he took me to the strip club, but now I *have* to spend time with him. It's bad enough when your mom is forcing you to spend time with someone you don't want to spend time with. I mean we never really got to spend any time with each other; we just sort of you know hung out. Sure he took me places and drops me off and picked me up. And sure we talked once in a while, but we never really spent any real time with each other. Now my mother wants me to go downstairs and help him and spend some time with him. So in the interest of being Goddamn nice I decided that I was going to go down there and help him out. Unless that is he didn't need my help and then hell I am all for it. But most likely he would not because he has a lot of shit to do, but he wants to spend some time with me too I can tell. I think that he said since I am getting older, and school wasn't going that great for me growing up, he wants to spend some time before I get to old or something. But I think what he really meant to say is that I am growing up in front of everyone's eyes and he would like to spend some time with me before it was too late. But who the fuck cares, I never *really* wanted to spend time with the guy, just wanted him to like me or something like that. I made my way downstairs and into the kitchen and asked Jeremy if he needed any help or anything. And can you guess what his response was, "Sure kiddo, I can use a hand, I am almost done cleaning up the kitchen. When I am done it is going to look like a million dollars." First of all I am fucking 18, and not a kid and I hate when he calls me that shit, sometimes I just want to… whatever there's nothing I can do now. So I decided to help him out, I grabbed the old boxes of the stuff he already put away and took them to the backyard patio. There were two large blue containers so I opened one of them, tore down the boxes down to size and threw them in there, and closed the lid. I waited before I went back inside; the weather was so calm and so uplifting. I could tell that today was going to be a good day. I headed back inside fast because I left the door open, in nice warm weather bugs usually tend to fly around and I don't want any to come in the house. I closed the door, walked over to the sink and quickly washed my hands with soap. Jeremy still needed my help with more boxes, so I tore them down again went outside, threw them away, came back in and washed my hands again. He asked me if there was a step stool somewhere in the house. And to be perfectly honest I had no idea, I yelled for my mom who was probably still in the bathroom. She didn't answer so I went upstairs again and looked for her; she was in her closet cleaning and shit. "Do we have a step stool in this house?" "I think there is one in the garage, did you look there?" I walked back downstairs and headed to the garage, now the garage was the only thing that was a mess. It wasn't that bad but I have seen worse. There were boxes everywhere, and old pieces of carpet that must've been left by the people who lived here before us. Finding the Goddamn step stool was so hard; I had to search around for everything and still had no luck. There were old buckets and more boxes in the corner, now I could tell that they were not ours because they were not labeled, but it was fucking disgusting. I mean couldn't the people who lived here before actually take the time to empty their shit out. I finally found the Goddamn step stool, it was behind more boxes and shit. It was a little smaller then I would picture it, but I guess that's why they call it a step stool and not a ladder. I grabbed it and brought it to Jeremy who was still working in the kitchen. I handed him the stool, and he just smiled. He opened it and straightened it out; he got on the very top, looked down at me and said, "Sport, can you give me those dishes please?" I handed him the dishes as he placed them on the top of the cabinet. He took each one and sort of dusted them off and stacked them on top of each other. My mom has these very expensive china dishes, and she is always taking care of them and making sure that they are clean. Now poor Jeremy has to clean them and make sure that they don't break as he is stacking them on top of the cabinet. They are used for when my mom has company over, but she never has that many people over at a time, actually I can't remember the last time she even had someone over to tell you the truth. She has all of this nice ass chinaware and never uses them. I swear it's like she is waiting for the perfect opportunity to use them or something. There was more stuff on the floor, which I needed to hand Jeremy so I guess that my job wasn't over just yet. Even though it just started and even though I wanted to do anything else but this shit right now. I hated spending time with anyone that I didn't need to spend time with, you know. It's like I am being forced to spend time with someone, well whatever I guess you get the idea. I handed Jeremy the rest of the stuff that was on the ground, it wasn't anything, just an old tea kettle and more dishes and shit. I threw the rest of the boxes away, the stupid containers were getting filled pretty quickly and I needed to put them in the front for the recycle guy. If they still do that shit that is. I was finally free to do whatever I wanted; I walked back upstairs and asked my mom if we were still going out. I was getting to the point where I was getting really, really hungry. She said yes, and told me to get ready or she will leave me. My mom loves to joke around sometimes, and no matter how bad they are I always laugh. Come on it's your mom, if she makes a joke and you know deep down it fucking sucks you have to laugh. My mom never was the type of person to actually make jokes on purpose. She wasn't funny or anything, and I can't remember the times that she tried to be funny and it didn't pan out. I can remember even at dinner when it was our real Goddamn family she tried to be funny. Now grant it some of the things that she says are funny, but that is once in a blue moon. Well I think that I had enough of bashing of my mother I decided to get dressed, and it was still pretty early too. I would say it was around 11:00 A.M., so it was just the perfect time, because it just the right time for breakfast and it wasn't too late for lunch. I rushed into my room, and just got undressed. I threw everything on the floor, since I didn't have a hamper or anything. And I just changed and threw on some cargo shorts with an old T-shirt. It wasn't old like dirty but old like I haven't worn it in a while. Some people usually get the wrong misconception of the word; I think it is pretty funny sometimes. I rushed back into my mom's room, and she was also getting ready. But since she was a woman she was taking longer than I expected, but I guess that happens when you are a girl and not a boy. We guys take pride that we finish getting ready faster than girls, it's in our genes or something, I don't know. Let me stop rambling on about some bullshit, like I said I have a tendency to do that sometimes. I left my mom's room and I can hear her say that she was ready. Now Jeremy was somewhere in the house, because when I got back downstairs he wasn't in the kitchen anywhere. I hope that he wasn't taking long, because it will go against everything I said. And like I fucking guessed, fucking Jeremy was taking forever, man he was slower than my mom when getting ready. Sometimes I wonder what the hell he does that takes him so damn long. Finally Jeremy was done, and not a minute to soon. It was already like 11:30, and breakfast was almost over. I kept on rushing Jeremy; it was pretty funny because my mom kept on rushing him too. What the hell is he doing, he is going to make us late. I was going to go up there and fucking say something but I don't want to get into any shit with him. He is not the best person to argue with, because if something is his fault he will never say sorry for it. Jeremy finally made his way downstairs and all he did was change his Goddamn shirt. All that shit for one person to change his Goddamn shirt, you have to be joking. We all rushed out of the house and into my mom's car. She always says that she is going to buy a new one, and with this job that is starting soon, she just might. Then my mom said something that just put a smile on my face, "Relax Mitch, the place we are going to serves breakfast all day. It's part of their special that they have all day. Awesome, I said, now I can take back what I said about Jeremy taking too damn long; well on the other hand maybe not. We all got in and closed the door, my mom started the car and we drove off. 24-7 breakfast here we come, well here I come I was hungrier than everyone in the car. I had no idea how far this place was from the house, but I couldn't wait.

We finally made to the breakfast joint and there were a lot of cars in the parking lot, great that can only mean one thing, service was slow. Well, I can't really make that judgment because many people could be finishing up or something. We parked near an old pickup truck, my mom stopped the car and everyone got out. We walked inside and walked to the front where the waitress was seating everyone. "Hello, she said, welcome how many?" "Three please; can we have the smoking section?" She smiled and led us to a booth that allowed smoking. Smoking, that can only mean one thing, Goddamn Jeremy. He has to smoke everywhere he goes I am surprised that he isn't dead. We all sat down, and the waitress asked us what we wanted to drink. My mom and Jeremy both said orange juice, and I said iced- tea. She wrote down the orders and gave us the menus as she said she will be right back. We all looked through the menus, and within the very first seconds I knew what I wanted to order. It was the basic food items but it was still good, it was basically eggs, toast, bacon, hash browns, and pancakes. It was like a freaking combo meal I loved it. My mom was still looking and Jeremy placed down the menu and pulled out a cigarette. I swear we are all going to die from second hand one fucking day, why doesn't that bastard just quit. I mean he came close one time, he went a whole year without smoking but then the little monkey on his shoulder told him to start up again, now he hasn't put them down. I really don't give a shit if he smokes or not, if he dies then it will be my mom and I like the good old times. But I will feel sort of sad, I mean he has been nothing but nice to me. But the one problem that I can't stand is when he blows a lot of smoke and I know that he doesn't do it on purpose but I swear he blows it in my face. If I had the chance one day I am going to grab the cigarette he is smoking and make him swallow it and watch him puke it up. The waitress came back around and with her little white note pad. She gave us our drinks, and took out her little white note pad. "Are you guys ready to order?" I didn't wait until my mom or Jeremy to go first. "I would like the combo meal thing, the toast, pancakes and stuff." My mom ordered next, "I will have the pancake special." And Jeremy was the last one to place his order, figures. "Yes, sweetheart can I get the bacon and eggs combo, with extra toast." She wrote down everything and walked away. I was so thirsty I nearly finished my damn tea in one sitting, not knowing if there were refills on them or not. I put the cup back down because I don't want to get full on tea, and then use the bathroom like minutes later or something. All this talk of food and then speaking of food our shit finally came. I can smell the steam coming from our plate's man I couldn't wait. The waitress placed our plates by who ordered what, and as soon as she was done she smiled and said, "Is there anything else I can get you guys today." "Yes, can I get another refill on my iced-tea please, smiling when I said it?" "Sure, no problem I will be right back." She took the cup and walked away. And I started eating, my mom and Jeremy traded portions of their food with each other, they were laughing and having a good time. I smiled but then it was getting to the point where they didn't even touch their food for minutes at a time. I started eating the pancakes first, I always used strawberry syrup, because it is my favorite and tastes good. There was only like three pancakes so it wasn't that bad. Then I ate the toast and the hash browns. The hash browns were not the regular ones, but scrambled up. I guess it taste better that way, I remember having it like this one time and it was actually better. My mom and Jeremy were still sharing each other's food but they were eating their food. I finished my pancakes and then finished my toast and hash browns. I took a second to rest and washed some of the food down with the iced-tea. I still had some of the eggs left, I never really liked eggs that much so I asked my mom if she wanted them and she said yes. My mom and Jeremy were finally done eating their food, as they finished up by both drinking their juices and waited for the check.

The waitress came around again, and my mom asked for the check, as the waitress said that she will be right back. She walked into the back, as my mom and Jeremy tried to calculate the price. And I know this may sound weird but all I can think about is Beverly and what she was doing. The waitress came back and handed my mom the check, and she said out loud that the price was about $16. My mom pulled out a twenty and three single dollar bills as tip. I don't know why she decided to pull out three dollars but she did, as she held on to it in her hand. She put the twenty on the bill and waited, the waitress came back and took the twenty and gave her the change back. Everyone got up and my mom placed the three dollar tip on the table, I guess that is all the money she had in her wallet at that time. So it was nice instead of keeping it she decided to tip the waitress. We all left and started walking to the car as everyone had a look of full on their face. My mom unlocked the door and everyone got in, she looked at me as I was getting in and said, "I have to go my interview today, so I am going to drop you and Jeremy back home and leave. It is around 2:00, but I need some time finding the place." "Okay, that's cool I have no plans today anyway. I was lying, I really wanted to hang out with Beverley but it was a long time since I relaxed at home, so I was going to do that. My mom started the car as everyone was in and getting situated. She reversed and drove off, Jeremy pulled out another cigarette, and he discarded with the first one pretty fast. We hit a few red lights but it was a smooth and quite ride home. My mom pulled into the garage, and waited for Jeremy and me to get out. Jeremy was the first one to get out, he kissed my mom on the cheek and left. I hated seeing that shit, I hate when Jeremy fucking makes Goddamn moves on my mom in front of me. It was only right when my dad did that because my mom loved my dad. Not saying that my mom doesn't love Jeremy because they have been together for a few years now, and that broke ass bastard still hasn't found a job, but my mom doesn't seem to care one bit. I got out and closed the door, Jeremy walked inside and I walked around to his side and closed his door. I waved to my mom as she reversed and drove off. Jeremy and I both walked into the house and he walked right to the kitchen and grabbed a beer and a sandwich. It was amazing that we just ate food and he is still hungry. I swear fucking Jeremy is so lazy, all he does is fuck my mom, eat all our food and lie around and shit. Sometimes the shit he does I just want to… whatever it's not like I am ever going to do that anyway. I walked to my room, and I heard the cap of the beer bottle open and the crinkling of the sandwich wrapper, as he was about to eat. I walked over to the door and closed it, he tends to the TV loud and I can hear it all the way in my room. "Hey kiddo, that fucking word again fuck you Jeremy, can you grab me another beer? I am almost done with this one." Oh yeah, that is another thing, he is always bossing me around, telling me to get him shit that he can easily get and shit. I walked to the fridge, opened it grabbed another beer and closed it. I walked to the room and handed him the Goddamn beer as he was laughing at some damn TV show. I walked back to my room, and closed the door so I wouldn't have to hear him having a good old time. I hopped on my bed and rested my head on the pillow and took a deep breath. I can hear Jeremy laughing it up, and laughing it up some more. Mitch, he yelled I didn't want to get up but he will keep yelling and fucking yelling. I took another deep breath and fucking got up from the bed. All day he has been bossing me around, and I was getting sick and tired. I walked to his room, and he was still drinking and being a pain in my ass. "What" I said. "Can you fetch me something to eat?" "Fetch", what am I a Goddamn dog, get up from your lazy ass and get something to eat yourself." "I don't like that tone, Mitch I am in charge when your mom is gone." "you" I said, you can't even take care of yourself" I am not listening to you." "Boy, I will get up and slap the shit out of you." "Okay, I am going to let that one go because I know that you're drunk, but I will knock the fuck out of you if you touch me." And knowing how people act when they are fucking drunk, Jeremy got up and started following me. He pushed me once and I warned him not to push me again. He didn't listen, obviously, he pushed me again, and then he tried to swing but I ducked and punched him right in the mouth. He started bleeding seconds later, screaming you busted my lip. He grabbed my shirt and threw me on the floor, he tried to stomp on me but I grabbed his foot and flipped him off me. I got pretty fast and he was still getting up, thank God he was intoxicated because people tend to be little slower with their functions. I fucking kicked him in the ribs, not once, not twice but fucking three times. He screamed "My ribs" I think they are broken. He got up and rushed me and tackled me on the floor, he got on the mount position and started punching me in the face. Jeremy that stupid drunk fucking bastard broke my nose and I was bleeding all over my shirt and shit. I got up and head butted him off me and he fell off, I picked him and threw him against the living room table. The table broke, I felt bad for the table at that point. He got up and followed me into the kitchen, still wanting more. I led him into the middle of the kitchen, and Jeremy was still talking shit. He tried to kick me but he missed, he was drunk more than I thought. He grabbed me and threw me on the floor again, he kicked me and stomped on me a couple of times. He waited for me to get up, that was a mistake, and I walked over to him and punched him in *his* nose and broke his shit. He walked back to his room and walked out with a baseball bat. He tired swinging it breaking everything in is sight, but he missed me completely. I grabbed him and kneed him in his stomach and threw him on the floor. Without thinking clearly I needed something to defend myself. I opened a drawer and grabbed a knife. I grabbed the biggest and sharpest one, I wasn't going to stab him or anything but just enough to scare him. I walked outside in the living room, and threatened him with the knife, and I don't know if Jeremy sobered up or it was the huge ass knife I was holding, but he didn't want to fight anymore. "Okay, fuck, take it easy don't do anything that you are going to regret." He dropped the baseball bat, and I put the knife back in the kitchen drawer. Jeremy walked back inside the room and I walked outside to my car. I still needed to buy something for my mom's birthday. I mean for God sake it was today, and I didn't want to give her a lousy card. I just didn't think that was going to be good enough. Jeremy walked outside as I was opening the door. "Where the fuck are you going?" "Shut up" I said, and if you must know I am going to buy my mom a birthday present." Jeremy just smiled and walked back inside the house; I got in and closed the door. I started the car and fucking drove off; I didn't know what to get her. My mom is never the person to care about what the fuck she gets. I guess celebrating birthdays for her got old fashioned. Now I can see where I get that from, growing up celebrating birthdays was the best day ever. And now when you get older it doesn't have that same feel to it anymore. Whatever, I never really cared after a point I'm just in for the damn gifts. But a gift is what makes birthdays special. I got tired of getting shit for my birthday; you know when you have an aunt who gives you crappy ass sweaters with like dog pictures sowed into the fabric. I hated getting that shit; for once I wanted something good. I had no idea what my mom needed or what she wanted. Then it hit me, nice jewelry that's what I can get her because she doesn't have one pair of good jewelry to go with any of her outfits. So I decided to buy her a nice necklace, so she can wear with all of her nice dresses and shit. Now finding a place shouldn't be hard I just have to be careful of not getting something phony. Because living in New York, oh did I tell you how happy I am about that, but anyway you tend to run into people often selling shit that isn't real. And I can't tell you how pissed off I would get if I bought something that was fake and I spent all my money on it. I found a place and from the outside it looked decent, so I slowed down and pulled in behind a black SUV. I turned off my car and got out, it was pretty cold and I was wearing a short sleeve, not a wise move on my part. I checked my wallet and I am glad that I cashed that check from the clothing store before we moved. Thinking about this clothing store, got me thinking about Alison, and thinking about Alison got me thinking about Kristen. Man what did I do to deserve this, why is it every time I think that my life is going good we have to get up and Goddamn move. But whatever I can't spend all day thinking about the past or I never going to meet someone. See I have this philosophy if I spend all my life thinking about the past and what could've been with say Alison or Kristen, I am going to miss the opportunity to meet someone special now. So I have to stop thinking about the past, and I know that is going to be hard but it is something that I have to do. I walked inside the jewelry place and started looking around a bit. "Can I help you" a guy said behind the counter. "No" I said, I am just looking for now. I looked and looked and then finally I found something that my mom would really like. "Excuse me" I said, I need some help with this one please? The guy from behind the counter walked over to me. "Yes" he said, I noticed that you were looking at this one, really nice selection. "How much" I said to the guy. "Well, considering that this is the last one, and it is a hot item, the original price is $400 but you seem like a nice kid so I will give it you for $200 and not a penny less." I was so happy I can't believe he just did that, and I had just enough money too, my mom was going to be so happy. I told the guy that I wanted this one, and he grabbed it gently from behind the glass display. He put it in the box and sealed it shut. I told him that it was for my mom's birthday and it had to be special. So he wrapped it up and put a red ribbon on it. I gave him the $200 that I had and he gave me the box. "Thank you" I said. "No problem" he said back, I hope your mom really likes it. He smiled and I walked away to my car, the weather was getting colder, so I needed to get back home before my mom does. That way it would mean more when I surprise her, then I do it while she is at home. I got in my car and started it; I placed the jewelry box in the passenger side and drove off. I wonder what the fuck Jeremy was doing; I wasn't gone for a long time. I wonder if he really did something for my mom, and then again how could he because he is always so damn cheap.

I finally arrived at my house, and it was getting late and my mom's car wasn't in the driveway so she wasn't home. I turned off my car and grabbed the present and got out. I slammed the door by accident and walked to the front door. I opened the door and I saw lights coming from the street, and I looked closer and it was my mom. Shit I said to myself, I rushed into house and took off my coat and hung it on the rack. I rushed into my room, not giving any attention if Jeremy was home or not. I placed the box in my drawer and rested on my bed. I wonder if my mom saw me coming in, or I wonder if she saw the present I was holding. I mean it was wrapped with a red ribbon and a bow, which I forgot to mention. No, I am being paranoid I am fine she didn't see anything. I rested my eyes until I awoke to the sound of my mom's car alarm. She locked the doors. My mom came into the house, yelling "Guys I'm home!" I walked out from my room, and walked to my mom. She was smiling, must be good. Jeremy came out and he stood by the table. We both cleaned ourselves up from the fight, and when my mom asked what happened, we lied and said that we played football with a couple of guys and got hurt a little. "I got the job" she yelled. Jeremy walked up to my mom and kissed her on the cheek, and congratulated her. I hugged my mom and also congratulated her. "Be right back mom, I have something for you." I walked back to my room and grabbed the present, and walked back outside holding it behind my back. I waited for a second, my mom waited patiently. "Happy birthday mom" I said, giving her the jewelry box. My mom's eyes lit up and she opened the box with amazement gazing upon the necklace that I bought her. And of course had a card, don't know where the fuck he got a card from but that's all he had. He presented my mom with the card and simply said, "Happy birthday Lauren." My mom took the necklace holding it with one hand and hugged and kissed me on the cheek. "Thanks guys the both of you, this really means a lot." She took the necklace and tried it on; she hugged me again and ran into her room. Jeremy looked at me, sort of smiled and walked inside the room. And I was standing there, I was happy because my mom was happy. And somewhere in heaven, my dad was watching and smiling down upon me. I think for the first time I out did myself, great how am I ever going to top this, smiling sarcastically.

Chapter 26
Progression

The next morning finally came, and not a minute to soon. Oh did I tell you that my mom was excited about her new necklace. I think that beside the cake, music, and people in which we had none of those. She was pretty excited about just being appreciated, and loved. And did I tell you also that I never slept. Yep, I stayed up all night because I couldn't sleep, because I was thinking about Alison, and Kristen. And thusly got me thinking about Beverley. See no matter how hard I tired not thinking about them it always comes back. Maybe it's like a bad dream, whatever it was it was ruining my life. And I had to take care of this problem. I got up from my bed, and walked outside. I walked to my mom's room and both of them were still sleeping. It was pretty early in the morning, and I decided to change and get ready. I had to see Dr. Ross; I needed to talk to her about what was going on. Maybe she can help before this thing progresses, and gets worse. I got undressed and threw on some shit that I had lying around. I wanted to be quite as possible without waking up my mom or Jeremy. Even though Jeremy sleeps like a Goddamn rock and will practically sleep through anything. I grabbed my keys and slowly and quietly opened the door, without making any noise. It was still pretty early around 10, and I kept thinking to myself if Dr. Ross was in her office or not. I mean it was like the middle of the week, I am sure she will be in today.

I closed the door behind me and walked to my car. I opened the door and got in; I pulled out my cell phone, dialed her number and started the car. I drove off and her number rang a couple of times until she finally picked up. Well, it wasn't her it was her annoying ass secretary. I asked the same questions that I always do, and sooner or later Dr. Ross got on the phone. "I need to see you it is an emergency." "Okay" she said, come on in I am almost finishing up with a client and I will be free for a couple of hours." I told her I was coming now and hung up the phone. I got at her office, after a few red lights but was able to park and get out. I walked to the front door and walked inside, I walked directly to the main counter. And it is always the same Goddamn procedure everywhere you go, so after the same questions I was able to see Dr. Ross and not a minute to soon. I followed her into her office as usual, and she sat down as usual. "Okay Mitch" she said, you have seen me a couple of times throughout the months, and tell me what's on your mind *this* time. "I feel urges and want and needs from things that I know I can't have." "What do you mean, explain." "It's like the dream I had, I think it had something with me being sexually abused by my mom." "Do you think that is causing you to feel obsessive and having all these urges with every girl you meet?" "Yes" I said, I tend to act differently when I am talking with girls. And I think that this also has to do with Alison and Kristen and they both led to Beverly." "I feel very different when I am with Beverly than I was with Alison or Kristen." "All of this is so confusing right now; I don't know what to do?" "Okay, so you feel different how is your relationship with Beverly going as of now?" "Good" I said, I just bumped into her after months of not seeing her and we are catching up. "I feel like I let Alison and Kristen slip through my fingertips. And I don't want to do the same thing with Beverly, because I love her and she loves me back I think. The last time we were together we told each other we loved one another, but now I don't know what it is." "I don't know if she even loves me now, we never talked about it since we saw each other again." "But in your mind you still love her and will always love her, am I right?" "Yes" I said, I mean no, I mean I don't know." "I don't know if I do love her, because I still have these feelings for Alison and Kristen" "Fuck" I said, sorry, I guess I just have to endure it." "What it seems like to me is you're feeling guilty, and you love all three girls equally." "You know by trying to find yourself, you got mixed up with all these girls and that is causing all these problems." "I still think that me being obsessed with girls has to do with that dream I had about by mom." "You think that you're obsessed with girls, is that how you feel." "Yes" I said, it's been like that for a long time, ever since I was 13." "I am sorry I have to go, I can't talk about this anymore it is getting uncomfortable, and I don't want anything bad to happen." "Bad" she said, what do you mean?" "I have to go." And with that I stormed out the Goddamn building, and I looked with the corner of my eye that Dr. Ross was a little worried. And I know that she was trying to help but I needed to figure this out for myself. I headed straight for my car, unlocked the door and got in. I didn't start it right away I just sat there with both my hands covering my face and took a deep breath. All I kept thinking about was fucking Alison and Kristen, and what they were doing and if they still remembered me. Whatever I didn't care, I got to stop thinking about the Goddamn past, the only person that I have to start thinking about is Beverly. Even if she doesn't love me back I still need to tell her how I feel. I started the car and decided to drive home again and get some fucking sleep. I just needed to relax before this *thing* progresses even more and I am lost within myself.

But before I actually went home, I was a little hungry so I decided to stop off somewhere and get me a sandwich and a cold drink. I was looking and looking until I finally found a place, the place was smaller than I would've pictured it but as long it gets the job done, I really don't give a shit. I pulled in and parked right in the Goddamn handicap spot, and luckily for me I stole one of those blue handicap things you put on your mirror. So people can see that you are actually handicapped. It worked out perfectly because there was no other parking anywhere and I wasn't going to fucking drive around the whole parking lot looking for a spot. I got out and checked my wallet, still had some money left. Food shouldn't cost that much at this place I don't hope so that is. I walked into the place and started looking around for some food, there was cute ass girl walking around the store. She was the first thing that I noticed when I walked in the place. I was going to follow her and ask her for her name but this is how this whole fucking problem started, me going around and chasing these fucking girls. But I couldn't help it there was something about this girl that I couldn't stay away from. It was probably her scent; she did smell good I could smell her as soon as I walked in. I walked around the store looking for something to eat and not knowing it the girl was walking in the same isle. I didn't intentionally walk up to her or nothing but I did walk pass her and kind of looked at her for a second. She noticed that I was noticing her and I quickly turned away. I started walking away and I could see from the corner of my eye that she started following me. I wondered if she saw me looking at her, I mean it was only for a second though. I stopped so I wouldn't tired myself out and shit, and then she stopped near me, "I am sorry" she said, you look familiar I tired stopping you before I guess you didn't hear me. "Sorry" I said back, for staring at you, it wasn't anything creepy just you smelled very nice." She didn't say anything for a minute neither did I, this was one of those awkward moments. She smiled at me and said her name, my name is Jessica and you are?" I smiled back, "Mitch" I said. "Well, it is very nice to meet you Mitch; I have to go that's my mom honking the horn." "Okay, nice meeting you to Jessica" And like a bullet she left the store and walked to her mother's car. She looked back at me and smiled one more time and then she got into the car and took off. I nodded my head as I just realized that I was supposed to get my sandwich. I grabbed any sandwich and a soda to go with it and quickly walked to the register. There was an older gentleman behind the counter reading an old comic book. It looked pretty funny because you would expect a teenager behind the counter reading a comic book, not an old ass geezer, but I didn't want to be rude and say anything. I will just laugh to myself about this one. I paid for my food and he put it in a bag, I grabbed the bag and left the store. I unlocked my car door and got in, closing the door but rolling down my window. I decided that I was hungry and there is no point to drive few more minutes. So I was going to eat in my car, I just hoped that the owner of the store doesn't mind me eating in the parking lot. I took the plastic covering off the sandwich and started eating it, being extra careful that I don't spill it all over myself. I took small bites instead of huge ones like I usually do. I took some sips of my soda to wash down the food. When it comes to drinks I am usually picky, even though its soda and no one even gives a shit about. But to me it makes a difference of what you drink to what kind of food you have. If you are eating something spicy as hell, you want to have an ice cold drink. That is pretty much common sense right there. But certain sandwiches have certain drinks, like for instance I got a B.L.T. and my drink of choice was lemon iced-tea. I could've gone with the soda but I needed a drink that was refreshing and a smooth mellow drink. Iced-tea is good with food; it's not too cold but not too sweet or sour. Anyway before I start explain the history of fucking drinks; I quickly took more bites of my sandwich. I looked around and outside my window to see what the rest of the world was doing. It was a pretty quiet afternoon, pretty mellow and slow. There weren't a lot of people walking around, just a few cars driving in the streets. I took more bites and then finished my sandwich, and finished it down with the last couple of sips of my drink. I gathered my trash and got out from my car and looked for a trash can. I found one, near two girls smoking. They were both pretty cute, so I walked to the trash can and threw away my shit. I asked one of the girls if they had a smoke. I have never smoked in my life and I never planned to start, I didn't know what the hell I was doing. She offered me a cigarette and I took it, thank God I saw Jeremy smoking all the time, so I won't look like a jackass holding it wrong or something. I had a lighter on me for some apparent reason so I lit the cigarette up and took a hit. I didn't cough or anything and the cigarette actually tasted pretty good so I took another hit and slowly blew all the smoke out my mouth. The two girls smiled and one of them looked at me and then turned away to look at her friend. "You're kind of cute" one of the girls said to me laughing and giggling. I smiled back taking another hit. "Thanks, you're pretty cute too" I said, taking one more hit and slowly exhaling it out. "My name is Rebecca, and this is my friend Courtney" she said. "Mitch" I said, my name is Mitch, nice to meet you girls. Rebecca, the one that offered me the cigarette, smiled as she took another hit. Just standing there for a second with two complete strangers I felt different for the first time in my life, you know. I felt like I was accepted, and it was kind of funny because it was two cute ass girls smoking cigarettes on the corner store. I didn't have to act like someone else when I was with these girls, I just walked up threw something away and asked for a cigarette, and they didn't tell me to get lost. Or reject me in anyway. I think that was my problem with all the other girls that I have met. I think that I tried to be someone else, but not really being me when I needed to be me the whole time. I finished the cigarette, I told them that I wished I could stay but I had to run. They smiled and both said bye at the same time, it was funny. I walked to my car smelling like smoke and shit, fuck I said my mom is going to kill me. Well I can just tell her that I met some people and we got to talking and they were smoking around me and shit. I made it to my car and unlocked the door, the first thing that I did is grabbed some gum from the glove compartment and chewed the shit out of it. I waited for a few more minutes and then I started the car and drove off. Luckily for me I was only a few minutes away from my house so I was almost home. I reversed from the parking lot and drove off, man the only thing that I was thinking is the smoke from my breath and clothes will go away soon. See the one thing that I don't understand is that my mom fucking smokes and she tells me never to do it because it causes all this bad shit. See I am not genius or anything but I think that my mom is a Goddamn hypocrite, because she tells me not to do something all the Goddamn time and then she does it. Sometimes it makes me really mad because it's annoying when she does that shit. I don't know how long or when she started smoking, but that is not the only thing that she does. She fucking drinks too and one time I got grounded for two weeks because I went to this party. And you see the party wasn't even the fact that I got in trouble, even though I snuck out and it was the middle of the night. No what I got in trouble for was there was beer there and I took a couple of sips. And when I got home, don't get me wrong my mom got a little upset that I came home late. She was crying because she was worried that I wasn't in my room when she walked in. I told her that I was sorry for sneaking out because there was a party. And you never let me go out and have any fun. But she calmed down and hugged me; I said I was sorry again. And she smelled the alcohol on my breath, and then she flipped out. Saying shit like I can't believe you were drinking and shit. You're going to become an alcoholic when you grow up, and alcohol is addicting and shit. She grounded me that night for two weeks because I took two mother fucking sips and shit.

I finally got home and the smell of cigarettes got off my clothing, and my breath smelled more and more like mint from the gum. So I think that I was good, I hope so. I pulled in and I was so fucking tired. I don't know why I didn't do shit but all I wanted to is go to sleep, I checked the time and it was pretty early in the afternoon around 2:00

so it was good. I turned off the car and walked toward the fucking door, and hoped and prayed that my mom didn't smell the cigarettes on me. I walked and I heard noise coming from the kitchen, so I closed the door and walked toward the kitchen. It was fucking my mom making all that noise, I couldn't believe it; she was being so damn loud. She started cleaning up the kitchen and moving shit around, and honestly I didn't care at all. I said hi and kept it moving, I didn't want to stand in the kitchen and watch my mom clean while I have a long ass boring conversation. I headed straight to my room and lay on the bed. I tired going to sleep, it was getting late into the afternoon, but I didn't bother to check what Goddamn time it was. That really wasn't important to me right now. I tried not to think about any of the fucking girls that I have met in my life, and how each and every one of them caused me some kind of pain. I closed my eyes and threw my damn covers over my face. I got up from my bed and closed and locked my door. I quickly unlocked it and kept my door close. My mom has a habit of always knocking before she comes into someone's room. Yeah, I know what the fuck you are thinking, that is good manners. But you really don't know my mom at all; if the door is locked or closed she will knock. If the door is locked she will fucking knock and knock until you answer it, and if the door is closed she will knock and knock and open it. I jumped back into bed and threw the covers on me again. I took off my shoes from my bed and tossed them along the wall near all my other shit. I took off my jeans and threw them with my shit also. Sometimes it gets really hot in my house and I have to be forced to strip down to almost nothing and sleep. I kept my shirt on because the covers I use is really itchy. And it feels weird against my skin when I am not wearing a damn T-shirt. I smiled to myself, because I fucking complain about shit too much. I closed my eyes and just fucking went to sleep. I had my eyes closed for a couple of minutes until I woke up. Of all the girls I thought about Beverly, maybe I am really obsessing over Beverly. And not just Beverly but every girl that I come across with, what exactly is wrong with me. I closed my eyes again and forced myself to go to sleep. I took a deep breath and another. I was sleeping, and this time if I was going to dream about Beverly I wasn't going to wake up and sleep through it. Maybe my dream will tell me something. And I was right about something, I did dream about Beverly again. Bu the dream was really strange. I saw Beverly standing in a meadow, she wasn't doing anything but she was just standing there. She looked like she was upset, she was crying about something. Her clothes were a little fucked up, like someone tore them apart, and her hair was all puffy and shit. I was standing on the opposite end watching her. I walked a little closer, but the closer I got the further she was. I tried yelling her name, and she didn't hear it. She didn't even move or anything, she was just crying and holding herself tightly. She was saying something but I couldn't make it out, I couldn't hear what she was saying. Then she started crying more and more, and she looked back and started running. She tripped and fell and just continued to cry. I try to run over there but it was to no avail. Then I saw something that I would never imagine in a million fucking years. I saw me in my own dream holding a Goddamn fucking knife. The dream me came closer and closer to Beverly, and I couldn't do anything. At this point I didn't want to wake up because in a weird way I wanted to see what was going to happen, and if I could stop it somehow. He came closer to her and then he did something, he stopped and looked at me. He smiled and started walking. I was yelling and yelling but it wasn't doing any good. Beverly stood up slowly; I could tell that she was hurting. This son of a bitch hurt my baby. Then she stopped and looked at him. "Mitch" she said, still crying and out of breath. "Mitch" she said again, but he didn't listen and he kept on walking toward her. And then she tried to walk but she was to hurt, it looked like she had a broken ankle or something, she must've gotten it when she fell. My poor baby, I said to myself. She couldn't walk anymore, and she fell to the ground. She tried to get up but she was crying and she was in a lot of pain. She staggered to her feet and within a second, he put the fucking knife right through her stomach. I still didn't want to get up because for some strange reason I wanted to see what was going to happen. And I know that sounds weird but I still had a feeling that I could do something. But I knew that it was too late. Beverly started crying more now, and she was screaming for him to stop. But he didn't listen, it's like he wasn't human, like he didn't respond to anything. She started crawling, and it felt like she was crawling towards me but she didn't see me there standing there. He just walked up to her and playfully kept slicing her, and slicing her. I swear she looked back at me and then Beverly died right in front of my eyes, and I screamed out Beverly and then I fucking woke up sweating and breathing heavily. I was in fucking complete shock that I had a dream like that. That wasn't even a dream it was a Goddamn nightmare. At this point I didn't know what to do, it was getting early into the evening, so I decided I will go to Dr. Ross. Maybe she can help me figure out what the fuck is wrong with me and why I am obsessing over Beverly, Alison and Kristen. And why I am doing it all the time, every time I think of either of them. I got up from my bed and walked out to the kitchen. I told my mom, who was still working, that I was going out and go get some air. I really didn't care what the fuck that Jeremy was doing at this point. More importantly my mom doesn't know that I have been seeing a psychiatrist behind her back for a few years now. I didn't want to tell her because she gets too involved in everything I do. And then she will ask a lot of questions, and she will bring in Jeremy to see if he can help. And then she will want to see Dr. Ross, and stay during the fucking visits. And right now I didn't want all that shit anyway. But one thing that I like about my mom, she doesn't care that much where I go and what I do sometimes. It's probably I am her only child that she trusts me to do whatever I want. And if that's the case that is fucking cool as shit. Too bad everyone's mom was like that then everyone will get along with everybody. Well that is just a fucking theory. I grabbed everything I needed and left. I walked to my car, unlocked the door and got in. I pulled out my phone and called Dr. Ross' secretary. I think you know the whole freaking procedure by now. I got a hold of Dr. Ross, and in record time, "Hi Dr. Ross, this is Mitch; I was wondering if you were not busy today, I need to come in and see you it is an EMERGENCY." Come on in and hurry." She hung up the phone and she sounded like she was really worried about me. I started my fucking car and took off, I was speeding a little but it was a quite road so I had no chance of getting pulled over for anything.

I finally arrived at her office, and she was standing outside near the door. She was talking to some people. I found a spot behind this old red truck and turned off my car. I got out and Dr. Ross was smoking a cigarette. Wow, I said to myself I would never picture Dr. Ross a smoker. I walked up to her as she was finishing up her cigarette, or what was left of it. The people that she was talking to left and started walking down the street. "Hi, Dr. Ross, I am here." "Please call me

Elizabeth or if you like call me Liz." "Okay Liz, well, you're still not busy are you?" "No" she said, come on in. I followed her into her office and it is always the same fucking routine. We both sat down and she sat a little closer to me this time. I leaned in a little and smelled her a little bit. She smelled so good, I didn't know what she was wearing but it was intoxicating. "How are you feeling today, Mitch?" "Not so good, I had a nightmare but this one was weirder than any dream or nightmare that I had or might have had." I explained the whole nightmare to her and for a minute she didn't say anything. "Okay, so let me get this straight, Mitch. You are obsessing with these women, and you want to figure out how to stop it." "Yes" I said, and it is slowly eating me apart, please help." "Okay, this is what I am going to do, and I don't do this with everyone, but I think you really need help." "I will do anything" I said. "I want to put you through a program. I will medicate you daily and evaluate you daily." I thought about it and I said yes. I didn't want to tell my mom just yet but I know that sooner or later she was going to find out. But I was going to tell her what is happening to me, just not right now. The doctor walked over to her desk and grabbed some papers and a clipboard. "I want you to read over this and sign this for my records. It's like a contract basically saying that you're going to comply with all the rules and understand that the doctors here, including me, has the right to make you stay longer if needed. I read over the contract and signed my name, and since I am 18 I don't have to have my mom sign the paper. I handed the papers back to the doctor, and she took them off the clipboard and put them in the filing cabinet. "Okay, stand up and follow me please. There is a pay phone down the hallway go and tell your mom everything, and why you are going to stay in this building for next few weeks." She handed me fifty cents and I walked to the pay phone and put the money in. I called my mom's cell and it rang for a couple of seconds and she picked up. I can feel my heart beating, I was so nervous I didn't know what to say. "Hi, mom how are you doing." "Fine" she said, what's up." "I have to tell you something important." "Okay" she said. "I am in a psychiatrist's office with Dr. Elizabeth Ross. I have been seeing her for a few years now." There was a sudden moment where my mom didn't say anything. And then she said, "Is everything okay? Are you feeling okay?" "I don't know" I said, I couldn't be a hundred percent honest with her because I didn't know myself what the fuck was going on. "Mom, the doctor is waiting on me; I will explain everything later I promise." My mom started crying, I guess she wanted me to be okay. Honestly I didn't know if I was okay or not. Hopefully the doctors can figure it out, before it this thing progresses even worse. The doctor walked to me and showed me where I was going to stay for the next several weeks. I was walking with her and I was thinking to myself. How could I get myself into this fucking situation? I wonder what my mom is thinking right now. I wonder what Alison, Kristen and Beverly are *doing* right now. Liz showed me to the second floor of the building where there was a lot of other people in a psych unit also. I thought to myself that for the next several months this was going to be lots of fun. Of course I was being Goddamn sarcastic just in case you didn't get it. But I am pretty sure that you got it because you're smart. She made me wait in small room and told me to take off my clothes and put this hospital gown on. And I have to tell you something that these gowns are the ugliest things that I have ever seen in my life. I fucking took off my clothes slowly and put the monstrosity of a gown on. Liz came back in the room and gave a smile, "Cute" she said. "Thanks" I said back. She told me to follow her and check up with one of the nurses in the front. Liz walked away and went to talk to other doctors, while I was in line waiting to talk to the nurse. "Are you new?" someone said behind me. I turned around and there was this girl. She looked like she was really sick or something. She looked very cute in a punk rock- gothic chick kind of way. "Yes" I said, I am new I am going to be here for a while. She smiled at me and said, "I have been here for a while now, little less than a year. This place isn't that bad once you get used to it." I smiled back and said, "I'm sure". There were still a couple of people in front me. So I decided to talk to that girl that was standing behind me for a while, and see what her story was. "My name is Mitch, nice to meet you." She smiled and looked at me with piercing eyes. "Lindsay Thompson" she said. "That's a nice name" I said to her. "Thanks it was my mom's name. "Was" I said. "My mom died last year." "I am sorry" I said. "I am not" she said back to me, my mom and I never got along that well, so one day I got sick and tired of her and killed her." I was shocked, how can a cute and innocent girl be capable of doing that. I looked at her and she was looking away for a second, I turned back around and just continued to look in the front. "Hey" she said. I didn't want to turn around but the girl was really cute even after the fact of what she just told me. The line was moving and I was next. I walked to the front and gave the nurse my name. "Yes, Mitch, I have all your stuff. Take this and go to Room #15. It was a bottle of toothpaste, one toothbrush, shaving cream, one comb, hospital slippers and socks, and other shit too. I forgot to mention that in this place they don't fucking give you anything sharp; because they don't want to you to fucking commit suicide or something. So that's why they didn't give a razor and anything else sharp. I took my stuff and walked to my room, and I saw the other girl walking down toward me. I hope that she isn't going to live with me. She ended up living one room before me. Great, I said we are neighbors. I was still in the fucking dreaded hospital gown, I put all my shit on top of a dresser they had. The good thing about this dresser was it had wheels. Oh, I forgot to mention also I was allowed to keep a notebook, but I snuck in the pen, so they wouldn't take it. I wanted a notebook so I can keep a journal of all my fucking days here at this psych unit. I closed the door halfway and grabbed my pencil, and I was able to sneak in a mini sharpener too. I will just flush all the pencil shavings down the toilet. I sat down on my bed, and hoping that I wasn't going to get someone else in the room. I looked at the other side of the room and there was another bed. I wanted to sleep alone for one night so I can get used to sleeping in a place like this one time by myself. I opened the notebook and took out the pencil. I looked the blank page before me and took a breath. I smiled and said to myself, where do I start?

Chapter 27
The First Entry

I was so glad that the pencil was sharpened, I was still looking at the page, and it was blank. There were so many thoughts going through my head, I couldn't figure out where to begin.

Dear Journal,

This is my first time in a mental hospital, and I am starting to hate it. I don't know why I have only been in here for a few hours. My room is quite big; my bed is along the wall when you first walk in. There is another bed along the left hand side of the room. There is a small bathroom, which I know I am going to have to share with someone, and there is one fucking closet. The closet is small with one hanger rack and a few shelves inside. The floor is tile, and it is really cold. There is a window, but the view is of another Goddamn building. Outside looks so fucking peaceful, I can't believe that I have to spend the next few months in this Goddamn hell hole. Maybe it won't be that bad, just maybe. I looked around the room and prayed that I am in here alone for one night, tomorrow, or maybe for the next few weeks. I really don't want someone else in here. Especially if he is the type of person who fucking talks a lot, he will want to know my whole story. I guess I have no choice; I got myself into this mess I have to get myself out of it.

I heard someone coming so I quickly hid the pencil under my bed, and placed the notebook under my pillow. I would expect just enough privacy from these guys not to go through my shit. It was Liz with a couple of doctors; I guess they were here to ask me some fucking questions or something. And judging by the clipboards in their hands I guess I was right "Hi Mitch, said Liz, are you doing alright? Do you want to talk about anything?" "No" I said, I am fine. Liz smiled and she left the room and the doctors left except one. "Hi Mitch, my name is Valerie, and I am going to ask you some questions. I hope you don't mind." She started asking me really fucking boring questions, like I was going to fucking commit suicide or going to kill someone else or something. I think that I am sane enough and am Goddamn stable enough that I am not or probably never going to kill anyone. After a few more questions she smiled and left the room. And that wasn't a bad idea, it's not like I am fucking restricted to stay inside my room all day so I decided to leave and walk around and possibly see Lindsay again, if she was around. I started walking down the hallway, and I didn't know where I was going or if I was going to bump into anyone. I hope that I didn't bump into anyone because if they start talking about something, honestly I don't want to hear it. I didn't see Lindsay around anywhere but I saw a TV and it was inside this room. And no one was inside this room so I walked in and sat down on a chair. The chair was really uncomfortable, the back of the chair was stiff as hell but it was the only chair that looked half decent. I picked up the remote and turned on the TV, I didn't know what to watch and before I got a chance to flip through the channels, Liz came into the room. "Mitch" she said, there you are I was looking everywhere for you. Come with me please we have to check for your vitals." "Vitals" I said, what is that. "I have to check your blood pressure, to see if everything is okay. I smiled and just followed her to where everyone was getting their vitals checked too. I was walking behind everyone, and Liz walked around the opposite corner and walked inside the doctor's office. I saw a girl in front of me and it was Lindsay, I didn't want to call her name because I didn't want to slow down the process for everyone else. I will talk to her when everyone is done with their shit. Lindsay sat down and a nurse wrapped something around her left arm, I couldn't see it clearly. I heard the nurse squeezing it; I guess that's how if they check if your blood pressure is good. The nurse unstrapped it and Lindsay got up and I heard the nurse say that her blood pressure was okay. She started walking away from her and I was next. She slowed down just a little and smiled at me and I smiled back at her. I was next. I sat down in the chair and the nurse proceeded to repeat the process with me and said that everything was okay. I didn't want to hurry up and walk away it would make me seem rude. So I started slowly walking away and walked where Lindsay was. She was sitting in a quiet room reading a book. I knocked on the door and asked if I can come in. She smiled, "Of course silly, it's a public place." I just laughed and walked inside the room. "What are you reading" I said, pulling up a chair next to her. "Nothing really, I just found something and started reading it, I got really board." She just continued reading, and I just watched her. It wasn't anything creepy or anything, but something about her was mysterious and I liked that. I didn't want to bring up anything too personal. I didn't want to make Lindsay upset in anyway, but in some weird way I wanted to know her story. I was really intrigued that they would let a person like her, and the condition that she is in to be in a place like this. Usually a girl like this is in jail or something, but she is in here with me. But her problem is far off worse than mine, but I am her with her too. I couldn't understand why. She put the book down and left the room, she started walking down the hallway, and that is when they announced that food was ready to be served. I guess it was lunch time, and it was about fucking time I was getting hungry. But I really couldn't think about food right now, even though I was hungry. I wanted to find out how long I was going to stay here for; I didn't want to spend the rest of my life here. I walked to the office until I saw Liz on the phone. I swear that women is always busy, I have never seen her not have time for herself. She hung up the phone and walked out the office. I got her attention before she went anywhere else. "Liz" I said, I just wanted to know how long do I have to stay here? Do you know? She smiled at me, "Not long, Mitch, just less than a week five days I promise. Now go eat your food I will give you your medication. But I have to warn you it is pretty strong." I went to get my food and the only thing that I worried about is what the fuck I was about to take. She said that my Goddamn medication is strong. Now I am worried that I am going to be drugged up and become some fucking robot and not respond to anything. Food, it smelled so good, I wonder what they were serving. Since today is the first day they just had sandwiches, pizzas, burgers and all that good stuff. I was waiting in line and Lindsay was behind me, she cleared her throat and I turned around. I think that she did that on purpose just because she knew it was me standing in front of her, or maybe she just likes to clear her throat. Liz was walking down the hallway and was making her way towards me. She arrived, looked at me and said, "I know that the food is not what you expected, some people like to eat healthy. Tomorrow the nurses are going to come around and ask you what you want to eat. So you have a choice of what you want." "I get a choice now, sarcastically, okay that sounds good. She walked away, and I was standing for a couple more seconds. Until they called out my name and I walked forward, I grabbed my tray and sat down by myself away from everyone else. At this point I really didn't want to make any friends, I didn't care about their problem and I know that they didn't care about mine. Lindsay was next and she also grabbed her tray and walked around until she found a seat. I was hoping that she will sit next to me, and she did. She pulled up the chair and sat down. She smiled as she pulled herself closer to the table and cleared her throat again. At first we both just started eating and neither of us was making any sounds. It felt weird eating with someone that I just met, and not say anything, but it didn't bother me. There was something about Lindsay that didn't bother me. She was chewing on her bite, when I finished mine and I asked, "So, how do you like being here?" She smiled as she was done chewing on her bite. "It is okay" she said, I don't really talk to any of the people here that much." "What made you start talking to me?" "I don't know, honestly, you where the only person around my age so I felt more comfortable talking to you then adults." "Fucking adults is the reason why I am in a place like this." "I know what I did was wrong but I was only a child, I don't have to be punished like this." She finished eating her food, or what was left of it anyway. There was still some food left over, and she didn't care that she was wasting any food. I had some food left on my tray to, but the majority of mine was in my stomach. I got up and she followed me by doing the same thing. We both put the trays on the table and went into the bathroom. Of course since Lindsay is a girl she went into the girl's bathroom. I washed my hands and got out and Lindsay was still in the bathroom. A few seconds later she came out and her hair was down. She was wearing it in a pony tail the whole day. She looked so much better with her hair down. She should wear it like that more often. We both started walking towards our room, and she went into hers and closed the door. I walked into mine and closed it halfway. I sat on my bed and took out my journal. I took out my pencil in which I hid so they don't think I am going to fucking stab someone or kill myself with a Goddamn pencil. The thought of me killing myself with a fucking pencil was really funny. I got comfortable and sat along the wall; the curtains were open and giving in a lot of sun. So I was warm sitting where I was, on my bed. I opened my journal and continued where I left off.

Dear Journal,

I didn't like the food that I ate today. I had some pizza but it wasn't good. I couldn't taste any of the cheese or sauce or anything. But I am not writing because of the food, I am writing because of Lindsay. I think I like her but I don't know how to approach it. Better yet, I don't know why I like her but I do. She seems a little crazy, but I have no right to judge. There is something about her that I like. She is mysterious but she is open with everything. She is stronger than I am, and I could use a girl like that by my side. All this talk about Lindsay got me thinking about Beverly and Alison and Kristen. I wanted to tell Beverly how much I still love her. I want to tell her that I want to spend the rest of my life with her. It has only been the first fucking day and I am already starting to go crazy. I can't believe I have to spend a fucking week in this shit hole. Well maybe it won't be that bad because I made a friend, Lindsay, well just maybe.

I put the journal away, not because I heard someone coming, I just didn't feel like writing anymore. I just continued to sit on my bed with my journal still in my hand and open. I put my pencil in between the pages and closed the book. I hid the book under my bed and got up from my bed. I was board and in this place you couldn't do anything fun. There are groups that you have to go to. They make you do all this stupid shit that I know that no one wants to do. If I start missing all the groups I will get in trouble. But thank God there is no group for another hour or two so it gave me some time to do whatever the fuck I wanted. I walked out from my room and walked where all the books where and sat down. There was another person sitting across the way and he was reading a magazine on travel guides. He looked up and he didn't say anything but smirked a little bit and continued reading his crappy ass magazine. I looked towards the left, which is where I saw the bookshelf. It had a lot of books but I bet all the money in the whole Goddamn world that none of them were good. I started from the top shelf and worked myself from left to right until I hit the second shelf. And I did it again until I hit all the shelves. I found nothing really good to read. The titles of the books didn't seem to catch my eye, so I got up from there and left. I wanted to see what Lindsay was doing. So I decided to visit her in her room. I wondered if she still had the door closed. I went to her room and knocked on the door. She answered and she was wearing a long T-shirt. That got me thinking what was under that T-shirt of hers. All I wanted to do is lift up her shirt and see what she was really hiding. Don't get me wrong Lindsay had a great body, but I guess she didn't know how to use it. She just stood there still standing, "Hey Mitch, what can I do you for?" She can *do* me for something but that wasn't the point. "I just wanted to see what you were up to, I hope you're not too busy to talk or something." She smiled and simply said "Nothing really you want to come in, my room isn't that special I am still decorating." I walked in and I was a little surprised at what she had done with her room. I mean it looked very nice she had posters and other stuff on the wall. My room was pretty empty because it was spur of the moment thing. This means I didn't have time to go poster shopping. I really didn't care it's not like I was going to spend my whole life in this fucking hell hole, unlike some people. I sat down on Lindsay's bed and I was jealous for a second. Her bed was actually more comfortable than mine. She walked to her closet and opened the door. "You have to excuse me for one second as I get changed." "Okay no problem" I said as I was getting up from her bed. "I didn't mean you have to go you can stay if you want. It is not going to bother me or make me feel any less uncomfortable." I can't believe it was she going to change in front me. You know I am getting tired of all the girls always changing in front of me. This is why I am always obsessing for them because of this shit. I was surprised to know that she had shorts under her shirt, but they were short. She unbuttoned the shorts and walked to her CD player. She took out a CD and popped in a new one. I didn't know the song or the artist at all, she smiled and said. "You will like this, it is a personal favorite of mine." I wasn't sure if she was talking about the song or the actual band. But then she started walking up to me and started dancing slowly. As if she was putting on a show. She started moving her hips very slowly, and grabbed my hair and ran her soft, smooth fingers through it. She walked back a little and started pulling off her shorts of her. She slid them down her legs and threw them in a corner. She walked to me again and grabbed my right hand. She made me go under her shirt and feel her tight stomach. My hand went all the way up until I could feel her bra and then her firm breasts. She smiled and laughed just a little as she playfully pushed me on the bed. I was lying there and she was playing with her T-shirt. She grabbed the corners and slowly started pulling it up and up until I could see her underwear. She completely lifted her shirt up until she was standing there in her bra and panties. She walked towards me again, as I was still lying in her bed. She put one leg across my left leg and the other across the right. She leaned in and started kissing me softly on the cheek. I tried pushing her off, but something about this felt right. Even though in my mind I know that if someone came in we could get in trouble. I didn't know what to do, she was still kissing me and now she moved to my lips. And she started kissing my lips; she put her tongue down my mouth and grabbed my hand. She placed the hand on her breast as she continued to kiss me. At this point I did what anyone else would do. I kissed her back and there we where kissing on her bed. I rolled her over gently on her back and I was on top of her, still kissing her. I kissed her on her lips and started moving down her neck, and started feeling on her breasts. She pushed me off for a second, and unhooked her bra. She was lying on the bed with a come and get me look in her eyes with her beautiful breasts exposed. She grabbed my shirt and started unbuttoning the buttons and threw it on the floor. We started kissing again and then I got up for a second and took off my pants. She smiled and said, "Oh yeah". She got up and took off her panties, and then we stared kissing more and more. She leaned in and started kissing me on my chest and she went lower and lower. She grabbed my dick and started feeling around, and it felt so good, she slid down my boxers and started to stroke my dick. I grabbed her by the hair and made her lean forward until she put my whole dick in her mouth. At first she started gagging and coughing, but she didn't stop. She spit on the tip and proceeded to do it over and over. It felt so good, but I was worried that someone will come in and we will get busted for sure. I grabbed her and placed her on the bed, and she started laughing. "Hey keep it down; we are going to get in trouble." "Will you relax; they have to knock before they can come in because my door is closed." She smiled and just said, "Fuck me". I started kissing her on her stomach until I got lower to her pussy, and she started playing with my hair. I put my tongue in her pussy as she moaned and screamed, "That feels so good, don't stop baby" I licked her pussy more and more and, honestly this was the first time I have ever done something like this. And I was surprised I wasn't messing up and she didn't say anything as if I was doing it wrong. I grabbed her and placed her on her stomach but she was on all fours. I just saw her small, but firm ass starting me in the face. I proceeded to fuck her from behind. At first I started slow and then sped up little by little. Then she said, "Harder, come on" So I fucked her harder and harder. "Come on" she said, what are you my dad, fuck me. And when I heard that I immediately stopped. "What's wrong" she said. "What did you just say, please don't tell me you said what I thought you said?" I got off from the bed and put my clothes back on. I quickly left the room, and walked inside my room and closed the door. Man I can't believe what happened, she went from changing to us having sex. And then she said, what are you my dad, come on fuck me harder. I couldn't believe it. This whole thing was crazy and pretty ironic. Because I was in here to get some help because I am obsessed with girls and then Lindsay and I fuck. But I guess it is pretty funny because I always get myself into this kind of fucking situations. Even with Alison, Kristen, and Beverly. They all had their moments where it just felt right, but in my mind it was wrong. But for no matter whom it was I never wanted it to stop, I wanted it to go on forever. But I guess forever is a long time and sometimes forever isn't meant to be. It was getting late, and they announced dinner over the intercom. I wasn't hungry, I was tired. I got up from my bed and closed the lights, and then got on my bed again. I got under the covers and closed my eyes.

It was fucking eight in the Goddamn morning and they called everyone for vitals, and then we were allowed to get some breakfast. I wasn't hungry that much, so I decided to write an entry in my journal. Before they came and got me, and drug me to get my fucking vitals done.

Dear Journal,

Last night was one for the fucking ages, and it went both good and bad. I still couldn't believe that Lindsay and I had sex. And what was shocking is what she said about her dad. Now I strongly believe that Lindsay was sexually abused when she was little, and that is why she said that. But there was something about last night that just clicked. When I was with her I forgot all about Beverly, Kristen and Alison. I have never been with a girl who was so controlling, but also at the same wanted to be controlled. I don't know if that makes any sense, but that is how I feel.

It was day two in this piece of shit and I still hated it. I can't wait until I got out less than a week. The first thing that I am going to do is go see Beverly. I would see my mom but she is the type of person who is going to squeeze and love you, and ask you a hundred fucking questions. Don't get me wrong that's not bad but I just need some space. And I need to be with a girl that understands me for me. I heard someone coming down the Goddamn hallway, so I had to hurry and hide my notebook and my pencil. I quickly threw it under my bed. And waited for another day where I can right down my thoughts.

"There you are" said, Liz. Come on you have to come with me so I can check your vitals. And if you are hungry get something to eat. I got up and smiled, as I walked towards her and out my room. We started walking down the hallway together and just got to talking. "Are you enjoying your time here so far?" I looked at like are you fucking serious, what kind of stupid ass question is that. "I have no complaints; I just want to get out of here." "Well, almost me and the other doctors are still evaluating you. And after we discuss your status, then you can go home." She smiled and told me to get your vitals checked, and then get something to eat. As I watched her sexy body walk inside the office. I walked around the corner and waited. And within a second someone came up from behind me and tapped me on the shoulder. It was Lindsay, and for a second neither of us said anything. "Hi" she said, I think that you're next. She smiled and I smiled back as I walked to the front of the line. I sat down and did the same ass procedure. After a few seconds I got up and the nurse smiled. "Your blood pressure is good, honey" she said. Lindsay was next and the nurse did the same thing, and told her that her blood pressure was also good. I waited around to ask her if she wanted to get some breakfast together. I walked up to her and tapped Lindsay on her shoulder. "Hey, are you hungry? You want to get some breakfast?" She smiled and said sure, we walked to the room where they serving the food. It wasn't a café or anything but it was just another boring room with the walls painted white. Lindsay and I found a table near a window. We both sat down, and I looked out the window, it was raining, the rain looked very peaceful. The rain was just sliding down the window, and I saw some people with umbrellas and some people running down the street, with newspapers covering their heads. I wish I can be them, outside and free. Lindsay got a simple breakfast just eggs and toast. I had French toast with hash browns. I have to admit one thing the fucking food here is better than any food that I have ate in a long time. It is even better than my mom's cooking, and sometimes she does wonders in the kitchen. And other days we have to order out because she either fucks up or burns the food. It's not her fault she tires but sometimes it is funny. We both finished about the same time, and got up and put the trays on the table. Now it was time for fucking groups. How did they expect us to have groups when we just ate? I just hope it wasn't anything boring like an exercise group or something. I have to tell you every time I eat breakfast or even eat anything and do something where I have to move a lot I fucking throw up. And believe me it is not a pretty site. But there was something that was running through my mind and it was bothering me all day, even throughout breakfast. And that is the fact that is I in love with Lindsay. I know that we had that night, and from that point on it has been a little weird sometimes to even say hello. I walked up to Lindsay who was standing against a wall. "Hey, let's skip out on groups and go talk or something." She smiled, "Okay" she said, these groups tend to get a little boring. We started to walk away from the groups and walked inside her room. I made my way to the bed and hoped that what happened last night doesn't happen again. She stood against her wall and looked outside her window. "Last night was... I didn't know what to say, I waited to see if Lindsay was going to say something. She just continued to look out her window. "Yeah, that got a little strange" she said, sorry about that. "What do you have to be sorry for, we both did it and if you feel a little uncomfortable how do you think I feel." "No not about that" she said, that was great, you know, but about the whole dad thing." "That probably freaked you out in some way." I got up and stood beside her near the window and looked at her. "Well, it did freak me out but if you want to talk about it I am here for you. I can't believe it I am actually falling in love with fucking Lindsay and I don't even know the girl. I don't know a Goddamn thing about this fucking chick. The only thing that I know is that she killed her mom and she was or I believe she was sexually abused by her dad. "My dad drinks a lot and one night he came into my room and started touching me. I tried to fight him off but he was much stronger than I was. He got on top of me and pinned my arms down. He started kissing me and unbuttoning my shirt. He grabbed my breast and started rubbing them. He took off my bra and started sucking on my breasts. I continued to fight him off but he slapped me across my face. And that is when I got sexually abused. "I have never forgotten that night, and up to this day I hope that mother fucker rots in hell that fucking stupid bastard. She started to cry a little and then I got closer and hugged her and held her close. She leaned her head on my shoulder, and started to cry more. I told her that everything was okay. "How long are you staying?" "I am not sure; the doctors are still talking it over. I didn't want to tell her that I am leaving in a couple of days, then she will be alone and she will have no one to talk to or to hang out with. I mean who she is supposed to make friends with, the Goddamn doctors. They don't know shit all they tell you is the run around of what is really matter with you. And let me see the other patients here don't know shit and they don't look trustworthy at all. And some of these people look like they can hurt Lindsay, and she has been through enough already, or that is what I think, I am no doctor. I had to tell her the truth, because she was going to find out some time. "Hey, I have to tell you something?" She looked up at me and waited for me to say what I had to say. "I am leaving in a few days,

I spoke with the doctor today and she said that I can home soon. I didn't want to tell you, but I felt that I needed to. I am sorry for telling you this way." She stopped crying and got out of my hands. "Okay, whatever I don't care, go then go home with your loving family." "Why are you getting all upset?" "I am getting upset because you're like every boy who I have met in here. They say they care for me and then leave whenever they have the chance. And they all think that I am fucking crazy." "First of all, I really do care about you, and I never thought you were crazy." She turned away from me and looked out the window. "Whatever, I don't want to hear it, please leave my room I want to be alone." I didn't have anything to say, I don't understand why she was getting all upset. I left and closed her door; at least I had the courtesy to give her privacy. I walked back to my room and opened the bathroom door. I walked in and used the restroom real quick. I was finishing up when I heard someone come into my room. I hurried up and washed and dried my hands and opened the door. It was another person, great there goes that shit, now I have to share my room with someone else. Well, I didn't want to be rude so I introduced myself. "Hello, my name is Mitch, and you are?". "Hi" he said, my name is Jermaine. Jermaine was tall; I have to say about 6'1 and black. He had a long white T-shirt on with blue jeans on. He had golden brown shoes, they look like timberlands I wasn't really sure. He had a scruffy beard on his face and his hair was in corn rows. He put his stuff down on his bed and left the room without saying a word. This is great, it's not that he is a bad guy I just wanted a room by myself, you know but I guess it won't be that bad. I mean I am never the one to judge, you never know Jermaine might be a really good guy.

They were calling for groups; I guess I had to go before they come to my room and fucking drag my ass to the room. I walked out my room and down the hallway. And I saw Lindsay coming from her room. I was going to walk over to her and talk to her but I didn't want to bother her, she seemed preoccupied about something. I wonder if she was still mad at me for what happened. I mean if you think about it, it really wasn't my fault. Actually we were both to blame for what happened. She enticed me and then I started, I mean I am a fucking guy and when you get placed in a situation like this by a girl you have no choice but do what you have to do. But that didn't matter because it wasn't important anymore. I just didn't want Lindsay to be mad at me forever. I walked up from behind her and tapped her on her shoulder, like I usually do to get her attention. She turned around pretty hastily, like she was afraid or something. "Oh it's you, what do you want?" She started walking again, faster like she was trying to purposely avoid me or something. I couldn't understand why she was so mad at me for, just because I wasn't going to spend the rest of my fucking life in here. You know what I just fucking realized that this wasn't my damn fault. And even though I love Lindsay I am glad that I am not spending my whole Goddamn life in this shit hole. Well, good I didn't even want to talk to her now, I just decided to go to group and not pay any attention to her. When I walked into the fucking room they were doing fucking exercises. And come on how many times we have to fucking exercise in the morning or afternoon or whatever time it is. I was getting sick and tired; thank God no one saw my face when I walked in so I fucking left and decided to go back to my room. I was bored so I was going to write for a while. And I knew exactly what I was going to write about. LINDSAY I FUCKING HATE YOU!!! YOU STUPID BITCH!!!

I put my fucking journal away because I didn't want to write anymore, I think that I got my fucking point across. I slid the fucking book under my pillow and just sat on my bed and closed my eyes for a second. I tried to think of a happy time, because I was so frustrated and I wanted to stop myself before I do something stupid. I thought about Beverly and what she was doing with her life now. And that is when I realized that I had enough of this fucking shit. I got off from my bed so I can go talk to Liz. I walked outside and to the doctor's office; she was talking on the phone. So I waited penitently along the wall. And that is when Lindsay came up and waited along the wall too. We didn't say anything to each other for a few minutes, I guess she was still mad at me and I was a little mad at her too. Liz got off the phone, and walked up to me before I got a chance to say anything. "Good news, Mitch, I spoke with the doctors and you can go home. But you have to stay for one more night, and then you can leave tomorrow afternoon. I just need to evaluate you for one more day before I can make a final decision, I hope you don't mind." "No" I said, I can't wait until I go home, but if you excuse me there is something that I must take care of first." Liz smiled and walked away and I walked up to Lindsay, who was still standing along the wall. "Hey can we talk" I said, trying to get her attention but she was doing her best to ignore me. I tried to get her attention again, "Hey can we talk" I said. "Fine, make it quick, I have nothing to say to you." "I still don't understand why you are so mad at me, but I have to tell you something. I am leaving tomorrow afternoon." "And you think that is going to make me feel happy. Why don't you just leave?" She tried to walk away but I grabbed her hand. "Listen, I meant it when I said I really care about you. "If you really care about me, why don't you show me?" "I don't understand what you are talking about, why you won't just be clear with me for a change. Sometimes you are so fucking confusing I don't know what you are saying. "Forget it" she said, I guess you will never know how I feel. She walked away and I didn't do anything to stop her. I am going to leave and Lindsay is going to be fucking pissed at me. I couldn't think straight right now, I needed to lie down and clear my fucking head.

When I woke up again, Liz was in my room with some doctors. "Good morning sleepy head" she said, you slept the whole night. "I'm sorry I was really tired and I had a lot on my mind." "You want to talk about it?" "No" I said, I am fine, can I go home now. "Yes" she said, you have to come with me and sign some papers at the front desk and collect your belongings. I had a huge smile on my face, I was supposed to stay longer but I guess she talked to some doctors and I get to go home earlier. But I was still thinking of Lindsay, as I was getting up and following Liz to the front office, I really do care about her and it is funny because we just met. Now it is different with Alison and Beverly because I got to know those girls, and Kristen I knew her but not that long. But there was something different with Lindsay that I liked, something different than with the other girls. The nurse gave me the papers to sign; I quickly reviewed them and sign it. I have to read over everything before I sign something, because you never know when they are going to fucking screw you in any situation. I gave the papers back to the nurse, and she gave me my belongings. Oh I forgot to mention, they took all my shit, and if I did then I am telling you again, and if I didn't well now I am. I grabbed my stuff and walked back to my room. To make sure if I didn't forget anything, I wanted to keep my journal here, I am going to write one more entry and slide it under Lindsay's door. I wanted her to have it so she can write down how feels and everything. And it was something in which she can remember me by. I pulled out my journal and got ready for my last entry.

Dear Journal,

Well, I am leaving now and I can't wait. I have too much time in this fucking place. This is my last entry and I am going to give it to Lindsay, so she can remember me by it. Well, I have to make this short and sweet, so here it is. Lindsay if you choose to read this or not. And if you're still mad at me or not, I just wanted to tell you that I really do care about you. And well, how I can put this. Lindsay I love you. I just hope that one day you can see it in your heart to forgive me for any pain I have put through. I never meant to do anything like that. I never meant to mess up your life, honestly I didn't. This is my chance to tell you that I am sorry. So I am giving you my journal, you can read over some of the entries I have written already. I want you to have this so you can your thoughts and stuff. And so you can always remember me. Goodbye Lindsay, I hope that one day you will get out and we can see each other again. Take care Lindsay, I love you.

And with that I threw away the fucking pencil, and closed the notebook. I got up from my bed and walked out the hallway. I checked to see if Lindsay was there and the coast was clear. I grabbed the notebook, and slid it under Lindsay's door. I walked back to my room to make sure if I had everything and I did. Sometimes I have to double check, because I forget shit all the time. I walked out my room and started walking down the hallway. I said bye to Liz, as I passed bye, she was on the phone, but she waved. I waited for the nurse to buzz the door so I can go through. I walked out and down the hallway. I looked for the sign that said exit and walked through the double doors. I made my way to the front of the building, the front entrance. I walked out and I was finally out. I turned around and looked at the building one more time. I wonder what Lindsay was doing right now, or even if she was thinking about me. The most important thing was that I was a free man. And I couldn't wait to go home.

Chapter 28
Happy 21st Mitch

I couldn't believe it, as I was at home thinking about everything. It was three years ago, and I can still remember it like it was yesterday. I remember first walking into that place and more importantly I remember Lindsay. Man, it has been three years I wonder if she is out or not. And I wonder if she remembers me. But I didn't want to think about that right now, my 21st birthday was coming in a couple of days and I couldn't wait. Oh, did I tell you the good news; I got into a fucking college. It's about time, right, well it's a community college, but it is better than nothing I guess. It is only a few miles away from our house. Well, my mom's house, she still lives in New York and of course Jeremy is with her too. I worked for three years and earned enough fucking money to actually get a small house for myself. It has been crazy the last few years; there has been talk of my mom and Jeremy getting married and having kids. Yeah, can you imagine fucking Jeremy raising a child? He can't even take care of himself, how the fuck is he going to raise a baby? But these years has been good to everyone, including Jeremy. He got a new job working as a contractor, or something. He doesn't build houses anymore he is like a supervisor now. So he is making really good money. My mom and Jeremy decided to spruce up the house a little bit. They painted all the rooms, but decided to leave mine alone. They couldn't bear the thought of messing up my room. My mom got a Jacuzzi in her room now. God knows what she is going to use it for, one can only guess. I didn't want even want to think about that shit right now. Anyway, my house is really nice. It is small and one bedroom, two baths and a backyard, a garage, an attic, and other shit too. But that wasn't really important to me now; I just couldn't wait until I started school. I know that I am a little old, but I started school late when I was little. And when I told them that I was home schooled for most of my life that wasn't appealing to them one bit. But the school I am going to was nice enough to let me register but I have to get my shit together if I wanted to make something out of myself. I wanted to do this so I can show my mom and my dad that I am growing up and becoming a man. More importantly I am doing this for my dad, may he rest in peace, and I wanted to show him that I am responsible and not just a fucking goofball. I started thinking about a whole bunch of shit at the same time. I thought about Beverly and Alison, and Kristen and more importantly Lindsay. It was time for me to move on so starting now I am going to forget about Beverly and Alison and Kristen. Even though I know that was going to be fucking hard but I needed to. I just needed to focus on Lindsay, now even though finding her was going to be hard. I wonder if she is still in the place. My mom or Jeremy wasn't home they were probably out shopping for my birthday present. I hope it was something nice. Well at least I can drink now legally, even though I don't drink that much anyway, but it is always there I guess. I decided to leave and go back to the place, and see if Lindsay is still there. I still had my piece of shit car, but as long as it gets me from point A to point B I really don't care. I left the house, and walked to my car. It was so hot and I was wearing a long sleeve, I don't dress well with the weather, I swear I wear the opposites when it comes to the season. For example, I wear pants when it is hot and shorts when it is cold, but whatever I don't care, just complain but you probably know that already. It was crazy that I still knew the fucking address to this place. It has been such a long time, I wonder if Liz still works there. Speaking of Liz, it would be nice to see her before I see Lindsay, I decided to go and visit her now. I got in my car, started it and drove off; I still remembered where her office was. It was crazy, I complain a lot but I am good with remembering shit.

There wasn't that much traffic in the road so getting there wouldn't be a problem.

I got there in record time, and there were no cars around, it was a pretty quiet day so parking was a breeze. I got out of the car and walked inside. Liz was standing outside her office talking to the receptionist. There were not a lot of people inside, just a few. So I shouldn't have any problem talking to her without making an appointment. I walked to Liz, and within a second she remembered me. "Oh my God" she said, Mitch how are you? I just smiled, "I am fine, thank you for asking." "It's been such a long time, how is everything? What have you been doing with yourself?" I smiled again, "Nothing really" I said, I bought a small house, and I am going to college soon. "Why don't you step into my office so we can catch up." I followed Liz into her office and closed the door. "About school, I know it's been tough, and I am already 21 and I know it is a little late but I got into a community college. It is just down the road from my house. So I am hoping everything goes well there." "I am sure that everything is going to work out just fine, you just have to believe in yourself." I smiled, and we started talking about my experience in the fucking psych unit. And we also started talking about the girl that I met in the place, Lindsay. "So you really like this girl? She said, what makes this girl different than any of the other girls that you have met?" "I don't know" I said, lots of things like she isn't afraid to express her feelings about everything. She is very open minded, and doesn't really give a shit about what people think about her. And she has had a messed up life, stuff didn't go the way that she expected, but that didn't bring her down. She is strong, stronger than any of the other girls that I have met." "I am sorry I know I am talking about her too much" Liz smiled, "It is okay it sounds like you really care about her, and that shows a lot of compassion and strength." "So what else is new, Mitch it has been such a long time. How are your parents doing?" "Good" I replied, my mom and Jeremy are talking about getting married. I don't know if soon or what but they are talking about it. They have been together for a long time, and even though I don't like it, it does make sense" "Why don't you like it?" "Well Jeremy is a nice guy, but we had our problems in the past and even though we worked most of it out. I feel if they do get married that those problems are going to arise again." "Well maybe Jeremy getting married to your mom will give him a chance to change and mature a little bit. Maybe you will see a new Jeremy after the wedding, you never know." I smiled, "Yeah" I said. "So how have you been" I said. "I've been good" said Liz. Just working here, and still working at the psychiatric unit. "Wow, you still work there" I said. It has been such a long time, I am impressed. And with that being said I decided to cut the meeting short and see if Lindsay was still there. "Hey, Liz I am sorry but I have to go, I am really busy today." "It is no problem" she said, it was really nice seeing you again Mitch. Take care and tell your mom and Jeremy congratulations. "I will" I said, as I got up from the chair and left Liz's office. I wonder if she is still there, man I was so nervous. How about if she is still there and we bump into each other or something, I wouldn't know what to say. I walked to my car and got in, I forgot to fucking lock the doors. Somebody could've stolen my damn car. I mean hot wiring a car isn't that hard, even I know how to do it. I don't know how but I do, I guess one day it will come in handy, wouldn't you say so. I got in and started driving. I wasn't going to let anything distract me from the place. I was determined to see if Lindsay was still there. But how about if she wasn't there, I mean they have no right to hold her there forever. How about if she checked out? Then what was I going to do, how will I ever find her again. I don't even know her last name, and Lindsay is such a common name. There is probably like a hundred fucking Lindsay's all around New York. But that wasn't important I had to take it one step at a time. I continued to drive and realized that I was running out of gas. Great, I said to myself a Goddamn distraction. Well I guess this is important without gas I couldn't get anywhere. I saw a gas station on the right hand side, so I got into the right lane and made that turn into the gas station. I rolled around and parked my car near a tank. I turned off the car and got out. I walked around to damn pump, and before I took the pump out I checked the prices. It was expensive as shit. Well I guess that is what you get when you fucking live in New York. It was $3.38 a Goddamn gallon. Luckily for me I had a debit card with some money on it, I am so happy I got that freaking job. Oh yeah my job, I forgot to tell you I got a job. Everything has been so crazy these past three years. It isn't that bad, I just got a job working at a bank. I know that isn't that great but I make a decent amount of money. And I don't have to travel far because it is a few miles away from my new home. I pulled out the pump and put it into the car. As I was filling my car I started thinking about my life. And how so far it hasn't been where I thought it would be. I always saw myself going to a real good university, and working for fortune 500 companies. But I guess that didn't go like how I planned. But I guess I couldn't be that mad, it's not like I am on drugs or any crazy shit like that. I am happy with my life; I am not in jail or fucking better yet killed. I am working and I got a good house. I got a good relationship with my mom and sometimes with Jeremy. Yep, my life is exactly where I want it to be.

I looked at the pump and it was done, I pulled it out and placed it back in the holder. The total ended being like $40 to $50 so it was expensive just like I thought. I paid by debit, I swiped my card through the machine and got a receipt. I got into my car and stared the car; it went from empty to full in one second. So I was good until it ran out again, and since I drive to work and home and other places, it will be soon when I have to fill it up again. I drove off again, and this time I was focused. I hit a few red lights, nothing too long, but annoying nonetheless. I finally arrived and parked my car near an old black truck. I stopped my car and got out, and started walking toward the front entrance of the building. I walked inside, and walked to information, to see if Lindsay is still here. "Hi, my name is Mitch, and I am here to see Lindsay? "Are you family" she said. "No" I replied, just a friend, I am only visiting. She filled out a visitor pass and handed it to me. "Do you know where building one, floor two is?" I smiled, "Yes" I said. I started walking around the corner and being here brought old memories of when I first came here. I found the place and I was so fucking nervous, my heart was pounding. I waited until the nurse buzzed the doors, and I walked in. The place still had the same smell and strangely enough the same people. I walked around and all over the place, until I saw her. I stopped and my heart was still pounding. I couldn't believe it, it was Lindsay. And sadly enough she was still here, I thought she would've gotten out by now. She was standing in line with everyone else, I guess waiting to get her blood pressure checked. I walked up quietly behind her and tapped her on her shoulder. She turned around and saw my face; she stood there and didn't say anything for a second. She just walked up to me and gave me hug and didn't let go. I hugged her back, and I didn't let go either. We just stood there and continued to hug each other, holding tightly, and not letting go. "I can't believe you came all the way back just to see me." "I told you that I care about you, and I love you." "But more importantly what are you still doing here, it has been such a long time, I thought you would've got out." "They are still doing more fucking research on me; they said that I am not ready to go outside yet." "Goddamn it to hell, fucking bastards, what do they know." "Relax, will you, you are getting bent out of shape." "Sorry I just really want to spend more time with you and well I can't since they have you trapped in here like some fucking animal." She just smiled and finally let go because she was next in line to get whatever done, I don't care anymore I am pretty sure you already know what the fuck happens. It is always the same shit all the same fucking time. I am just happy that I got out when I did, but I couldn't tell Lindsay that, otherwise it will ruin the relationship. It was funny because I think that I care about her more than I did with any other girl. But I am just saying that shit, don't get me wrong I did care about those girls a lot, but Lindsay is different. And I know I Goddamn say that about every girl, that I am always comparing them. How one is different than the others, but Lindsay is really different. And I am starting to grow and appreciate it more and more. She finished getting her vitals fucking checked. And then she walked up to me again. "Let's go and take a walk." "Are you allowed to walk outside of the building?" "Yes" she said, sometimes I go and sit outside on the benches and think about when you are coming back to see me." "Now you don't have to think about it anymore, I am going to visit every day until they let you go." And with that my phone started to vibrate, I stopped Lindsay mid sentence to pick it up. I know that was rude, but this might have been important. It was important, it was my mom, and I wasn't allowed to pick up fucking cell phones in this place. They frown upon it. "Hey I have to go, it is my birthday today and my mom is calling." "Oh my God, today is your birthday" she said, as she leaned in and kissed me on the lips saying happy birthday. I thanked her and told her that I had to go. "Come back tomorrow and see me, promise." I smiled and hugged her before I left, and simply said okay. I walked toward the door and waited until I got buzzed. I looked back and waved back at Lindsay who was still standing there. And looking at her, while I was leaving to go outside, she looked so sad. I can't believe that these mother fucking assholes kept her in this shit ass place for so Goddamn long. You think that she had learned her lesson, she made a mistake and everyone fucking does. I just wondered what kind of thoughts and shit is going through her head. And then I thought about my journal, and wondered if she started writing. Maybe one day I will ask her, no I am not going to do that. I wanted her to surprise me like how I surprised her when I gave it to her. I had to remind myself not to bring it up in any of our future conversations. I made it outside and I couldn't ask for better weather, even though it was fucking blistering hot, but good nonetheless. I walked to my car and unlocked the doors and got in. I had to hurry to see what my mom wanted. Or better yet or what she got me, you know I hope that she knows that I am not a fucking baby anymore. I am a man. And I am turning 21, and with that come a few things. I am an adult and I have responsibilities, and the most important thing that I can finally, finally drink. And that means only one thing, the first chance that I get I am going to get FUCKED UP, out of my mind. I drove off and couldn't wait to get home, to see what my mom and Jeremy got me.

After a few stops, Goddamn red lights, I made it home. Not my home but my mom's home. I pulled in and I can see Jeremy peeking out the freaking window. He turned away and walked away from it. I just nodded my head as I stopped my car and got out and started walking toward the door. I was about to get my keys until my mom opened the door and hugged the shit out of me. "Mitch" she said, happy birthday baby. Come on in Jeremy and I have some great news to tell you, and we have something for you." I came in happy, and closed the door behind me. "Okay, close your eyes honey I have your birthday present for you." I closed my eyes and waited. "Hold out your hands" she said. And I did just that, hoping for a set of keys to go with a brand new car, and my mom placed the gift in my hand." "Open your eyes" she said. And I did just that, and it was a old gold watch." "It looks like the same one that dad had?" "It is the one that your dad had; I found it and restored it just for you, happy birthday Mitch." I just smiled and a tear came to my eye, and I hugged my mom and Jeremy handed me an envelope. Knowing him he probably gave me fucking money or something. And I opened it and I wasn't surprised, it was but it was a lot $200. "Happy birthday, kiddo, now don't spend it all at one time." I smiled again and thanked him. "Now are you going to tell me the good news or am I going to have to wait." Well Mitch" said my mom, you know that Jeremy and I have been together for a long time and well we decided after a long talk, and well we are getting married." I was stunned and honestly not surprised. I was just stunned that they would do it so fucking soon. "That's great, wow, I can't believe it. When are you guys officially getting married?" "Well, Jeremy proposed today and the wedding is in two weeks." "Two weeks wow, which is great, well congratulations to the both of you and best wishes for the future." My mom started crying, oh yeah she is very sentimental when it comes to sad shit. She hugged and kissed me all over like moms usually do, and Jeremy didn't cry, no he is a man, but he did shake my hand and said, "Well thanks kiddo." I tried on the watch and it was a perfect fit, I couldn't believe it. This is the nicest thing that my mom had ever gotten me. I got more comfortable and took off my shoes and socks and Jeremy went into the room and turned on the TV. "How did Jeremy propose?" "Well it really was so romantic, but I guess for Jeremy something that had never done before. He baked a cake and put the ring inside the cake. And let me tell you something it was a real funny watching Jeremy bake a cake. So he brought this cake to me and told me to cut in a specific place, because he has present for me. But the funny thing was Jeremy forgot where he put the darn ring and we ended up tearing up the whole cake." "It was really funny when you think about it. There was cake all around the place and all over our faces and everywhere. He proposed and I said yes, as we laughed the day away while feeding each other cake." I just laughed with my mom, as Jeremy gave a little laugh from the room. I guess Jeremy overhead my mom's story. I continued to laugh some more and looking at my watch, I just realized that I had to go. "Mom, I love you and tell Jeremy thanks for the money, and thank you for the watch. But I have to go, I will call you tomorrow. And congratulations again best of luck with everything." My mom hugged me one more time and told me to visit more often. And I put my socks and shoes on and left. I walked in my car, and thank God I left it unlocked, and got in. my mom came out to the front porch and I waved at her, and I reversed and took off. I couldn't believe that my mom and Jeremy were finally getting married. You know it is about time, Jeremy needs to settle down, and he picked the perfect women to do it with. The reason I was hurrying because I had to be at work, it was my first day and I didn't want to be late. I guess I am growing up right before my own eyes. I smiled as I just drove off.

Chapter 29
Family Is Forever

There was heavy ass fucking traffic, but I finally made it to work, well the building. It was quite bigger than I had imagined but I wasn't that excited about working in a fucking bank. I mean it's a fucking bank, who the fuck works at a bank. But I mean it was money and I needed some right now. I need money to pay for my car and for my small ass house. I got out of my car and walked to the fucking building. I walked in ready and confident that one day I am going to get promoted and be the CEO of this Goddamn place. I was a little confused, I mean I walked into banks all the time, but never actually worked in one. I found whom I believed is someone who worked there, but I could be wrong because this person was wearing like a fucking suit or something. Well, I walked up to him and before I could say the next word, he said, "Mitch"? I followed by saying, "Yes." Good, he said I am your boss, Mr. Johnson, let me show you to your work space. Now I am glad you're part of this team, let me tell you something we work hard Johnson and Global Bank. He led me to where I was going to work. See I filled out this piece of shit resume, and luckily I got the job fast as hell. I have always had a good people skill that's hard to believe right, but he decided to put me as a bank teller. So he put me behind the desk, and told me everything that I needed to do. "I am starting now, I said, are you sure I am ready?" "Kid, come on, don't ask too many questions, you will be fine and if you have any questions ask me." Fucking Mr. Johnson walked away, and I was alone and thank God that no one was coming to my line. This gave me the perfect chance to see how the other tellers do the job. Since Mr. Johnson didn't want to teach me that bastard fuck. I watched them for several more minutes, and continued to watch them for several more minutes. I started to get the hang of what they doing, and with that said someone came up to the window. It was an older lady; she walked up to the booth and said that she wanted to cash a check. So I guess that wasn't that hard, I took the check, and she gave me her driver's license. You have to show id, to cash a check; they want to make sure that it is you and shit. I took the check and gave her the cash, and a second later she smiled and said have a good day and she left. And I was standing there thinking to myself that was easy and if that is all I have to do I am going to be good. More and more people came to cash checks and one person actually wanted to make a withdrawal. He gave me his account information, and I looked it up. After a few seconds, I gave him his money and he thanked me and walked out of the bank. Wow that was easy I said to myself, maybe working here wasn't going to be that bad. I noticed that the girl at the far end put a sign up; she looked at me and walked past me, looked at me again and walked to the manager. I wasn't trying to overhear but they were right next to me so I heard everything. It wasn't that special she was just taking her break and I heard her say "The new guy". I guess she was referring to me, as I tried to play it off like I wasn't listening, but she looked at me looking at her and I quickly turned away. When I turned to her again she was smiling and standing in front of me. "Hi" she said, my name is Valerie. You must be Mitch right?" "Yes" I said, it is nice to meet you Valerie. "Thanks, but you can me Val, I hate when people call me Valerie it makes me sound old." I smiled as she was just so cute. "I convinced the manager to give you break, so I can show you around a little bit. I hope you don't mind." I smiled again, "No" I said, I would like that, thanks. I walked from around the booth and towards Val, who looked amazing close up. It wasn't so much what she was wearing, but her body. What the fuck, why is it that every time I meet someone new, especially a girl, I act all weird and obsessed. It's a problem that I can't still figure out. "How long have you been working here, Val?" She paused and thought it about for a second, "About two years, but honestly I really want to quit." I was confused when she said that. "Why" I said, why you want to quit." "You see don't get me wrong I like working here and all but after two years of doing the same thing, I really want to do something different something exciting." "So why don't you ask the manager you don't want to work here anymore, I am sure he will understand." She laughed, "There is one problem, Mr. Johnson isn't just the damn manager here he is my dad." "Shit" I said, sorry I didn't mean anything by it. "It's okay I know you didn't, he won't let me quit, I have to do something to get fired. "Let me ask you a question, do you like working here, even though it is your first day and all. And please be honest and give me your answer." I thought about it for a second while starting at Val. "No" I said, I just got this job to make some money, I hate working in banks, no offense. "None taking" she said, I think I have an idea that could get us both fired, but you have to promise me that if we do this you have to go all the way and no backing down no matter what." I looked a little confused but ready for whatever comes my way. "Sure" I said, are we robbing this place. "Better" she said, we are going to do something more fun. "Follow me" she said. I followed her into a room where there was a camera and it was looking right at us. She pushed me in front of a stack of boxes that were on shelves, and started messing with my hair. She leaned in closer, and I already knew what was going to happen. And for the first time I wanted to be in control. I grabbed her and re-positioned her where I was and started kissing her. "Who is watching this camera anyway" I said, as I kissed her more and more and started feeling on her. She said, "All the cameras go into my dad's office, so he is probably watching us right now." I got off from her and said, "What the fuck your dad, you mean we are making out while your dad watches." "Hey, you promised remember, you have to do this." And that is when I realized that I did promise and I had to do this. This felt wrong in so many ways, but Val tasted so good that I couldn't stop. I leaned in closer and ran *my* fingers through her hair this time. I started unbuttoning her shirt and I can see her bra, she was wearing a red color bra. We started kissing more and more, until I heard a door slam. I believe that was Mr. Johnson, and I was right. "What the hell is going on here, Mitch what the hell do you think you are doing?" And I said like a dick, "I believe I am making out with your daughter sir, do you mind we are in the middle of something." Val just laughed, as she still had her hands around me. "Well, this is how it's going to be Mitch, well son your fired." "Well if I am fired, then I quit, and you know what and so does Val." "What, he was surprised, Val, you too." "Yes" she said, dad I hate working here and you never let me quit or work somewhere else." He was still mad, "Fine" he said, quit I don't care, but we will talk when you get home." Val smiled and Mr. Johnson walked away, and Val just looked at me and kissed me again. She started to walk away and I followed her so, I was still confused and horny about this whole thing, you want to hook up. She just laughed and said, "With you please, I just needed someone to help me get fired, thanks a lot kiddo." And then she walked away and out of the door. And I was standing there fucking confused and mad. That bitch, I can't believe she just did that. She fucking used me and the worse part of all this is that I can't even get my fucking job back. I was so furious that I didn't want to stay here any longer. I left and walked to my car. I still can't believe she just did that, well I guess it wasn't that bad because I never had the chance to be someone's last stand. Even though that is something that you should never be proud of, but I just made out with a hot ass girl. So in my eyes there was nothing wrong with that. I got into my car and decided to go back home and fucking relax. I think after what just happened I needed to relax and not to think about fucking Val.

I got home and it wasn't a minute to soon. I turned off the car and got out. I grabbed some CD's from the car and put them in my pocket. I just needed something I can listen to when I take a shower. I walked to my door and was about to unlock it, when my mom called. I sighed and answered the phone. "Hi mom" I said, what's up. "Mitch honey can you come home for a while, Jeremy went out with his friends and I am all alone." I just laughed a little, it wasn't anything rude, and it is just that my mom tries to make me spend time with her as much as possible. "Okay mom, I will come over just give a few minutes." She hung up the phone and I walked to my car again. I got in, because I didn't lock my doors the last time, and started the bitch up again and drove off to my mom's house. I didn't have to stop for gas but I was getting a little hungry, so I decided that I was going to wait until I got home. I got home and boy was I hungry. It felt like my appetite grew, I was trying to walk in and make it to the kitchen before anyone notices. I walked and my mom was sitting outside in the living room, and she was drinking. I can tell because they were empty bottles of beer everywhere. I don't know how many she had and I wasn't going to count. She came up to me and put her hands through my hair. "Mom I think you had too much to drink. I think you need to sit down and just relax a while." "Mitch, you know how much I love you, you are my only son and we never get to spend any time together. This was getting fucking weird, this was like my dream that I had a few years ago, now I think it is becoming reality. I tried pushing her off but she came closer and closer to me. She was fucking staggering she couldn't even walk straight. "Mitch, I need you, you have always been such a good son to me. Please come to your mother." I didn't know what to do; I mean this was getting weird. She got closer and I was trapped against the door. She leaned in and stared whispering in my ear. She leaned in and softly kissed me on the cheek, and then she started softly kissing me on the lips. I tried to push her off but I couldn't. I grabbed my mom and we both fell in the middle of the living room floor. I was on the bottom and she was on top of me. She started unbuttoning her T-shirt. She threw it angst the door, and I started to take off my shirt, and my fucking pants. She slid down my boxers and she unzipped her blouse. And she was on top of naked. She put my dick in her wet pussy and started riding the shit out of me. This felt so good, I grabbed her from the back and forced her harder and harder. She leaned in and I started sucking on her big breasts. She continued to ride my dick more and more. She started screaming and moaning. She got up and rotated so she was facing the other way. She bent over and she was sucking my dick. She put her ass lower in my face and I started licking her pussy. She sucked my dick so fucking good and hard. She started moaning, and then she laughed a little. Jeremy used his keys to open the door, and he was in complete surprise. I guess neither of us heard him pull in. "WHAT THE FUCK IS GOING ON!" he said, slamming the door. "Honey, you're home" my mom said. Jeremy walked up to my mom and slapped the shit out of her. I got up and got fucking mad as shit, and ran and tackled him. We started fighting again. We grabbed each other and started throwing fists. He was a little drunk because I can smell the beer on him, so I had an advantage. I threw a hard ass punch and hit him right in the fucking lip, it busted and started bleeding. He grabbed me and fucking threw me half way across the Goddamn room. I got up and he ran and tackled me into the kitchen. He got up before I did and he started fucking kicking my fucking stomach. He kicked twice and once more until I grabbed his leg and tripped him off. I was fucking losing, and I needed to do something fast. I opened the cabinet drawer and pulled out a long, sharp butcher knife. Just enough to scare him, he got up and I started walking with the knife. He walked up to me and I tried to slice him but he ducked and wrestled the knife away from me. He threw me on the ground and picked up the knife and started walking toward me, I walked back out to the living room, and my mom was moving around, he started walking closer and closer and then he tried to run and stab me at the same time. I moved and threw him off of me, and he dropped the knife. I kicked it aside and I punched him right dead in his mouth, breaking his jaw, and he grabbed me by the shirt and punched me right in the nose, breaking it and it started bleeding. He kept on kneeing me in the stomach and kneeing me, I got desperate I was fucking losing. So I punched him in the face a few more times and kneed him in his fucking Goddamn balls. He immediately fell to the ground. I was so fucking furious I walked back to the knife and picked it up. Jeremy was trying to get up but I fucking stabbed him in his stomach. My mom was getting up to her feet. Jeremy was crying out, and bleeding all over the place. My mom just saw what happened. She started crying and yelling, PUT DOWN THE FUCKING KNIFE! I couldn't hear what she was saying, I was so mad at Jeremy for hitting my mom. He tried to crawl away and I watched him bleed from his fucking stomach. I walked towards him and fucking stabbed him a few more times in the face and chest area until that mother fucking asshole died. I watched over his body still holding the knife and covered in blood, as Jeremy took his last Goddamn breaths. I continued to watch over his body for several more seconds, and I don't know what it was but something about this felt good. Stabbing that asshole Jeremy with a knife felt good, I felt different, and I have never felt this kind of way before. I finally dropped the knife and walked over to my mom and tried to explain everything to her. But she was crying and screaming, GET THE FUCK OUT OF MY HOUSE NOW! I tried to explain what happened. "Jeremy hit you, and I wasn't going to stand for it. I got carried away with the knife." And again she didn't want to hear it. GET THE FUCK OUT OF MY HOUSE BEFORE I CALL THE COPS. I was so fucking mad that my mom was acting like a baby, I fucking left. I got into my car and fucking drove off.

I made it home and decided to clean up and wash all the blood off my hands and shit. I grabbed some wipes from the glove compartment and wiped my hands. I cleaned the inside of my car, just the damn steering wheel. I got out and shut the fucking door. It was getting pretty late so I decided to go and take a shower; I just needed time to think about everything. First thing in the morning, I am going to visit Lindsay. If I go visit Liz and tell her what happened, she is going to send me to the psych unit for fucking ever. I walked to the door and opened it with my keys; I got inside my house and turned on the Goddamn light. The light turned on and I closed the door. I took off my shoes and my coat and walked inside the fucking kitchen. I cracked open a beer and took a couple of sips. I hated this kind. I took more sips and put it back in the fridge. I closed the door and walked to the bathroom. I started undressing and then I started thinking about what happened. I was still a little shock and fucking scared. I can't believe I just killed a person. And to make it worse it was someone that I knew and well honestly somewhat liked here and there. But on the other hand, I felt nothing at all when I killed him. I turned on the water and set it to warm. I hate taking really hot showers it burns the fuck out of my skin, because my skin is so sensitive. I waited for several more seconds and got in. I turned facing the shower and let the water hit my face. I stood there for a couple of minutes thinking about my mom. She told me leave but she didn't call the cops on me. I wonder if she was going to call the cops on me. I washed my body with soap and finished up. I didn't want to spend all night in the fucking shower because I will prune up. I got out and wiped dry with my towel, and wrapped it around me. It was a little cold when I stepped out of the shower, but after I get dry and put some clothes on I will be fine. I walked to my room and finished up getting dry and threw on some fucking clothes and just fell onto my bed, and closed my eyes. I woke up and I felt like I was sleeping for days, but I was only out for about an hour. I woke up because my phone kept going off. I didn't want to pick it up, but it will keep on ringing and after a while it will get annoying. I fucking answered the phone, and it was Liz. And at this point I was thinking that I was in deep shit. How about she heard what happened. Could my mom have told on me, no I was acting fucking paranoid. "Hey Liz, what's going on?" "Nothing much Mitch" she said, how is everything? I paused for a brief second. "Good" I said. "Mitch, I was just calling and checking up on you making sure that everything was okay." I breathed a sigh of relief, "Everything is okay Liz, no complaints here." "Okay, well if you ever want to talk about anything you know how to contact me or stop by." "No problem I will, take care Liz." And she hung up the phone. I placed the phone back on my dresser, and thought about if she knew or not but didn't want to tell me. I mean I told my mom that I saw a psychiatrist, and she could've easily told her what I did. Great, now I couldn't sleep and I checked my watch, and it was around 9:30 and it was late. I sat up from my bed and put both my hands over my face, and breathed a sigh. I got out of my bed didn't even bother to make it when I got out of it. I walked to my closet and took off what I was wearing and threw on something else. I grabbed my fucking car keys and my wallet and my dad's watch. Well my watch now, shit, I can't believe that my mom gave me this watch and I turn around and do something like this. But fuck it I didn't care anymore about anything, I just didn't care anymore. I opened the front door and walked out; I closed it and locked it. I walked to my car and opened it and got in. I didn't know where I was going, I know it was too late to go visit Lindsay. So I decided to go home and try for the like the third Goddamn time explain to my mom what the fuck really happened. I just hope that she is sober enough to know it's me this time and can actually sit down and hear what I have to say. I drove off, and driving to my mom's house one day I found a shortcut, so I decided to take that. It took about five to ten minutes off the actual time to get there so it was good.

I finally got there and hurriedly parked the Goddamn car and got out. I didn't bother to lock the doors because we lived in a safe neighborhood; well I guess I don't know. I rang the doorbell and it took a while until someone came and finally answered. My mom wasn't too happy to see me, she tried to close the door in my face but I stopped it with my fucking foot. "What the fuck mom, how many times do

I have to try and explain myself? Will you sit down, as I was coming inside the house, so I can tell you what happened? I can tell by her facial expression that she didn't want to hear it right now. She started walking toward the kitchen, and yelled out; "I arranged a funeral for Jeremy tomorrow. The police came to the house, don't worry I didn't tell on you." She came back into the living room. "I told the police that Jeremy committed suicide, for a second they almost didn't buy it, but I *convinced* them otherwise. So you have to come to the funeral service tomorrow, and wear something nice, something in black." She walked back into the kitchen and said, "Now go home Mitch it is getting late." I was so fucking confused about what the fuck was going on. I left and closed the door behind me. I got into my car and fucking drove off. I made it home and it was starting to pour rain, so that wasn't a good thing. I hate driving in the Goddamn rain. I got out and this time I locked the doors and walked to the fucking door. I got out my keys and opened the door; I walked in and shut the door behind me. I took off my shoes and walked straight to my closet, to see if I had something in black. And I did, so that was good, now I have something for the service. Even though I really didn't feel like fucking going. But I guess I had to go and pay my Goddamn fucking respects to a guy whom I liked and disliked at times. It was getting later in the night, and I didn't bother to check what time, I could just tell. I didn't want to do anything else but fucking sleep. I walked into my room, took off my pants and shirt and still had my socks on. I turned off my phone and didn't set an alarm on my clock. I didn't anything to fucking bother me when I went to sleep. This was going to be the best fucking sleep in my fucking life.

Chapter 30
The Service/Lindsay

I woke up refreshed and ready to go, man I have to tell you that was the best night of fucking sleep I had ever gotten. Even though today wasn't the day to celebrate, now that I think about it my mom had to spend a Goddamn fortune to get the funeral service the very next day. Usually funerals take about a couple of weeks. I guess she wanted this to be over and done with. I mean they were to get married and shit. I got up from my bed, because I was still lying down in my bed. I walked to my phone and turned it back on; I got a missed call from Liz. I was in no mood to call her back right now. I undressed and decided to take a shower, and then I was going to go to my mom's house and see how she is coping with everything. I just hope that everything is going okay with my mom; I know it has been a crazy couple of hours for her. I mean all this shit happened within a day and shit. I got into the bathroom and turned on the shower, I set it for a little hotter than before. I needed to fucking relax more, I was to fucking tense. After I see my mom I was going to stop by and see how Lindsay is doing. I just hope that everything is going okay with her as well. I stood in the shower and just relaxed as the water felt good hitting my body. It was so warm and gentle, it felt more soothing and I really needed that shit right now. I didn't want to stay real long in the shower so I hurried up and soaped my body and washed off, I washed my hair with shampoo, some got in my Goddamn eye, and got out. I was dripping and I forgot my fucking towel. So I had to run all the way to my room and I was dripping everywhere I went. I didn't care about the water all on the floor right now. I walked to my closet and got some clothes; I brought a bag and folded my funeral clothes in there. I changed and decided that I wasn't going to blow dry my hair. I was going to let it air dry. I grabbed my keys and the rest of my shit, and decided to leave my house. I didn't know where I was going to go first, I thought it about it for a second, and I decided I was going to go to see Lindsay and see how she was doing. I got into my car and pulled out my phone. I should really call Liz back, but I really didn't want to talk to her right now. I called the place where Lindsay was staying, and told one of the Goddamn incompetent nurses that I was coming to visit Lindsay. She hung up the phone and I put the phone on the passenger's side. There weren't a lot of cars today so I got to the fucking place really quick. I pulled in and stopped my car, and got out. I walked up to the fucking building and walked to the front entrance, the information booth, and told them that I was visiting. "Hi, I cleared my throat, Mitch I said, and I am here to see Lindsay." She looked at me and gave me a visitor's pass. I already knew what to do and where the fuck I needed to go. I walked all the way down the hallway. It took me about a minute to get there. I waited for one of the nurses to buzz the door open so I can walk on through. I walked around and tried to find Lindsay, I couldn't find her anywhere. Someone told me that she was eating lunch so I walked into the room. I saw her, well recognized the back of her head. I walked up behind her and cleared my throat. It's like she had sixth sense or something, because she knew it was me. She got up and turned around and saw me. She hugged me and didn't let go for several seconds. I guess she was happy to see me. I hugged her back and kissed her on top of her head. "I knew you would come back and see me" she said. "I told you that I was going to come back at least every day and see you. I love you Lindsay." "But there is something that I need to talk to you about" I said, this is very important can we go somewhere?" She looked kind of worried and upset I could just tell by looking into her eyes. We walked to a room and no one was inside. "I did something that I am not proud of." I said, I killed Jeremy at my mom's home. She didn't say anything for a second and then something that was surprising even to me. "Now you know how I feel, welcome to my world Mitch." There was a moment where she felt that my actions were justified, and that she was Goddamn proud of the fact that I killed someone. I mean honestly, it did feel good, I told you that he called me kiddo again I was going to kill him. I just had no idea it will feel this good. "What did your mom say about the whole thing" she said. "Nothing really, the police came and she told them that Jeremy committed suicide and shit. And they fucking believed my mom." "Then my mom got all mad and told me to fucking leave the house, but then she also told me that she was having a service for him, like a funeral and shit today. I was going to say more, but Lindsay cut me off. She told me that she will be right back and told me not to go anywhere. She started walking and I started thinking about her more and more. She was talking to an adult and then she walked into her room. I really do love her and I will do *anything* to be with her. She came back and said; "I have good news and bad news" I smiled and asked for the bad news first so I can get it out of the way. I am sorry but you have to go because they are going to vitals, then groups and then I am going to be meeting with the doctor today. They might let me go home today." I got sad for a moment. "What is the good news" I said? She smiled, "Thanks for the journal it was really sweet. And I knew you didn't mean it when you wrote Lindsay I hate you, I knew you were just upset." "You read that, I am sorry I was upset about something but I am over it now." "Anyway, I started writing in the journal, so there is some entries for you to read." She handed me the journal and hugged me and told me that I had to go. I hugged her back and gave her a kiss. I thanked her for the journal and left. I folded the journal and put it into my back pocket. I walked to the doors and waited for the nurse, to buzz me out. She buzzed the doors, and I left. I walked outside and found a bench near my car and took the journal out of my back pocket. I found the page where I stopped writing and she began writing. The journal entry started like this.

Dear Journal,

Hi baby, it is me Lindsay, you're one and only. I am just kidding. I am writing you in your journal you gave me. That was really sweet. But I didn't like it when you wrote Lindsay I hate you. I know you didn't mean that so I am going to let it go. I don't know what to write about so I am sorry if this entry seems short in any way. I can't believe that I am still in here it has been such a long time and the people in here aren't friendly at all. I want to go home and see my dad. I miss him a lot, I wonder if he is thinking about me right now. This place hasn't change one bit since you were here. They still make you do the same old shit. I started talking to the doctors more and more, but they are not convinced that I am ready to go home. But they talked it over and told me that I needed to stay just a little longer. Longer right, I mean how long I have to stay in here; it has been three mother fucking years I want to go home. Baby, I am going to go now, sorry, I am too upset to write anymore, with lots of love, Lindsay.

I folded the notebook back up and put it back in my back pocket. I just smiled and thought of her. I got into my car and decided to go my mom's home. I took the notebook and put it in the glove compartment, for safe keeping. I will read more when I have time. I wanted to make sure that my mom was doing okay with everything. I drove off and went to see my mom and to check up on her. I got to the house, and she was sitting outside in the porch area just sitting there doing nothing really. I pulled in and she stood up, I turned off my car and got out. Hi, mom how is everything?" She smiled and hugged me when I walked toward the top of the steps. "I am just glad that you came today, and remembered." "I brought some extra clothes; well it is the funeral clothes so I can change into, for the service." "Good the service is today at 4:00 P.M., so don't be late. Won't you come in? I know it has been a long and stressful day for you." It really hasn't but at least my mom wasn't yelling at me or better yet didn't tell on me on the police. I wonder why she wanted to keep that a secret. Well not really a secret but not tell anyone, even the police. She could've easily told on me to the fucking cops. I walked in and sat down on the couch. Everything felt so different, and so quite without Jeremy in the house. I can still remember that night, everything was happening so fast. I remember fucking my mom and that was crazy. I knew that she was my mom and she was very drunk but that didn't stop the both of us. And when Jeremy overreacted and slap the hell out of my mom, I just snapped. All I remember is that we started fighting, and then the next thing that I remember doing is stabbing the shit out of him with a fucking knife.

And then the next thing that I remember is standing over him watching as he is gasping for his last breath and he looked right into my eyes and then he died. But it was something about that night that I will never forget, something about that night just felt right. My mom walked over to the door and closed it, because I forgot to when I walked in. "Do you want something to drink or eat or something." "No I am fine, mom, if I am hungry or thirsty I will get it myself." My mom walked to the kitchen and opened the fridge door; she started messing around with shit. I got up and walked into the kitchen too. I checked the time and it was around 2:00, so maybe it was a good idea of everyone to start getting ready. I told my mom that since I already took a shower and everything that I am going to go and see an old friend. And when I met that I of course meant Lindsay. "Just make sure that you come back here around 3:00, so we can make it to the service around 4." I smiled and hugged my mom and I left. I walked to the car and unlocked the car door, I got in and started the car, and I drove off and let me tell you it was a relief to get out my mom's house. I mean it's like she has been acting different now. She isn't full of life anymore; I believe that I heard that she got fired from her job for drinking problems. I wouldn't blame her for that shit. I mean I did stab the fuck out her fiancé with a large and sharp butcher knife. And stabbed him again in the face and chest a couple more times, but that bastard deserved it for hitting my mom. Anyway before I get into the whole fucking story again, I do somewhat sorry for what happened and for my mom now. Now she has to live with all of this shit, I just she doesn't kill herself from drinking to Goddamn much. I found a spot near an old car and just parked my car. It was in this old ass parking lot for some store. I wanted to park there because I can read another one of Lindsay's entries she wrote in my, I mean our journal. I pulled it out from the glove compartment, and stared reading where I left off.

Dear Journal,

I am getting really sick and tired of this place, baby I miss you. When are you come and visit me. I miss the way you taste baby. I miss kissing you and being with you. I really want to go home now. The food is getting better day by day, but the people are getting worse. I mean there is this one old creepy guy who keeps looking at me weird. I don't know what his Goddamn problem is, but he is scaring me. Baby, I need you to come here and fucking punch is fucking lights out for me. That is what I need you to do for me. I spoke with the doctors today and they still haven't said anything yet whether or not I can go home or not. It is starting to get really, really annoying. I mean I have been complying with all the rules, taking all the medications and being nice to everyone. But the doctor said, get this, and I quote, "It is just we haven't spent time with a girl of your status, and we need you to stay here upon further treatment." Can you believe that shit, they swear like I don't know what is going on but I do. Baby, I got to go they are calling everyone for food, and I am hungry. I miss you and I love you, come visit okay, your girl Lindsay.

I smiled and folded the notebook back up and put it into the glove compartment. I started my car up, and it didn't turn on. I turned it on again, and again it fucking stalled. I tried one more time and finally it came on. I got worried for a second, because if my car fucking stops I am really screwed because I would have no way of getting home. I reversed and pulled out and man was I fucking tired, I don't know why but I really was tired. Not sleepy tired because I was wide awake but like emotionally tired. I am just tired of all the fucking bullshit that happened in my life and with everyone else I have met. I feel like all the Goddamn shit always happens to me and to no one else. But you know what forget it I guess I just have to endure it, I don't give a shit about it anymore. The only thing that I care about now is Lindsay and yeah, my mom, sometimes. And as soon I said Lindsay's name, I thought about her more and more. And I guess I did the one thing that I wanted to do for a very long time, even though Beverly is the girl that I wanted to do it with. I checked my wallet and my mom gave me a credit card, you know for fucking emergencies. I pulled it out and I called the number on the back of the card. I just wanted to make sure how much money was actually on the damn card. After I punched a few numbers in a voice on the other side told me, your balance is $4,400. I was in complete fucking shock. I can't believe I have over $4000 on a credit card. I mean did my mom call and find out and find out how much freaking money was on the card. I mean she wouldn't give me a credit card with that much money on it. I checked the time and it was around 2:45, so I had time. I was still contemplating if I should go to the service, I mean that bastard fuck wasn't my dad and what the fuck did he ever do for me. I mean sure he did one or two things for me and tired to be my friend, but still that doesn't constitute Jeremy being my dad. No one in the whole fucking world can replace my dad, and my mom well the only thing that I go to her now is either food, or fucking sex. I drove around and around until I finally found it, it was a jewelry store. I was going to buy Lindsay an engagement ring. I was going to ask her hand in marriage, I just have to wait and see what her dad says. I pulled in and parked my car I turned off my car, praying that next time I turn it on it will start, and walked to the front entrance of the building. I walked in and walked to the place where they had a glass display right in the front of the store. "Hi" a tall gentleman said, how may I help you today? "I am looking for a ring for my girlfriend" I said, and I want it to be special, she deserves something nice. "Well we have this ring that would be perfect for your girlfriend" he said. "It is a cubic zirconium 14kt gold, with diamonds across the outside boarders with a heart shaped diamond in the middle." I looked it at for a second, and it was better than any of the rest of the rings. "I will take it, how much is going to be?" The guy simply said $8,999. "I only have $4400, can you please give it to me for half, I know that you guys don't do that, but that is all I have." He looked at me and smiled. "You really must care about this girl. Tell you what I will give it for half." I smiled and thanked the guy. "That would be perfect" I said. He took the ring and put it in a box and gave me the box, I gave him my credit card and he swiped it and after a few seconds, it went through. I signed the receipt and he gave me my copy. I couldn't believe it I bought a nice ass ring, and the guy gave it me for half. He was so nice; I would have to thank him one day. I got into my car and opened the glove compartment, and put the box on top of my journal. I started my car and decided to go visit Lindsay, and see how everything is with her. I drove off and hit a lot of fucking red lights. Since I had time, I opened the glove compartment and took out the ring box, and closed the glove compartment door, and put the ring box on the seat. I got there and Lindsay was sitting outside alone, she didn't see me pull in. I pulled in and parked behind a blue truck. I stopped my car, again praying that it would start the next time I turn it on, and got out and walked toward Lindsay. Who immediately shot up from her seat and ran into my arms. "Hey baby, what are you doing here?" "Wait, she cut me off again, I have really good news." I smiled, "What is it" I said. "I spoke with the doctor today and she said that I can finally go home." I am leaving Mitch, baby I am finally leaving." I hugged her and told her that I am so happy for her. "Now it is my turn" I said. "Close your eyes and hold out your hand." I saw her face lit up as she had a huge smile on her face. She held out her hand as I got on one knee. I took the box which had the ring inside and opened it. I began by saying, "Lindsay I met you for the first time when I came here and I knew that I wanted to be with you forever. There was something special about you the day that we first met. I love you Lindsay and well, open your eyes now." She opened her eyes and saw that I was on one knee holding her hand. And you can only guess what happens next. She started breathing heavily, and crying a little. I finished what I had to say, "What I am trying to say is Lindsay I love you, and I know that you love me too, and well will you marry me?" And I placed the ring on her hand, and she lifted up her hand and looked at it. She started crying more and more and I got up from my knee and waited. She looked at for several more seconds, and then she looked at me and hugged me and said, "YES." I was so happy that she said yes, I kissed her and continued to hug her. "I love you so much" I said. She looked back at me and said, "I love you too." "Wait right here for me, promise, I have to go back inside and get my stuff before I forget it. She left and started walking towards the building. This would be a good time to tell everyone the good news. I called my mom first and told her. "Mom, I have good news I just asked Lindsay, the girl that I have been dating for the last three and a half years to marry me. And she said yes." "Can you believe it, she said yes." And of course my mom wasn't too happy about it. She started going on about how young I am. And how am I going to support the both of us with no job. I guess she heard about what happened at the bank, I am still mad at fucking Val for that shit. She went on and on about other shit that I didn't want to hear anymore. "Mom, I am not doing this for you, I am doing this for me. I love her and that is the only thing that fucking matters." And the last thing she said before she hung up was, "Okay if you want to throw your Goddamn life away on some girl, go ahead but don't come crying to me when everything you wished for doesn't work out." And then she hung up. I couldn't believe that she would say something like that. My relationship with my mom is started to slowly fade away. I called Liz back, finally right, and told her the good news. Her stupid receptionist picked up, and I told her if she can pass me on through. I waited for about a couple of seconds, and Lindsay was taking forever to get her shit. Liz finally came on the phone, and she said, "Finally you return my calls. I thought something terrible happened to you." "Sorry about that, I have been really busy. But I have good news I just asked Lindsay, the girl that I told you about in the psychiatric unit to marry me, and she said yes." Liz paused for a second, "Congratulations Mitch, I am so happy for you. I am so happy that you found someone who can share in all your memories together. When is the wedding?" "I just proposed, you have to give it some time, I said laughing, maybe not for a couple of months, maybe." "Well I am just thrilled for the both of you, I am sorry a client walked in, I have to go, but congratulations again to the both of you." She hung up the phone and Lindsay finally came out the building. "Who were you just talking to?" I smiled. "My mom, I called her and told her the good news." "Oh yeah, what did she say?" "She was happy for the both of us." Lindsay smiled and we walked toward my car. I unlocked the trunk and she threw all of her shit in, she closed the trunk and got in the passenger side. I got in and closed the door. "Where do you want to go" I said. She simply looked at me and said, "Home".

We drove off, and being with Lindsay I just felt so much better about everything. I don't know why, I just did. "Where do you live" I said. She gave me the address while resting her head on my shoulder. She lived what sounded like in the suburbs of New York. Or did she even live in New York I had no idea. "Where do you live again, asking again for reference?" "You forgot already, I just told you where I lived. "I live in Long Island. And then she gave me the street address and I quickly asked for a pen and some paper so I can write it down before I forget. She said she was going to lie down for a while because she was really tired. She rested her head on my shoulder again, and closed her eyes. I got my MP3 player and plugged it into the car jack and turned it on. I put it on shuffle so I don't have to mess with it. I lowered the volume so Lindsay can rest. It felt like hours of driving, because it was a lot of traffic but I finally got to Long Island, and from the psych unit to Long Island it wasn't that long of a drive, just about one hour and fifteen minutes. I called Lindsay's name and told her that we were here. I grabbed the paper which had her street address on it and followed it. Of course Lindsay was still sleeping, so I turned up the music, and then she woke up. She playfully punched me in the arm, and said jerk. She looked out the window, and said wow; I can't believe it I am home. Well, not home, home but home. She said that her house was just around the corner of the street I was on. I drove around the tight corner and finally we were at Lindsay's house. Her dad came out the house and started walking down the steps. I pulled in and turned off my car, and got out. I was so fucking nervous, I walked to the other side and opened Lindsay's door. She got out and I closed, and locked the doors. Lindsay ran to her dad with open arms. Her had hugged and kissed her on the cheek. I walked slowly to them; Lindsay turned around and introduced me to him. "Mitch" she said, I want to introduce you to my dad. Dad, this is Mitch, he is a boy I met when I was in the place. I walked up to him and extended my arm. "Hello sir" I said, it is a pleasure to meet you. He smiled and looked at me, and then he said, "Please you don't have to call me sir, it makes me sound old. Please call me Frank." "Okay Frank." "Dad" Lindsay said I have good news now I don't want you overreact but just think about this. I am not a baby anymore and I am ready to move on meet someone special and live my life. Well Mitch is the special person that I am talking about. I just smiled and slowly looked away and looked back at Lindsay and Frank. "I went to get my stuff from the place and when I stepped out again he surprised me with this." Lindsay lifted up her hand, and showed her dad the engagement ring that I got her. "Dad" she said, he proposed and I said yes. Frank looked puzzled but overjoyed with everything; he looked at me and then looked at Lindsay and gave her a hug. "I am so happy for you sweetheart, I am so happy that you finally found someone who will love you with all the respect that you deserve." Of course Lindsay started crying, and I was tearing up a little too. Hey, I might act like an insensitive asshole but I got a sensitive side too. It just doesn't come out that much, that's all. I walked up to Frank, and told him like a man looking into his eyes. "I want to ask your hand in blessing sir, as I ask your daughter's hand in marriage sir." He shook my hand and smiled, and yes even Frank was crying too. He invited me into his house. I walked in holding Lindsay's hand, as we were making our way up the stairs. There was something that I needed to go but I couldn't remember what it was. I walked inside his house, and closed the door behind me. He walked into the kitchen and asked if I wanted anything to drink. Lindsay walked over to me, and said something about iced-tea. So I asked Frank, if I can have a glass of that. And I am not drinking it because Lindsay said something. Iced-tea is always been my favorite drink for the longest time. Okay, I lied; I am drinking it because Lindsay mentioned it. Frank came back with a glass and I started drinking it. I yelled out to whomever, "This is really good." Lindsay was in the other room and said I told you as she was going upstairs. She came back down, with nothing in her hand. "What did you go upstairs for?" "Nothing really I just had to check on something." She smiled and walked and sat down on the couch. My phone went off but I didn't bother to pick it up. The only thing that I was focusing on was Lindsay. She looked so much different now. She got up and yelled out, "I am taking a shower." It was funny because no one answered back, and she didn't even care. I checked my watch because I wanted to see what time it was. And it was around 3:30. There was something I needed to do but for the life of me I couldn't remember what the fuck it was. I followed Lindsay who was walking up the stairs. She turned back around and looked at me. "You following me?" she said. "I got bored sitting in your living room all by myself." "Well I am going to take shower; you are welcome to come in and sit down and talk if you want." Oh yeah this I remember, I believe it was Kristen who told me same exact thing. Lindsay walked into her room and grabbed her towel, she walked into the bathroom. I followed her into the bathroom and closed the door. She turned on the water, and let it run for a while. She looked right at me and started undressing. It's not like I haven't seen that before, I can recall plenty of times a girl undressed in front of me. When Lindsay stepped into the shower, my phone went off again. I was getting sick and tired so I decided to answer it. It was my fucking mom, FUCK I said to myself the funeral service it was already like 4:00. "Mitch, finally you know how long I have been trying to call you." "Where are you you're missing the Goddamn service." "I am with Lindsay at her house; I am waiting for her to get out of the shower." "Always with that fucking girl, and then that is when she hung up. I was so mad that she just hung up on me that I didn't even care to even call her back. Lindsay was singing in the shower and it was so cute. I don't know if she realized that I can hear her. She probably thought I was still on the phone. I didn't say anything for a while, and just started laughing. And that is when she realized that I wasn't on the phone anymore. And Lindsay just started laughing too. She turned off the water and grabbed her towel. She took a minute to get dry and stepped out the shower. She smelled so good; I could just eat her up. As soon she stepped on the mat I swooped her up like on our honeymoon. She started laughing and telling me to put her down. I didn't and carried her to her room and gently placed her on her bed. And I started smiling as I looked at her getting up from her bed and walking to her dresser. She closed her bedroom door and locked it. "I am going to change real quickly" she said. "What do you want to do when you're done getting ready or something?" I said. "I don't know" she said do you have any plans?" Plans like unintentionally missing Jeremy's service which is probably still going on. "I was supposed to go to my mom's fiancé's funeral service right now. It started at 4, and it is already like 4:20. I didn't want to miss it but I lost track of time." Lindsay finished getting ready and grabbed her wallet. "Come on you are taking me to the movies" she said. I am taking her where, I said, the movies now when I am supposed to be with my mom. But I guess my mom didn't want anything to do with me right now. I guess I don't blame her, I mean I killed her fiancé, unintentionally, and now I am missing the service. But fuck it, what did Jeremy ever do for me that I owe him like my fucking life. I smiled at Lindsay, as she started walking down the stairs. I told her to wait up, but I guess she didn't listen. I walked down the stairs and followed her she was standing near the door. With a hurry up let's go face, so I hurried up and got my stuff and walked to the door. She yelled out for dad but he didn't answer. "I am going to the movies with Mitch." "I will be home soon."

We started walking to my car and I unlocked it, and Lindsay ran to the passenger side and got in. I got in and closed the door. "Lindsay can you pass me my journal." She opened the glove compartment and took out my journal. "I remember this" she said. "What are you going to write in it now?" "I am going to write one more entry, I just feel like I should write this one in there to seal the deal." I took out my pencil and began writing.

Dear Journal,

My baby is finally out. My Lindsay is finally out and now I can see her. I can spend all my days and nights with her, because for the first time in my life I took control. I didn't listen to what anyone else had to say. With Lindsay's dad blessing I asked Lindsay to marry me and she said yes. I can finally live my life now. There are still a couple of things that I feel uncertain about. But we are going to fix that, because I believe strongly that Lindsay and I can get through anything. With a lot's of hard work we can get through anything. For the first time in my life, I am sure about something. I am so happy that I met Lindsay. Don't get me wrong the other girls; I miss them, especially Beverly. But I wanted more with Beverly but she didn't want to go any further. And I don't feel sorry about that for one bit. But I do feel sorry about my mom, and what I did. No, fuck that I don't feel sorry for what I did. For the first time I am taking control of my life and with Lindsay by my side anything is possible.

I closed the book and folded it back up and handed it to Lindsay. I asked her if she can put it back in the glove compartment. She was going to put the journal back, and asked if she can read what I wrote. I told her that it wasn't anything special but she still wanted to read it. She flipped open where I wrote the last entry and started reading. In the meantime I started the car, and I am so happy that I know where a theater is, there is one just a few miles away from my mom's house. Speaking of my mom I have to go and see her before I go to the movies. I could tell that Lindsay was done reading because she folded up the journal and put it back. She leaned over and kissed me in the cheek. "That was so sweet" she said. "Hey I have to stop by and see my mom before we go to the movies." "I feel bad that I missed the service, so I have to go and apologize, even though I don't want to do but it would be the right thing to do." I started driving towards my mom's house and it didn't take that long as I expected. I got there and pulled in. "Hey wait in the car, unless you want to come in" I said. "Okay I'll wait in the car it is no problem at all." I got out and kept the door halfway open and walked towards my mom's house. I rang the doorbell and of course knowing my mom it took a million fucking years to answer. I rang and fucking rang the fucking doorbell and she never answered. I was walking back to my car until my mom finally answered the door. "What the fuck do you want?" I was so upset at myself that I completely missed the Goddamn service. "What the hell mom, I am sorry that I missed the service but I had other important things that I needed to do." "Let me guess, you are with that girl again." "First of all her name is Lindsay, and she is not some girl, she is my fucking wife. And I don't appreciate you talking about her like that, if you don't have anything nice to say... "Yeah yeah I know the fucking speech. If you want to come in you can I am not doing anything." I smiled and motioned back to Lindsay to come here. She got out of the car and closed the door, and walked around to my side and closed the door. She walked towards me, and waited by my side. "Mom, this is my Lindsay, Lindsay this is my mom, Lauren. "It is nice to meet you. Mitch talks about you all the time." My mom smiled because obviously she didn't want to say anything rude at this point. "I hope that they are good things I hope." Lindsay responded by saying, "But of course, he really loves you and wants you to be happy." My mom's smile quickly faded as she walked in. I turned back to Lindsay who looked like she just said something that she wanted to take back. "I am sorry, I forgot I didn't know." "It is okay, I just smiled, just come on in." We walked inside and my mom was in the kitchen, rummaging through the fridge. "Do you want something to drink?" I said. "No" Lindsay replied, I am fine. She sat down on the couch and I sat next to her. My mom came back with a beer in one hand and a cigarette in the other. She lit up the cigarette and started smoking. "When did you start smoking again?" "I thought you fucking quite." "I don't care; smoking helps relieve my Goddamn stress." She started drinking and walked back into the kitchen, again looking through the fridge. My mom didn't come out for several minutes. It got pretty quiet and somewhat awkward. I turned to Lindsay and softy said, "Let's get out of here, I think that my mom wants to be alone." We both got up and started walking towards the door. "Mom, we are leaving I am going back home, and Lindsay is coming." No answer for a second, I know that she heard me but I didn't want to repeat myself again. She finally yelled out, "Well take care and you can call from time to fucking time." I said okay as we both walked out of the house and started walking towards my car. I unlocked it and we both got in. "Your mom seems sweet." I laughed, "Sweet, she is sometimes but I feel like our relationship is started to slowly fade away. But I don't care; I mean I don't feel like talking about it. We drove off and we decided to go to my house, so I can take a fucking shower and change. We drove and fucking drove and finally we got my house. It started to rain not hard, but it was drizzling, so that only means one thing. It was going to rain hard as shit later. I stopped the car and got out; Lindsay got out too and closed the door. I closed my door and locked the car. "You have a nice house" she said. "Thanks" I said. We walked to the front door and I unlocked it. We both walked in and Lindsay began by taking off her shoes and her coat. I also took off my shoes but I kept my jacket on. I was going to take that off when I go to my room. The first thing that I did is head into the bathroom. I turned on the water and took off my pants. I walked to my room and took off my jacket. I had on a pair of boxers and one black tank top. And I also was wearing gray and black socks, which I took off when I got into the bathroom. I took off my tank top. I grabbed a towel from the closet, because the one I was using was dirty. Or I thought it was, but nonetheless I threw it in the hamper and got a new one. I closed the door halfway just in case Lindsay wanted to come inside. I took off my boxers and I was standing there naked and cold waited for the water to get hot. The water finally started to get hot because I saw steam coming from the water. I stepped in and lowered the temperature a little before I get burned. I stepped in and closed the curtain. Lindsay came in and closed the door. "I got bored walking around your home." I laughed, "My home is boring" I said. "No nothing like that" she said. "Do you ever think that your relationship with your mom is ever going to get better?" I sighed, "I don't know to tell you the truth" "I don't know what went wrong with my mom." I quickly soaped my body and washed my hair. After I rinsed my hair I got turned off the water and got out. I grabbed my towel and wrapped myself; I stepped out from the shower and quickly dried off. I walked to my room and Lindsay followed me. I got changed, and then she said, "I don't feel like going to the movies." "I have a better idea, why don't we just rent a movie and watch it here." I looked at Lindsay and told her that was a good idea, as I was putting on my T-shirt and jeans. I got finished getting ready and walked out of my room. I walked back into the bathroom and closed the lights. I walked back into the living room and Lindsay just followed me and sat on the couch. She smiled, "I am so bored and it is raining so it is not like we can go anywhere." I smiled back at her, "Well you want to start planning for the wedding. It is in a couple of months you know." She just started laughing, "That is something we need to do with my dad, and your mom and all of our friends." I walked into the kitchen, and started thinking of all of my friends. Beverly, Kirsten and Alison, wow, it has been such a long time since I thought about them. Wouldn't it be something, if I told them that I was getting married? I don't know if they would even handle it like adults. This is really funny because I thought that I had everything set in my life. When I first met Beverly, I knew that she would be the one, and then she dumped me. Do you know how it feels to be with a girl that you can honestly say you can spend the rest of your life with, and then she dumps you? That really fucking crushed my spirits; I thought I was never going to get over that. That is until I met Lindsay, she is so special. She is different than any of the other girls that I have met. I know that I keep talking about her, but I can't help it.

I walked back out and sat on the couch, I don't know why I walked into the kitchen, and I thought I needed something. I sat next to Lindsay who put her arm next to me, and instead of turning on the TV, she just rested her head on my shoulder and closed her eyes. I just looked at her while she was sleeping. And I knew from that point on that everything was going to be okay. Because no matter how tough it got or bad thing got, I could tell that we were going to work it out. To tell you the truth I was getting tired too. I just put my head on the back of the couch saw out the window. It was still raining, it stated to pick up a little, but not as hard. I looked at Lindsay and smiled, and just closed my eyes and went to sleep.

Chapter 31
Uncertainty

I could hear birds chirping outside, morning has finally arrived. But I didn't want to get up. I just wanted to lay here with Lindsay. Lindsay woke up and I was still sleeping, or pretending to be sleeping. She told to wake up but I wasn't moving. She leaned over and kissed me on the lips, and then I woke up. I tackled her on the couch and then the both of hit the floor and stated laughing. I got up first and then Lindsay got up next. I was pretty upset that she didn't want to go to the movies last night. Or that we both forgot to rent or order something and we both fell asleep on the couch. "Hey what do you want to do today?" "I don't know" I said. "Are you hungry at all?" Lindsay smiled, "A little why you are going to feed me?" I smiled back, I was wondering if you wanted to get some breakfast or something." "I am sure that we can find a place somewhere around here that serves breakfast. "That sounds nice" she said. I walked into the kitchen and Lindsay came up from behind me and grabbed me. "If we are going out, why are looking through the fridge?" I tried to push her off, playfully, but she was strong. "I just wanted to see if I had anything in the fridge that I can make." I couldn't even get a chance to look inside, because of Lindsay. I turned around and picked her up, I walked with her to the couch and gently placed her down. I was on top, and leaned in and kissed her on the lips. And I kissed her again. "Okay, you win, let's go out and get something to eat." She pushed me off and I fell to the ground again. I was pretending like I was hurt. Here Lindsay comes, "Poor baby, let me kiss it and make it feel all better. "Just tell momma where it hurts." I got up and told her that my elbow hurts. She stood up and walked to my elbow. And she gave it a kiss, and then smiled. Just looking at her while she smiles and laughs and plays around, I knew that I found the perfect girl. And I couldn't be happier. None of us knew what we wanted to do, so trying to figure it out was going to be fun. I mean we are still going to breakfast but after that, you know what the hell we are going to do after that. "Come on if you still want to get some breakfast you'd better hurry up" I said. "I am coming, I am coming don't rush me Mitch, said Lindsay smiling. Both of us looked like crap, I mean it was the Goddamn morning and neither of us were in the mood for taking showers and getting ready. I mean all I had to do is just change and throw on some deodorant, but for Lindsay she takes fucking forever to get ready. And sometimes she takes longer when she is not in the shower. But I wasn't going to have any of that today, if we still wanted to get some food before the dawn of the new civilization. "Please, baby don't take forever I really want to get some food by today." She smiled, "Okay, I won't I promise. And about ten minutes later she was finally done. I mean ten minutes it is not that hard to change and throw on some clean clothes and maybe brush your teeth. We both left and started walking toward my car. I couldn't ask for better weather, the sun was out and everything. I unlocked the car and Lindsay shouted out, "I think I know this place, I am not really sure of where it is but if you drive around for a while I am pretty sure that we can find it." I looked at her like she was crazy; I wasn't going to drive around all day looking for some breakfast place. But I guess a girl can make you do crazy things, and in my case I will do anything for Lindsay. We both got in and I started driving, I didn't know where the hell I was going but all I knew is I wanted some breakfast and my baby was with me for this adventure. I backed up slowly and took off. "Keep an eye out for any restaurant or corner store that might be serving breakfast." She smiled and said okay, as I was both driving and trying to find a place myself. We finally found something like it would serve breakfast, or I just hope so. It was small and it was just on the corner next to these other stores. I pulled in and parked behind a red pickup truck. The truck was old and it had some pieces of lumber and a tire in the back. The paint job was fading and rusty and it was painted with two different colors. Now who in the hell paints their car in two different colors. Sorry, I know that I am going on and on about the fucking truck, but when I see something this bad I have to say something. I got out and Lindsay got out next. I locked my car and we started walking towards this place. Some of the letters of the name were not lit up, so we couldn't get the name of the restaurant. Now I can tell already that this place was suitable. Again I was being fucking sarcastic. I walked in and Lindsay was by my side. We both walked all the way in and there was this lady who was seating everyone. We waited until she came to us and told us to follow her. She put us in a small table, just the two of us, and then she said, "Can I start you off with something to drink?", while she was giving us our menus. I let Lindsay order first since I am a gentleman and all. She ordered orange juice, and I was the next one to order. I asked for iced-tea, with no lemon. I looked through the menus, and Lindsay put the menu down and she had a look of worry on her face. "Baby, what's the matter, if there is something wrong you can tell me." She smiled, "it is nothing, and you don't have to worry yourself about it." She quickly looked up and noticed that our waitress was coming back with our drinks, so she quickly tried to change the subject. "Our drinks are here, finally, I am so thirsty." I just smiled but I did wonder what was bothering Lindsay. See girls always say that there something wrong with them, and then try to change the subject. And then they get all mad when you get too involved. Well here is my take on this, and especially Lindsay, she brings up things all the time and then doesn't want to talk about it. The waitress put our drinks down, and we were both ready to order. Well I already knew what I wanted, I don't know about Lindsay over there. She took out her little white pad and her little black pen and wrote down our order. Lindsay got the all day special, which consisted of eggs, hash browns, two pancakes, and toast. That looked so good what I was going to get didn't even compare to what Lindsay got. So I changed my order when it was my turn to order. I ordered the same thing. She wrote it down and walked away. I looked at Lindsay and held her hand and smiled. "So what was bothering you before?" "I don't know it is a number of things, first I feel like we are rushing into this very fast, I feel like me saying yes was a bit premature." I looked at her, and she started crying, but just a little not a lot to make a Goddamn scene. "What is the matter, please tell me?" She just looked at me her crying stopped for a minute, and then she got up and ran out of the restaurant. I got up from my table and the waitress was coming over with our food so I had to make a quick decision. "I am sorry" I said, my girlfriend ran out crying and I have to go see what's wrong. I am willing to pay for the meal and whatever else." "Don't worry about it" the waitress said. "Go and talk to your girlfriend that is more important." I put down some money on the table and walked out of the restaurant. People were fucking staring, sometimes I just wish that people would learn to mind their own Goddamn business and don't stick their noses in other people's shit. Lindsay was waiting by the car when I walked to her and she was still crying. "If you were feeling like this before why didn't you say anything before?" "I didn't know how you would handle the situation." "I just didn't want you to get all upset and then get mad at me for rushing into things." "I am not going to get upset; you know that, if you feel like this you should've told me." She walked up to me and hugged me and stayed in that position. "Okay we don't have to get married; we don't have to rush into this if you don't feel like it." "All I want is for you to be happy. She kissed me and told me to unlock the door. I unlocked the car door and I had no idea what the hell we were going to do now. It was still pretty early, as we both got into the car, and I closed the door. Lindsay closed her door and said, "Let's go back to your house, we can watch a movie on your TV or something." I looked at her and she was wiping the tears away from her face. She looked so cute even when she was crying; I leaned over and kissed her on the forehead. "Everything is going to be alright, the important thing is that I love you." I started my car and drove off.

I made it home, and not a moment too soon. It wasn't like I was hurrying or anything to get home. But I heard on the weather report that it was going to rain today, and since it was pretty early in the afternoon and it was kind of muggy outside, and whenever it is really muggy and there is no breeze, it usually rains. I hate that because it never rain any other time. I don't mind any other weather but rain is something that I can't stand. Let me stop I have a tendency to talk about bullshit that no one fucking clearly thinks or talks about. And I also have a tendency to talk about one thing a lot. Some people find it annoying but sometimes I find it really funny. And by the way if you know anything about me already, you know that I don't give a fuck what people think. But anyway I pulled into my house, and it was starting to rain. When it is really muggy outside the rain will drizzle and then pick up. Lindsay and I both got of the car and I locked the doors. We ran inside before the rain started to pick up, and walked into the living room and sat down on the couch. I sat down first and then Lindsay sat down next to me and rested her head on my shoulder. We both sighed at the same time; I wonder if you can die from chronic boredom, I wonder if that is really possible. We didn't look at each other for a few minutes; you can tell that we were living an exciting life style. I grabbed the remote and was about to turn on the TV, until Lindsay said something that I was so happy to hear, well I guess. "I want to have sex." For a minute I had to think to myself because I just wanted to make sure that she said what I thought she said. "What" I said, please repeat that I didn't hear you. "I said let's have sex." "Oh okay I knew you said that." "Then if you knew what I said why did you ask?" "I was just wondering, because you kind of caught me off guard the first time you said it." She looked at me and was waiting for a response. I kissed her on the lips and then I said, "Not in the mood baby, I am tired." Her sweet happy face turned mad and then she stood up. "What the fuck Mitch" she said as she walked into my room slammed the door and locked it. Well supposedly locked the door. I got up and fucking sighed, and walked to my door. "Lindsay open the door please, I think you are overreacting to this whole situation." "Oh now it is a situation" she said. "I didn't mean it like you and you know that but you're overreacting." "I am not overreacting I am being completely justified." "I want to do something with you, and you throw an excuse in my face." "It is not an excuse, what the fuck Lindsay open the door." "No" she said, not until we have sex." "Why the hell do you want to have sex so badly?" "Oh now I need a reason or an explanation to do something." "Mitch, you will never understand." "Open the door I am tired and I want to lie in my fucking bed." "No" she said, you are sleeping on the couch tonight." "No the fuck I'm not, open this Goddamn door now." "No" she said again. I didn't even want to fucking stand there and argue with her right now. I walked back to the couch and lay down; I couldn't believe that fucking Lindsay would overreact to this whole situation and make me sleep on the couch. Bu whatever I was tired, so I grabbed the couch pillow, and closed my eyes. I was getting comfortable until my door opened. I didn't want to get up because she might close the door on me fast as hell. So I pretended like I was sleeping, and I could hear her creeping. She walked to me and then I opened my eyes and within a second she jumped on top of me and kissed me on the lips. "Wake up sleepy head" she said. "I know you were pretending to be asleep." "I was only joking around we don't have to have sex, well not right now." I grabbed her and playfully threw on the floor, she got up laughing and then she grabbed my arm and threw me on the floor too. We were both laying there on the carpet looking at the ceiling laughing, and smiling. To tell you the truth, in some way Lindsay was right. I guess getting married was too early. We both had our lives ahead of us, and if she felt that we were rushing into this, then that meant we didn't have to get married. I want to experience more with my life, and there is so much more to Lindsay that I need to find out. I wanted to do everything with her, and we getting married will get in the middle of all that shit. She grabbed my hand and held it tightly, she looked at me and I looked at her. We were still on the floor, looking at each other smiling. She got closer and said, "I love you" I gave a little smirk and got closer too, "I love you too" I said.

Chapter 32

A Special Visitor

Lindsay got up from the floor, and she stood up scratching her arm and back. I got up and started scratching my arm. I just realized that the rug that I had bought for my floor is very old. It's not old like its' been around for hundreds of years, it is old because it is an antique. And the stupid rug, now realizing it, is very itchy. She walked into the kitchen and opened the fridge, and started looking around for something. I walked into the kitchen too and watched her rummage for food. She looked like a little pack rat looking through my fridge. She closed the door, pretty upset, and turned back to me and said, "You need to go grocery shopping." I smiled and started laughing, "I know I was going to go today." She walked into my room and grabbed my keys and my wallet. "Well, you are not doing anything anyway might as well get some food." I looked at her and told her that wasn't a bad idea. I grabbed my stuff from her and started walking out and towards the front door. She walked to her shoes and put them on, and walked to the front door. We started walking out and the rain started picking up. It started raining hard but not that hard. I guess Lindsay picked a perfect Goddamn day to go shopping, when it is raining and shit. We both ran to my car and got in. We closed the door and I started the car, and took off. I had no idea where the grocery store was, or how long it was going to take us to actually get some shopping done. I started driving and started driving until I found something. And let me tell you something, the more you drive around anywhere the more places you are bound to find. And the good thing is that it is a few miles away from my house, well I am not sure about that a hundred percent but I can guess. The rain stopped and it looked like the sun was coming out. So that was good I hate walking or being in the rain. It was funny because it never bothered me to watch the rain. I guess to some people that is soothing and to me too. But I just hate being in the rain because I hate getting wet. And you hear the same old shit all the time, but you take showers all every day. That is true but how often do you take showers with your clothes on, my fucking point exactly. I pulled in and stopped the car, and Lindsay and I got out. The sun was beaming its bright rays upon my car. So I knew that today was going to be a good day. Lindsay and I both closed our doors at the same time. We started walking and the place was called, One Stop Shopping Center, now how lame of a name is that for a grocery store. I got a cart, but I forgot the most important part, I forgot the Goddamn list. Now I am going to have to walk around the whole store looking for shit. I hate when that happens, when you don't have what you need and you have to walk around looking for everything in every single aisle. I got the cart and Lindsay was waiting by the glass doors that open automatically. I walked into the store and it felt like a breath of fresh air. What I mean by that is the store was air conditioned, and it felt so good. I stopped and Lindsay suddenly stopped to. "What is the matter" she said. "Nothing, I just don't know where the hell to start." She looked at me and started laughing, "Well what do you need" she said. "Let's start with that and then work our way up." I smiled, "Baby you're such a genius." We started moving, I decided to go from aisle one all the way to aisle 15 until I have everything I need. I walked into aisle one and that is where the good stuff was. That's where all the milk and frozen food, and other frozen products. I grabbed two gallons of milk, whole milk of course, and I grabbed some low fat yogurt. I never like drinking two percent or skim or any other type of milk growing up. And for the yogurt I guess I need to start losing weight, I mean I am not that fat, but everyone can feel better and look better. I started walking down the aisle more and Lindsay shouted out from the end of the aisle, "Do you need some frozen TV dinners." And the sound of that didn't sound that bad, I guess I can use some of those in my freezer. Just because I hate cooking and the thought of me cooking was funnier than my mom. I told Lindsay to grab some, and at this point I didn't even care what kind they were, as long as they tasted good. She grabbed like five of them, walked to my cart and grabbed a few more. I felt like I was poor or something, because I was fucking stocking up on frozen TV dinners. And I mean a lot of them, Lindsay already grabbed like seven or eight boxes. But they were good, cheap and the best news of them all they were on sale. Now it doesn't get any better than that when you have cheap food and they are on sale. She put more in the cart and started walking with me when I made my way into the next few aisles. Now I just started grabbing shit without even thinking if I already have it home or not. I grabbed some cleaning solution; don't ask me why, I guess I just like to have a clean house. I grabbed a fucking mop and a broom; I like to make sure my kitchen floor is clean too. I was going to grab some dog food. And I know that I don't have a dog but I always wanted a dog. I just thought that I could use a little best friend running around the house. Lindsay stopped and shouted, "You have to see this." I walked to where ever the hell she was and she was looking at hair accessories. "Do you need any shampoo or body wash or anything like that? I looked at the deal and even though it was generally expensive I told her that I had enough at home. See I went shopping earlier and bought some shit to stock up my house. She put the bottles down and wrapped her hand around my arm and we started walking. She was looking to her right as we were passing down the aisle. I quickly looked at her and she didn't notice that I was looking. I just smiled and continued to walk down the aisle. I grabbed few more things when I turned into the next aisle, like chips, soda, bread, milk, eggs and a whole bunch of other shit. I think that my cart was getting full and Lindsay looked toward me and said, "I think that you have everything you need, let's go to the checkout. I smiled, and proceeded to walk towards the checkout. Thank God the line wasn't that long, because I hate waiting in lines, for any reason. I checked the sign that said 15 items or less. I counted all my stuff and I had about 14 things so I was good. I proceeded to get all the items out of my cart and put them on the counter. I scanned each item and waited until the price showed up. I finished and Lindsay, being the sweetheart that she is, helped bagged all of the groceries and put them into the cart. The total came out to be $21.45, so I pulled out some money and paid for the food. And it is amazing right, that I still had some money even though what's her name screwed me out of the job at the bank. But I still have some money I don't know how but I did. After I paid for everything and everything was bagged up I walked to my cart and started pushing it down the aisle. I walked outside and started walking to my car. Lindsay grabbed my car keys and opened my car door. I made it to car and unloaded all the fucking groceries. I had to put them in the trunk because there was no room in the back seat. For some reason I had all my shit in the back seat and so I had to stuff everything in the trunk. And there is one problem my trunk is small, so fitting 14 bags of shit in there was a miracle in itself. I finally got all the groceries in the trunk and got in the car. Lindsay got in the car too and closed the door. We drove off. Now the very fun part begins, going home and unloading everything and putting everything away where the hell it belongs. See there is one thing that you have to know about me; I really don't care where the hell all the groceries go. I usually just put shit anywhere and find time to put them where they go later. Oh, Lindsay helped too, putting away everything, well sort of. I could tell that she felt because she didn't know where any of the stuff went. She looked around for a minute and then she put all the stuff on top of the counter.

She walked back into the living room and sat on the couch. I followed her and sat next to her. I sighed and looked at her and just started laughing, I don't know why I just couldn't control myself from laughing. She thought I was weird by the look in my face, but then she started laughing too and we were both sitting on the couch just laughing together. I got up and stretched and walked back into the kitchen. She got up and asked me if I was putting any of the groceries away, and I told her not this second. She got up from the couch and walked into the kitchen with me. "So what do you want to do?" I looked at her, as she was taking some of the groceries out of the bag and putting them on the counter. "I don't know" I said, what do you want to do? "Let's go out" she said. "Let's go and have some fun." I smiled at her, "Okay sounds like a great idea, but where and what do you want to do." She stood there, hand on her chin, and blurted out, "Let's go a really good music store." Now my first reaction was why music. She could've said anything else like the movies or dancing, or hell even mini golf or something. But I wasn't complaining, because I love music and I know that Lindsay loves music too. Well, music to me is very important. I am always trying to expand my taste in music and going to a music store was a good idea. "Where are we going" I said. "What music store are you talking about?" "I am talking about like a really good CD store, where they have all types of genres and everything. I wanted to go one day and see if they have a record player, because I wanted to get some really good Vinyl's and stuff." "Do you know where the hell it is?" Lindsay just laughed, and said, "No." "But I am sure that we can find it if we just look hard enough." I started laughing, "Great this means I am going to have to drive everywhere and find this shit." I hate fucking driving around everywhere because I never know where the hell I am going half the Goddamn time. We started walking towards the car; we got in and closed the doors. I started my car and we took off like a bullet in the fucking wind. I drove around for a few minutes until I found something that looked like a CD store so I stopped and parked my car. She got out and walked to the store and later realized that it wasn't the right store. They sold CD's but it wasn't the store she was looking for. She got back into the car and we took off again. We drove for several for minutes and then she said, "Stop." I slowly stopped my car and parked it behind another car. I stopped the car and we got out, she walked over to me and said, "This is the one I was talking about" she said. "This is the right place." I looked at the name and didn't bother too much about it. We both walked in and started looking around. She went off to her own little world and everything. I started looking around myself; I was looking in the rock section of all the CD's. I started looking when Lindsay was walking around; I think that she was trying to find me. I wasn't going to say anything for a second, because I thought that would've been funny. But I didn't want to be an asshole and have her look for me all day. I called out her name and then she walked over to me. "Jerk" she said. "You probably knew that I was walking around and shit". I just laughed as she was showing me her sweet collection of music she just picked up. I looked through her albums and she had some good taste. She told me to hang on to these and she walked away to I guess look for more CD's. I mean, honestly, how many CD's one person can possibly buy. I looked around some more and I really didn't find anything that got my attention. She came up to me and got more CD's and then she said that she was going to pay for them. She walked over to the counter and waited until she got seen. I walked over to her and waited at the front of the line. When the cashier asked if I was in line, I simply said "No I am waiting for my girlfriend." After two people Lindsay was finally up and she couldn't wait until she was seen. She placed all the CD's on the platform and pulled out her credit card. After a simple swipe and a smile she was the brand new owner of like seven CD's. I guess her taste in music is one for the record books. She got a bag for all CD's and she walked to me. She grabbed my hand and said let's go. I just smiled as we were walking out the store. As we were walking I passed by this girl that looked very familiar. As if I seen her before somewhere but I don't know where. I wanted to stop and see what she looked like. But I think that Lindsay would've gotten mad and jealous a little. Did I tell you guess who is the jealous one in the relationship, yep Lindsay. She gets really fucking jealous if I stare even talk to another girl. That's why I didn't stop and see what that girl looked like. But I swear to you she looked very familiar. And the crazy thing is in that one second she turned her head and looked at me. It wasn't like a regular look you give someone, but more like a look, like I haven't seen you for a long time kind of look. I know that doesn't make any sense but that's what it was. We started walking to my car and I couldn't stop thinking about that girl. I mean she really did look familiar. I just swear that I have seen her before; this is going to make me go crazy thinking about that girl. I couldn't let it bother me then Lindsay is going to know that I have been thinking about this girl, and then she is going to get really jealous. I unlocked my car door and we both got in. She looked through her CD's and told me that she got a really good collection. She opened one of the cases and popped the CD in the player and pressed play. The music started playing and I couldn't understand what it was or who was singing it. She smiled; I knew that she wasn't going to tell me anytime soon so I really didn't care too much about it. I drove off and now I can finally go home. "I am so bored" said Lindsay. "Let's do something." "We did just do something" I said. "What do you think we were doing when we went to the CD store?" "No silly, the CD's were for me I mean let's do something that we both can do." I continued driving and suggested what we should do. She came up with a few ideas, and I was listening to all of them trying to pick out the best ones. She mentioned something about a movie or something. Honestly I really wasn't paying any attention, sometimes I just pretend that I do. And I know that is bad but I really do love Lindsay, but she can be a handful. "Do you want to go to the movies?" She thought about it for a second, "Not really no, but I want to do something with you." I was almost home, and neither of us made up our mind of what we wanted to do today. I got home and still neither of us made up our mind of what the fuck we wanted to do. I pulled into the driveway and stopped the car. I turned and looked at Lindsay who was smiling and pretending not to look at me. I was about to open my door and she interrupted me by saying, "Let's go visit your mom." "I don't want to go visit my mom because I called her a few days ago and she fucking hung up on me." Lindsay was quiet, she just looked out the window and then she got out. She closed the door and walked to my side; I got out and closed my door. I locked the doors and walked to Lindsay. We held hands as we were walking to the door. Then my phone started ringing and I saw who was calling me and I couldn't believe it. I was really nervous about picking it up though; I told Lindsay that it was my mom. She just smiled and looked at me and then waited. She took the keys from my pocket and opened the door. She walked in and closed the door halfway. I walked away from the door and answered the call. It wasn't my mom. "Hey" I said. "Long time no talk, how is everything?" "Good" she said. "It has been a long time, what's new?" "Nothing really" I said. "I met someone and she is very special to me." "Things are moving pretty seriously right now between us." "That's nice to hear, I just wish you were still single." "Well it has been a long time and I needed to find someone." She just laughed and said that she had to go because she was busy or something. "Well it was very nice talking to you Mitch." "It was nice talking to you to Alison" I said. "I hope that everything goes well for you and say hi to your dad for me." She hung up the phone and Lindsay walked to the door. "Who was that" she said. "I didn't want to lie and tell her that it was my mom, because she would never believe that. "It was an old friend" I said. "She just called to say hi and see what's new with me." Lindsay just looked at me and then walked back inside. She didn't say anything. I was a little confused and I walked in. "Are you okay" I said.

Again she didn't say anything. Then she finally said something. "A friend huh, like what kind of friend an old girlfriend or something." I could tell that she was getting really upset and more importantly jealous of Alison calling. But she didn't know that it was Alison calling. "If you really fucking must know, it was Alison calling to say hi." "And yes we did date for a few months but it wasn't anything." Even though I was lying, but I couldn't tell her the truth that I really did like the girl. "Okay, what do you want me to do, like pretend this didn't happen?" "How would you feel if all my ex-boyfriends started calling, what did you call it, just to say hi." I couldn't understand why Lindsay was getting really upset about this. "Why are you overreacting, she is just a friend, and so what we dated but that was before I met you." "Oh yeah like that is supposed to make me feel a whole lot fucking better." Lindsay pulled out her cell phone and called for her dad to come and pick her up. "Baby" I said, I am not going to apologize about what happened, but I think that you just need to relax." "Don't tell me what the fuck to do Mitch; you are in deep shit as it is, so I wouldn't be saying anything." "If you need me for anything, like I care, I am going to be waiting outside for my dad to come and pick me up." I was so Goddamn confused about everything; I didn't know what to do. "Fine then if you want to get mad about every little thing that happens in this Goddamn relationship and leave go ahead." I didn't mean to get mad but I was so frustrated because she does this shit all the fucking time. She just smiled sarcastically and started walking to the door. She opened the door and walked outside, and sat on the porch. I was so mad that I didn't even try to make up or even say that I am sorry. I walked to my room and closed the door. The good thing about my room is that I can see outside the window, and see if anyone is pulling up. I lay on my bed and closed my eyes and waited until I heard a car pulling up. After a few minutes I heard a car pull up and I saw Lindsay walk to the car. I guess her dad was like in the neighborhood or something, because he got here pretty fast. I was so mad at Lindsay, as she got in the car and was driving away, for overreacting to this whole Goddamn situation. I got up from my bed and I heard the car driving away from the driveway. I walked out from my room and into the fucking living room. I needed to clear my head and not think about fucking Lindsay right now. I got my stuff and started walking towards the front door. I need some coffee or something, I just need to drive somewhere and do something. I opened the door double checked that I had everything and closed the door on my way out. I walked to my car and unlocked it. I got in and started the piece of shit up, I really need a new car, and I drove off. I just needed to drive somewhere and do something, like I said before. I started looking everywhere for a decent place to get some Goddamn coffee, and I found like a hundred Starbucks so I decided to go there. I mean they have really good coffee, so it was a no brainer. I found one that was next to a clothing store, which reminded me of Alison's store. I pulled in and parked behind a truck. I stopped my car and got out. I closed the door and breathed a sigh; this is exactly what I need. I walked inside and started looking through the menu. They had so many choices it was making my head spin. There were a few people in line so the wait wasn't that long. I am glad that everywhere I go I have just enough money. And don't ask me how when I don't even have a job but you will be surprised, sometimes I even surprise myself. I was second in line so it wasn't that bad. The guy in front of me ordered a small coffee and stepped out of line. I was next in line. I got to the front and I felt as if someone was behind me. Did you ever feel that like you were doing something and someone just came from behind? I didn't care enough to turn around and another thing if I turned around it would've made me look fucking nosy as hell. I stepped to the front and ordered a small coffee too. I guess that guy and I have pretty good taste in ordering the same exact shit. I stepped out of line and I tried to sneak a peak of the person standing behind me. I tried to look but there were people there so I couldn't see. My coffee was ready and I paid by credit card. She gave me back my card and a receipt. I thanked her and she smiled and walked to the other people waiting in line. I bought a newspaper so I can be one of those important people who sip coffee and read their newspapers all day. I am just kidding, I am sure those guys really are important. I found a small table and sat down. I unfolded the newspaper and cleared my throat to be a jackass. I put one leg across the other and scooted up my chair closer to the table. I folded down the newspaper to see if anyone saw it. No one did I guess everyone is in their own little world. It was pretty early in the afternoon so I guess they were on lunch or something. I continued to read and then I heard someone pull out a chair and sit down. And I know what you're thinking, so the fuck what someone sitting down big deal. But the only problem with that was it was at my table. And okay I wanted to sit in privacy and enjoy my Goddamn coffee and read my newspaper. And I know that coffee places tend to get busy and this is a free country, but come on I bet there are plenty of other seats available. I tried to lower my newspaper enough so I can see who it is, without giving the impression that I really want to see who it was. All I saw was light brown hair and nail polish. She was scratching her head when I saw. And it is a she because of the nail polish. Unless guys started wearing nail polish all of a sudden and I didn't get the memo. Cool, it was girl so I am not that mad after all. I didn't want to be rude, so I put the paper down and she was looking around. I wanted to introduce myself to her but I waited. When I saw her face she looked very familiar. You know what this is the same girl that I passed coming out from the grocery store that day. This is the same girl that I said that looked very familiar. She turned back to me and just stared at me for a minute. I wanted to say something so bad but my mouth wouldn't open. So I sat there looking at her like a fool without saying anything. "I am sorry, but you look very familiar have we met before?" The mysterious girl just smiled and didn't say anything. "I think that we have met before, and I am not just saying that because I want to talk to you or anything, but you really do look familiar. She again smiled, and put both her hands under her chin. "You really don't know who I am do you?" I was confused now, for some reason this girl knew who I was. Wait a minute, she did stare at me when I was leaving the grocery store, but I thought she was just staring just because. The girl laughed and said, "Mitch." She knew my name now this was getting weird. First of all places in New York, of all the Starbucks, and of all the tables I get the one with a hot ass girl that knows my Goddamn name. She continued to sit there, she reached into her purse and grabbed out Chap Stick and started putting some on her lips. For some reason that was turning me on, fuck now, why is it every time a girl does something regular I have to find it sexual. She finished and put her back into her bag. She started wetting her lips and she finished. Fuck, this girl is really hot and she is sitting there and playing around and she doesn't even know it. She laughed again, "Mitch" I can't believe you don't know who I am. "Okay, how do you know my name?" She just nodded her head and started laughing." "Man dude you are so cute when you don't know anything." "It's me Bethany." My mouth opened wide, and my heart was racing. As if time and space stood still for a whole second. I couldn't believe it, Bethany, my first girlfriend before I moved to Ohio. "Oh my God, how have you been?" Bethany just smiled, "Good" she said. "It has been a long time Mitch, a very long time." I just smiled I still couldn't believe it, Bethany. It was like fate or something, this was crazy. She stood up and pushed the chair in. "Leaving so soon, but I just saw you." "I am sorry but I have to go to work." "Give me your phone?" I gave her my phone and she put her number in my phone. I stood up and took the phone back and put it in my pocket. She walked over to me and gave me a hug and a kiss on the cheek. "Call me sometime; I am town for a few days." And like that Bethany started walking towards the door and she left. I grabbed my phone and scrolled down to her name. I stared at it for a second and then I put the phone back in my pocket. I still couldn't believe it. Bethany, this was fucking crazy as hell. I looked back and then I just realized the most important thing in the whole world. My fucking coffee was getting cold. I sat back down on the chair and scooted the chair back to the table. I grabbed my newspaper, took a sip of coffee put it back down cleared my throat again, and started reading.

Chapter 33
Bethany

I finished my coffee and got up from the table. My mind was still buzzing from this whole Bethany thing. I grabbed my phone, and I just realized about my *current* girlfriend. I wanted to call and see how Lindsay is doing and if she is still mad at me for today. Even though this is her fault for getting mad, but I wanted to call and make up. I was sure that she will still be mad about the whole thing and that I will be in for it later. I left Starbucks and headed for my car that was still parked. I couldn't believe that I didn't get a ticket for it or something. I got in and decided to go and go home and just take my fucking mind off things for a while. I was contemplating about calling Lindsay and see how she is doing, but I thought it would be wise just go give her some space. I drove off and after a few minutes I made it home, I almost got lost because I took a turn that I didn't need to take. But luckily I knew where I was going so I was perfectly fine. I got home and pulled into the driveway and stopped the car. I didn't get out just yet; I just sat in my car and thought about my whole Goddamn life. I thought that I was never going to see Beverly again and then she just pops into my life. And now Bethany, all of a sudden all these girls are coming out of nowhere. All that got me thinking about Alison; even though that relationship was short it *did* mean something. And the same with Kristen she was different than Alison and I guess that it why

I like her so much. Correction liked her so much, because I am in a relationship and her name is Lindsay. I finally got out of my car, because I didn't want to spend my whole fucking day in there. I walked towards my door and unlocked it; I turned around and locked my car with my alarm. I opened the door and sighed as I walked in my house. I walked towards the answering machine because I noticed that the light was blinking red. I pressed the button and it read, "Hey baby it's me Lindsay, I am sorry that I got all mad earlier, I didn't know what I was thinking." "I hope you get home soon because I want to see you, call me when you get this." I deleted the phone message and picked up the phone and I hesitated about calling her right away. It's not that I didn't want to talk to her, but I was still kind of upset that she got all mad at me for no reason what so ever. But I guess I had to be the bigger person in this so I called her and waited. She finally picked up the phone after several rings; "Hello" she said. "It's me Mitch" I said, I got your phone message. "I miss you can you come over so we can talk or something." She sounded pleased or something, because she jumped to saying yes and she said she will be over soon. I smiled and hung up the phone and put it back on the charger. I got my cell phone out and decided to call Liz and to check up on how things are going with her. I called and of course her annoying ass fucking receptionist picked up. She already knew it was me I guess because of the caller id, and transferred me over. Liz got on the phone and the first thing I said was, "Can I please get your direct number, I hate calling and waiting." "I normally don't do this but she did, she gave me her number and I wrote it down in on a piece of paper. "So what's on your mind" she said. "Anything new happen in your life that you want to share, I am listening." "Well" I said. "It's like this, I really love Lindsay but you wouldn't believe who came and visited me out of nowhere, Bethany. She was my very first girlfriend that I ever had." I loved her so much, but now these feelings are coming back, and I don't know what to do." She paused for a second and then she suggested, "Why don't you explain to Lindsay about Bethany. Even if that means telling her how you feel for her, don't try to bottle this up inside or you are going to do more damage than you think." "It is not that easy it is not like I can just tell Lindsay, "Hey I forgot to mention that my old girlfriend came back and I think I love her." "You see what I mean it wouldn't work out. And Lindsay is the type of girl who would get really jealous and probably have a fucking fit or something." "Okay, well I don't know what to suggest, but to tell Lindsay about Bethany. I know this may sound weird but introduce Lindsay to Bethany and see what she thinks of her." "I don't know, I'll try it but I don't know if it is going to work. I don't know what to do with my life, everything is so overwhelming." "Don't worry I'll figure it out, and I will let you know what happens." "Okay sounds like a plan, well don't worry I am sure that everything is going to work out." "If you need anything just call me on my direct number." I thanked her and hung up the phone. I was so stressed and I had no idea what time Lindsay was coming over. I hope I have enough time to take a shower; I rushed to my bathroom and started undressing. I took off my clothes at the same time turning the faucet to hot. I jumped in the shower and at first it was hot as I was hopping around in my bathtub then I got used to it. And after that it was pretty relaxing. I stood there for several minutes and let the warm water hit my body. I quickly soaped up all over my body and my face. I rinsed off as some soap got into my eyes as it was burning. I grabbed the shampoo bottle and quickly washed my hair. I didn't care about using the conditioner because I didn't want to spend all day in the shower. I rinsed off and turned off the faucet. I let the water drip off for a while, and then I forgot my fucking towel. I stepped out the bathroom and ran across the hallway to the closet, naked, and grabbed a towel. I didn't bother going to back into the bathroom to dry off so I dried off in the other room. I walked to my room with a towel wrapped around me and grabbed my clothes. The Goddamn phone started ringing as I was about to take off my towel. I wrapped it back up and walked to phone and picked it up. It was Lindsay. "Hey" she said. "I will be there in a few minutes." "Okay I just got out of the shower so I am going to get dressed and I will see you soon." She hung up the phone without saying goodbye. But I guess that is the kind of person she is, I guess I am not used to her just yet. And of course you are going to get dressed after you get out of the shower. That was just stupid what I said. Like what the fuck, I am going to walk around my own home naked or something. That would be pretty funny if like I answered the door and Lindsay saw me naked in front of her. She will probably do one of two things, knowing her, one she will be freaked out because I am naked and leave. Or two she will want to have sex because I just turned her on. Anyway, I walked back to my room and started getting dressed. I wanted to wear something nice this time so I threw on some jeans and a good button up T-shirt. Sometimes it is good to get dressed up and not to wear the same shit over and over again. I finished getting ready like putting my socks on and the doorbell rang. Lindsay was here, I took my time to answer the door because if I would've rushed she would've expected me to see her or something. I answered the door and said hi. She walked and gave me a hug. She took off her coat and placed it on the side of the sofa. She sat down on the sofa and crossed her legs and looked at me. I smiled, "Well it is nice to see you to." She just sat there still crossing her sexy legs and waited. I closed the door and sat down next to her. She leaned over and kissed me on the lips. "I am sorry for getting mad before." "Funny you said that, there is something I need to tell you." Now she uncrossed her legs and moved closer to me holding my hand. "This is not easy to say so I am going to say it. "And I need you to promise me that you are not going to get upset." "You can tell me, and I promise I won't get mad just tell me. "Okay, well before I moved to New York I used to live in Ohio, and before I lived in Ohio I lived in some small ass town. And in that town I met a girl named Bethany." Now Lindsay was lying back on the couch and this time she had her arms crossed. "Keep going I want to hear the rest." She said. "Well after years and years she came and we bumped into each other in a coffee shop I went to after you got upset the first time." "I told you I wasn't upset." "I know, please let me finish , well back then I had feelings for her and now after seeing her after all this time, these… "Let me guess these feelings are coming back and now you don't know what the fuck to do." "How did you…" "I had experience like that before someone pulled the same shit on me." "Well I have to tell you Mitch, it is either me or her." Lindsay stood up and grabbed her coat. "I can't believe I wasted my time coming all the way out here so you can tell me that you love another girl." "First of all I haven't told you anything; you assumed that I love her." "Whatever, like I said, as she was opening the door, it is either me or that fucking slut." She slammed the door and walked outside. I didn't even care enough to check if she got a ride from someone or drove here herself. I can't believe it; I fucking took Liz's advice and it fucking backfired on my ass. Now

Lindsay was mad at me even more and all because I told the mother fucking truth. I should've done what I am good at and just lied. Then she would've been happy, I would've been happy and everyone would've got along great. But no, I had to tell the Goddamn truth and now Lindsay is mad at me. I wanted to call Liz back and tell her that her stupid advice didn't work. But we both knew that it wasn't her fault, I was just mad and I needed someone to fucking blame. And I knew it was wrong to blame her but I couldn't help it I was so mad. I was about to walk into my room until the phone rang and I walked back and I picked it up. I said hello and said hello again and no one answered on the other side. I fucking hung up the phone and walked back to my room. Well now Lindsay fucking left, she is probably still mad; I had the whole day to myself to do whatever the hell I want to. There is only one problem I had no idea what the hell I wanted to do. I grabbed my car keys and walked outside the door, and closed the door and walked towards my car. I got in and closed the door; I turned on the radio and put it on full fucking blast. It was some really good music blaring through the speakers. I closed the door and started up the car. I still had the music on, but I lowered it just a little. To tell you the truth I was getting a headache and all the loud ass music wasn't doing me any favors. I still had no idea where the hell I wanted to go or what I wanted to do. Then I had an idea, even though that Lindsay would get mad, but she wasn't here so I don't give a shit. And I mean I love her and always will, still speaking about Lindsay, and where it is written that a guy can't be best friends with a girl. I grabbed my cell phone and decided to give Bethany a call and see what she is up to. I called her number, if I forgot to mention or if I already did she gave me her number so I was obligated as her best friend to give her a call and see how she is doing. It rang several times and then she finally picked up. "Hey Mitch" she said. "How is everything, what are you up to?" "Nothing, Lindsay and I got into it again and she stormed out my house pretty upset." "What did she get upset about?" "Nothing important, the reason I called is if you wanted to hang out and do something." "Sure I am not doing anything; I am at a clothing store with some friends. I didn't drive so it would be nice if you can come and pick me up. "Sure" I said. She proceeded to give me the address to the store as I was writing it down. "Okay see you in a few minutes then, just hold on tight and don't go anywhere." She started laughing as she knew that I was joking around, she hung up the phone and I started thinking. Does everyone I talk to never say goodbye when they are done talking, they all just fucking hang up the Goddamn phone. I put the phone down as I needed to concentrate on driving before I get into a Goddamn car accident. I grabbed the piece of paper and looked at it one more time. I put it down and kind of knew where it was because the name sounded familiar. Or I remember passing it one time when I was driving or something like that. I was driving fine until I got into a few red lights. It wasn't that bad, the wait that is, and I started driving again. I checked to see if I needed gas and I did. The gage was running on empty not literately but you know what I mean. I drove some more and saw a gas station on the right hand side. I pulled in slowly and pulled up to one of the pumps. A guy walked from inside a booth and walked towards my car. I rolled down my window and gave him a twenty and told him regular please. I kept the window rolled down because it was really hot outside. And since my car was off I couldn't use the air conditioner. He grabbed the pump and put it in my car, and I waited until it was done. The pump was finally done and the total came up to be like $30, so it wasn't that bad. I paid by cash, and again don't tell me where I am getting all these fucking money from because I don't know. I gave him the cash and he walked away smiling. Well of course he just got paid like $30 in cash he better walk away Goddamn smiling. I kept my window down and I turned on the car. As soon the car turned on I blasted the air conditioner on full fucking blast because I was really, really hot. I rolled up the window so all the cool air doesn't escape. I grabbed the piece of paper one more time and looked at the directions to the store, that Bethany was in. I put it back down again and I was going to give Lindsay a call and see how she is doing but I guess she needed her space or something. I finally made it to the store, and pulled in behind a black truck. I stopped my car and got out. I closed the door but I didn't lock it because I was only going to see Bethany for a little while anyway. I walked towards the store and walked in. I was going to scream out Bethany's name like a jackass but I guess I would be only the one in the store who would've thought that would be funny or something. I started looking around and to tell you the truth this clothing store looked very familiar to the one that Alison worked in. I just realized that I am not over her or any other girl that I have met, but you know what in some way or another they all fucked me, so fuck them. There is only one girl that I love and her name is… "Mitch" said Bethany. "Hey you finally made it; I thought you weren't going to show or something." "I was started to get a little worried about you." I lost my Goddamn train of thought when Bethany interrupted me. "Hey I told you that I would show." She grabbed my hands and made me walk with her as she had some clothes in her hands. My guess she was about to go to the fitting rooms. And I can only guess what I was going to do next she was going to ask me if they looked good on her. I mean if you saw Bethany's body, anything that she would wear would look very good on her. She just had such a great body; I guess she works out or something.

We made it to the dressing rooms and it was pretty busy. Bethany walked up to the main counter and got a ticket so she can go change. Her friends were probably still shopping or something. Or they left and Bethany and I are alone in the store. The last time I was alone in a store with a girl, Kirsten, we sort of made out. But that was in the past, and I can't concern myself with that. Bethany finally got a room, she walked in and she made me walk inside but not inside the room. Just in the hallway, where the people can't say anything. She tried on the first piece of clothing that she had on and it looked very good on her. It was a small black top with straps in the back going in a zigzag design. She spun around and at that time something was happening, my feelings for Bethany were getting stronger. She spun around and started laughing. "Well what do you think?" "You look amazing." She stopped and looked at me. Maybe I came on her just a little too strong. She walked up to me and looked into my eyes, and then she leaned in and kissed me on the lips. It was very spontaneous; I was shocked I didn't know what to do. My heart was telling me that this wrong but my mind was telling me to kiss her back. So I kissed her back and kissed her for a long time. Then I pulled away, she was kind of upset. I didn't mean to pull her away, but this was wrong. But why didn't I want to stop, something inside kept telling me to keep going. "I am sorry Bethany but I can't to do this." "I have a girlfriend whom I love very much." "No I am sorry I guess I wasted all these years to have you and now I can't." "It's okay it's not all your fault." "Just pay for your stuff so we can go home or something." She grabbed the rest of her stuff and walked up to the register and put all of her clothes down. I walked behind her and waited in the front of the line. She pulled out her credit card and paid for everything. The lady was nice she was fast too she rung her up and put everything in bag. Bethany grabbed her stuff and started walking towards me. She grabbed my hand and, I let go. I felt very badly treating Bethany like shit, but I can't have any feelings for her. I have feelings for Lindsay, and Lindsay only. We started walking towards my car, I unlocked the door and Bethany got in, I followed next. "Where are we going?" she said. She placed all of her stuff on the floor near her feet, and closed the door. I closed mine too. "My house" I said. "I hope you don't mind just for a little bit. Then I will drop you off if you want." She smiled as she buckled up and I started the car. I made an illegal u-turn in the middle of the street, because first of there was no traffic and I didn't give a shit. I drove and drove and Bethany fell asleep on the seat. I made it home and slowly pulled in, and to be very funny I started messing with her hair to wake her up. She didn't get up at first, so I honked the horn and she jumped from her seat. I laughed and she started laughing too after she realized what happened. We both got out and closed the doors. I grabbed my keys and open my door. She walked first before I can get one foot into the door. She put her bags down and took of her coat and sat down on the couch. "I was going to say make yourself at home, but I can see you already done that." She just smiled as she was taking off her boots. When she rolled up her pant leg and I could see her legs and they were so toned and tan they looked very amazing. She took off her boots and placed them on the side of the couch. I closed the door and sat down next to her. She turned towards me and leaned in and said, "Show me the bedroom." "Don't you want to see the rest of the house?" She smiled again and stood up and grabbed my hand. I took the lead and showed her the bedroom. She walked in and I closed the door behind me. She found the bed and sat in the edge and then she fell back. "Your bed is so comfortable, I can just fall asleep all day." I smiled and started laughing, as I walked towards my bed and lay next to her. I know that this was sort of uncomfortable but nothing was going to happen right. She leaned over and got on top of me, "Let's do something fun" she said. "What do you have in mind" I said. She leaned in closer, and now this was getting uncomfortable, but I couldn't find it. It was like I was searching my whole life for Bethany and now she was right in front me and now I am not going to lose her again. I grabbed her and pulled her closer and started kissing her. I rolled her on the bed so I was on top now and I started kissing her more and more. She grabbed and started messing with my hair. I started unbuttoning her shirt and kissing on her chest and stomach. She leaned up and took off her shirt and bra. She fell back down and I started kissing her more and more. I took off my shirt and kissed her more and more. The whole time I was kissing her I thought about Lindsay, and how wrong this was. But Bethany tasted so good that I couldn't resist it anymore. After we kissed for several minutes we started having sex. We both took off our clothes and started fucking in the bed. And then as we were into it, someone rang the doorbell. I didn't want to answer it but it could be something important. I told Bethany that I had to answer it. I got up and put my boxers and pants back on, I didn't care that much about putting a shirt on because it was in my own home. I looked through the peephole and it was Lindsay. Oh shit, fucking shit, I opened the door but I had it halfway open. I didn't want to Lindsay to see Bethany if she comes out or something. "Lindsay what you doing here." I said. "I just felt bad for getting upset and I wanted to come here and apologize." "Mitch" said Bethany as she was coming out of my room with my T-shirt on. That wasn't a good sign. "Who the fuck is that in your house" said Lindsay. "I can't believe this shit, I felt sorry for you and drove all the way down here to apologize and now you have another girl in your home." "It is not what you think, please let me explain." "No, you need to explain a Goddamn thing." "Mitch we are fucking over." She closed the door and walked back towards her car. I saw from the window and opened the door and walked out to the porch area. I was screaming her name she just got into the car and just drove away. Bethany came out apologizing and saying that she will make it up to me, but I think that the damage was already done. She walked back inside and I walked back inside too and closed the door. I couldn't believe that it was over, why the fuck didn't I listen, I know that what I was doing was wrong but I didn't listen. Bethany walked back inside my room and I followed her. She kept on apologizing to me and saying that she will make it up or something. But she couldn't just fix it, Lindsay is different than that.

Saying sorry wouldn't bring her back to me. "Hey I am kind of tired do you mind if I go to sleep in your bed for a while." I told her yes, and I was going to be in the living room thinking. She lay down in my bed and closed her eyes and went to sleep. I closed the door slowly and walked back into the living room. I sat on the couch and put both hands on my face. I couldn't believe that I messed her everything up with Lindsay. I think that she was serious about leaving this time. I grabbed my phone and decided to give her a call try to explain things to her. It rang and rang and then it went to her voicemail. I guess she knew that it was me calling and didn't want to pick it up. I slammed the phone down on the couch; I was fucking pissed off at myself. I had to do something to show Lindsay that I need her and she is the one for me. It's crazy how I almost married a girl who has a history of psychotic problems. I knew that her mind wasn't in the right place when I met her, but neither is mine so that's why we are so perfect for each other. And this is the same girl that killed her mom and I fucked things up. I had to prove that she was the girl for me; I had to show Lindsay that we belonged together. I got bored sitting on the fucking couch and blaming myself. I walked into the kitchen pulled out a large butcher knife and closed the cabinet drawer. I looked at it and walked into my room. I slowly opened the door and closed it halfway. I saw Bethany just sleeping there on my bed. I walked up from behind her and hid the knife behind my back. I started messing with her hair. And she moved around saying my name and started smiling and laughing. I started messing with her hair more until she told me that I was hurting her. She stood up and told me what the fuck I was doing. I wasn't saying anything back. She got worried. "Mitch" she said. "What the fuck do you think you're doing?" "Mitch" she said again. I grabbed her hair and pulled her closer. "Mitch" she said again. "What the fuck you are hurting me let go." "Mitch" then I pulled out the knife from behind me and fucking stabbed her in the fucking stomach. Immediately she held with both hands two her stomach and looked right into my cold dark eyes. I stabbed her again and she fell out of the bed crying and in tremendous pain. She started crawling and I was right behind her. She started crawling more and more trying to escape, I walked towards her and picked her up from her hair and started slicing her and threw her back on the floor. She started crawling but she was slowly crawling and then she stopped crawling, she was gasping for air and then she died. I walked past her body and grabbed my cell phone and called Lindsay back. Of course she didn't pick up so I decided to leave a message. "Now we can be together forever, Bethany won't get in the way ever again." "Lindsay, I love you. I guess now I can say that Lindsay and I have one more thing in common.

Chapter 34
The Clinic/Lindsay

I had to clean up the mess before it starts to smell, and I have wooden floors so it would seep through and get into the basement. I walked back into my room and took all the sheets from the bed and curled it into a ball and threw it in the garbage can. I got a mop and some cleaning solution and started cleaning the floors. All the dirty water I drained into the sink and cleaned the areas around it. I cleaned the rest of the floors and started carefully picking up the body. I got an industrial size garbage bag and grabbed a few more and stuffed Bethany's body inside. I carried the bag and it was fucking heavy as shit. I carried her body all the way outside towards the back so no one in the front can see, and stuffed her body in the garbage can. I threw some old newspapers and some boxes I had sitting along the side on top to make it seem like I had garbage instead of one heavy ass container. I closed the lid and drug the mother fucking container in the front of the street so the garbage people can collect it the next morning. I was hoping that I don't get caught for this shit and go to jail. I walked back inside my house and closed the Goddamn door behind me. I got the fucking mop and started cleaning up the rest of the Goddamn mess. I squeezed all the water into the pale and carried it to the sink and poured it down the drain. After several minutes of cleaning I was finally done and now I can go with the rest of my day.

It was funny because I was acting like I was doing fucking chores or something. Now that I am done I can go play or something. I knew that what I did was wrong and I did feel some sort of sadness in what I did. But Bethany was in the way of what was really important to me. And in that second my phone rang and I saw the caller id, it was Lindsay. I picked up but I didn't say hello at first. "I got your message Mitch, what do you mean that Bethany won't get in the way again." "I am coming over don't go anywhere." I hung up the phone and walked towards the kitchen and cleaned off the knife and put it back in the drawer. It was a perfectly good knife I wasn't going to throw it away. I walked towards the front door. I opened the door and kept it open; I sat down on the front porch and waited for Lindsay to come. I waited for several minutes and Lindsay finally came, and it was about time. I stood up and walked towards her car. She immediately got out without turning off her car and kept her car door open. "Are you okay" she said. "I was confused about your phone message earlier." "I will explain things later" I said. "I am just glad to see you" I walked up to her and gave her a hug and didn't let go. I wanted to be with Lindsay for a long ever I was willing to do anything. I guess I just fucking proved my own point wouldn't you say. I let go of her and just started into her eyes and didn't say anything for several seconds. "What's on your mind" she said. "You seem preoccupied" "Nothing" I said. "Don't worry about it right now I will explain when the time is right. She seemed worried, I mean why wouldn't she be she had no idea what I had done and what the fuck I was thinking. I mean I couldn't even understand what I did or what I was thinking. All I know is that what I did for some strange reason beyond my own control I wanted to do more of it. This is only the second time that something like this had happened and I felt so empowered. I walked over to the porch and sat down. Lindsay followed me and sat down next to me. I mean where is she going to go back home. I can tell that she wanted to spend the rest of her life with me and to tell you the truth I wouldn't have it any other way. But I had this feeling like I wanted something badly. You know what I am talking about, when you want scratch that, need something or someone in this case, Lindsay, very badly you will do anything to get her. Fuck it, I guess never mind I don't know what the fuck I am saying sometimes. I confuse the fuck out of myself sometimes; I tend to do that from time to time. "I have to go and visit Liz." "I just wanted to tell you in person rather than over the phone, I thought it would be better that way. "I wanted to see you in person before I leave." "What are you saying, you are talking about like you're never coming back or something." "It's all confusing right now and I don't know how to tell you." I stood up and Lindsay got up also. I turned towards her and kissed her on the lips. "I have to go and see Liz, I will be back." She hugged and kissed me back. "I am so confused; can you please tell me what's going on?" "I will in due time, please do not stress over it okay can you promise me that for once." I walked Lindsay to her car and she got in, I held her hand outside the window and kissed it. "Everything is going to be alright, I will be back." She held my hand tightly and looked at me. She let go and blew a kiss to me and drove off. I waited for a few seconds to watch her drive away and then I got into my car. I didn't want to waste any time so I didn't bother calling. I had no idea if she was even if her office or not. I was going off a gut reaction that she would be in her office or something.

I drove for several minutes and the more I drove the more I felt bad about not telling Lindsay what happened. But I guess in some weird way this was the right thing to do. I didn't want to worry her about what I did and what the fuck I was thinking. When the time was right then I will tell Lindsay everything. I made it to the office and Liz was walking out of the door. I honked my horn and got her attention before she went anywhere and I drove here for no fucking reason. I pulled in and parked my car, I turned it off and got out and closed the door. I walked around my car towards her and she was very surprised to see me. "Mitch" she said. I was just leaving, what can I do for you?" "I have to talk to you, it is very important." She paused for a second swung her purse around her shoulder and grabbed her keys. "Alright come on in, I can make time for you." I followed her into her office and the receptionist saw me as I was walking in and I just waved to her. She smiled and nodded back and went on talking on the phone. I walked into her office and sat down on the couch. "What is on your complex mind this time?" I could tell by the sound of her voice that she was joking around. Liz was never the type of person to say something mean about someone and actually mean it or something like that shit. She was always nice to everyone especially me even with all my fucking problems and everything like that. "I did something that I am not proud of and I don't know what to do now?" Liz could tell that I was being very serious because I was choosing my words very carefully. "Tell me what you did I am sure that I can handle it." I took a deep breath and sighed I covered my face with my hands and I wanted to just tell her but I was having a hard time. I needed to tell her because I would feel better if I just did. "I did something very terrible that I feel very bad but at the time I felt like I had no remorse, I felt like I enjoyed what I did. "Okay tell me what you did?" "I was at home with Bethany, and Lindsay got all mad that I was spending all this time with her." "You see it wasn't anything like that, and well you see I wanted to be with Lindsay and I was willing do anything to be with her. Well, Bethany was sleeping and I got really bored so I walked into my kitchen, grabbed a knife, and stabbed my girlfriend to death." Liz dropped the pad that she was holding in her hands and just stared at me with her jaw wide open. "What the fuck Mitch" she said. That is the first time I heard Liz curse, I didn't know that she curses. But I guess that is beyond the fucking point here. "What do you have to say for yourself Mitch?" "I don't have anything to say for myself I told you I was willing to do anything to be with Lindsay forever." "What did you do with the body?" "I disposed of it and put it into a garbage container. "There is only one thing that I can recommend now, and that is maximum security at a mental hospital, and it is manta dory, no exceptions. For some reason that sounded good, and another thing was very weird is that even though to anyone else this but to Liz she was perfectly fine. Well I wouldn't say perfectly fine she did curse and get all upset at me but what can you do. She stood up and walked over to her desk. I also got up and followed her to her desk. She grabbed some papers and told me to sign. I guess they were like fucking wavers or something, I skimmed through the page and then I signed. I really didn't care what it said because at this point what's done is done and there is no turning back. I gave her the papers and walked back on the couch. "When do I start" I said. "Soon don't you worry; look I am not doing this because I am mean. "I am doing this because I care for you and I don't want to see this problem get any worse." I stood up from the couch and walked towards her and gave her a hug. "I really appreciate everything that you are doing for me; most people would've thrown me in jail." "I don't want to do that because even though you made a mistake, a huge mistake, you're a nice kid and well I don't know. "I am going to be evaluating you myself to see how the program is going and everything, can you please follow me." I followed Liz and she took me to the elevators. From there she pressed the third floor button and the doors closed. She didn't say anything or even look at me the whole time. I guess she was still pretty upset, and the worst news is I haven't told my mom yet. I wonder how she is going to take this news. Knowing her she will probably commit suicide or something. She is never taken very bad news well in her life, and sometimes I think that affects her but she tries to hide it from everyone. The doors opened and we walked out, I followed Liz still, and still she didn't even look back or say anything to me. There were a lot of rooms on this floor but she took me to a room that was far away from everyone else's room. I guess I was special or something. She opened the door, and told me to wait inside someone will come and see me in a few. And like that Liz closed the door and she left.

Now I am fucking trapped here like a fucking rat. It was funny I just got in here and I wanted to get out already. The room was very plain. The walls were made out of concrete, and the floor was tile. The floor and the wall were like a white color. But it wasn't a bright white sort of like dirty or something. I guess they really didn't care about this room to much. There was one sink, a chair and a table, and one bed. At least the bed looked comfortable. But as soon as I sat down the bed wasn't that comfortable, but it was doable. I just lay on the bed and waited for the person to come that Liz was talking about. I was worried about one thing though, and that is my mom and how she is going to handle everything. But there was another thing that was bothering me and that is how long I was going to have stay in here for. I wonder if I will see Lindsay ever again. I was about to close my eyes and I heard someone walking down the hallway. I guess that was the fucking person that Liz was talking about. It got closer and closer and then I heard keys. So I was right that was the person that Liz was talking about. There was so much shit on my mind I didn't even want to talk to anyone right now. The person opened the door and it was a older gentleman, he had gray hair and glasses. He also had a gray beard and he was dressed in slacks with a leather jacket covering his T-shirt.

"Hi" he said. "How are you doing today?" "Good "I replied back. "So Mitch Liz has told me a lot of about you in these few minutes, how are you handling things?" "Fine" I said. "Not much of a talker." I didn't say anything. He walked in and closed the door and sat down on the bed next to me. "Mitch I don't want you to see me as a doctor but as a friend, someone who you can talk to if you're having problems with something." "Okay" I said. "What about Lindsay" I said. "Yes Lindsay" he said. Don't worry Liz told her everything, she is fine and she can come and visit anytime." "What about my mom?" "Liz has kept her in the loop with everything." "I want to go home now." "I am afraid you can't go home now, you can't go home for a while Mitch, I am sorry but don't get mad at me." "This wasn't my rules, it was Liz's rules and she is the boss." The gentleman got up and walked towards the door, he opened the door and walked out and closed the door. I lay on my bed and closed my eyes and the only thing that came to my mind was Lindsay, and how she is dealing with everything. Now I am mother fucking restless and I couldn't even get some Goddamn sleep. Someone came back and opened the door; it was Liz with my mom. I stood up fast as hell and my heart was fucking pounding, I was sweating a little bit. They both walked in and my mom was crying a lot and Liz looked sad to but she was a professional so she to maintain her composure. Or I guess that is what professionals do; I don't know I have no knowledge in a field or something like that. My mom walked in sat down next to me and didn't say anything at me she just looked at me and was crying more and more. She finally leaned in didn't say anything but hugged me and kissed me on the cheek. "I love you I always will I just want you to be safe." I looked back at her and for some reason I had nothing say to her. She waited for me to say something and then nothing, she got up still crying and then she walked towards the door. She stood behind Liz who was next. She sat down and put her hand on my shoulder and said, "Your mom came all the way over here to see, are you going to say something." I was silent. It wasn't that I was being inconsiderate I just had nothing to say at this point. And I am not going to say something if I don't mean it. Then it wouldn't be true and I would be just wasting my mother fucking time. Liz got kind of disappointed and walked out with my mom. She closed the door and saw me standing up and looking at her with a pale expression on my face. I sat back down and lay back on my Goddamn uncomfortable bed and didn't close my eyes but all I could think about is Lindsay. And how everything I did up to this point was for her. I couldn't explain it but it's like I waited my whole life for a girl like this. And now she is here I am fucking screwing it up every fucking chance I get. It was funny because it was like roles were fucking reversed. What I mean by that is like Lindsay was in the same situation I am in now and I was the one who came in and visited with everyone and met her. Now it is my turn to be in here and now it is Lindsay's turn to come in and see me. At least when she comes in we have something to talk about. It is always better when you have stuff in common with other people especially if they are your girlfriend. You don't want a girlfriend who you don't have nothing in common because every fucking conversation would be awkward. Whatever I know that sometimes I don't make any Goddamn sense you get used to it. I wonder what Liz told Lindsay. I hope that she didn't like stretch the fucking truth or something like that. I just hope that she didn't make up any lies to make Lindsay not come and see me. But I have trust in Liz because I know her, and she is not the type of person to go around and spread rumors about someone, especially someone like me. I am not saying I am special or anything like that; all I am saying is that we know each other and formed a relationship over the years. But it was strictly professional, nothing intimate, but Liz was a very attractive woman for her age and she did have an amazing body. But that was beside the Goddamn point. I stood up and as soon as I did that, Liz came back with the gentleman again. He walked inside and stood next to me. "Are you hungry, Mitch?" "A little" I said. "Follow me" he said. I followed him; I guess he was leading me to the cafeteria. I was a little hungry but I didn't want to say that I was starving. If I did that it would give him a reason to start up a conversation with me and I was in no mood to talk to him. We made it to the café, or what I thought was a café, it wasn't it was a small ass room with a few tables. There was one table set in the middle in the room where I followed him to the one in the middle. He sat down and I sat down next to him. A nurse came by and he told her what he wanted and she nodded her head. "What can I get you honey?" I didn't say anything and just looked straight ahead without moving. She waited and said, "I guess someone's not hungry, it's okay you don't have to eat." She walked away and the older gentleman started talking. "How are you doing Mitch?" Again I didn't say anything. He didn't ask another question for a few more seconds. And as soon he was about to open his mouth, I interrupted him. "I want to see Lindsay." "Okay I can see what I can do to have her come in and visit you. The nurse came back with a cup of coffee, apparently he didn't order any food, and I guess he wasn't hungry either. He started drinking the coffee slowly taking loud and obnoxious sips. But luckily for us there were only the two of us in the room, it would've been embarrassing if there were more people. He put the coffee cup down and looked at me. "I know you are not going to talk to me, but if I bring Lindsay in will you talk to her." "Yes" I said. The older gentleman got up from his chair and walked out the room and I waited for several minutes.

After I waited and fucking waited to my surprise Liz walked in and told me that it was okay if I called Lindsay so she can visit. Apparently she already knows everything, so explaining it to her shouldn't be that hard. I quickly got my cell phone and called Lindsay, and soon she picked up I hurriedly told her to come over I needed to talk to her. The phone hung up and Lindsay slowly walked through the door, I hung up my phone and placed it on the table. She stood there in the middle of the room and I was standing there across from the table. And I saw everything that I ever wanted in my whole life standing in front of me. And this time I wasn't going to ruin it by making any stupid Goddamn mistakes. I walked up to her and she stood there not moving just staring at me. "I missed you so much" I said. She walked to me and hugged me and didn't let go. She looked up at me and said, "Why did you do all this?" I looked back at her and I told her that I did it for her. In my mind I was thinking that she might not get it why I did what I did, but in all honestly I did it for the girl of my dreams. "Did you do this to prove a point or something?" "Look I know now it might seem very difficult for you to understand but trust me on this." "One day I will explain everything to you, right now everything is so fucking complicated it is giving me a fucking headache all the damn time." Lindsay just smiled and laughed. She still stood there and I hugged her. I looked at her and said, "No matter what happens with me, with us there is one thing that I need to tell you." No matter what happens, Lindsay, I just wanted to tell you I will do anything to be with you. I want to spend the rest of my life with you and what I wanted to tell is that I love you." Lindsay looked at me and kissed me on the lips and hugged me, and said, "I love you too." I held her close, and I saw in my mind that everything was going to be alright. The only thing that was important to me was Lindsay.

Chapter 35
Goodbye Forever

Lindsay pushed me off, playfully, and started laughing. "Sometimes I think you are too emotionally attached or something." I laughed back, "Whatever sometimes I think you want me badly you can't control yourself." It was funny, as Lindsay and I were walking out the room and down the hallway, no matter how bad things got every time I am with Lindsay I just feel like everything is going to be alright. It is weird I act differently when I was with Alison, Kristen, Beverly and even Bethany. But Lindsay brings out something different out in me and I think I like it. She grabbed my hand and I grabbed hers, and she turned away from me and started looking the other way. "What's the matter" I said. I Worried about Lindsay, because she didn't seem like herself. "Nothing" she said. But she was lying because there was something wrong with her, I just had a feeling in the pit of my stomach that Lindsay was preoccupied about something, and there was something that she wasn't telling me. I stopped walking and turned towards her. "There is something that's on your mind just tell me." "It's nothing; I told you don't worry about it." "Let's just enjoy the time we have together now." What did she mean by let's just enjoy the time we have tougher now. She was talking like she didn't want to be with me anymore or something of that nature. We started walking down the hallway and she walked to the door where you have to get buzzed out to leave. "Can you please let us out; I want to take Mitch out to get something to eat." The nurse behind the station looked at us pretty funny, and then she finally hit the fucking buzzer. The door opened and Lindsay and I left. I was surprised I can just leave like this with whomever I choose to. I am surprised that Liz or any of the other nurses weren't stopping me. But I am a grown ass person; I should be able to do whatever the hell I want to. And I think that Liz trusts me enough to make my own decisions in life and her and I are both fine with that. There was one thing that was bothering me though, as we started making our way to the front entrance of the building, is my mom. I wonder how she is taking the news, I mean her only son in a place like this for the second time. I couldn't imagine in her wildest dreams that I would do what I did. But I needed to, don't you see I need to be with Lindsay, and I am willing to do anything to be with her. We made it outside and the weather was absolutely beautiful, I forgot how nice the weather was. Well I was only in the place for a few hours but you tend to forget being in there how amazing the outside world is. "Where are we going to eat?" "We aren't, I said that so they can let you leave and get some fresh air." I just laughed; I can't believe Lindsay just lied to let me leave. But I guess that is not the first time she surprised me. We found a small table, but it was still in the same compound, but it was nice. Lindsay started making her way to the table so I followed. She sat down and crossed her legs and sighed. "What a beautiful day to be outside" she said. "Don't you think so Mitch?" "It is a nice day, but I know that is not the reason why you brought me out here and I know that is not the reason why you came and visit, so why don't you tell me what's really on your mind." "For the last time Mitch, there is nothing on my mind." "Is it a sin for me to come and visit and bring you outside without getting fucking harassed?" "You know I didn't mean it like that, why are you being so difficult?" "I am not being difficult, you just keep on harassing me all the time, and I can't breathe." "Sorry I'll stop, I thought something was bothering you and you weren't telling me." "Everything is fine now sit down and enjoy this day with me please." I sat down and got close to her. I grabbed and held her hand as I just looked at her while she was looking around. Lindsay was right about one thing, it was a beautiful day outside. The sun was out and it was nice and warm. The birds were chirping and there was a nice cool breeze flowing in the air. Something about today in my mind was the perfect day. "Okay well I know that there is something bothering you, and I won't ask anymore but I am glad that you came." "Me too" she said. "It is nice to see you." "Can I ask you a question?" "Sure" she said. "What's on your mind baby?" "I was just wondering if you were still mad at me from before because of the whole Bethany thing." "I know how jealous you can get sometimes if you see me talking to another girl." "First of all Mitch, I don't get jealous I am just protective and I don't want anything to happen to you." I just laughed and stood up and started walking around. "You sound like my mom" I said. "I appreciate that you feel protective of me but I am capable of taking care of myself thank you very much." "All you *boys* are the same all the male bravado you guys think that you are the fucking shit." "First of all I don't think that I am the shit *I am* the fucking shit, just joking, but anyway I do appreciate you being here and everything. Lindsay got up and walked towards me and wrapped her hands around me and pulled me closer. "I am here because I love you and to me that is the most important thing in the whole wide world. I smiled and kissed her. "We should be going back inside; I think they are beginning to get worried like I ran away or something." Lindsay just laughed and walked me back inside the building. We held hands all the way into the door and all the way down the hallway. We walked to the elevators and down the hallway again. We made it to the door and the nurse actually had a smile on my face. I don't know why she is so fucking grumpy all the damn time. But I think that she was actually relieved that I didn't fucking runaway or something. And she is always giving Lindsay a look. But now she wasn't, I guess she saw, like me, how amazing of a person Lindsay is. And another thing the nurse should know her because Lindsay was once hospitalized here, but I guess the nurse isn't a very sociable person. The door buzzed and we walked in, Lindsay directed me to my room and came inside with me and sat down on the bed. I closed the door and sat down on the bed next to her. I just hope that no one walks by and gets the fucking wrong impression that I have a girl in my room with my door closed. I mean first of all its Lindsay, but you know how nosey some Goddamn people are. Once they see something out of place they go run and fucking tell someone. They probably think that since I am crazy, because I am pretty sure that they heard of what I did, that I am going to rape Lindsay or something. I can see how one can come to that conclusion because we are in a room far away from everyone else's room. And I am a boy and Lindsay is a girl. But fuck them and what they think. I don't care about what anybody fucking thinks. The only thing that I care about is me and what I believe in, and of course Lindsay too, can't forget that. Lindsay got closer to me and looked at me. "I have missed you so much; I can't imagine what my fucking life would be like without you." "I missed you too, but Liz and the older gentleman said that I can't go home for a while. "And I don't know how long that is honestly." "Well I am here now" she said. "What do you want to do?" I looked at Lindsay who was looking right back at me holding my hand. "We drew closer and closer to each other and we all of a sudden started kissing. We started kissing more intensely she pushed me off and she started taking off her shirt. Then she took off her bra. I got up from her and begun to take off my shirt also. We were about to have sex when someone knocked on the mother fucking door. I shouted as I was hurrying to put my shirt back on to hold on for one minute. Lindsay was hurrying to put her clothes back on too. I got up from the bed and Lindsay was sitting on my bed with all of her clothes on. I walked towards the door and it was my mom. She was by herself this time Liz was nowhere to be seen. I didn't want to be rude so I invited my mom in. I don't think she ever had the chance to meet Lindsay so this was the perfect time to introduce each other. My mom walked towards my bed and I began by saying, "Mom I would like to introduce you to my girlfriend Lindsay." "Lindsay this is my mom, Lauren." My mom smiled and walked up to Lindsay and she stood up from the bed and she gave her a hug. Lindsay sat back down on the bed and I sat down next to her. My mom stood on the other side of the bed, and looked at us. A tear came to her eye, I guess she was happy that I finally found someone but I could be wrong. "I miss you baby" she said. I miss you to mom" I said. "Did Liz say when you are coming home?" "No" I said. "She told me that I am not going home for a while." My mom just stood there with a sad look on her face, she was pretty upset about the whole situation. But I think that she was more upset about me and how I decided to live my life. It is funny my dad never judged me for anything I did, but trying to prove something to my mom is the hardest thing that I ever had to do in my life. I feel like no matter what I did in life it was never good enough for my mom. And Jeremy well I don't know if even gave two shits to even fucking care about me. I mean don't get me wrong he did come through when I needed a "father figure" in my life, but in all honestly he was no one to me and I never cared about him that much anyway. Sure he took me out and sure he showed me a great time, but he wasn't my father and the only good thing about Jeremy that I can say is that I think he knew that. Jeremy was never the person to sit me down and fucking give me lectures about growing up or being a man. I can never recall once him giving me the Goddamn birds and the bee's speech. Luckily for me sex is something that I figured out myself with no one's help. "Mom what's wrong you seem very upset?" "Are you sure that there is anything on your mind that you would like to discuss?" My mom just stood there and looked at us and walked towards the door. "I am just happy to see you that's all I just want to you to be careful." I stood up from the bed and walked towards my mom, "Of course I am going to be alright, nothing is going to happen, everything is going to be fine." My mom smiled and hugged and kissed me and then she opened the door and walked out. I turned back towards Lindsay who was sitting on my bed with her hands on her knees curled up. "Are you sure that your mom is going to be alright?" "I am sure that she is going to be alright" "She tends to worry about stuff like this for a while and then she gets over it pretty quickly." Lindsay stood up and walked towards me and kissed me on the cheek. "I have to go, I have to head home my dad is probably worrying sick about me." "He called but I had my phone on vibrate and he gets pretty fucking upset when I don't return his phone calls." She hugged me and then she left. And just like that the two most important women in my life just left. Well the two most important women in my life right now. I had girls that really meant a lot to me in my life but none who impacted my life as much as my mom and now Lindsay. And I know that I haven't known Lindsay for that much but it is something about her that we connected and we have clicked ever since. There is something about her that makes her so different than any other girl that I have dated. We can talk and we just click on stuff that it was hard for me to talk to other girls about. I walked back to my bed and lay down. The only thought that was coming to my mind at this point is if I am ever going to leave. All I can think about is spending time with Bethany before I killed her. She was so sweet and innocent she didn't deserve to die. Someone knocked on the door, and I got up and answered it. It was Liz and she seemed pretty upset about something. She asked me if she can come in and I said yes. She made her way towards my bed and sat down. "What's wrong" I said. "Is everything okay?" "I talked to your mom" she said. "She seems pretty upset more than usual." "When I talked to her she was flipping through an old family album and going on and on about your dad, and if he was still alive you would've become a better man than you are today." "So what are you trying to say, my mom is blaming my dad that I am not the person that she expects me to be today." "I don't know but she was crying and going on and on about everything." "I swear we talked on the phone for several minutes before she hung up quite rudely." "Well I don't care" I said. "She's your mom even though she is blaming you or not blaming you she still loves you." "I don't care" I said. "If my mom wants to blame my dad or blame me than let her I just don't care anymore." "Now I know you don't mean that" Liz said. "I do" I said. "Who the fuck is she blaming my dad, my dad has nothing to do with this." "I am a man and I am responsible for my own actions not my dad not my mom not anyone." Liz stood up and then she walked to the door. "I don't know what to say to you anymore Mitch." "Everyone does care about you and I think it is about time that you see that." Liz opened the door and walked out. I walked towards the door and closed it. I wish I had a Goddamn do not disturb sign right now I can hang it on the damn door knob and everyone will leave me the hell alone. I still couldn't believe that my mom would do something like that. I can't believe that she would stoop so low to blame my dad for me not turning out the way that she wanted. I was so mad that I couldn't even think straight, I tired going to sleep. I got on top the bed messed it around in hatred and tried to go to sleep. I got under the covers and just fucking closed my eyes, hopefully a good rest will calm my nerves.

I don't know how long it was but I was sleeping for a while. It was fucking night time and I think that I missed dinner. I think that I heard someone calling over the intercom that dinner was being served but I didn't hear it. I woke up and stood up from my bed and walked to the window. I looked outside and the Goddamn view never changed.

It felt so fucking boring outside, like the whole world was empty or something. I walked to the door and looked out the window to see if anyone was in the hallway. Luckily for me there was no one walking the hallway so it was safe for me to leave. I quietly opened the door and walked out and soon as I took one damn step outside, Liz came by and she had something in her hand. It was a letter. It was probably from my mom. I wonder what that was all about. She came up to me and said how I was doing, and asked me if everything was okay. "Mitch I have something for you" she said." "A letter came for you not to long ago." She gave me the letter and just smiled and walked away. I looked at the letter and it wasn't from my mom but it was from Lindsay. Why did she write a letter I wonder why she didn't just come and stop by. I took the letter and didn't waste any time. I walked to my room and closed the door halfway. I waited one more second before I tore open the letter. Still wondering why she wrote to me. I softly tore open the letter being careful not to damage the letter. I got the letter from the envelope and threw the envelope away. I unfolded the letter and begun reading, it read:

Dear Mitch,

Hi baby I hope that everything is going okay with you. I am sorry that I am writing. I hate writing but this was hard enough as it is, and I wasn't able to do it in person. I have been waiting my whole life to find a guy that truly understands me for me and I finally found him in you. You were the best thing that ever happened to me in such a long time. Baby my life wasn't some fantasy tale; I had a rough life growing up, with me killing my mom and all, and my dad sexually abusing me and verbally abusing me all the time. I thought that my life was never going to get better but it did. The day you walked in I could tell that there was something about you that was different. I could tell that I wanted to be with you for the rest of my life and I was determined. I loved you the day that you first walked in and I will always love you forever. But if there is one thing that my dad has been good at before he turned into an alcoholic fuck is giving me good advice in life. And well baby I know that this is going to be really hard for me to say but here it goes. I don't know how to say this; this is so hard for me. Mitch, honey, baby, I am leaving. And I am probably never going to see you again. I don't want you to get upset. It is actually funny my dad of all people got a job working somewhere I can't remember right now. But we are moving in a few days. Actually there was a reason why I wrote instead of not seeing you in person. I just didn't want to see you get all upset and blame yourself for me leaving. Because baby it is not your fault. I am trying to be as strong as possible about this. I don't want to write anymore because the more I write the more I am going to think about you. And the more I think about you the more I am going to cry. So I just wanted to say before I go is that I love you and I want you to promise me one thing. And that is that you will never forget me. I love you Mitch, forever and always, I love you.

Love

Lindsay.

I just stared at the letter for a few more seconds and covered my face with my hands. I can feel the letter slipping from my hands and it hit the floor. I couldn't believe that Lindsay is leaving me. I stood up from the bed and picked up the letter and looked at it one more time, I wanted to do nothing but fucking throw it away but I folded it up and put it in my pocket. I want this of all things to be the last thing that I remember Lindsay by. Because I am never going to see her again, I started crying and walked towards the window. I stared and saw the world unfold. It was just crazy because I felt like the world just didn't make sense anymore. I quickly dried my tears off and walked outside. I needed to find Liz. I walked to one of the offices where she is generally working and she wasn't there. I walked around and saw her on the phone in one of the other offices. I knocked on the door and she put the phone on the side. "Hey Mitch, what can I do for you?" "I need to speak to you it is very important." She told the person whomever she was talking to that she will call her back. She told me to come in and I walked in and sat down on the chair. She told me to close the door so I stood up and closed the door and sat down again. "What's up" she said. I didn't even want to tell her. I went for my pocket and grabbed the letter and gave it to her. "What's this" she said. "This is the letter that you gave me today." "It is from Lindsay, I want you to read it." She took the letter, slipped on her glasses that were on top of her head and begun reading. After a second or two she read the letter and placed it down on her lap. "Mitch I am so sorry" she said. "When I got this letter I had no idea that this is the way that it would turn out." "Are you okay?" "I am fine, I guess this is good thing right." "If you love something the best thing you can do is set it free." "All I want is Lindsay to have a happy life with whomever she may meet; I don't want to hold her back anymore." "Do you think that you are holding her back?" "Yes" I said. "I don't want her to worry about me being in here you know, I just want Lindsay to live her life." Liz stood up and handed me the letter. I told her thank you as I stood up also and put it back in my pocket. "Can I have a hug" I said. Liz walked towards me and gave me a hug. "Don't worry everything is going to be alright." "I know, thanks for always being there for me when I needed a friend." Liz smiled and we continued to hug. In my mind, even though Lindsay was leaving I had a feeling that everything was going to be alright.

Chapter 36

I Love You Mom

I left Liz's office and they were announcing food over the intercom. Even though it was still late and I missed dinner I was hungry. If I was correct they were serving snacks. See at this place they serve snacks after dinner. Because fucking people complain that they are always hungry all the Goddamn time. I walked over to the line and the snacks line was very long. I guess people were very fucking hungry tonight. After waiting for several minutes I finally got the chance to get my fucking food. I was so hungry I got two things of cereal, two milks and a piece of fruit. I gathered my goodies and walked to an empty room by myself. It's not that I don't want to eat with anyone else right now, wait that is the fucking reason I don't want to eat with anyone else right now. I walked into the room and found a table in the corner. I sat down and on top of the table was a TV remote. There was a Goddamn TV in this room. I didn't care enough to pick it up and turn it on, because I didn't want to see what was going on. I was tearing up my cereal cover and about to pour the milk inside and eat when a girl walked in and made her way to the table. The funny thing is that every time I try to get away from someone or try to do something by myself someone always comes and fucking ruins it. But it wasn't that bad because this girl was so fucking hot. I mean she is the hottest girl that I have seen in such a long time. She is hotter than any of my previous girlfriends. I was nervous to talk to her, I mean we are both in the same place so it's not like she is fucking special or something. "Hello" I said. She looked at me with her food at hand and looked back down giving me a fucking snotty look. I didn't want to say anything because she might say something back and then instead of being nice to her, whom I was going to do, she would've said something smart. I continued to eat my food and she looked up, and sighed and said, "Hi" in a prissy ass fucking voice. I just laughed and continued to eat my food. She looked up again, "What is so funny?" I looked up and some milk dripping from the side of my mouth. I wiped it off with my sleeve and smiled. "Nothing" I said. "My name is Mitch and you are?" I was trying to be polite even though she was acting like a total bitch. "Well even though it is none of your damn business, I will tell you because I don't want to be rude." "My name is Ashley." "Hello Ashley it is very nice to meet you." She smiled but this smile was different than her usual facial expressions. I could tell that in her smile she was very sincere. We finished eating around the same time and shit, so we had time to do whatever we wanted before *I* went to sleep. I really wasn't too sure about her, and what she likes to do in her spare time. Well I guess that this is a perfect time since we are both sitting here and not saying anything. "So Ashley if you don't mind me asking, why are you in here?" "I don't mind" she said. "I am in here because after my mom died, life has been very tough on me." "I was on drugs and I used to cut myself a lot in the bathroom of my house." "I am sorry" I said. "It's okay; it has been tough on my dad too." "So why are you in here?" she said. "It is a very long and complicated story Ashley." "I have time" she said. "Well it goes like this" I said. "I stabbed and killed my mom's boyfriend soon to be husband because he was a total dick. I ended up here the first time and then I met my girlfriend Lindsay. Well she is not my girlfriend anymore she left me but that is beside the point. And to prove that I loved her very much, which I still do, I stabbed and killed my very first girlfriend so she wouldn't get in the way again." "So that is my life in a fucking nut shell Ashley, I hope you are satisfied." And of course she was a little upset. I mean when people tell you why they are in a psychiatric unit it is something less severe than my problems. But I guess I am the fucking exception to the rule. "Oh" she said. "That is different." She got up from the table and left, and walked out the fucking door. I guess I scared her off or something. Well she wanted to know why I am in here and I didn't want to lie, and make a bad impression. I got up from the table and left the room. It was getting late but I was determined to find out why she left without even saying goodbye. I turned my head and looked down the hallway and I saw her walk into her room. Wow I forgot to mention that I live in a place where there aren't that many people on my floor. I have a room that is far away from everyone else's and here she is lives in the same hallway as me and shit. Now that is some crazy ass shit. I walked down the hallway and knocked on her door, I was determined on why she left without saying anything. I knocked on her door and she answered pretty surprised to see me standing in front of her face. "Ashley" I said. "Why did you leave so abruptly without saying anything?" "You kind of freaked me out and well you also made me realize something too." "Oh yeah what's that" I said. "That you are special and shit." "First of all I don't appreciate the fucking attitude, and second me and you have something in common." Oh great not another one, as I was still standing by her door, are you telling me that this is another Goddamn Lindsay. Next I believe she is going to tell me that she murdered her mom or something. "When I said you and I have something in common what I meant to say was we both had to prove something in our lives." Man that was a relief I thought for a second she was going to say that she never mind you already know where the hell I am going with this. "Would you like to come in and sit down?" Come on the girl is fucking hot and in this place no one ever bothers checking you for anything, so what the hell do you think I was going to say. I walked in and she closed the door all the way and dimmed the lights a little bit. I found my way to her bed and sat down. She started talking, "So you were here before right?" "Yes" I said. "A while ago and then I left, and then crazy shit started happening in my life so I came back." "Oh" she said. I can tell that she wasn't really interested in what I had to say. I mean who is; my life is but so Goddamn interesting. I hope that you can tell I was being fucking sarcastic; I wouldn't take back one damn thing that happened in my life so far. I mean well you already know what the hell I mean. She sat down next to me and started staring at me but she wasn't trying to be rude in any way she was just pleasantly staring at me. And at first I didn't want to look her way but I turned towards her and looked at her back. Ashley was smiling so it was a good sign, I hope. She leaned in and said, "You know I never told you that you're kind of cute." I smiled; I didn't know what to say. I mean do I say she was cute back because I still am in love with Lindsay. "Well you're kind of cute yourself too." Fuck what the hell was I doing, was I cheating on Lindsay with Ashley. And I just fucking realized at this point that I really didn't care anymore. I mean how I know that she is not cheating on me with someone else right now. I am in here and she is probably miserable and needs a shoulder to cry on. She probably met someone and didn't tell me. No, what the hell no I sound all fucking paranoid, I love her and she loves me back we were going to get married. But there was no hiding the fact that Ashley was hot and I am a guy so there is no denying the fact that I wasn't going to tell her regardless. I wanted to kiss her so badly, was that so bad I didn't want to but again I couldn't help it? I mean we were alone in her room and no one ever bothers or checks up on us. I got up from her bed and she stood up too and walked to her window. She opened the curtains a little and looked outside. "Doesn't it look very pretty outside?" I walked to the window next to her and looked outside also. "Yes" I said. I really didn't give a shit how it looked outside I just wanted to talk about something else. She turned towards me again and smiled and walked to her bed. All this fucking tension is killing me. I walked to her sat down next to her and leaned in and kissed her on the lips. Luckily for me she was looking at me so it wasn't fucking awkward or anything. "What was that for" she said. She seemed pretty surprised that I did that. "I am sorry I just… she cut me off and smiled. "You don't have to apologize to me; I was hoping that you would kiss me. I smiled and we both got closer and just like that we started kissing. We got into it pretty intensely when someone fucking knocked on the door. I stopped kissing her and fucking panicked. I ran into her closet and closed the door. I could hear her laughing in the background. She got up from the bed and answered the door. "Hi have you seen Mitch anywhere?" She started laughing more, "Yeah he is my closet, he panicked and ran in there." I came out and I saw that it was only Liz. I started laughing, and walked towards Liz. "Hey Mitch care to explain to me what you were doing in her closet?" "Long story" I said. "Come with me the nurse wants to see you before you go to bed. Great I wonder what the fuck this can be about.

I wonder if it was even important enough to waste my fucking precious time. I walked with Liz down the hallway and we made it to the nurse's office. Liz walked in and sat down. The nurse got up and walked towards me opening the door further. "Mitch, I know that you don't want to hear this, but I want you to stop hanging out with that Ashley girl." "I think that you are making so much progress that she is going to bring you down." "Why" I said pretty upset about what just happened. "No I am not going to stop hanging out with her just because *you* say so." Liz got up from her chair and walked towards me. She told the nurse that she could handle it from here. "Mitch" said Liz. "It is not that we are trying to be mean in any way." "Then why are you doing this to me?" "Ashley is special, and I don't think that you should be hanging out with her." "And I have a surprise; your mom is coming up to visit tomorrow morning." "That's great news, but that is not that point." "I am still going to hang out with Ashley okay I like her as a friend and I need friends right now. I was so mad that I fucking stormed out of their mid sentence of Liz. I walked back to Ashley's room and knocked on her door. She answered and she could tell right away that I was fucking upset. "Mitch" she said. "What's wrong?" "Can you fucking believe these Goddamn nurses here?" "They told me to stop hanging out with you because they think that you are fucking unsafe or something." "What" she said. "They said that shit." "Yes" I said." "Well obviously they don't know me very well." "If they think for one second that I really give a shit of what they fucking think they have something else coming." I walked in and closed her door. She sat down on her bed but I didn't make my way to her bed just yet. I was still mad I was pacing around in her room for several minutes. "Sit down Mitch" she said. I know you're tense and I can make you feel a *whole lot* better. I stopped pacing in her room and looked at her. She was smiling and this can only mean one thing. I slowly walked to her bed, I didn't want to walk fast then she would know that I wanted to fuck her. I sat down on her bed and she made her way around to the back of me. She started rubbing my shoulders. "Don't worry, momma knows how to make you feel a lot better." I laughed. She started giving me a massage, and it felt so good. I could feel all my tensions going away as my body was completely relaxed. She stopped for a second. "Take off your shirt?" I looked back. "Trust me I know what I am doing." I took off my shirt and threw it on the floor next to her dresser. She started rubbing my shoulders and working her hands into my lower back. And I do have to say one thing the girl did know what the fuck she was doing. She was hitting all the right spots. She started laughing while she was rubbing my back with her hands. "What's so funny?" I asked. "Nothing really, it has been such a long time that I gave a massage to anyone I thought I was going to mess up." "You mean I am not your first?" "No" she said. I didn't want to keep asking fucking questions because I didn't know if they were too personal or not. "I had a boyfriend once" she said. "But he died a few years back by a drunk driver. "Sorry" I said, as she was working her hands lower and lower. She stopped and told me that it was my turn to give her a massage. Now I don't know how to. I know that it is very fucking easy right all you have to do is rub some fucking shoulders or something, but it is more complicated than that. We switched positions and I got behind her on her bed. She stood up halfway and took off her shirt. I didn't have to ask her to take off her shirt she just did. I started giving her a back rub with my hands and she was making these sexy ass moaning sounds, I think she was doing it on purpose just to get a rise out of me. And to tell you the truth it was working, she was actually turning me on a little bit. I turned her whole body around and I leaned in and started kissing her. She didn't fight it at all then she started kissing me back. Her hands made her way down my pants and started unbuckling my belt. She unzipped my zipper and pulled it down slowly laughing while she was doing it. She started pulling my pants down and then she felt inside my boxers. "What's this, you have been hiding this bad boy from me the whole time, naughty boy." I just laughed, I guess she was getting way into this, but I didn't give a fuck. She was about to pull down my fucking boxer shorts when again someone knocked on the mother fucking door. Ashley told the person to wait as I hurriedly put my clothes back on and sat on her bed. Ashley walked to the door and it was Liz again. "Mitch I had a feeling you would be in here." "Come with me please there is something that I need to talk to you about." I got up from her bed and again walked with Liz down the hallway. We started walking and talking. "Before you go to bed, I have great news, your mom is coming up to visit and spend a few hours with you." "That's great" I said. "But there is one thing that is bothering me." "What's that" said

Liz. "Please don't talk about Ashley, she is going through a very hard time and I don't appreciate everyone talking about her." "She is my friend" I said. "Okay if it bothers you that much I, I mean everyone won't talk about her." We walked to the main nurse's station, Liz walked in and I stood outside. Ashley walked out of her room and saw me down the hallway. She walked up to me and kissed me on the cheek. "Goodnight I am going to sleep, see you in the morning." I smiled and hugged her back. As she was walking back to her room she reminded me so much of Lindsay. And then I just fucking realized that I am in a Goddamn relationship. I think that I was cheating on Lindsay with Ashley, but I didn't mean to. Ashley was so fucking hot and there was something about her that I liked but I couldn't put my finger on it quite yet. I mean yes we were fooling around but we were not serious. I am still in love with Lindsay, if Lindsay is still in love with me is the important question. I mean I acted like a total dick to her and not telling her about all my other previous girlfriends doesn't fucking help matters. It was getting late and my mom was coming to visit so I might as well get some sleep. I walked down the hallway to my room and closed the door as I walked in. I lay in my bed excited about my mom visiting and just closed my eyes.

I thought I heard something when I was sleeping. I woke up and it was morning. I couldn't believe that I fucking slept the whole night. I got up from my bed and walked to the door. I still swear that I heard someone knocking. I answered the door and it was my mom surprising me early in the fucking morning. I walked towards my mom and hugged her and kissed her on the cheek. She hugged me back. "Mom what are you doing here so early?" "I wanted to visit my baby, what is there a law that says I can't." "No" I said. "Exactly" she said. "Come on let's walk and talk I want to know how you are doing." We started walking and I walked back to my room and closed my door. I walked back to my mom and we started walking again. "So Liz has been telling me about Ashley?" "She seems like a pretty interesting girl." "Great you heard to." "Look I am tired of everyone talking about her." "I am not saying anything Mitch, but don't you have a girlfriend already." "I do Ashley and me are just friends." My mom stopped talking about it I guess I made my fucking point. We walked into the café and she found a table for us. "Are you hungry" I said. "Not really" she said. "I ate before I left the house." "Well I am not that hungry either but I'll order food just in case." We sat down and my looked at me. She started talking but this time it was about my dad. "Why are you bringing him in the fucking conversation?" "Mitch, watch your mouth." My mom was pretty mad at me I can tell by her eyes. She was staring at me with these fucking eyes. "Why are you talking about dad?" "It is funny" she said. "I couldn't believe it you were such a nice kid, what happened?" "What the fuck do you mean what happened." "I am still the same mother fucking kid." "I told you to watch your mouth." "No" I said. "If you *are* my mom then you would stop blaming dad for my fucking mistakes. And my mom didn't say anything; a nurse came into the room with coffee and a newspaper. I guess that was for fucking whomever. She placed it down, and another nurse came into the room with a tray of food. The food here was fucking disgusting, but I guess it is better than nothing. The nurse put the food on the table and smiled and walked away with the other nurse. My mom was going on and on about how my dad was never around enough to mold me into the perfect Goddamn gentleman. She was going on about some other shit but I guess it wasn't important enough. I couldn't believe that my fucking mom was going on and on about blaming me for my actions. "You know you are a fucking disappointment." She picked up the coffee and turned the other way. I grabbed the tray and started playing with my food. I was holding the knife, clutching it in my hand, and cutting my food. I was so fucking mad at my mom for saying all this. She wasn't saying anything but drinking her stupid coffee. I was still holding the knife in my hand; I wanted to walk around to the other side and fucking stab her in the side of her fucking neck. I put the knife back down on the tray and folded my arms. She put the coffee cup down and turned towards me. "Look I am sorry for fucking blaming you." "I know that it was wrong and I shouldn't have done it." "Apology accepted" I said. "I still can't believe you said that." "I am sorry I guess I am still dealing with the whole Jeremy thing." My mom didn't say anything after that for several minutes. And I didn't either. I guess she was taking this whole thing pretty hard. My mom stood up from the table and looked at me. "Honey I have to go" she said. "Don't worry I will stop and visit soon." I stood up from the table. I walked to the other side and gave my mom a hug. I didn't say anything because I had nothing to say. My mom kissed me on the cheek and smiled and just like that she left. She started walking down the hallway and making her way to the elevator. I didn't walk out to see her off, because I couldn't handle it. Ashley poked her head into the room. "Was that your mom?" "Yes" I said. "She seems pretty nice, I would really love the chance to meet her next time, and tell her that she has an amazing son." "I wish I can tell her about you, but apparently she has already heard." "Let me guess more people talking shit about me I suppose." "You know it" I said" "Don't let it bother you babe." "What did you just call me?" "What" I said. "What did you just call me?" "I called you Ashley." "No you didn't, you called me babe." "My boyfriend was the only person to ever call me that. "Sorry I won't call you that again." "No I don't have a problem with it." "I just caught it as a surprise, because every time I hear it I think of my boyfriend, and the mother fucker that killed him." "Sorry" I said. She walked over to me and wrapped her arms around my body. "It's okay; you know you are more sensitive than my boyfriend was." She leaned in and started kissing me on the lips. I started kissing her back. I pushed her off. "Wait, wait, wait, I have a girlfriend, whom I love very much." She didn't seem to be bothered by it. "Well she is not here is she, so she doesn't have to know." "And besides I saw the way that you have been staring at me, I know that you want me." "Most guys do I have the "it" factor." "Well don't get me wrong I like you, as a friend, but that is it." "I am in a relationship with Lindsay." Ashley started laughing, "Well let's see how long that lasts." She started walking out the room and down the hallway. What the fuck, could my mom, Liz and the nurses be right? Is Ashley really like fucking crazy or something? I stood there just thinking about what just happened. And with that thought I had to move or get another room away from Ashley before something terrible would to happen. I started walking towards my room and Liz was walking down the opposite side of the hallway. I didn't want to talk to her and tell her that she was right about the whole Ashley thing. Because I didn't know if she was the type of person to say I told you so or not. I tried to avoid her as much as possible. We crossed paths and she said hi, but I didn't say anything back. She didn't wait for me to say anything, I just kept on walking and headed straight to my room walked in and closed the door. I thought she was going to come and see if everything was okay but she didn't. I could hear her footsteps getting further and further away the more she walked down the hallway. I turned off the light, even though there was light coming from the window and the fucking curtains wasn't helping fucking matters. I did my best to cover the light and lay on my bed and just closed my eyes. I thought about my whole life. I couldn't believe what happened so far in my life. Everything was going fine until my dad passed away. No matter what happens that is always going to be the hardest part in my life. And for my mom I still love her, sometimes, but I can't help the fact that she still blames my dad for me turning out the way I am. I mean there is nothing wrong with me. I mean I think there is nothing wrong with me. I am a mother fucking normal person just like everyone else. I am not retarded or physically deformed or something. I have a normal face and a normal body and a normal state of mind, sometimes, and yes I have done things in my life that I am not happy about. But it's a life lesson and I have to learn from that, I have to embrace the fact that I am Mitch. And that is the only person that I am. I have to stop caring about what other people think of me, or what they have to say about me. If there is anything that my mother has told me is that listening to other people and trying to do what they tell you or whatever is never going to get me far in this world. I opened my eyes and just realized that everything that my mom was saying was right. Family and my friends are the only people that I need to care about in my life. I smiled as I put my arms under my head and sighed. And then I said something that I thought I would never say in a long time, to myself, I love you mom.

Chapter 37
Free/the Decision

After being in this fucking place for a few months now I was already getting fucking sick of it. Sick to my Goddamn stomach where I just wanted to fucking puke all over the place. I couldn't believe if my calculations were correct I have been in this God forsaken hell hole for about 15 months now. And every day felt like fucking shit. I got up from my bed, and luckily for me I have been in the same room, and decided to go and see what Ashley was doing. Oh yeah, I totally fucking forgot she's gone. She left a few months ago. Some old lady came and picked her up or something. It must've been her aunt or something. Well anyway a lady came and got her she packed up all of her stuff and left. Now I am walking out of my room, wondering the fucking hallways, alone and with no one to talk to. There is always Liz but our relationship has been off again on again over these last year. She has tried talking to me about stuff regularly but I have nothing to say to her anymore. I think we talked about everything we possibly can growing up and shit. I just felt the need to stop talking to her; I just don't want to talk to anyone anymore. I was walking down the hallway when I *saw* Liz, I was going to say something but she saw me and didn't say anything. She kept on walking and I stopped for a second and looked at her. I guess she knew that I had nothing to say to her. I mean it has been such a long time since we said anything to each other, I guess she figures might as well give up. Well if that is the way she wants it then I don't give a shit, I don't need her help, one day I am going to get out of here. And I am going to live *my* life. There were announcing food over the fucking intercom, but I wasn't that fucking hungry. I mean I was hungry but I didn't want to fucking eat anything at this moment. I was walking to my room and Liz was walking right behind me. "Mitch" she said. That is the first time she has spoken to me in such a long time. "Mitch" she said again. I stopped walking and turned around. I heard her calling my name and I didn't want to be rude by not answering her. "What's up" I said. "Your mom is coming over again today to visit but just for a short while." "She said she had something to do." "That's fine" I said in a low toned voice. I wasn't really eager to see my mom right now; I just wanted to get the fuck out of here. I walked back to my room, and I didn't even thanked Liz for the good news. Well I doubt that you can call it good news or not, seeing my mom when I am in this place really fucking sucks. I made it to my door and just stared at it for a second, and then I walked in and closed the fucking door. I didn't close it all the way because just in case someone needed something, I just wanted to let them know that I am in the Goddamn room. Even though I really don't care who the hell comes to my room and asking me for the most random bullshit ever. I lie on my bed and put my hands behind my head and fucking sighed. I still couldn't believe that my mom was coming over. I mean she had her whole fucking life to come over and visit and spend time with me. I mean we "hung" out growing up, but now since I am older. This is like the first time she came and visited me in such a long time. That's another thing the relationship with my mom and I haven't been that great either. Honestly I really don't want to see her right now; we haven't sat down and talked about anything in such a long time. I would have no idea what to talk about if we did have one of those lame ass mother fucking mother to son talks. I was so fucking bored that I got up and started thinking about Ashley. I can't believe that she left. It seemed like only yesterday that we met and became friends, and started hanging out all the Goddamn time. I wanted to leave my room and walk around so I wouldn't get so Goddamn bored. So I decided to leave my room and go for a walk. But in this place there is only so much where you can walk to. I got up and left my room and stated walking down the hallway. I walked to the fucking library section; well I don't know if you can even call it a library section, there was only like a few Goddamn books. I sat down and started reading, all I wanted to do is sit the fuck down and read, but I couldn't even get that. Liz walked towards me and sat down. "Mitch" she said. "We need to talk." I put my fucking book down I didn't get as far as reading the fucking title of the book when I sighed. "What" I said. "What's the matter with you?" "You have been acting really strange lately." I looked at not saying a word I got up and started walking away from her. She stood up and yelled down the hallway, "I am only looking out for you." I walked back into my room and shut the door behind me. I walked toward the window and I sort of felt bad for completely ignoring Liz like that. So I decided to go back and apologize. I opened my door and my mom was standing in front of the door. "Mom" I said. "What are you doing here?" "Don't act like that you know I came to visit my baby." "Would you like to come in?" "Or are you going to stand all day." My mom walked in not very happy about the attitude I was giving her, but who can blame her if she would have any sense how long I have been fucking stuck here she would give everyone fucking attitude too. My mom walked to the window and quietly said, "Liz has told me that you have acting different." "Why is that?" "I am me, and that is the only mother fucking person I can be." My mom turned around with a smile on her face and said, "Well as long as your happy that is all I am asking here." I looked at her like she wasn't serious or something. "Happy" I said. Now I know that my mom has gone off the fucking deep end. Then out of fucking nowhere my mom started crying for no reason. She turned back to the window and started fucking crying. I was going to ask if she was okay or something but she started talking about something, I couldn't hear because she was crying so much it was hard to understand. "I am going to go now, I am going home." She abruptly got her belongings and walked out of my room. I was so fucking confused about this whole thing right now. Did I do something wrong? Did I say something wrong? I couldn't figure out what I did wrong. I walked out of my room and my mom was all the way down the hallway. She turned around and saw me looking at her. She smiled and waved goodbye. The door buzzed open and my mom left. Was this the last time that I was ever going to see my mom again? But the strange part I didn't cry or anything, I guess she smiled because she saw that I was okay and shit and not fucked up or worse fucking dead. She smiled yeah, but there was something about that smile that didn't seem to hit home. Like as if she didn't mean it, because she saw that I didn't smile back or anything, I had a pale expression on my face. I stood in the hallway, and Liz poked her head out of her office and noticed that my mom left pretty quickly. She looked down the hallway and saw me still standing there. She smiled and waved at me and I was still standing there. I didn't smile back or wave or did anything. I just stared at her and all I kept thinking about was Lindsay. And how much she had to fucking overcome to be where she is today. Even though, in my opinion, she is really not where she needs to be, but who I am to fucking judge because we all are a little crazy sometimes.

A few hours went by and then a few more hours went by. I was getting to the point where I was getting really fucking tired. I wasn't getting bored because I'd rather be here than home with my mom. I had to do something to fucking entertain myself so I walked to the room where the TV was and turned it on. I channel surfed for about several minutes and then turned off the TV. There wasn't really anything on anyway. I just sat on the chair and thought about my life again. I tend to think too think about shit to much that's why I get stressed out so fucking much. I couldn't believe that Ashley went home before me and I think that she has been here longer than I have. What the fuck, why I am still here. It has been a little more than a year and a half and I am still here. I am fucking 21 and I am in a place like this. I should be with fucking Lindsay, how about if I never see her again. I wouldn't know what the fuck I would do if I never saw her again. And then it fucking hit me. I don't have to be held down anymore. I am going to fucking leave one way or another, whether they like it or not. I was getting hungry and they were serving food. I thought about an idea that might work. Everybody was being called, everybody on my floor, was being called for food. In this place they give you actual silverware and real fucking knives. But they always watch you so you don't cut yourself or ending up stabbing someone to fucking death. And then they take your tray and collect the silverware. Don't ask me why they don't use fucking plastic. I guess they don't want to be fucking cheap. I was standing in line, and got my tray. If this going to work I had to make sure that I fucking timed everything just right. I hurried up and started eating, to fool them like I was actually hungry, and started eating fast. There were nurses all around so I had to time this. I looked at this lady who was about the same age as my mom, and she was staring at me. But she wasn't being rude or anything like that. I didn't mind the stare at all. She looked at me with these eyes like all she wanted to do is get the fuck out of here. But she wasn't scared at me because I was starting at her. See, most people in my hallway are scared because I am tall and big. But she wasn't scared, not one bit. She kept starting at me, and she noticed that I was holding my knife very tightly and wasn't letting go. I was starting at her but again she wasn't scared not one bit. I slowly started dragging the knife towards me and trying to slip it into my pocket. She got up and started screaming about something. I couldn't believe it she had caused a fucking diversion. This was my chance. I slipped the knife into my pocket and stood up from the table. A few nurses came in and helped her up and escorted her out of the room. I gave my tray and as I was walking by I took the lady's knife and placed it on the tray when no one was looking. Because they would know that I was a knife short. I gave the tray to the guy and he got the silverware and he let me go. I started walking towards my room slowly and when I made it to my room I smiled. I couldn't believe that fucking worked out like that. I couldn't believe that lady helped me out like that I mean she didn't even know me or anything, yet she helped me grab the knife. I walked into my room and slipped it under my pillow. I am just glad that no one saw me do it; otherwise I would've gotten in some serious fucking trouble. I was smiling and then Liz came up to me crying. That is when I stopped smiling and started looking concerned. "Mitch" she said. "I have some bad news." She told me to sit down; I sat down first next to my pillow so she didn't feel the knife. "I don't know how to say this but your mom is dead." I was in shock; I couldn't believe the fucking news. My heart was pounding and my eyes were tearing up. "What" I said. "I am so sorry Mitch" she said. "Police arrived at the scene when a neighbor heard a gunshot go off." "The witness said that there was no one in the house but your mom." "I am sorry to tell you this, this way Mitch, but I didn't know any other way to tell you." I didn't say anything and I was looking at Liz crying. "I know that you would like to be alone right now." "But before I go I wanted to give you this." She handed me a letter and I didn't grab for it right away. Liz stood up and placed it on the side of my bed and again apologized and left my room. I grabbed the letter, still crying, and opened it. It read:

Dear Mitch,

Hey baby it's your mom I am so sorry that I left so abruptly, I just couldn't stand seeing you there. I know that you want to get out. I know that all you want is to come home and spend some time with your mom. The whole time that you are in there all I kept thinking about was your dad. Baby I am so sorry that I blamed you for everything. You know that I would never blame you for anything in the whole wide world. You are my sweetheart, my only child and the only thing that I want is to make you happy. I am not mad anymore about what happened in the past with you and I. I am not mad anymore about what happened to Jeremy. That was a thing of the past and I am looking toward the future now. I am looking towards you. I just want you to do great things in life and make me proud. Can you do that one little thing for me, baby, can you make me proud. I was looking through some old photos and I found your dad's old gun. I checked if there were still bullets in there, and there was one left. I grabbed it along with the photo album and started looking at old pictures of the family. You look so cute when you were a baby, and there's daddy holding you and taking care of you. I know that you miss your dad and I miss him too. But I miss you too, and I can't take this anymore. I can't take coming down and seeing you all fucking miserable all the Goddamn time. Just thinking about you and your dad I started crying. I closed the Goddamn album, and picked up the gun. Baby I am so sorry that we never had a family. And I am so sorry that we never got along that well growing up. But I just want you to remember one thing. I love you and I always will. Bye baby.

And with that that the letter stopped, and all over the letter was water, probably from when she was crying. I just stared at the mother fucking letter and started crying more. I wiped the tears away with my sleeve and crumpled up the letter and threw it on the fucking floor. I couldn't take it anymore, and I couldn't bear to see the letter. It was getting late and all I kept thinking about was getting the fuck out of here. They were announcing something over the intercom but I wasn't listening. I grabbed my fucking knife and put it in my pocket. I walked out the room and started at the letter on the ground as I turned around one last time. I noticed that there was more on the bottom before I crumpled it up. I walked over to it and unfolded it. I read the bottom and it said, "I love you Mitch, and I know that you and Lindsay are meant for each other, now go show her that you too belong to each other." I started at the letter and placed it on my pillow. I walked over to the light switch and turned it off. I looked back one more time and closed the door. The hallway was empty and I was examining the area making sure that were no people around. I was walking down the hallway and I noticed that there was only one guard and two nurses on duty. Everyone, including Liz went home, so leaving place wasn't going to be that hard. I walked back down the other side of the hallway and there was only one nurse working, so she was in control of the door. I had no time to waste; I walked back to my fucking room and yelled out for the nurse. One of the nurses from the other room, not the main room, but from the other side of the hallway, left her office and started walking down the hallway. I walked back inside my room and busted my light. She walked in the room and said, "Son you called me?" she tried switching on the light, and it didn't turn on. "There must be something wrong with your light." "Let me go and get a step stool and a new bulb. She left my room, as my hand was in my pocket gripping my knife. She came back with a step stool and a bulb. She positioned the stool under the light, and started unscrewing the old bulb. "It's a good thing you called me when you did." "I was about to go on break." She was about to put in the new bulb when I kicked out the stool from under her legs. She immediately hit the floor, screaming. "Why would you do that?" "What the hell is the matter with you?" she was about to get up when I took out my knife and walked over to her slowly. She was about to scream when I quickly covered her mouth, and began stabbing the fuck out of her mother fucking chest and face. After a few stabs she was dead, and I waited just in case anyone else heard that. I walked into the bathroom and cleaned off the blood off my hands and knife. And turned back around and saw her on the floor dead. I put the knife back into my pocket and grabbed my door handle. I locked it and closed the door. The security guard was walking around and I noticed that he went into the bathroom. I followed him and closed the door. The good thing about the bathroom that it was in a corner all by itself and it wasn't near any of the rooms where the nurses worked. He picked a stall and unzipped his pants. I got close to him, and he sort of jumped. "Whoa" he said. "You almost gave me a heart attack." He started laughing as he was pissing. I took out my knife and grabbed him. The good thing about these security guards they didn't carry guns only pepper spray and handcuffs. I roughed him up a little bit and grabbed him closer. He tired to fight off but I was much bigger and stronger. I turned him around and slit his mother fucking throat. He immediately fell to the ground and I stabbed him a few more times in the face and chest area. I didn't bother to clean off the knife, just my hands, because the knife was going in my pocket. I waited for the other nurse to come and wonder why the security guard was taking a long time. I walked to the door and turned off the lights and locked the door from the inside and shut the door. I stood outside the bathroom door and waited for any of the two nurses to come. I waited for a few seconds and then I started to walk down the hallway. I passed the booth where the nurses were, and one of them was gone. She had her coat on the back of her jacket. She must've gone for a break or something. The good thing about living on this fucking floor was there were no cameras. Actually there were no cameras on any of the floors. I guess that would invade some type of fucking privacy law or something, I really wasn't a hundred percent sure on that. But I didn't care one fucking bit, because having cameras everywhere would make you go fucking crazy. I knew that if they were any cameras on my floor or in my room I would go paranoid as hell. I told one of the nurses that someone locked the bathroom door and I had to use the restroom very badly. She got up and pleasantly smiled as she grabbed her keys. She left and started walking down the hallway. She grabbed her keys and started to unlock the door. When she opened the door she turned on the light and she noticed that the security guard was dead. She began to scream; I quickly pulled out my knife and covered her mouth. I grabbed her fucking ass and slit her throat and threw her in the Goddamn bathroom. She started coughing and I walked over to her and stabbed her a few more times to make sure she was fucking dead. I peaked my head out to make sure that the other nurse didn't hear anything or if she came back. I put the knife back in my pocket, and it was fucking amazing I was thinking the whole time I was fucking killing these people. Everyone else in the rooms was letting this happen. Even the crazy old lady, that looked the same age as my mom, was letting this happen. I guess I was doing all these miserable people a Goddamn favor or something. I turned off the light and closed the door. I walked down the hallway and I walked to the door where the nurse's office was. The other nurse didn't come back yet. I walked inside and hit the mother fucking buzzer button and the door swung open. And the doors here they stay open until you hit the buzzer again. A smile came to my face and I left the office and started walking down the hallway out of the door. I made it to the elevator and the guard there wasn't there, I guess he was in the bathroom. Well I wasn't going to wait for him one fucking bit. I hit the elevator button and took it all the way down to the basement. I wanted to leave through there instead of the first floor because there might be people there and I would never leave. I made it to the bottom and the elevator door swung open. There are no cameras down here either, I hope. I found the door that said exit and walked to it. I still had the knife in my pocket just in case. Everything was happening so fast, I couldn't even explain it. I just killed a number of fucking people and it didn't bother me one fucking bit. I opened the door and fucking left. It was raining and I was getting soaked, all the blood off my hands and clothes were getting washed away. Now that I am finally fucking free I had a huge decision to make. Be with Ashley, try to find her or be with Lindsay the girl that I am love with. Now that I am free everything was going to work out the way that I want it to be. I started walking down the side of the street, and the rain started picking up. I knew that I had a big decision to make but the only thing that I wanted to do now is get far away from that place as I could. I stopped walking and turned around one more time. I stared at the building and gave a little smile, so many good memories, and turned around and continued my path down the side of the street. I knew that no matter what happens this was going to be a long journey and I was looking forward to it.

Chapter 38
Trick or Treat

Five years later and I couldn't believe it. So let me catch you up to date, there have been news conferences and shit like that about a mental patient breaking free and police has recovered five bodies at a local mental hospital. I guess it is no surprise that I fucking killed each and every one of those people. You are probably thinking what the fuck I have been doing with my fucking life so far. Well I will tell you, it hasn't been nothing short of fucking disappointing. Ever since my mom died everything in my life has been going downhill. I have been living in my mom's old house and only come out when it is fucking night time. It has been so fucking long that I forgot everything and mostly everyone. But it is funny because no matter what happened I still remember Lindsay. I guess I still do love her. But it has been five years I think that she finally moved on with her life. I haven't cut my hair, well I did but it looks all fucked up because I got it cut myself. I let my beard grow out though because I was too fucking lazy to get it shaved. But enough about me, my favorite time of the year is coming up, Halloween, it is my favorite time of the year because I get to dress up and go have some fucking fun in my life. I guess I can count on this day to have fun because God knows that my life wasn't full of it growing up and shit. It was getting late so I decided to come out and go have some fun. I never worried too much about the fact that someone is always looking for me or something like that. I closed the door to my mom's house and continued to walk down the pathway to the street. I still had the knife in my fucking pocket. It is funny because I feel in some strange way that the knife has become sort of like my best friend, besides Lindsay and Ashley and all of the other girls that I have met. I continued to walk down the Goddamn street when it started fucking raining again. And at this point I really didn't care it is not like I had any money to buy new clothes anyway. I started walking and some old couple was having a yard sale. I walked up to the people's yard and there was a box full of old clothes. I looked through the box and I picked up a black sweatshirt. The husband probably came out and walked towards me. "Found something you like?" I didn't smile or anything. But on the other hand the guy was fucking smiling his ass off. I held up the sweatshirt and I said, "Yes, I would like to buy this." He took it from me and said, "Good choice this used to belong to me a few years back." "It might be a little big on you considering you are a big boy. I smiled. I told the guy how much and he told me three or four dollars. I reached in my back pocket and I forgot since it has been so fucking long I forgot I had no fucking money. "I think someone has stolen my wallet." "I am sorry." The guy looked at me and smiled again. "Here just go ahead and take this one." "You seem like a good kid." Yeah, a good kid if he really knew me and knew how my life has been so far. He knew that it wasn't a fucking walk in the park. He gave me the sweatshirt and I didn't wait. Thank God it only rained for like a few minutes. I really felt sorry for the guy with the yard sale. But this guy was smart, he put like a tent thing in his front yard so all of his shit wouldn't get ruined. I took off my old shirt because it got dirty and threw on the sweatshirt. It was a little bigger than what I expected but I think I will manage. I thanked him for the sweatshirt and continued to walk down the street. I didn't know where I was going or what the fuck I was going to do honestly. The sun finally came out after it rained for about a few minutes and wearing this sweatshirt was a bad idea. Luckily for me I had an old T-shirt under this so I took off the fucking sweatshirt and wrapped it around my waist. I guess this used to be some sort of style or something because I know a lot of people used to do this back in the day. I was getting later in the night and I didn't have a fucking costume to wear or anything. Then I decided in a matter of seconds that I didn't want to go as someone. I was going to go as myself, because honestly that is the best costume there is. And I didn't have to waste any money on it or anything. Because to tell you the truth it's not like I had any money to spend on it anyway so what the fuck was I going to do you know. I was walking down this street and I could already see people putting up decorations on their front lawns and shit. I guess some people were really in the mood. The reason that I am saying that is because most of the houses were decorated a lot and some of the houses just had second-rate decorations. I saw kids running around and screaming trick or treat all day with their little costumes on and everything. And then I saw a house that took my fucking breath away. But there was something else to this house. It was the girl that was coming outside of the house. I couldn't believe my eyes it was Ashley. I can't believe that she lived here. Of all the houses that I could've seen walking down the fucking street I picked the one where she came out of. I walked slowly to her house and then stopped. Wait, I said to myself. It has been about five years, how about she doesn't recognize me anymore. I walked and hid behind this tree that was on the sidewalk and just watched her as she kissed and hugged her dad. I knew that right then and there that her dad was going to get in the way of Ashley and me. I never got the chance to meet her dad but I could just tell by looking at him that he wasn't an approving person. I mean look at me and look at Ashley. Five years has gone by and she looks more beautiful than ever and I look like a Goddamn fucking homeless person, begging people for fucking change on the streets. I watched her walk down the street and some of her friends met up with her and got her attention. I made a mental note of where her house was and continued to walk down the street where she was walking. I wasn't trying to stalk or anything because it wasn't anything like that but I just wanted to know where she was going. I was walking down the sidewalk when a door opened. It was Ashley's front door of her house. Ashley's dad came out and walked in the front yard. He stood there and put his hands on his hips and took a deep breath. I stopped walking and started walking the other way towards Ashley's house I walked around the other way so Ashley's dad didn't see me. I slowly took out my knife and as soon as he was about to go back inside I followed him and he opened the door and took one step inside. I grabbed him and slit his throat and threw him back inside the house. I dropped the knife because I was getting tired of using such a small knife. I walked into the kitchen and started opening drawers and took out a butcher knife, now this was more like it. I turned off the lights in the house, just the ones in the living room, and locked the door from the inside and shut the door. I made sure that no one saw me leaving; I mean who would since it was so dark outside and I was dressed in black and dark gray. It would've been hard for anyone to see me coming from a house. I continued to walk down the same sidewalk where Ashley was walking before maybe I'll get lucky and see her again, or one of her friends.

Ashley never told me how old she was once we first met, as I was still walking down the street, I wonder how old she is now. I mean it has been five years and everything. It's been crazy it felt just like yesterday we met and shit. I know that I said that before and everything but it really has been. Five years went by so fucking fast and everything. I didn't even have time to stop and smell the fucking roses. I was still walking down the street and it was getting later in the night, I didn't know how late in the night it was getting though, since I wasn't wearing a fucking watch. I guess the time wasn't my biggest Goddamn concern right now. My concern was Ashley. I continued walking and then I heard laughing. But it wasn't kids laughing, it sounded like teenage girls laughing. I walked closer and it was a group of three teenage girls. If I would bet money on it, I would say that Ashley was in that group. I wasn't a hundred percent sure I was going with my gut feeling. I got closer and closer to the girls without giving away to much attention to myself. There was a street light shining on the corner of the street and I saw that it was Ashley and her friends. They were trick or treating late at night. I couldn't fucking believe it, it was like my lucky night I keep on bumping into her by accident. I followed her as she was walking with her friends. One of her friends stopped and went the other way. She was talking pretty loudly as she was in the middle of the street. "Hey, remember my parents are away for the weekend." "So don't forget party at my house later tonight." I stopped my path and followed Ashley's friend to her house. She got all the way up her stairs and opened the door. She didn't bother to close her door and I walked in and quietly closed the door. She didn't hear me close the door as she was listening to music. I followed her upstairs and I heard sounds coming from a room I quietly walked to her room and slowly and walked inside. She walked inside her bathroom and opened her medicine cabinet, and she turned around and saw me. Now anyone's first reaction in this case is to run. But she started screaming and luckily for me her parents weren't home so I grabbed her and tore her shirt off. She was panicking and half naked. She tried to run but I grabbed her by the hair and pulled towards me. She started crying and yelling and shit. I grabbed her towards me and held tightly on her hair. She started crying and I threw her roughly against the side railing of the steps. She hit it pretty hard. She started getting up slowly and coughing. She ran down the steps so I followed and grabbed her by the hair again. I ripped off her skirt and threw it on the floor. She was running around screaming and bleeding when she hit the side of the railing. She went for the phone but I grabbed her by the hair again and threw her against her mirror in the living room. She hit it pretty hard and she had cuts all over her arm. I was getting tired of this little cat and fucking mouse game. I pulled out my knife and walked over to her as she was getting up. She looked so cute all half naked and everything it was a shame that I had to kill her. I grabbed her by the hair and some stands fell out. I stabbed her in the stomach and let go of her hair. She immediately grabbed her stomach crying and coughing up blood. She started crawling and I walked over to her and continued to slice her body and legs and thighs and back. She started screaming more and more, but no one could hear her. She crawled all the way to the door and eventually died. I stepped over her body and walked to the door. I slipped the knife back into my pocket and left. I walked outside, and closed her door and walked outside. I heard more teenage laughing coming so I decided to go back to where Ashley's dad's house is and wait. I didn't know how long I was going to wait but I waited.

I waited and waited and finally I saw someone coming toward the house. It was Ashley. She opened the door and turned on the light. She was in shock when she saw that her dad was fucking murdered. She started screaming and I was hiding behind the door. She walked slowly towards her dad and I slowly closed the door. She turned around afraid. "What the fuck." I didn't say anything for a second. "Answer me you mother fucking asshole before I call the cops on you." "You better answer me you stupid mother fucker." "Are you responsible for

my dad being dead you stupid son of a bitch asshole mother fucker."
Again I didn't say anything for a second, but Ashley was crying and
looked towards her dad and looked back at me. I was holding my knife
out and was about to stab her when I stopped. I put the knife back
into my pocket. For some reason I couldn't do it. I couldn't muster up
the courage to kill Ashley, no matter how badly I wanted to. "Trick or
Treat" I said. And then she dropped her bag of candy and said "Mitch."
She didn't say anything for several seconds. And I got closer to her
without saying anything to her at first. "What the fuck Mitch how the
fuck can you do something like this." "I thought you were my mother
fucking friend." "I can't explain myself Ashley" I said. "I didn't do this
for me." She got closer to me and said, "You are not going to hurt
me are you?" I didn't say anything and she leaned in and gave me a
hug. I don't know why she would give me a fucking hug after I killed
her dad. I guess she was having mixed emotions about me killing her
fucking dad or something. If I am right I think that she told me that
her and her dad weren't having the best of relationships and he used
to hit and sexually abuse her and shit. She continued to hug me and
then I grabbed my knife and then stabbed Ashley right in the back.
She started screaming and coughing up blood. "What the fuck" she
said. "Mitch I thought you loved me." I didn't say anything and just
continued to stab the shit out of her until she hit the floor dead in
front of me. I stepped over her body and closed all the lights in the
living room and shut the Goddamn door. I walked down the side of
her driveway and down the street with the knife still in my hand. Trick
or treat Mitch, trick or treat.

Chapter 39
Together Forever

It was finally fucking morning and I was still walking around and still trying to figure out what the fuck I was going to do. I decided to go to my mom's house. I waited for several minutes and then I decided to leave and go walk around for a while. I needed to clear my fucking head. I walked outside, and then I opened the door and shut it. I just realized that I had the knife in my hand. I walked down to the basement and hid it under the fucking floorboards. I walked back upstairs and then finally I was ready to leave. But there was only one huge problem I didn't know where the fuck Lindsay was. I wouldn't know where to begin to look for her. It has been so long I don't think that she will even remember me now. I left and closed the door behind me and started walking. I really had no idea where the fuck to look. I started walking and found some change along the side of the street. I decided to pick it up; this can come in hand, just in case I needed to make a phone call and shit. It wasn't a lot of money only a few quarters and dimes here and there but it was enough to make a phone call. I slipped the money in my pocket and I started walking down the street. I saw a pay phone and a phone book. Maybe I will get lucky and find Lindsay. I remember her telling me her last name one time but she never mentioned it to me again after that. And since it was such a long time I probably forgot. I walked to the pay phone and gathered all the change from my pocket to make sure that I had enough. I flipped open the phone book and started looking for her name. It was so fucking hard because there were so many Goddamn names that started with Lindsay. If I can only remember her fucking last name and then it hit me. I started looking through all the names that started with Lindsay and I believe if I am correct that she told me that her last name was Thompson or something. I looked up Lindsay Thompson and luckily for me there was only a few of them. But I didn't have enough change to make all these phone calls. So I decided to go in order and try the first Lindsay Thompson. I got the change from my pocket and inserted it into the pay phone. I called the number and waited and praying that this was the right Lindsay. I waited and fucking waited and nothing. I hung up the phone pretty pissed off and everything. I waited for several minutes by the phone and everything. I didn't know what was happening to me. I couldn't explain these feelings that I was having. I never expected that my fucking life would turn out this way in a million Goddamn years. My heart was pounding and I didn't know why. I wasn't nervous or anything. I mean it was Lindsay, my girlfriend, I mean I almost married the chick for Christ sake. This is the girl that I want to spend the rest of my life with, and no one else. I wanted to pick up the phone and tell Lindsay everything. All I wanted is to tell her everything but I didn't know how. All I wanted is to tell her everything but I didn't know if she was willing to except this "person" that I have become. I mean I am still the same fucking person it's just that shit happened and my life just got very, very mother fucking complicated in a Goddamn heartbeat. I picked up the phone, took a deep breath, and called back. Luckily for me there was no one in line behind me waiting to use the phone otherwise I would bash the fucking phone upside their head. I called back and again waited and waited. And then a voice on the other side of the phone, so sweet and innocent simply said, "Hello." I froze I couldn't believe it was her, it was Lindsay. I had to say something before she thinks this is some type of Goddamn prank call and hang up. "Lindsay" I said. Very nervous, hoping she recognizes my voice or something. "Yes" she said. "Who is this?" I waited again and took another deep breath. "It's me Mitch" I said. "It's me Mitch." I waited for a second to see if Lindsay was going to say something but she didn't. There was a pause and then she finally said, "Mitch is this really you?" "Yes" I said. Again there was pause and neither of us said anything for several seconds. It was getting pretty late in the morning and the weather was getting colder by the second. It was warm outside, yes, but there was a breeze that was coming in and it was cold. Luckily for me I had a long sleeve shirt on and I still had my sweatshirt wrapped around my waist. Since Lindsay wasn't saying anything I put the phone on the stand, took my sweatshirt from my waist, and put it on. I picked up the phone and said, "Lindsay you still there?" "Yes" she replied back not sounding the same as she did when she first picked up. "I missed you so much; it has been such a long time." "I thought you would have forgotten me by now." "I miss you too" I said. "I want to see you so badly" "Where are you can we meet?" I waited for Lindsay to say something. I don't think that she wants to see me now. I mean it has been so long and how about she found someone, then what the fuck was I going to do. Again there was a fucking pause; I was getting sick and Goddamn tired of these pauses. I wish that she just would say something and tell me anything about how she was feeling or anything. "I want to be with you forever" I said. "We were meant to be together forever." Lindsay sighed. "Is everything okay?" "Mitch" she said. "It has been such a long time and I was tired of waiting for you." "Please don't take this the wrong way but I still do have feelings for you but I have moved on." "I just couldn't deal with the pain; I just couldn't deal with the fact of not seeing you anymore." "What are you saying?" I said. "I don't understand what you are saying." "I am saying that I am moving on and I think that you should do the same." Lindsay said bye and she hung up the phone and there I was standing there in the middle of the fucking day, fucking heartbroken and confused. Lost in this crazy ass messed up life, I slammed the mother fucking phone and walked away pissed off to hell. I couldn't believe that she met someone. I guess this is good for her, I guess she is right it has been way to long time and I am happy that she did finally find someone. I wish that she would just give me another chance. There were so many mixed emotions running through my veins, I felt like my head was telling me something and my heart was telling me another thing. I didn't know what to do anymore. I felt like my whole fucking life was over now. The girl that I have loved since the day that we first met said that she doesn't want to be with me anymore. I didn't know what the fuck I was going to do now with my life. I guess life isn't worth living anymore without the girl of my dreams beside me. Rooting me on and helping me with everything in my life. I started to walk home, well to my mom's old home, and started thinking that why Lindsay all of a sudden didn't want to be with me anymore. I started thinking that I did something wrong.

I made it to my mom's house and walked around the back. I walked to the back because I wanted to check if the fucking lock was still working. And to my surprise, well it really wasn't, but it wasn't working. So I grabbed a fucking rock and busted the window and opened the door by sticking my arm through the window, but being extra careful of not cutting myself. I opened the door and walked in. I had a terrible feeling in the pit of my Goddamn stomach. I couldn't explain why or for what fucking reason I was feeling this way for. I have never felt this way before in my whole life before. I just wanted to end my fucking life right here and right now. I wanted to end my life the same way that my mom ended hers. No I don't want to be like that mother fucking slut. She can rot in fucking hell. I blame her for messing up my relationship with Lindsay. I fucking blame my mom for messing up everything with Lindsay. I blame Liz for messing up things between me and Lindsay. I blame all the fucking nurses staff for putting me in that fucking place. That mother fucking hell hole. But no matter how mad I get, or how many times I fucking curse, or no matter how many Goddamn people I fucking blame I know that in the bottom of my heart, in the pit of my stomach it isn't going to bring Lindsay any closer to me at all. No matter how mad I get at the world and how many terrible things that I have done or will probably do in the future it isn't going to bring Lindsay and I closer one bit. I do feel bad for my mom though, and I do take some of the stuff back about what I said. I know that all she wanted was to help and she really thought that Lindsay and I were going to be forever together. But if there is one thing that my mom has taught me, is advice. And the best advice that my mom ever gave me was, "No matter what happens in life, just remember one thing you will always have your friends and family by your side." And in some weird way I think that still holds true to this day. And as for Lindsay, I *am* glad that she found someone who can love and respect her the way she deserves to be treated. And I am happy for her. But in my heart Lindsay is always going to be my friend. I love you Lindsay, I love you.

Chapter 40
The End/Bar

What kind of fucking beer do you want" the bartender said. As I was drinking and fucking drinking, I told the guy to give me another bud light. I wasn't counting and I think that I am literally fucking drunk out of my fucking mind. The bartender gave me another bud light and said, "Man after hearing you tell your story for about a few hours, I thought my fucking life was messed up. I laughed and then I took another sip. I finished the bottle and he said if I wanted one for the road and I told him no thank you. "Thank you for that very fascinating story." "I really learned a lot about you." "No problem man, thank you for listening. It's always hard to make someone listen to you when they don't want to. And especially if it is about something that they don't want to fucking hear. I got up from the bar and started walking. I was a little wobbly because I had been drinking so much fucking beer. I shook the bartender's hand and stared walking towards the door very carefully. Well it is nice to always make a new friend. Well here I am, twenty six years old and I have nothing to fucking show for it. My fucking mom is dead and my girlfriend isn't my girlfriend anymore. I guess that is what I get for being a complete dick my whole Goddamn life. I started thinking and I immediately walked back to the Goddamn bartender and got his attention. "Hey everything I told you was one hundred percent the mother fucking truth." "Don't worry I won't tell anyone about you or anything that you have done or may do." "Look don't worry about it okay, can you imagine how many fucking people come in here saying that they did something awful." "Or how many times I get husbands come in here that abuse their wives and still come in for a drink." "I never ask questions, they all come in one by one and spill their fucking guts out and I listen and sometimes give advice." "That is good to know" I said. "But listen before you go no matter how many people have come in, and no matter how many people I have given advice too." "You are the first person that I never had to tell anything." "You are the first person that I had no advice for, you seem to answer all your own questions and I am proud of you." I smiled and shook his hands I finally left the mother fucking bar. I wasn't too thrilled that he said that he was fucking proud of me, like he was my fucking dad or something. But I didn't care one bit about that shit right now; all I wanted to do is go home. I walked home very intoxicated and stumbling over my own fucking feet and shit. I am so glad that I can walk properly and shit without falling over. I checked my wallet and no money. I wasn't that far from the bar so I walked back in and got the bartender's attention again. I asked him if I can borrow some money to catch a cab. He graciously handed me some money and told me good night. I smiled and waved back to the guy and left. I waited in the blistering cold for a taxi and I finally found one. I hailed him down and he stopped him. He pulled in front of me and stopped the car. I opened the front door and told the guy, as I was getting, the address of my mom's house. As I was getting in I don't know how the fuck I ended up where the hell I am now. I closed the door and he left. I rested my head on the back of the seat and after a few miles of driving we arrived. I was still sleeping and he slowly pulled up to the house. He said, "Buddy come on we are here and I am tired of waiting." I awoke and saw that we finally made it to the house. I apologized to the cab driver and took out my money and handed it to him. He thanked me as I opened the passenger door and walked out. I stepped out and closed the door and like a fucking bullet he was gone. I stood there and saw my mom's old home. Well my home for my life growing up. It is crazy everything that happened in this house. I am surprised that no one has bought it or even renovated it yet. I mean it has been five long fucking years and the house is still there. They way it was from the beginning, untouched. I walked around the back and opened the door because I knew that the back of the door was opened. Man being in this house gives me so many good memories but also at the same time so many bad ones. And with that there were so many mixed emotions going on. It was fucking overwhelming. I walked around the house and started thinking about everything. I walked into the kitchen and found a piece of paper and a pencil in a drawer that I opened and took it out. The tip of the pencil was kind of dull so I couldn't do much. I took the paper and the pencil and walked into the living room. I sat down on the couch, and it was dusty as shit, and placed the paper on the fucking table and began writing.

Well this is my life; everything that happened in my life had to happen for a reason right. I mean everything happens for a reason. That is fucking fate and you can't challenge fucking fate. I just wanted to take this time to say I am sorry for everything that happened. And say sorry for my mom who selfishly fucking killed herself. I just wanted to say sorry to Liz. I treated her badly and fucking blamed her for Lindsay leaving me and shit. I can't take back what I have done and nor can I take back what I am destined to become. I know that I did many terrible things in my life growing up and all the people that I have hurt and all the people that I have killed won't bring them back. What the fuck am I saying? I don't know what the fuck I am saying anymore. I am just saying some mother fucking random bullshit. I was going to fucking kill myself, which is how bad I wanted to just do it. Nothing was making sense anymore. I felt like everything in my life was falling apart. No matter how hard I tried in everything I felt like it wasn't good enough for anyone. I didn't mean to mess things up. I didn't want to mess things up anymore. Fuck, I can't write anymore, I stood up from the couch, brushed all the dust from my clothes and walked into the kitchen. I frantically opened all the drawers and finally found a butcher knife that I picked up and brought with me back to the table. I laid it on the table and just fucking started at it. I picked up the pencil and looked where I left off and began writing some more. I laughed to myself, everything is happening so fast. I said that to myself a million times, and it never gets old. I didn't know what the fuck to do anymore with my life. I felt like I let everyone down in my whole fucking life. I was tired of letting people down. I felt like that is all I did is let everyone down. I mean I try so hard in life and nothing good happens to me. Everyone else gets all the fucking show for it. I bust my ass in everything and I don't get mother fucking Goddamn shit for it. I am sorry I do have something to show for it. GUILT is what I got to show for it. And not to mention a dead mother fucking mother and a slut for a fucking girlfriend, but you know what fuck that slut. I am the better man, way better than whomever she chose to spend her fucking life with. If Lindsay want to ruin her life by throwing it away on some fucking loser asshole than it is fine by me. From this point on, no from this day on I am never going to speak the name of Lindsay ever again. I guess people can move on, no matter who they are or what they do in life. I am tired of writing; I am going to take Lindsay advice for the last fucking time and fucking move the fuck on. I guess everyone needs to change and forget about the Goddamn past and just think about the future and what it can hold for you. I guess I need to embrace the fucking fact that life is full of surprises.

I stopped writing and just threw the mother fucking pencil on the floor. I stared at what I wrote and to tell you the truth I was pretty happy about myself and what I wrote. I think that I got the fucking point across. There was something in that letter that did make a lot of fucking sense. And that was that life is full of surprises and sitting at home or wherever you are you may missed them. I guess I don't want to miss them. From this day on this is going to be a different and new Mitchell James. I stared at the knife and slowly picked it up and started looking at it. I walked to the window and used the blade to slide open the drapes. It was dark. And there were people walking around at night, not a lot only one couple but they were going the opposite direction of where my mom's house is. I stepped away from the window and stared at the knife again. I slowly put it in my pocket and walked to the front door. I turned around and looked at the piece of paper and smiled. I turned around and slowly opened the door, and waited for a second. I smiled, life is full of surprises, as I gripped the knife in my hand, and I wasn't going to miss any of them. I slammed the door and pulled out my knife and started walking down the mother fucking street. I stopped and turned and looked at the house on more time, turned around and kept on walking. I walked down the street with my sweatshirt on me and my hood over my face and said, "This is for you mom."